SHIFTING LOYALTIES

COMPANY OF STRANGERS, BOOK 4

MELISSA MCSHANE

Night Harbor Publishing

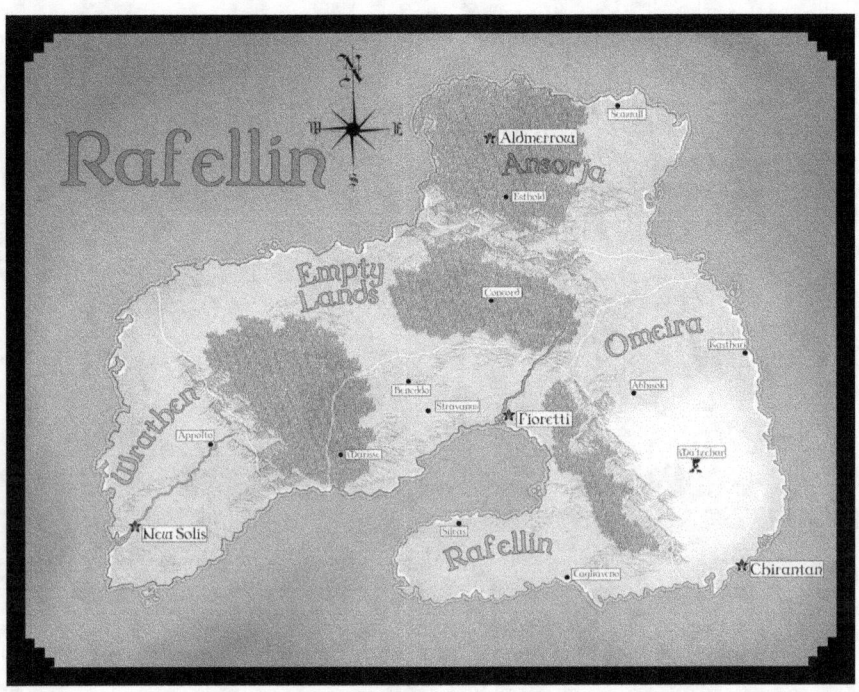

For my children,
most of whom will never read this book.
I love you all anyway.

1

Sienne's cold magical light reflected dully off the black stones of the corridor, as if they were made of something that sucked the light in and held tightly to it. Moisture slicked the walls, but despite the warmth and wetness, nothing grew on them. Water dripped, somewhere in the distance. The noise came at irregular intervals, probably from more than one source. Knowing that didn't make the sound grate any less on Sienne's nerves.

A regular *plink*, she could have ignored, but the erratic *tap-tap, tap, taptaptap* kept her on edge, listening for the next one. The smell of old stone, cold and damp, filled the air, mingled with a whiff of something sour that rose up with every step. It was like being inside the digestive tract of some oddly angular beast.

The stone swallowed up the sound of her footsteps and that of her companions just as it did the light. It was a strange corridor, as wide as it was high and seeming without end. Sienne pinched her nose against a sneeze and summoned another couple of magic lights. Their light banished the darkness a few paces, but didn't illuminate the corridor more than about ten feet away.

She sent the new ones flying ahead and heard Dianthe curse. "Too bright," her friend exclaimed.

"Sorry. This place has me on edge. No lanterns, no torches, not even brackets to hold lanterns or torches." She shifted her spellbook to a more comfortable position.

"Nobody's been down here but us for decades, maybe centuries," Alaric said without turning around. "There's nothing to be worried about."

Sienne eyed the giant Sassaven's broad back. "Then why are you tense?"

"Because I could be wrong, and someone's already retrieved the salvage from this place."

"Am I the only one who believes this corridor has gone on forever?" Perrin said. "With no discernable landmarks, I cannot imagine how we could tell if that were true."

"I have marked the walls," Kalanath said, demonstrating by drawing the steel tip of his staff with a *skree* across a stone at head height. "But there is no turn, or door, so it does not matter."

"It relieves my mind," Perrin said. "Pray, do not stop."

"The corridor turns here," Dianthe said, "and there's a door up ahead." She vanished into the darkness. Sienne came around the corner to see her examine the thumb latch, then try it. "Not locked."

"That could be bad," Alaric said. "Let's see what we have."

Dianthe pushed the door open and waited for Sienne to send her lights through before entering. Sienne followed Alaric and moved to the side to allow Perrin and Kalanath to enter. The sour smell was diminished in this room, which was vast enough Sienne's lights, clustered around the door, didn't illuminate the far end. Chairs with disintegrating cushions stood in groups here and there throughout the cavernous room. Damp, rotting tapestries whose subjects were lost to time hung from the walls, which for once bore patches of moss. They seemed the only healthy, thriving thing in what Sienne was increasingly inclined to call a lair. The ceiling was unexpectedly low, though no lower than it had been in the hall. In this vast room it felt as if it were poised to fall and crush them. Sienne shivered and stepped closer to Alaric.

"It's empty," she said. "Should it be this empty?"

"Reva Nocenti was killed before she could retreat with her possessions," Perrin said. "But there are records enough of her underground palace that other scrappers may have looted it in the hundred-odd years since her defeat."

"This was an entrance," Kalanath said, prodding one of the cushions with the tip of his staff. "A place for people who wish a thing to come."

"An antechamber," Sienne said. "That makes sense. Though not much else about this does. Why would a wizard care about ruling a dukedom? Particularly a wizard who was as interested in research as Nocenti was?"

"Power does strange things to people," Alaric said. "Why would someone spend three fortunes building an underground palace when an aboveground palace is half as expensive, and has windows?"

"There are two doors," Dianthe said. She'd crossed the room, trailing a light, and the far wall was now visible. "Anyone have a preference?"

"You sound like you're in a hurry," Alaric said.

"Aren't you? This place gives me hives. See, I'm scratching." Dianthe rubbed her forearm. "Let's find this salvage and get out."

"I apologize for not being able to direct us more, ah, directly," Perrin said.

"You got us this far. And figured out there was something here at all. I call that more than enough help," Alaric said.

Sienne brought a light closer to the door nearest her, the one on the left. It was nearly as tall as the ten-foot-high ceiling and half that wide, carved all over with scenes of a beautiful noblewoman dressed in the style of a century past, passing judgment on groups of people —merchants, peasants, even other nobles. "I think we should take this one."

"Why is that?" Perrin said.

"Because it probably leads somewhere interesting. The other one is plain and I bet it leads to the storage room."

"She has a point," Dianthe said.

Alaric nodded. "Then left it is."

The room beyond the carved door was as cavernous and claustrophobic as the first. More rotting tapestries hung on the walls, more mossy growth gleamed verdantly in the white light. Directly ahead, on a dais reached by three shallow steps, stood a throne carved of black marble, unrelieved by cushions, even rotted ones. The wall behind the throne was carved in a bas-relief whose details Sienne couldn't make out at that distance. She crossed the room to look up at it. It showed the same woman with her hands held out in a pose like the Mercy card in a hazard deck, water overflowing her cupped hands.

"I sense a theme," Perrin said.

"We already knew Nocenti was arrogant," Alaric said. "Though this certainly proves the point. Dianthe?"

"I see no signs of any concealed doors or rooms," Dianthe said. "But I'm not sure she'd want her treasury where so many outsiders go, even if it's well-hidden. The only exit is that archway over there." She pointed.

"I think perhaps we should be certain we are not leaving anything behind," Perrin said, removing his riffle of blessings from inside his vest. "Not to disparage your abilities, Dianthe, but Averran sees better than we do, and if the wizard Nocenti knew the *seeming* spell, it might be beyond all of us to find what she hid. I have several of these revealing blessings today, and I daresay that is a hint I should use them." He tore a purple-smudged square of rice paper from the little bundle and held it high, bowing his head and murmuring an invocation. Purple fire consumed the paper, and a bright violet light outlined all the stones of the walls, turning the moss a dusty gray color. When it faded, Perrin said, "Nothing."

Alaric was already headed for the archway, in which drifted shreds of a filmy curtain that might once have been red. "Between the two of you, I think we have an excellent chance of finding the lost treasury."

Sienne took up her place in the middle of the group, cradling her spellbook in the crook of her left arm. "I hope nobody else found it first. It's so disappointing when we make a find and it's been cleaned out already."

Once again, the walls of this corridor were clean of moss. She wondered what made the difference. Nothing obvious, at any rate.

"My augury blessing suggests strongly that whatever is here is worth our time," Perrin said. "I, for my part, hope it is a non-magical treasury. Selling off gold and silver is much easier than haggling over artifacts, however more potentially valuable the artifacts are."

"There's a door ahead, and the corridor branches right before it," Dianthe said. "The door's not locked. More specifically, it can't be locked."

"We might as well check it first," Alaric said.

The room beyond was clearly a barracks, with three rows of bunks devoid of mattresses or bedding filling the space. "Nothing worth looking at here," Dianthe said. She crossed the room to the door on the other side and reached for the latch, only to snatch her hand back as if she'd been burned. "Somebody trapped this door. Recently."

"How recently?" Alaric said, joining her at the door.

"Not that recently. A year or so."

"That's still recent." Alaric glared at the door as if that would disarm the trap by itself. "Can you disable it?"

"I could, but it will take time. We're probably better off seeing if there's a way around it. Though the fact that there's a trap there tells me somebody found something worth hiding."

"Or they intend to deceive other scrappers," Perrin said.

"Or that. In either case—"

"We move on," Alaric said.

They backtracked and took the second corridor, which ended in a T-junction where they went right. The next room they found was an armory, stripped bare of all but a few rusted swords and armor stands. Sienne examined the walls of the corridor outside the armory.

"Strange," she said. "There's moss growing here where there isn't any just ten feet away in the cross-corridor." She leaned close and sniffed the moss. It smelled reassuringly green.

"This place has mold growing all over it," Alaric said. "There's probably some quality of the walls that encourages it, or inhibits it."

"Probably," Sienne said.

Far in the distance, something went *thunk*. Sienne froze. "What was that?"

Alaric raised his head like a pointer scenting game. "I don't know. It didn't sound like something falling. Did you knock something over?" he called to the three still in the armory.

"No," Dianthe said, and a moment later she joined them at the door. "It sounded like a door slamming, or a portcullis dropping."

"Huh," Alaric said. "Did you find anything hidden?"

"No, and Perrin's blessing didn't either. Let's move on."

"Aren't we worried about that noise?" Sienne asked.

"There's nothing we can do about whatever it is," Alaric said. "We'll just have to hope it's not some gate trapping us in here."

Sienne shivered. "You could have kept that thought to yourself."

Turning left at the T-junction led them down a winding corridor to a dead end. "I guess we'll have to tackle that trap, after all," Dianthe said as they turned and headed back.

"We're not in a hurry," Alaric said, "and I don't—what's that *smell?*"

Sienne sniffed. A breeze brought the scent of something rotting to her nose. Something rotting, tinged with the burning, sour odor of a strong acid. Her heart pounded faster. "Could there be ghouls down here?"

"Nothing for them to eat," Alaric said. "I don't think anything could live down here except bugs and rats."

Dianthe stopped at the corner leading to the T-junction. "You know," she said in a too-casual voice, "we haven't seen any rats down here at all. Or beetles, or spiders."

Sienne drew closer to Alaric. "What does that mean?"

"It means we might be in for a fight," Alaric said. "Let's not be carried away by our imaginations, all right? Lack of vermin doesn't have to mean anything."

Sienne realized she was shaking and clutched her spellbook tighter. She was being ridiculous. She and her companions could defeat anything this lair could throw at them. She couldn't stop shaking. Her arms and legs vibrated with it. Just as she realized the vibration was coming from outside her, Alaric said, "Something's coming. Something big."

They had nearly reached the T-junction. Sienne's lights illuminated the short corridor clearly. No one was there. The vibration had grown to the point that it was audible as a low hum that sang through Sienne's bones and teeth, rattling her skull. She stepped in front of Alaric and opened her spellbook to *fury*. It sounded big, and anything this big needed more than one *force* bolt. She wasn't taking chances.

Behind her, she heard the rasp of Alaric's sword sliding free from its sheath. The sound comforted her. She held up a hand, reminding them to stay silent. It was possible whoever this was didn't know they were there.

The lights danced in the air, caught in the vibration. The smell of rot and acid was so strong Sienne could taste it. She swallowed hard and clenched her teeth together, blinked away tears from the stinging, acidic air, and focused hard on the T-junction corner.

The air rippled, and two of Sienne's lights went out.

She blinked. The rippling in the air didn't stop. Something was there, something almost invisible in the now-dim light. She made more lights and flung them down the corridor. As they sailed into the junction, they vanished.

"Kitane's eyes, look at that," Dianthe breathed. A rat danced—danced!—into view, reared up on its hind legs. Its fur was almost gone, and bone shone through in places. Sienne covered her mouth to hold back a shriek. She still had nightmares about undead monsters, and maybe this rat wasn't big enough to hurt anyone, but it still horrified her.

She brought up her spellbook and flipped back to *burn*. *Force* had no effect on the undead. But as she began to read, Perrin said, "Dear Averran, it is floating. There is something there, carrying it."

Sienne took another look. The air before them shimmered, and as another light went out, Sienne realized the rat wasn't moving its limbs. Perrin was right—something was carrying it, something nearly invisible that moved slowly into the T-junction. "What is that thing?" she exclaimed. Now that she was looking more closely, she could see other things embedded in the field, or mass, or whatever it was: tiny stones, wisps of what might once have been moss, more small furry bodies nearly eaten away, the twisted remnants of a lantern bracket.

Kalanath stepped forward, his staff extended. Its steel tip prodded the thing. "It feels like a jelly," he said. The thing reached the wall and stopped. Kalanath pressed harder, then yanked his staff back as the wood below the steel cap began to smoke. "That is fire-hardened oak," he said. "It is a powerful acid, whatever it is."

Sienne summoned more lights. "But what is it for?"

Alaric chuckled. "I think we just met the cleaning staff. Look—Sienne, shine a light up high there. It's exactly the same shape as the corridor."

Sienne did as he directed. With a dozen lights shining on it, the creature was visible as a cube of some thick, clear liquid, its skin shimmering with oily rainbows. It was almost pretty.

The vibration began again. Kalanath took another step back. "Ah," he said, "it is moving again. Toward us."

"It's not that fast. We can stay out of its way," Alaric said. Then a peculiar look crossed his face. "But this is a blind corridor."

They all looked at each other. "I think we should back up," Dianthe said.

They retreated around the corner, all the way back to the blind end. "Sienne, can you get us out of here?" Alaric said.

"I can get *some* of us out of here," Sienne said. Her palms were sweaty, and she surreptitiously wiped them on her trousers. "Moving all of us with *ferry* takes all my reserves, and I've already cast spells today, to get us in here. But I can try *force*-blasting it."

"We can fit two of us across the corridor," Alaric said. "Maybe if we hit it hard enough, we can get it to reverse its course."

They ran back down the twisting corridor. The cube hadn't advanced very far, though it had consumed more of Sienne's lights. Sienne opened her spellbook and read off the evocation *force*. The syllables of the spell were hard and etched with acid, burning her mouth the way the acid in the air burned her eyes. She kept from blinking until the spell shot away from her in a tremendous burst of force.

It splashed against the cube and vanished.

"Burn it," Alaric said. Sienne flipped pages and read again, tears trickling down her cheeks from the burning sensation. *Scorch* would be more powerful, but it would also burn everyone in the area, so she stuck with its lesser cousin *burn*. Dark blue fire shot away from her to strike the cube, flickering across its surface.

This time, she got the thing's attention. A high, wavering scream joined the low hum, creating a discordant melody that felt like needles being stabbed into her ears. Alaric grabbed her and pulled her back as the cube accelerated toward them. It still wasn't moving faster than a brisk walk, but the way it just kept coming, inexorable and ponderous, made Sienne want to flee.

Alaric squared up to the thing and swung his massive sword in a great two-handed blow. It struck the cube, which made no effort to get out of the way. The sword sliced through the membrane of its skin, and a thick, clear liquid spurted out, striking Alaric in the chest. He shouted and sprang backward, swiping at himself. The stench of acid redoubled. Sienne stepped in front of him and read off *burn* again. The blue fire struck the cube, turning it a translucent sapphire color briefly. It sped up again. Sienne saw no other indication that her spell had affected it.

Sienne turned to Alaric and nearly screamed at the sight of his chest, the jerkin and shirt burned away, raw red burns covering his chest and stomach. Alaric was paler than usual and grimacing with pain. "You need to get out of here," he panted. "Take Dianthe."

"I'm not leaving you. Don't be stupid."

"Sienne—"

They'd backed almost all the way to the dead end. Hands grabbed Sienne and pulled her away from the oncoming juggernaut. Then Perrin said, "O Lord, have patience in your crankiness, and grant me this blessing." A pearly gray wall went up between them and the cube, which was now only ten feet away and closing fast.

"Smart," Alaric said. "But will it last long enough?"

"I have no idea. We did not see this thing earlier, so perhaps once it reaches the end of its route, it will return to wherever it lurks when it is not on duty." Perrin stepped forward to the edge of the gray barrier. "Unless it does not consider itself finished until it touches the wall behind us."

Dianthe swore. "This is ridiculous. We haven't seen a single blind corridor in this whole damned labyrinth until now. I refuse to believe there's no way out of here." She pressed her hands to the wall and closed her eyes, feeling her way along it.

Sienne stood watching the cube advance. She felt Alaric put his arm around her shoulders and squeeze gently. "Get out of here," he said.

"Make me."

"I would if I could. Sienne—"

The cube pressed against the gray barrier, which started to sizzle. The scent of jasmine and mint mingled sickeningly with the stench of acid. Sienne and Alaric backed away. "I have one more shield blessing," Perrin said. "I will not go without a fight."

The shield popped like a soap bubble. The cube lurched forward. Perrin invoked the blessing, stopping the cube three feet from them. Sienne stared through the barrier at it. "At least we know which corridors are safe," she said. "The ones with moss still growing on the walls. I wonder why those don't get cleaned."

"If I remembered which ones they were, I could make a guess," Perrin said.

The barrier shivered. "Dianthe, if you're going to make a discovery," Alaric began.

"Shut up, mountain," Dianthe said through gritted teeth.

With a pop, the shield vanished. The cube once again advanced. "Well," Alaric said, "it's been—"

A whoosh of dank, sweet air free of acid taint blew past them. "Save it for later," Dianthe said, grabbing Kalanath and hauling him through the gap she'd just opened. "Move!"

2

Sienne darted through the opening, followed by Alaric, who immediately turned and shoved the secret door closed. It moved ponderously slowly, and the cube began to press through the opening before the door closed on it, leaving them all in blackness. Sienne leaned against the wall, not caring about the dampness, and waited for her heart to slow. Beside her, Alaric breathed more heavily than his exertions accounted for. She fumbled in the dark until she found his hand and clutched it. He gripped her hand tightly and drew her into his embrace. She felt raw skin and pulled back slightly. "Did I hurt you?"

"Not much. Make a light, will you?"

"Oh. Sorry." She made half a dozen magic lights and sent them spinning into the air. Her friends all blinked in the sudden light, which made them look ghostly, even dark-skinned Kalanath and the well-tanned Perrin. "I can't believe we're alive. I *knew* I should have made more of an effort to find *transport*. *Ferry* is just too exhausting with a team this size."

"Nobody's blaming you," Dianthe said. "Let's take a look around this place."

Sienne made more lights and shot them off into the corners of the room. It wasn't very big compared to the others they'd found, maybe twenty feet on a side and with the same low ceiling the entire palace seemed to have. Empty shelves lined the walls, with chests bound in corroded brass occupying the center of the room. All the chests had their lids flung open, and most were arranged in a way that suggested they'd been shoved around.

Kalanath peered into one of them. "Empty."

"So is this one," Perrin said. "I would guess they all are."

"Well, damn," Alaric said. "If this was the treasury, we're too late."

"We don't know that it was the treasury. It could have been an ordinary storage room," Dianthe said. She examined one of the shelves and shook her head. "Nothing here."

"An ordinary storage room wouldn't have been stripped bare," Alaric said. "Scrappers don't take what they can't sell, and they wouldn't burden themselves with the kind of ordinary things people tend to store."

"But why would Perrin's augury show this place had salvage, if it's already been taken?" Sienne asked.

"Possibly this was not Nocenti's only treasure chamber," Perrin said. "She was arrogant and clever, true, but she was also paranoid and mistrustful. I think we should be looking for a secret room."

"Go ahead," Dianthe said. She'd moved from the shelf to the room's only visible door and was staring at the latch with her hands on her hips. "Our friends, whoever they were, left us another trap. I wish I could find them so I could strangle them. This smacks of deliberate malice."

Perrin nodded and removed another blessing from the riffle. "Our thanks for the shields that warded us against that monstrosity, Lord," he said, "and if you would, have patience in your crankiness, and grant me this additional blessing."

Violet fire flared, and lines of purple light traced the stones of the wall, turning all of them a funny gray color. They showed the secret door as a brightly lit rectangle that continued to glow long after the rest of the light faded. No second hidden door appeared. "I have only one more of these blessings," Perrin said. "I hope I do not misuse them."

"I thought you said Averran likes it when people use their initiative to figure things out," Sienne said.

"He is also opposed to his worshippers leaning too heavily on his aid." Perrin went to stand near Dianthe, but not too near. "We should exhaust our other resources before calling on him again, I think."

Dianthe was crouched before the door, peering at the latch. She brought both hands in front of her face, cupped as if catching a stream of water. Then, with a twist of her left wrist, she caught something invisible to Sienne and drew it away like someone gathering up a rope into a coil. "That wasn't too bad," she said. "Though it would have been unpleasant if we'd just walked through the door."

"Locked?" Alaric said.

"No. They probably thought the trap was enough." She opened the door and stuck her head through. "No acid-filled cubes. It's another storage room."

"Dianthe, you start looking for a concealed door. Everyone else, let's be thorough." Alaric gestured for Sienne to precede him out the door.

It was a storage room, but not bare like the first. Barrels and crates lay piled haphazardly throughout the room, some of them split open to reveal moldy grain or rusted metal. There were shelves here, too, all as empty as in the first room, but in this case it was because someone, or several someones, had swept the crockery and casks to the floor to lie in shattered heaps around the shelves. The smell of decay and fungus was strong enough Sienne had to breathe through her mouth. "What are we looking for? Because I can tell you right now, there's no market for bolts of rotted fabric."

"We want to be sure not to overlook anything mundane that might have resale value," Alaric said. "Though I'm not betting on it. The idiots who came through here first had no idea this pottery was valuable. If it weren't shattered, we could get more than a hundred lari for each set. Old crockery is popular among the well-to-do."

"I could mend it, but that would take forever," Sienne said. She picked up a handle and the curving side of a jug and fit them together, using a small magic to repair the crack. "Though it is a perfect repair job."

"We're not quite so desperate for cash as to make you reassemble the lot." Alaric took the mended piece out of her hands. "Dianthe?"

"Still looking," came the reply. "I wish I had a better sense for how this labyrinth was laid out. I have no idea which of these walls could theoretically have enough space for a secret room behind it."

"There are two doors," Kalanath said. "I think the wall they are in is not it."

"Don't touch the doors," Dianthe said. "I haven't checked them yet, and those idiots might have thought it was funny to leave more surprises." She felt along one of the walls, then stopped. "This stone is a different color."

"How can you tell? It all looks black to me," Sienne said.

"I just can. There's something here, but I can't find it."

Alaric stepped up to the wall and began feeling along it with his right palm. His left hand, Sienne finally saw, was as blistered from the acid as his chest. "Do you need healing?" she said. "Your hand, and your chest..."

Alaric looked at his palm and the backs of his fingers as if he'd never seen them before, then touched his chest gingerly. "It's only just starting to hurt. I didn't realize how much I'd burned myself getting that stuff off me."

"I cannot repair your clothing, but flesh is another matter," Perrin said, coming to Alaric's side. Sienne watched as he muttered an invocation and green light spread across Alaric's chest and hand. The scent of jasmine and mint swept away the funk of mold briefly, making the room smell of spring. Alaric flexed his newly-healed hand and nodded thanks.

"I think it's time for that blessing, Perrin," Dianthe said. "I'm sure there's a door here, but I can't find a way to open it. Maybe a little divine light will help."

Perrin tore off the last of the purple-smudged blessings and walked around a shattered crate to close to the center of the room. "O

Lord, if you will, have patience in your crankiness, and grant me this blessing," he said, "and if it is not too much trouble, guide our hands in this matter."

The violet light traced the black stones once more. Sienne gasped. A thicker line of light like glowing mortar outlined a jagged section of wall, then vanished. She stepped closer. Now that she'd seen it, she couldn't imagine how they'd missed it before. The blessing had left the stones within the outline scrubbed dry, and the secret door was obvious.

"Perfect," Dianthe said. "Now we just have to find a way in."

"It doesn't look like it was made to open," Sienne said. "More like someone bricked it up when they were done. Thoroughly, so it blended with the other stones."

"That's possible," Alaric said. He ran his hand over the surface. "But I don't relish the thought of having to batter it down."

Dianthe was on her hands and knees, creeping along the base of the wall with one hand lightly touching the stones. Her eyes were closed. "Just give me a minute."

They waited in silence. Sienne was sure Dianthe could work despite distractions, but there was no point increasing the difficulty of her task. She watched Dianthe stand and brush moisture off her knees. "Perrin," she said, "I need your pastels."

"Certainly," Perrin said, removing the packet of colored sticks he used to mark his blessings. "May I ask why?"

"You'll see." Dianthe withdrew a pale blue one and drew an X low on the wall near the left edge of the dry spot. "Sienne, I want you to cast *force* on the wall, right where the X is."

"Are you sure? That could bring the ceiling down on us."

Dianthe handed the pastels back to Perrin. "I don't think so. There are marks just here, radiating out from the spot I marked, that look like what *force* does to stone. And I'm certain there's no other opening mechanism."

Sienne shrugged. "All right. Everyone stand back, just in case." She read off the evocation. The power built within her until it burst forth with the final syllables of the spell. The bolt of magical energy shot away from her to strike the wall in the exact center of the X.

A shuddering groan like two mountains colliding filled the small room. Sienne dropped her spellbook to hang loose in its harness and covered her ears. With a sharp crack, part of the wall popped free and swiveled toward the companions. Stale air rushed out of the dark space exposed by the spell. Sienne coughed and lowered her hands. She looked at Alaric, who'd stepped between her and the wall when it began to move. "Lights," he said.

Sienne made lights and sent them flying into the space. Their glow revealed a room no bigger than a closet, its whitewashed walls blinding after the darkness of the outer room. A chest big enough for Sienne to curl up in sat on the floor, its steel bindings and lock plate gleaming and free of rust. She let out a long, awed breath. "That has to be intact," she said.

"Let's hope so," Dianthe said, kneeling to examine the lock. "There's no sign it's been tampered with, and no traps. I bet Nocenti thought the secret door would be enough protection." Her fingers were busy with her lock picks as she spoke. "That, and this lock is fiendishly difficult."

It felt like hours before the lock clicked open. Sienne spent the time staring at the doors they hadn't yet opened, feeling superstitiously that another scrapper team might burst through them and attack. She found she'd opened her spellbook to *fury* without realizing it, thought about closing the book, and decided to embrace paranoia.

The sound of Dianthe lifting the chest lid dragged her attention back to what mattered. She pressed forward with the others, then took a step back when Dianthe said, "It's not going anywhere. But by Kitane's eyes, there's a *lot* of it."

Sienne dropped to her knees next to Dianthe to get out of the way of the men. She reached out to touch a silver mirror decorated with pale purple stones that winked in the white light. "This is the kind of treasure I dreamed scrappers always found."

"In nearly seven years of scrapping, I've never seen a trove like this," Alaric said. He reached past Sienne and Dianthe and picked up an ivory scroll case, carved with starbursts and capped with jet. "Sienne, see if there's anything wizardly in this."

Sienne scooted to one side and worked the cap off. Inside was a sheaf of parchment, tightly curled on itself. She shook it hard until the pages slid out into her hand, then spread the sheets flat on the floor. "Spells," she said. "The parchment's untreated...well, that makes sense, you can't turn parchment invulnerable without destroying it. Looks like...*break, cat's eye, shift,* and...this evocation is an old-fashioned variant on *shout.*" She smiled. "And I've never seen this summoning before."

"Is that good?" Kalanath asked. He had a pair of golden earrings set with agates in one hand and a silver bracelet in the other.

"Could be. A lost spell is worth far, far more than its market value. Well, it would have to be, because no one will know how much to ask for it. If I sold this to the university, or to Stravanus...depending on what spell it is, it could be worth the rest of this treasure combined."

"Don't get too excited," Alaric warned. "We have to get it home first."

"I know. Oh, that necklace is beautiful!"

"Blue star sapphire," Dianthe said, "and worth a minimum of a thousand lari." Dianthe always knew about gems.

"I believe this is Nocenti's personal seal," Perrin said, holding up a fat signet ring with an intricate pattern incised on the top. "A collector might find it valuable."

"Plenty of coin, too," Alaric said, hefting a small sack. "We'll count this later. Let's load up."

Sienne handed out more treasure, a silver comb, a crystal egg with a silver stand, a cloak pin of a white-gold metal Dianthe said was platinum, and several more bags of coin. That left only one thing at the bottom of the chest, something that glowed in Sienne's wizardly sight.

Sienne lifted it out. It was a slim ash baton about fifteen inches in length, with a smooth grip shaped to a hand a little bigger than hers— well, her hands were small, so that wasn't surprising. Tiny crystals embedded in the wood made a spiral from the tip to just above the hand grip. A few of them were dark, but the rest sparkled like diamonds. Sienne wrapped her hand around it and waved it, directing an invisible orchestra to attention. "It's pretty, but I don't know what it does."

"It's fancy, for a stick," Alaric said.

"No, it's a wand. An artifact. I've seen them before in Stravanus. They can let people who aren't wizards cast spells—or, rather, each wand has a spell imbuing it, and if you know how to activate the wand, you can cast the spell." She touched the darkened crystals, counted the rest. "But wands can only be used a certain number of times before the magic runs out. Looks like this one started with thirty spells, and eight have been used."

"So when you say you do not know what it does, you mean you do not know the spell on it," Kalanath said.

"Right. I know the masters at Stravanus have a way of learning which spell is on a wand, and it's sometimes possible to figure it out by experimentation, but that can be wasteful and potentially dangerous."

"I imagine I can request a blessing that will tell us," Perrin said, "if Averran chooses to help. He may consider the search for that knowledge a divine blessing in itself."

"Sometimes I wish your avatar weren't quite so devoted to seeing humans grow in wisdom on their own," Alaric said. "But it's a problem for another time. Let's get out of this place."

Sienne stowed the wand in her pack beside the scroll case. Now was the most dangerous time, after they'd succeeded in finding their treasure but before they were home safely. It was easy to become complacent despite there still being obstacles. She opened her spellbook to *burn* again. *No more acid-filled cubes of jelly*, she thought, *no undead, no swarms of diseased rats...*

Dianthe was studying the two doors. "They're not locked and there's no nasty surprises waiting. I don't know which to choose."

"Left," Alaric said.

"You always sound so decisive," Sienne said. "How do you know?"

"I don't, but assertiveness can cover a multitude of sins," Alaric said.

The left-hand door opened on a long corridor, at the end of which was another closed door. Dianthe swore. "Trapped. I think this is the door in the barracks. I can deal with it, but it's risky. Traps that sit around for a long time can degrade—bits go rusty, or shift, and that makes them more dangerous."

"But we know what's on the other side of this door, and what I like about it is that there are no horrible corridor-cleaning creatures there," Sienne said.

"Let's go back and try the other door," Alaric said. "This is not a risk I want to take."

Weariness struck Sienne as they trudged back down the hall. She'd lost track of how long they'd been in this subterranean palace. It was hard to imagine anyone living here voluntarily. Reva Nocenti had to have been slightly mad to think it was a good idea.

The second door led to another corridor that turned left almost immediately. "It's leading us back toward the barracks, or at least in that direction," Dianthe said. Sienne eyed the walls, clear of dirt or moss, and moved a little closer to Alaric. They were all walking faster now, not needing to say aloud what they were all thinking: *how soon before that thing comes back?*

They came to another left-hand turn. Sienne wished her internal compass, product of a small magic, was any use down here. She knew they were facing northwest, but that told her nothing about the more important question of where the exit was. She'd had the stink of rot and acid in her nostrils for so long she'd begun hallucinating nicer smells, like roses or even manure.

"Do you see that?" Alaric said to Dianthe.

"I see it." Dianthe sounded grim.

"What? See what?" Sienne demanded.

"A cube, way at the end of the corridor," Alaric said.

"Is it coming this way?" Kalanath asked.

"Can't tell."

"I think this corridor leads to the exit," Dianthe said. "Either that, or it's parallel to it."

"There seem to be no other doors along this hall," Perrin said. "Should we turn back?"

"The cube is definitely coming this way, Alaric," Dianthe said. "Not as fast as the other, but we need to make a decision."

Sienne looked past Alaric's bulk at the shimmer that marked the presence of a cube. She made a few lights and hurled them down the hall to light it up more fully. As they flew, they cast odd shadows on the floor—

"There's a side passage," she exclaimed. "On the right."

In the glow of her lights, the cube was clearly closer than she'd thought. Dianthe said, "I think that's the exit!"

"The thing is very close," Kalanath said.

"Run," Alaric said.

They pounded along the corridor, Sienne working desperately to keep up with her longer-legged companions. The stench of acid burned her throat as she gasped for air. Alaric blocked her view of the oncoming cube now, but she didn't need to see it to know it was going to be a close race. If the cube blocked the exit before they reached it...they could turn around, try their luck with the trapped door, but that was its own kind of danger. She pushed herself harder, grateful the cube's cleaning secretions didn't leave the stones slippery.

Dianthe made a sharp right turn, and Sienne tripped over her own feet trying to stop. Alaric caught her under the arms and gave her a shove in Dianthe's direction. The acid in the air was almost overpowering. Sienne kept running down this new corridor, praying the cube had a preset path and this wasn't part of it.

The path sloped gently upward, and Sienne's legs ached from running up the incline. Just as she registered the presence of moss on the walls, Alaric said, "It's passed us. We're safe."

Sienne stopped and crouched with her hands on her knees, breathing deeply. "This *is* the way out, isn't it?"

Fresh, warm air struck her by way of reply. "It is," Dianthe said, holding open the door at the end of the hall. Sienne walked past her into the shallow cave that concealed the entrance to Reva Nocenti's underground lair. The air smelled of stone and, faintly, animal waste, but she'd never smelled anything more delicious. It was dark beyond the cave mouth, but it was the beautiful darkness of a true summer night, not the pitchy blackness of underground, and tension slipped away from Sienne like water flowing down a drain.

Alaric came up behind her and put his arms around her. "One hurdle down," he said. "Back to Glorenze, then another two days will see us in Fioretti."

"Now who's looking beyond the mark?" she teased.

"Just planning ahead. I feel I could sleep for days, but the work is just beginning." He kissed the top of her head. "Let's start walking."

3

Every time Sienne returned to Fioretti, it felt like a different city. The capital bustled with life and energy no matter the season, and old buildings were always being torn down to make way for new construction. The people were different, too, thousands of men and women coming to Fioretti for a fresh start or leaving Fioretti to try their luck elsewhere.

But now the City of Golden Ways sparkled and shone as never before. Sienne reined her horse Spark in to watch a pair of men hanging strings of lights between lampposts using invisible fingers, and marveled at the colors, red, white, and gold. Every door they passed had a wreath made of thin, flexible vines woven with yellow forsythia branches or red or white berries. Some of those were probably poisonous, but it was unlikely anyone would try to eat them.

"We're not going anywhere for the next week, are we?" she asked. "I don't want to miss the festivities."

"I don't see why the celebration is so important," Alaric said. "It's not as if the city has done anything more than exist for four hundred years."

"That still makes it the oldest city in Rafellin," Perrin pointed out. "Nearly as old as the wars that tore civilization apart. It is a milestone everyone can find common ground to celebrate, regardless of income or religious beliefs."

"There will be food, and athletic events, and *dancing*," Sienne said. "You should enter the contests, Alaric. Wrestling, or I think there are tests of strength..."

"I'm not a citizen," Alaric said. "I think it might dampen things if I defeated a Rafellish contestant."

"Hmm. You're probably right. We're still going dancing."

Alaric clutched his right knee and pretended pain. "I think I pulled a muscle running from that cube."

"I am happy to heal whatever troubles you," Perrin said with an arch smile.

Alaric muttered something under his breath. Sienne said, "It will be fun, you know it will."

"Anything for you, sweetlove," he said, smiling in a way that warmed Sienne's heart.

They left the horses at the stable and continued on to their lodgings on foot. Master Tersus's house felt more like home to Sienne than the ducal palace in Beneddo, where she'd grown up, ever had. She looked forward to a good home-cooked meal and her own comfortable bed. Inns were never the same, no matter how expensive they were.

She shifted her pack to keep the ivory scroll case from digging into her spine and said, "Who should we approach to sell this stuff? I imagine we can't use that old coin as modern currency."

"Right," Alaric said. "This find is big enough, we should make it public knowledge, which will boost our reputation and get us more contracts in the long run. So we'll need to declare it with the government, to establish provenance. They'll want a cut, but we should still make enough to keep us going for a year even if we took no other jobs."

"Which will give us time to continue the search," Dianthe said. "Though we probably don't want to stop working entirely."

"And some of that money will have to go toward buying access to private libraries," Sienne said.

"Does not the University of Fioretti library suffice?" Perrin said.

"The three books I found there were only partially helpful. I haven't given up hope of finding a book that has the whole ritual we need." Sienne couldn't help feeling personally responsible for her failure, though she knew it was stupid. They needed to find a ritual that would free Alaric's people, the shape-shifting race called Sassaven, and although a year of searching had taken them farther than Alaric had gotten alone in ten years, they had hit a wall recently. The bulk of the research burden had fallen on Sienne, fluent in three languages and familiar with reading ancient books, and every time she left the university library empty-handed, she felt despair creep a little closer.

"We have the knife, the goblet, and the sedative potion," Kalanath said. "It is more than we had a year ago."

"And we've found pieces of the ritual," Alaric said. "Kalanath's right, we've made progress."

They were passing the world-famous Fioretti marketplace, home to hundreds of booths selling anything one could possibly want, and the noise was so great Alaric had to pitch his voice louder to be heard. Hundreds, perhaps thousands of voices argued and haggled and laughed, creating waves of sound that rushed over Sienne, making her wish she could cover her ears like a child in a thunderstorm. "What did you say?" she shouted.

"I said we can worry about it another day!" Alaric said.

Sienne nodded, not wanting to shout over the din. She took a few more steps to keep up with Alaric, whose powerful form parted the crowds like a battleship, and gasped as someone grabbed her arm and pulled her to the side. "Alaric!" she shouted.

Instantly he was there, breaking the grip of her assailant and twisting the dark-haired man's arm high behind his back. The man yelped in pain and said, "Let me go! Sienne!"

Sienne took a step back in surprise. Her hands and face felt as numb as if struck by *force*. "Rance," she said faintly.

"You're an idiot if you think you can attack people in broad daylight," Alaric snarled, and twisted harder. Rance let out a hiss and arched his back, trying to get away from the implacable grip.

"Let him go," Sienne said. "He's...let him go. He wasn't trying to hurt me." That, at least, she was certain of. Rance had only ever inflicted emotional pain on her.

Alaric released Rance, who took a couple of long steps away from the Sassaven and rubbed his wrist. "Do you know this man?" Alaric asked.

She felt a flash of anger and humiliation that left her wishing she could run away from all of them, anything not to let her two worlds meet in such spectacular fashion. "This is Rance," she said. "Rance Lanzano Verannus."

Alaric's brow furrowed. "*This* is Rance?"

The way he said it, as if Rance's identity were an impossibility, as if there were something shameful about it, made Sienne wish even more that she could hide. "Yes."

"It is the Rance who married your sister, yes?" Kalanath said, with an air of having solved an intractable puzzle.

"Yes." Her ex-lover, her first lover, who'd left her when the opportunity to marry her sister and become heir to a dukedom had fallen into his lap. She felt she needed a map and a guide dog to fully explain what he was to her.

Alaric still had that look of consternation on his face. "I thought he'd be taller," was all he said.

That made Sienne want to laugh. Rance was handsome in a dark, Rafellish way, with hazel eyes that twinkled when he laughed, but he was several inches short of six feet tall and compactly built. Alaric, at over six and a half feet tall, loomed over Rance like the mountain he was popularly compared to.

"Sienne, who are these people? Where have you been for the past year?" Rance looked bewildered, which made sense—he probably hadn't expected to just pass her on the street when she'd spent the last year staying thoroughly lost.

"In Fioretti. I'm a scrapper now. These are my companions." That was simple and straightforward, something she felt on solid ground with. "Why are you in the capital?"

"We came for the celebration. King Derekian summoned us. And —but I'm overwhelmed, Sienne. Don't you know how much your parents have worried about you? We all thought you were dead!"

"Well, I'm not dead." How had she missed how whiny he sounded? She'd thought she loved him, and love did strange things to the perceptions. "I thought the king would have told them I was safe."

"The king? Why would the king do that? Sienne, come with me. Your parents need to see you." Rance reached for Sienne and was arrested by Alaric's hand landing heavily on his shoulder. "Don't touch me."

"Don't touch *her*, and I won't have to," Alaric rumbled. "She's not going anywhere."

"Oh? And who are you, to make that decision for her?"

"I told you, he's my companion," Sienne said, interrupting Alaric's retort. "And I'm not going anywhere."

Rance hesitated, looking at Alaric, then at the others, who'd remained silent but watchful during this conversation. "You don't understand. They *really* need to see you. It's important."

"Why is it important?"

"I...you should speak to your parents. I can't explain it." His eyes flicked to her friends again, in a way that said clearly *I can't explain it in front of these people.*

"The duke and duchess are in Fioretti?" Dianthe said. "Sienne—"

"I don't have anything to say to them," Sienne said, but she felt her certainty slipping away. Seeing Rance made her carefully constructed world fall apart, made the illusion that she was simply Sienne the scrapper wizard and not Lady Sienne Verannus impossible to maintain.

"It is a small thing," Perrin said. He'd avoided looking at Rance and had his attention fully on her. "They cannot make you do anything you do not wish."

Sienne wasn't sure that was true, but if it wasn't, it was her own weakness that made it so. "Tomorrow," she told Rance. "Where are they?"

"Why not right now? I'm going there—just went out to pick up a few things for Felice."

The mention of his wife, her older sister, was like a splash of cold water to the face. She could bear seeing her father, could endure seeing her mother, and Rance himself...it was like their affair was a ghost of a thing, nothing that roused any current emotions except, perhaps, embarrassment. But coming face to face with her sister, knowing that they'd shared a lover—that was too much to bear. It hardened her heart against Rance's pleas. "Tomorrow," she repeated. "We're just back in town and I'm tired. They can wait a little longer."

Rance sighed. "They're at the Plaza of Sighs," he said. "Number four, across from the Gavant chapel. Can I at least tell them when to expect you?"

"Ten o'clock tomorrow morning. And yes," she added as Rance opened his mouth, "I'll come alone."

Rance looked swiftly away from Alaric, who looked ready to explode. "Thank you. I...thank you. Tomorrow at ten." He made as if to clasp her hand, thought better of it, and disappeared into the crowd.

Sienne stared blindly in the direction he'd taken until Dianthe said, "Sienne. Let's go." Then she turned and followed her friends toward home. She wasn't sure if they were being tactful, or if the noise was just too great to carry on a conversation, but she was grateful for their silence.

They walked as far as the bottom of the street where Master Tersus's house lay before Perrin said, "Are you certain you wish to go alone?"

"No, I'm not," Sienne said, "but I think I have to. I don't know why, but it feels wrong to have you all with me when I meet my parents for the first time in over a year. Like I'd be bringing a siege weapon to a knife fight."

Kalanath chuckled. "It is true, we are fierce in each other's defense. It is maybe not a thing you need."

"I know where that house is," Dianthe said. "We'll be waiting for you to return, and if you don't, we'll storm the place."

"I know. Thank you."

Alaric held the door for them all, and Sienne breathed a sigh of relief when it closed behind them. They'd had an uneventful journey back from Reva Nocenti's lair, but she hadn't felt safe until now, surrounded by familiar walls and with the smell of beef stew simmering on Leofus's stove.

"I'm going to nap before dinner," Dianthe said. "Carrying so much treasure through the streets makes me tense, and that makes me sleepy."

"That's a good idea," Sienne said. "Alaric?"

"I'll be up shortly," he said. "Leave your packs, and I'll store the treasure in a secure place. Master Tersus will let us use his safe."

Sienne dropped her pack at his feet and trudged up the stairs in front of Dianthe. At her bedroom door, Dianthe stopped her, her face still and worried. "You don't still...care about that man, do you?"

It was so ludicrous Sienne laughed, and controlled herself before it could turn into hysterics. "Of course not! Why? Did it look like I did?" The remnants of her laughter evaporated. "*Alaric* didn't think so, did he?"

"I doubt it. He just...he was awfully quiet all the way back, the way he gets when he has something on his mind."

"He's probably just tired. But I won't let it go at that, if that's what you're wondering."

"Thanks. Sleep well."

Sienne went into her room and took off her boots and socks, wriggling her toes in pleasure. Alaric couldn't be jealous of Rance. It was just ridiculous. Nobody sane would choose Rance over Alaric...all right, Rance was handsome in a roguish way, but Alaric was strong, tall, well-muscled, and had those hands that made Sienne shiver when he touched her. It was probably nothing.

She lay back and listened for the sound of Alaric's heavy feet on the stairs. Her muscles weren't tense anymore, but she didn't feel sleepy, just relaxed. Of course, when she thought of her parents, she tensed up again. They were the ones who'd arranged the match between Rance and Felice, the heir, and with a year's distance she could admit they hadn't done it to be cruel, because they hadn't known about Sienne's attachment to Rance. But she'd humiliated herself in begging them to let her marry him, and she'd never forget the pitying look in her father's eyes or the scorn in her mother's voice: *We can't insult the Lanzanos by offering them the lesser sister.* Lesser sister. It still made her burn with fury and residual humiliation.

And now she'd have to see them again after swearing she'd never return home. Technically, she hadn't broken that oath, but she felt the spirit of it had been, maybe not violated, but certainly stretched to the breaking point. Was her whole family here? Maybe she could see her siblings, whom she'd missed—not the younger ones, who'd been infants when she left home for her fosterage in Stravanus, but certainly her next younger brother Alcander. That was a cheery thought.

She heard someone coming up the stairs with a heavy tread and sat up. But Alaric passed her door and moved on down the corridor, and moments later his old bedroom door opened and shut. He hadn't used that room for over a month, not since they'd started sleeping together. It felt like a punch to the stomach. So he wouldn't come to her. Maybe she was wrong, and he was jealous. Or angry. She hated it when they were at odds; he was her heart, her dearest love, and when they weren't one she ached inside.

She left her room and went down the corridor to knock at his door, then opened it without being invited. "What's wrong?" she asked, closing the door behind her.

Alaric was seated on the bed, removing his boots. "I'd rather not talk about it."

"That never gets us anywhere. You're not jealous of Rance, are you? Because there's nothing to be jealous of. I wouldn't have him back even if I didn't love you."

He fixed his pale blue eyes on her. "Then why didn't you tell him I'm your lover?"

"I—didn't I?" She scrambled backward in memory. She'd called

Alaric her companion when Rance had asked who he was. She closed her eyes and thought about kicking herself. "I didn't. I don't know—no, wait, I do know why I didn't." She walked over to Alaric and took his face in her hands. "Rance is going to tell my mother every detail of our encounter, and I want the news that I've taken up with a giant Ansorjan scrapper to come directly from me."

Alaric raised one eyebrow. "Is that so important?"

"Love, if my mother is going to have a heart attack, I want to be there to witness it." She leaned down and kissed him lightly on the lips. "I assure you I'm not ashamed of you, or embarrassed to let my old lover know I've moved on, or...or still secretly in love with that slimy bastard. I can't wait for Rance to find out what you are to me, because you are superior to him in every way, and I think he knows it."

A smile touched Alaric's lips. He put his hands around her waist and pulled her down to sit on his lap. "I wasn't angry," he said, "I just had a moment of insecurity. Don't hold it against me."

"I never would. And now I think we should go back to our room and reassure each other. There's plenty of time before dinner." She squinched her eyes closed. "No, we can't. I've run out of the preventative. I'll have to find an apothecary first."

"Why are you using a preventative?"

"Because I'm not interested in ending my scrapping career early to take care of an infant. I didn't think I'd have to tell you that, love."

Alaric shook his head. "I thought I told you it's not necessary. Sassaven and humans can't interbreed."

She drew back, astonished. "I...had no idea."

"I could swear I told you. I'm sorry." His grip around her waist tightened. "I hope that's not distressing."

"Why would it be distressing? I had enough of raising children when my youngest sisters were babies. We were too poor to afford full-time nannies, and my mother enlisted Felice and me in shouldering our share of the burden. I'm relieved I don't have to worry about it."

"Oh." He looked thoughtful, as if he wanted to say something else, but just shook his head.

Sienne took the opportunity to kiss him, long and sweet, promising a world of delights. "Let's go. Sex in those seedy inns is never as satisfying as sex in our own big bed."

"I don't know," Alaric said, standing and swooping her up in his arms. "I find it satisfying wherever we have it."

4

The Plaza of Sighs was west of the palace and the estates of Fioretti's nobles. Tall mansions with pillared entries stood cheek by jowl along four sides of the five-sided plaza, facing an ugly marble fountain depicting all six avatars in their most heroic poses.

Sienne sought out the statue of Averran and stood looking at it for a while. Averran hadn't become famous until he was elderly, and his portly, bald statue comforted her in its ordinariness. The other five statues looked noble and beautiful, but the sculptor had depicted Averran as a grumpy old codger leaning on a walking stick, and it was so exactly how she pictured the avatar in her head she wondered if the sculptor had had some insight not granted to the average man.

She sighed and turned away from the fountain. The fifth side of the plaza was taken up by a chapel to the avatar Gavant, first of the avatars and a staple of Sienne's childhood. Like all places dedicated to Gavant, it exuded wealth, far surpassing the mansions on the plaza in its opulence. Its pillars and the frieze above the door were picked out in gold paint that was probably real gold, and the smell of very expensive incense floated from within. Sienne was happy to turn her back on it. Worshippers of Gavant didn't have to be proud or wealthy

—her own father was proof of that—but in general they cared more about appearances than Sienne felt comfortable with.

Brass numerals hung above each mansion's door, all of which were decorated with yellow wreaths of forsythia. The wreaths were so identical Sienne had an image of the householders, or renters, coming together to agree on a decorating scheme. It was fortunate the mansions themselves differed in construction and paint, or the effect would have been downright unsettling. Sienne rapped on the door of number four and waited.

Presently, the door opened, and a servant Sienne didn't recognize said, "Yes?" He might not have been Beris, her parents' steward, but he had the same air of upper-class superiority Sienne had always hated. He looked at her, assessed her appearance—she hadn't bothered to dress up for this—and dismissed her. It made her angry.

"Lady Sienne Verannus, here to see *my parents*," she said in her haughtiest voice. "If that's not too much trouble for you...what is your name?"

The man's eyes had widened when she declared her name, and he visibly controlled himself. "Pagani, my lady."

"Pagani. May I enter, or do your duties require you to keep me waiting on the doorstep?"

Pagani took several steps back and bowed. "My apologies, my lady. If you would care to step inside, I will show you to the drawing room."

Sienne sailed past him, forcing him to hurry to get ahead of her. She surreptitiously slowed her steps, not wanting to look like a fool for not knowing where to go. The entry hall rose two stories in the most modern fashion—this mansion couldn't be more than ten years old. Paint, not whitewash, brightened the walls, and four closed doors led off it. Stairs that curved back on themselves with a white ironwork bannister occupied the back of the hall, with another, smaller door tucked beneath them. It smelled of floor polish and the more biting scent of vinegar. Someone had cleaned thoroughly, and not very long ago.

Pagani opened the second door on the right and bowed again.

"Please make yourself comfortable, and I will tell the duke and duchess you have arrived."

Sienne nodded, the barest incline of her head she could get away with and not be rude, and Pagani shut the door behind her. Her feet made tapping noises on the freshly waxed floorboards, so shiny she could see her dim reflection in them. Antique chairs and a low table occupied the center of the room, atop a rug that might have been Chysegaran in make. The room had only two windows, and Sienne judged they faced the back of the mansion, which put them in shadow at this time of day. She almost made lights to illuminate the dimness, but decided against it. It was less off-putting when she couldn't see how opulent it was.

The chairs looked comfortable, for antiques, but sitting might make her look weak...or would it look like she was confident enough to behave like one of the family instead of an estranged daughter? She sat, discovered the chair wasn't as comfortable as it looked, and stood just as the door opened. She turned to face it, banishing the ridiculous guilty feeling that she'd been caught somewhere she didn't belong, and was for the first time in over a year face to face with her parents.

Dear Averran, she thought, *they look so old.* There was more gray in her mother's dark hair, her father's forehead was surely more wrinkled than it had been when she last saw him, and both looked so stern she had to quash an impulse to throw herself at their feet and beg their forgiveness. She swallowed to moisten a suddenly dry throat. She didn't want to be the first to speak, not least because she had no idea what to say.

Her father took a few steps forward. "Sienne," he said, his voice husky. Then he came to her, his arms outstretched, and enveloped her in a hug. "We're so glad to see you."

Startled, she reflexively put her arms around him and returned his embrace. He smelled just as she remembered, of dry paper and woody incense, and she found she was crying. "Papa," she said. "Papa, I don't know what to say."

"You don't need to say anything," Papa said, releasing her to arm's length. "We're just glad you're back."

Sienne looked past him at her mother, whose lips were still pressed together in a stern frown, and thought about that "we." Then her mother let out a deep sigh and reached for her. "Why couldn't you have at least told us you were safe?" she asked, clasping Sienne's hand and squeezing gently. "We imagined the worst."

Sienne's inappropriate guilt gave way to the real thing. "I thought King Derekian would tell you I was well. He knew where I was."

"Derekian knew?" Papa let out an explosive curse. "Damn him for keeping secrets. How dare he interfere in our family business?"

"I asked him not to tell you my location. I didn't want—I wasn't ready to return. But I told him it was all right to let you know I was well."

"He's a busy man, Pontus," Mother said. "And it *isn't* his business. Sienne, sit. You look so uncomfortable." She pulled a bell rope near the windows, and as if by magic, Pagani appeared. "Coffee, Pagani," Mother said, and Pagani did his disappearing trick again.

Papa sat on the sofa, and Sienne took a chair near his. Mother came to join them, saying, "Have you been in Fioretti this whole time?"

"Yes."

"Dear Kitane have mercy. And you're well? You look..." Mother's voice trailed off as she observed Sienne's plain clothing, her sturdy boots that had taken her on so many adventures. Sienne guessed she'd been about to say *common*.

"I'm well. I've been a scrapper for most of a year."

"A *scrapper?*" Mother imperfectly concealed her horror. She recovered herself and added, "That must be...interesting..."

"How did you fall into that line of work? We thought you'd become a scribe, or hire out as someone's court wizard, something you were trained for," Papa said. "No wonder we couldn't find you. We looked in all the wrong places."

"I chose it deliberately for that reason. I didn't want to be found."

She'd sounded too forceful, and both her parents recoiled slightly.

"And I wanted to do something unusual with my magic," she added, trying to soften the blow. "I've become so much more experienced, and I've learned spells I never would have learned if I'd...stayed home."

The door opened, and Pagani entered bearing a tray from which wafted the most heavenly aroma. He set it on the low table between Sienne and her parents and withdrew without another word. Mother came to herself and took up the coffee pot, pouring slowly as if playing for time. Nobody spoke. Sienne found she was tapping her right toe and made herself stop. She poured liberal amounts of cream into her cup and stirred, watching the patterns the light cream made against the black coffee.

"I love what I do," she blurted out, feeling the silence like a physical pressure. "I have friends—the best of friends—and my life is exciting. I don't regret anything except giving you pain." The last wasn't entirely true; she'd wanted to hurt them the way they'd hurt her. But that desire had faded as the months passed.

"Friends?" Papa said. "That's a relief. We imagined you alone, without support...Sienne, this is all such a surprise to us. You'd never been anywhere but Beneddo and Stravanus your whole life. We didn't think your sheltered existence had prepared you to survive on your own."

"Rance said you were with friends yesterday. Scrapper friends?" Mother said "scrapper" like it was a foreign word.

"They're my companions, yes. My scrapper team. We've been together almost since I left Beneddo." Was this the time to bring up Alaric? Not yet.

"And you...explore ruins? I'm sorry, I have no idea what scrappers actually do."

"That's right. Or we sometimes act as bodyguards for a caravan, or hunt monsters."

Mother's lips soundlessly made the word "monsters." Papa said, "That sounds dangerous."

"It is dangerous, sometimes. But that's why I'm part of a team. We protect each other." She felt defiant and afraid at the same time, anticipating the moment when her father would forbid her to continue and order her home. She didn't have a plan for if that happened.

"Giles wants to be a scrapper," Papa said. "I don't think he realizes what it entails. Maybe you can explain it to him better than I."

"I won't dissuade him, if that's what you want."

To her surprise, Papa smiled, though she'd sounded more belligerent than she felt. "Your brother takes up enthusiasms and discards them as readily. I think if you're honest about the difficulties of scrapping, he'll decide something else is more interesting. Gavant forbid he do any actual work."

"He's nineteen, Pontus, he has time to decide what he wants," Mother said.

"You were married at nineteen, Clarie," Papa said. "It's not too young to decide on a life's path." He turned back to Sienne. "The whole family is here. I know your siblings will want to see you. Will you stay?"

"Stay...you mean, here?" Sienne shook her head and set her cup down. "I have a home. But I want to see them."

"But you're back. You can't expect us to let you go so easily."

"You let me go easily enough a year ago. I know I'm good at confusions, but I can't imagine you looked very hard for me."

"That's enough, Sienne," Mother said. "You have no idea the trouble you caused us. We searched *everywhere* for you."

Tears pricked Sienne's eyes again. "I'm sure it looked very bad, the duke's daughter disappearing after a huge fight with her parents."

"Stop it, both of you," Papa said. "Sienne, do you think so little of us that you imagine it didn't tear us apart not knowing where you were? How could you do that to us?"

She blinked back the tears. She was not going to cry in front of them, damn it! "How could you treat me like I was nothing? Like what I wanted—the thing I wanted more desperately than anything —was irrelevant?"

Papa bowed his head. "I can't tell you how much we regret what passed between us. We didn't understand your attachment to Rance was so strong. It was cruel—we should have found a better way to tell you about the marriage."

"Not found a way to let me marry Rance?" Sienne couldn't stop herself from saying.

"That was impossible," Mother said. "We already had a marriage contract. The Lanzanos would never have accepted a change."

"Never would have accepted the lesser sister, you mean." It was out before she realized she'd spoken her thoughts aloud. Mother's brow furrowed, but she said nothing.

"The Lanzanos are proud people, and they were thrilled to see their son marry nobility," Papa said. "They might have...but things have changed, and what happened a year ago doesn't matter."

"Proud social-climbing snobs, you mean," Mother said bitterly.

"There's no sense revisiting the past," Papa said. "We need to move forward, not dwell on old mistakes. Gavant must have blessed Rance to walk to the market yesterday just as you were there. Something's happened, Sienne, and it involves you."

Cold dread crept over her. "I'm not coming back. I'm sorry if that hurts you, but I have a life here now. I'll want to visit, probably—"

"It's not that simple," Mother said. "Felice is infertile."

It was so unexpected it took Sienne a moment to remember who Felice was. Right. Her lover-stealing sister. "That's...too bad? I'm sure she's not too upset about it, she likes children even less than I do."

Both of her parents looked at her steadily, as if they were waiting for her to make some connection between herself and her sister's infertility. "Is Rance disappointed? We never talked about children, which in hindsight probably should have told me something."

Now her parents exchanged a private look, and Sienne got the feeling they were wordlessly arguing over who would speak next. Her father won the battle—or lost it, Sienne wasn't sure which. "We only found out two months ago," he said. "She and Rance hadn't been married long enough for anyone to be concerned, but Felice needed healing for a minor illness, and Lorne discovered her condition."

Lorne Macchari was her mother's personal priest of Kitane. "And he couldn't fix it?"

"It's beyond the scope of anything healing can do."

"I guess that saves them months of wondering if this is when she'll conceive. Is that..." More dread crept up her spine. Her father's expression said there was something awful he was working up to tell her. "She can't have children. What does that mean for the succession?"

"It means," Papa said, "you're going to be the next duchess of Beneddo."

5

Sienne's mouth fell open. A hundred possible responses choked her. What came out was, "How can *I* be duchess of Beneddo? I'm a scrapper!"

"You are our daughter, and next in line to inherit," Mother said. "This...adventure...you've been on may have been an exciting diversion, but you have a birthright you can't ignore. And a duty to your people."

"They're not my people! They're your people! I can't be a duchess!" She was breathing heavily and tried to calm herself. "Felice can adopt—it happens all the time—"

"Legally, only a child of the blood can inherit a ducal title." Papa clasped Sienne's unresisting fingers. "We have been over the problem with a dozen law-speakers. There's no way around it."

"That's not fair!"

"I realize this must be a shock," Papa said, "but we've redoubled our efforts to find you in the two months since this all came out, and if you hadn't run away, you wouldn't—"

"So this is my fault."

"I didn't mean it that way. I meant you'd have been better prepared to accept your new role."

Sienne drew in a deep breath and let it out slowly. "All right. All right. This is...I don't know what to say. It's a long way off, because you won't die any time soon, and Felice is likely to live a long time..." Her parents were exchanging meaningful glances again. "What aren't you telling me?"

"Felice will never be duchess," her mother said. "We didn't just come to Fioretti for the celebration. We're here to have her officially disinherited."

Sienne yanked her hands away from her father. "That is *sick*," she said. "She loses her birthright just because she can't produce a snot-nosed brat? How could you do this to her?"

"Stop shouting and calm down," Mother said sharply. "It was Felice's idea. Leaving the dukedom for so long in the hands of someone whose heir is a potential rival...you hate the idea of being duchess now, but who knows how you'll feel about it in ten years? Or even five? We don't want you breathing down Felice's neck, waiting for her to die."

"I would never do that."

"It's possible. And the law is on our side."

The room felt small and closed-in now, or maybe it was just the way her vision was tunneling to nothing. Sienne closed her eyes and wished she could cast *jaunt*, take herself somewhere far away where no one had ever heard of the dukedom of Beneddo. "It's still not fair. And what about Rance? He always wanted to be a duke. Is he willing to let that dream go?"

More meaningful glances. "Rance has asked for his marriage to be annulled," Papa said, "on the grounds that it cannot produce offspring."

Sienne wished she had Rance in front of her so she could smack him with half a dozen *force* bolts. She might have hated her sister for taking him away, but for him to desert Felice just when she needed him most...he'd done Sienne a huge favor in abandoning her. She never would have imagined he could be so cruel. "Damn him," she said.

"Language, Sienne," Mother exclaimed. Sienne bit back another, cruder remark.

"Rance and Felice discussed it, and they agreed it was the best course of action," Papa said. "It's an amicable separation."

"And..." Mother sat forward. "There's no reason Rance has to leave the family. You'll need a husband, and—"

Sienne laughed once, harshly. "Me, marry Rance? Not a chance!"

Mother's brow wrinkled. "Sienne, you begged us to let you marry him. I thought you'd be pleased at the idea."

"It's been a year, Mother. Things change. *I've* changed. Rance didn't love me, and I was stupid to make such a fuss over him. I wouldn't marry him now if you paid me."

"We will pay you," Papa said, "or, at any rate, you'll have his marriage settlement."

"I don't care. I love someone else, and Rance can go off and make a life for himself with anyone but me."

"You—" Mother's eyes grew wide. "Who is this man?"

Sienne swallowed. Defying her parents about Rance was one thing. Telling them about her love when they would likely be furious about it was terrifying, like opening her heart for them to stab it bloody. "His name is Alaric. He's my companion, the leader of our scrapper team."

"Alaric is an Ansorjan name. What's his family?" Papa asked.

"His family—his clan—doesn't use surnames because it's so small. And yes, he's Ansorjan." This was only partly true. The wizard who'd created the Sassaven had used Ansorjans for the root stock, so as far as anyone knew, Alaric was an ordinary Ansorjan man. If anyone could call him ordinary.

"So he's not noble?"

"No."

Her parents had exchanged so many meaningful glances it was almost funny. Sienne wished she could eavesdrop on the conversation they were sure to have after she left. "Is he your lover?" Mother asked.

"He is."

Mother's face whitened fractionally, and her lips compressed again, but she said nothing. Papa said, "I shouldn't have to say anything this indelicate to you, but...I hope you're taking precautions."

She was not about to share the details of her sex life with her parents. "I won't get pregnant, if that's what you mean."

"You can't be sure of that."

"At least you'd know I was qualified to inherit, if I did."

"Don't joke about it," Mother said. "You have no idea how traumatic this whole experience has been for all of us. Felice has been raised to be a duchess, trained almost from birth. You know nothing about ruling, you've run wild for a year, and you expect us to be happy that you've taken up with some nobody scrapper? This has very nearly been disastrous for Beneddo, and it's past time you gave up playing games with your life and came home to take up your new duties."

"Clarie—"

"Pontus, I'm sick of dancing around the issue. This is no game. This is real life. Sienne, you have a duty to your family and you have a duty to the dukedom. I'm no longer willing to endure your defiance."

Sienne shot to her feet. "I didn't ask for this. And, as you so kindly point out, I'm not prepared for this. Find someone else. I refuse."

"This isn't something you can refuse," Papa said. "Only a royal decree can disinherit someone who is otherwise legally and lawfully capable of inheriting a dukedom. And Derekian doesn't hand those out readily."

"Then I'll talk to him. Convince him."

"No, you will not," Papa said, rising to face her. "The dukedom has suffered enough turmoil for one lifetime. Derekian won't pander to your selfish wishes. You're the heir now, Sienne. And before you tell me you'll run away rather than face this, I want to remind you that you're also a grown woman who understands responsibility. You may not like it, but you'll do your duty."

He was so blurry. Sienne touched her face and realized she was crying. "I won't," she said, and had to stop. Papa reached out to her, and she backed away before he could touch her. "This isn't what I want."

"It's not what any of us wanted," Papa said. "Do you think Felice wanted to lose what she's been raised her whole life to be? Or that we wanted anything but a scholastic life for our wizard daughter? But the rules are different for the nobility. What we want isn't as important as what we owe the kingdom. You'll come to understand that someday."

"Sooner rather than later, I hope," Mother said.

"Stop it, Clarie," Papa said in a cold, cutting voice. "Sienne. Come to dinner. See your siblings. Talk to Felice. Let's for a few hours be an ordinary family. Please."

Sienne wiped her eyes. "I'll come," she said. "But I won't give up hope."

Her father had the good sense to say nothing.

She didn't remember how she got from the drawing room to the plaza, but when she came to herself, she was standing once more in front of the fountain, this time gazing at tall Kitane's well-shaped legs. "You wouldn't understand," she whispered. "You gave your life for the sake of someone else's dream. I can't do that."

She turned and ran out of the plaza and down the hill, not stopping until she reached the temple district. It was quieter than the rest of the city, if only because the festival decorations hadn't reached this far. Temples to all six avatars sprawled here, some of them bigger than others—Gavant's was half the size of the palace—but all masterpieces of architecture and art. She walked until she reached the round temple of Kitane, its golden dome gleaming in the sunlight. Passing through the portico, she stopped just inside to admire the giant bronze statue of the avatar, naked except for helmet, shield, and sword. Sienne had come in on the east side, and the altar on that side was not in use at this season. It was true summer, which meant the southern altar would be where the divines worshiped.

"Miss? Would you like to make an offering?"

Sienne startled and turned to face the young priest who stood eagerly at her left elbow. He was too young to be a full divine, and despite her agitation, she couldn't help smiling at him. "I would like to talk to the divine Octavian, if he's available," she said.

"I'll ask. Please, have a seat," the priest said, guiding her to one of the benches lining the walls. Sienne sat and watched the ceremony in progress at the south altar. It looked like a marriage, which should have cheered her, but the memory of her mother so casually assuming Sienne would leap at the chance to marry Rance made it bitter instead. All right, maybe Mother had meant well—she couldn't have known Sienne didn't love Rance anymore—but how could anyone treat another person like a commodity, or believe Rance wouldn't care who he married so long as he could be a duke? Sienne turned that last thought over in her head. It was possibly true, and if it was, Rance was even less principled than she'd thought.

A door behind the east altar opened, and an old man with a full white beard emerged. He wore a pale blue robe open over an ordinary shirt and trousers, not the garb Sienne would have expected of a divine. His sharp blue-eyed gaze fell on Sienne, and he smiled as he approached her. "I remember you," he said. "You were paralyzed by that lich. Congratulations on bringing it down."

"Your amulet helped us tremendously," Sienne said. "Thank you."

Octavian waved that off. "How can I help you today? I'm sorry, but I'm fresh out of artifacts," he added with a wink and a smile.

Sienne smiled back. "Nothing like that. But it is a delicate personal matter. I was...I need to know if I'm capable of bearing children."

He raised an eyebrow. "Forgive me, but normally when I receive that request, the person is not nearly so grim. Do you have reason to believe you are infertile? Family history, or a long succession of miscarriages?"

"No. I just need to know. It's about an inheritance."

Octavian nodded and pressed his hand to Sienne's stomach. "Our Lady of Power, bless this young woman," he said.

Green light flared, and flames flickered across Octavian's hand. Sienne didn't flinch. She felt no pain, just a trickling sensation of warmth. Then her skin glowed green for a moment, flashing bright and then dark a few times, and faded. Octavian smiled. "There is nothing wrong with your female organs," he said. "I hope that's the answer you were looking for."

"It's not," Sienne said. "You're probably not willing to lie about it, are you."

The smile faded from Octavian's face. "I choose to believe that was a joke."

"A bad one. Of course I wouldn't ask you to lie. But it would be so much easier if I were infertile."

He sat beside her on the bench. "Children are a gift of God. Even if you don't choose to have them, you should still be grateful that She made you capable of bearing Her gift."

"It's not that. I've just learned that I'm going to inherit a title because my sister, the actual heir, is disqualified on those grounds. It's stupid, I know, but I thought...anyway. I'm not prepared for this."

"We rarely are prepared for the surprises life hands us. I'm sorry for your sister. She must be devastated."

"I guess. I don't know. I haven't spoken to her in over a year."

"Well. Your life seems considerably more complicated than just an unexpected inheritance. Is there strife in your family?"

"It's too long a story for me to burden you with, sir."

Octavian shook his head. "One of my duties is listening to people's long stories. I won't pry, but I think you could use someone to talk to. Someone who isn't a member of your family."

Sienne hesitated. Then she said, "A little over a year ago, I was a graduate living in Stravanus..."

She told him everything, even her most shameful memories of pleading with her parents to let her marry Rance that made her cringe just thinking about them. She told him about Alaric and her friends and her new life. And she recounted the conversation she'd had with her parents that had ended with her leaving in tears. When she wound down, Octavian said, "I can see why you're in turmoil. What a nightmare for all of you."

"I don't know what to do. I can't be a duchess."

"You mean you don't want to be a duchess. You're too intelligent not to be able to learn the skills necessary."

"I mean I have another life now. I'm happy with who I am and what I have. And I'm not giving up Alaric just to marry some...I don't even know who my parents would want me to marry, except it's not a Sas—an Ansorjan scrapper from nowhere. And *he* can't have children, so even if I did marry him, we'd still be in the same position." It was the closest she could come to explaining why she and Alaric would never have children. No one knew of the existence of Alaric's race, and he wouldn't thank her for sharing the secret.

"I admit that seems the sticking point. As far as I know, there is no law requiring a Rafellish noble to marry a citizen, your parents' objections notwithstanding. You...I won't insult you by asking if you're sure he's the one for you."

"Thank you."

"I wish I had a solution for you, but as with much of life, the most profound solutions come from within ourselves." Octavian patted her hand. "But I think you already know you need to reconcile with your family, whatever else you decide to do."

Sienne bowed her head. "I know. I was selfish to run away. I mean, I don't regret it, because it brought me to where I'm loved and appreciated by my friends, but objectively, it was the wrong thing to do. I put my family through terrible pain. But they hurt me, too."

"Neither of which excuses the other."

"Yes. I know that too."

"Do you have an avatar you worship more than the others?"

"I'm not very religious. I suppose I depend on Averran a lot, since my friend is a priest of his and his intervention has saved my life more than once."

"Averran is a good choice for your situation. He was cranky and recalcitrant, but he also believed strongly in the human capacity for choosing wisely, even in the most dire of circumstances. You might speak to your friend about receiving Averran's guidance for you personally. If he's already taken an interest in you, as I conclude from your story, he might have a hand in this test you're undergoing, and the avatars never give us tests without giving us the means to pass them."

The idea that her life might be at the whim of the curmudgeonly Averran made her nervous, but she said only, "Thank you. I'll do that."

Octavian helped her rise. "Good luck," he said. "I'll pray for you. And be open to the possibility that this new challenge is actually for the better."

"I'm not sure that's true, but I'll remember."

"Oh, and one more thing. You say your relationship with your young man is permanent?"

"Of course."

"How does he feel about the prospect of no children?"

"He's fine with it. He wasn't at all disturbed when he told me—he was more worried that I'd be upset."

Octavian looked skeptical. "Be certain of that. Sometimes we don't know what we want until we've lost it."

"I'm sure. Thank you for being concerned, though." She waved goodbye and left the temple.

She passed through the celebrating streets without noticing the festivities, her mind fully occupied with memories and plans. She simply could not be her father's heir. She'd worked too hard to get where she was to give it up. And Alaric—there was no way she was going to leave him, especially not to marry someone she didn't love. A perverse imp at the back of her head muttered *You might learn to love someone else,* and she almost smacked herself in the forehead before remembering it was her imagination.

It was well after noon when she reached home. Delicious smells filled the back hallway, drawing her to the kitchen, where Leofus presided over three huge pots bubbling on his stove. "Bread and cheese," he said.

"What? This all smells so good!"

"It's for the feast tonight. Master Tersus is hosting friends. And yes, I'm feeding you lot, too. But I don't have time for a midday meal. So—bread and cheese."

Sienne grumbled, but helped herself to both. "Where is every-one?" she asked, feeling vaguely disgruntled that her friends weren't there to listen to her news.

"Out. I don't know where. Nobody tells me nothing."

"That's not true. We told you we were going after Reva Nocenti's treasure."

"I suppose so." Leofus stirred one of the pots, then tasted its contents. "Perrin might have said something about registering a trea-sure trove for provenance."

"Oh. Yes, we were supposed to do that." She sat at the table and munched in silence. Even the bread and cheese were excellent. Master Tersus loved the finer things in life. "So what's for dinner?"

"Standing rib roast, broiled rosemary chicken, poached fish in lemon sauce, sautéed vegetables, herbed rice, and sweet rolls. Dates in spiced honey for dessert."

"Sounds delicious. But it can't be what's in those pots."

"I'm rendering beef stock for the roast and testing a new lemon sauce. You're not really interested in the details, are you?" His voice had the same resigned tone it always did when he tried to get them to appreciate his genius in any way other than the gustatory.

"I'm not. Sorry." She bit into her bread and cheese fiercely. What could she do? She *wanted* to spill her story to her friends and maybe weep a few self-indulgent tears, but she could hardly roam Fioretti looking for them. She ought to see about selling the spell pages, or even figuring out what the mystery spell was, and that would use up a few hours of waiting time...but no, if Perrin was registering them as treasure trove, they weren't here to be disposed of. Which left her, once again, stuck at home with nothing to do but think unpleasant thoughts and glare at Leofus. She ought to go upstairs before she inflicted her bad mood on him.

The back door opened, and Sienne heard Dianthe say, "...even if it is a little strange."

"We're used to strange," Alaric replied.

Perrin said, "I am intrigued by the possibilities of this job," and then they were all crowding into the kitchen. Leofus waved his spoon at them.

"No sneaking bites," he said. "Dinner will be at seven. Bread and cheese on the counter, then take yourselves off, if you please."

"We won't disturb you," Alaric said. He dropped into the chair next to Sienne and kissed her soundly. "You look like you've had a terrible day, and it's not even full afternoon yet."

"You have no idea," Sienne said, scooting closer so she could lean against his comforting bulk. "Did you register the treasure already?"

"We did, and the Crown took their percentage out of the coin, all of which they bought. No haggling needed," Alaric said. "At a better than fair price. A little more than ten thousand lari, *after* taxes."

Sienne's eyes widened. "Ten *thousand*? Just for the coin?"

"We were right that this would make our fortune," Dianthe said. "And some of those objects will go for a lot of money. Not to mention the gems." Her eyes gleamed at the idea.

"What did they say about the mystery spell? Did they put a price on it?"

"It was the one thing I wasn't sure of," Dianthe said. "Neither were they, though. We had to go through the records of similar findings and agree on a historically-determined value. I don't know which of us was cheated, but we probably won't know that until we find a buyer. They also valued the wand higher than I'd expected. But we're not selling that, are we?"

"Not until we figure out what it does. It might be a useful spell. And if one of you can use it, even better." New spells. The scholar in her, buried deep, sat up and cheered at the prospect of being named the discoverer, or recoverer perhaps, of something that had formerly been lost to history. "What was Perrin saying about a new job?"

"Don't you want to tell us what happened with your family?" Alaric asked.

Now that they were actually there, she found her desire to share the story was diminished, as if refusing to talk about it could make it not true. "That's...a long one," she said. "Job first."

"Someone left us a message while we were gone," Alaric said. "I forgot to mention it last night, because I was...preoccupied...and then you left before I remembered it this morning. They said they were looking to hire us, us specifically, for a job out near the Bramantus Mountains. I didn't think we'd be interested, certainly not immediately, but it seemed polite to at least turn them down in person."

"That doesn't sound like a new job. It sounds like a dead end."

"That is not the peculiar part," Perrin said, his eyes alight with mirth. "We went to see the gentlemen after dealing with the treasury, and they went straight to Dianthe and asked, 'Are you the duke's daughter?'"

Sienne blinked. "They what?"

"It seems you are the draw for them," Perrin said. "When we explained that you had a prior commitment today, they were very polite, but it was clear they did not wish to discuss business without your presence."

"That's ridiculous. Why would they care about me? It's not like I have any special benefits—" She stopped, conscious of her changed status. But how could they have known she was now the heir? Total strangers with no connection, as far as she knew, to Beneddo or her parents?

"I have not seen Alaric so...I do not know the word, but it is when you cannot believe what your eyes and ears tell you," Kalanath said. He looked as amused as Perrin.

"Mystified, perhaps?" Perrin said. "Perplexed? Flabbergasted?"

"It is all of those," Kalanath said. "He has the look of a man whose dog sits up and asks with words for a seat at the table."

"It wasn't that funny," Alaric said. "But I'll admit I'm not used to being passed over when I'm not actively pretending to be stupid."

"I wish I'd been there to see it," Sienne said. "Though I guess if I had, it wouldn't have happened. So will we meet with them later?"

"We agreed on a time tomorrow morning," Dianthe said. "Unless you need to be with your family."

The mention of her family brought back everything she'd experienced that morning. Alaric frowned. "Something happened, I can tell," he said. "Can you talk about it? It might do you good."

Sienne let out a deep breath and took his hand. "I don't know where to start."

"Then let's go to the sitting room and get comfortable, and you can start from the beginning." Alaric helped her rise and kept hold of her hand afterward.

"All right," Sienne said, "but I'm afraid this is the kind of story where no one will be comfortable no matter where we sit."

6

S ienne held up a skirt to her waist and surveyed herself in the mirrored surface she'd created on the wall. It was more wavery than an actual mirror, but the image was clear enough for her purposes. She sighed and tossed the skirt on the bed. It was the only one she owned, but she hadn't worn it in seven months because it made her look like a street vendor, selling oranges off a cart.

"Wear the dress," Alaric said. "You look beautiful in the dress."

Sienne picked up her red dancing dress and held it up to herself. "What if it's too fancy?"

"Then you'll be the most beautiful woman there."

"All I know is I can't wear my usual clothes to supper with my family. Mother always insisted we dress nicely for dinner, which for us girls meant a dress. But this—" She brandished the dress at him —"is too formal, and it's the wrong kind of formal, too."

Alaric sighed. "Which would be worse, being underdressed, or overdressed?"

"You ask impossible questions." She thought about it. "Being underdressed would be worse."

"Then it's either the orange-seller skirt, or the dancing dress."

Alaric eyed her and smiled, a wolfish gleam in his eye. "I'll help you take it off later."

"The thought of that will get me through this evening." She shrugged into the dancing dress, which slid over her head and settled perfectly over her hips and chest. One of the advantages to being a wizard with the *fit* spell was never having to pay extra for made-to-order clothing; she could alter anything to fit her exactly.

Alaric came to stand behind her and put his hands around her waist. "Are you sure you don't want me to come?"

"I still don't know how the rest of my family will react to my returning to the fold. They might feel entitled to be rude, or insulting, and it would just make you angry. Plus, if Rance is there—"

"You're right. I couldn't sit through a meal with his smug face staring at me. I still owe him a beating for how he treated you." He turned her around in his arms and bent to kiss her. "But I'll have to meet your parents sometime."

"I know. Just not tonight." She leaned her head against his broad chest and closed her eyes. "It won't be so bad. I love my siblings, mostly, and I didn't realize I missed them until I saw my parents. I wonder if Liliana is still a brat?"

She walked through the noisy streets, which bustled with celebrating people dancing, singing, and kissing in the middle of the road, feeling as if there were a sheet of glass separating her from them, or an invisible wall of *force*. No one accosted her, which relieved her mind; she was on edge enough she might have used magic on anyone who stopped her, wanting a dance.

A whiff of warm honey caught her attention, and her stomach growled at the idea of honeyed figs, or roasted sausages, or even a mug of ale. Her tastes had become so low in the last year. No doubt her parents would be horrified at the thought of their daughter preferring street food to an elegant four-course meal.

This time, when she rapped at the door of her parents' mansion, Pagani opened it immediately and bowed low. Did he know she was the heir, or would be soon? She walked past him without acknowledging him, still feeling miffed about her earlier reception. This time, the doors on the left and right were open, and golden light from candles, not magic lights, spilled out into the entryway. Pagani bowed again and extended a gloved hand. "This way, my lady," he said, and guided her to the second door on the left.

Sienne made it as far as the door before she stopped, stricken with unexpected shyness. It was another drawing room, identical to the first except for the antiques being of an even earlier era, and it was full of people who all stopped their conversations to stare at her. Feeling awkward, Sienne stared back. She'd forgotten how overwhelming the Verannus clan was en masse. Seven brothers and sisters, her parents, and, ugh, Rance...and every one of them no doubt angry with her for having run away.

She found her next younger brother Alcander, standing near another door on the far side of the room, and stared at him in mute pleading. They'd been so close, once, and of all her siblings she'd missed him the most. If he hated her...

She almost turned and left, but pride kept her rooted to the spot, pride that she wouldn't let them drive her away. Maybe running away had been wrong, but she'd had plenty of good reasons for it, and if anyone should feel guilty, it should be Mother and Papa. And Rance, but she no longer cared what he felt about anything.

"Sienne," Alcander said. Then he smiled. "Sienne!" He crossed the room in a few swift strides—she'd forgotten how long his legs were—and threw his arms around her, hugging her tight. "Thank Gavant you're safe. I couldn't believe it when Rance said he'd seen you. Where have you been? Here, all this time?"

"I...yes," Sienne said, stunned at his unqualified happiness to see her. She returned his hug and blinked away tears. "I'm sorry I ran—"

"Never mind that," Alcander said. "We all want to know what you've been doing."

"She's a scrapper now," Giles said, his eyes gleaming with excitement. "I never thought you had that kind of courage, to take off and leave everything behind. Are you successful? Do you have a permanent team, or do you hire out on a job by job basis?"

"She probably doesn't want to talk about that," Giles's twin Quentinus said. "Respectable people aren't scrappers."

"Oh, shut up, Quent," Alcander said. "As if you know anything about it."

"Alcander, don't be vulgar," Mother said. "Sienne, your dress is lovely."

"Thank you," Sienne said, though she suspected her mother had suppressed a comment about being dressed for a ball rather than a family meal.

"I like it," young Liliana said. "It sparkles like diamonds. Mama, may I have a dress like that?"

"Trust you to turn a compliment into something about you," her next older sister, Phebe, said with a sneer. Liliana's face fell.

"You already have a lovely dress for tomorrow night," Mother said. "Phebe, don't be rude."

"But, Mama!"

"Let's all go in to dinner, shall we?" Papa said, his deep voice cutting across the rest of the conversations. Sienne turned away from Alcander and found herself facing Felice. Her older sister was as beautiful as Sienne remembered, her honey-blonde hair tawny in the candlelight, her perfect face and rosy lips a masterpiece of the sculptor's art. She regarded Sienne silently, with no hint of how she felt evident on her face. Beside her, Rance was equally silent. His dark eyes held a question she couldn't interpret, and it made her feel awkward again, like the interloper who'd ruined their lives, even though none of this was her fault. Then Felice turned and followed Papa into the dining room, with Rance close behind her.

Sienne dithered about where to sit, but in the end it turned out her family's normal seating arrangements, come to by unspoken consensus over years of Verannus dinners, hadn't altered in the time she'd been away except to add Rance at Felice's left hand. Her own usual place midway along the table, between Alcander and Quentinus and across from Erianthe, was empty as if waiting for her. What a reminder, if they'd left it empty the whole time she'd been gone. She sat, and was struck so hard by the familiarity of it all she had to swallow to keep from tearing up. She hoped she remembered her table manners. At least she hadn't fallen into the habit of propping her elbows on the table in the year she'd been gone.

Servants emerged from concealed doors in the paneling, bearing tureens of aromatic soup. Sienne leaned back for them to serve her a clear, rich beef broth sprinkled with herbs. Her stomach chose that moment to announce its hunger. Liliana giggled. "Liliana," her mother warned her, "we don't draw attention to such things."

"Sorry, Mama," Liliana said. She didn't look sorry. She stared openly at Sienne. Sienne ignored her. She remembered Liliana mostly as an infant she'd had to care for, and then as a child she saw once a year at High Winter when she returned home for the end of year festivities, a child prone to giggling when she got her way and pouting and screaming when she didn't. She couldn't remember how old she was now—ten? eleven?—but her parents' policy of training their children in etiquette and good behavior by including them in family dinners didn't seem to have had much effect on Liliana.

"Sienne, tell us about your adventures," Giles said. His green eyes, jade-pale and just like their father's, gleamed with excitement.

"I'm not sure that's appropriate conversation for the dinner table," Mother said.

"Of course it is! Don't we want to know what Sienne's been doing? You'd ask her to talk about her experiences as...as a wizard at a duke's court, if that's where she'd been, right?"

Mother pinched her lips tight and turned her attention to her soup. Sienne glanced around the table. Everyone except Felice and Mother were watching her like a family of foxes surrounding a vole's den. "Um," she said. "I...it took me some time to establish myself as a scrapper. It's hard to find the right jobs and even harder to convince clients to take a chance on you when you don't have any experience. I was lucky to find the team I have now." She didn't want to share the details of how that team had come together, how Alaric had hated her for being a wizard and Perrin had been drunk all the time and Kalanath had been independent to the point of isolation. All that was well in the past.

"But you're successful now, right?" Giles hadn't yet touched his soup.

"Yes. Very. We just made a major find, big enough that we can support ourselves for a long time. It will bolster our reputation among potential clients, too."

"What does a major find look like?" Papa asked. "Money?"

"Old money is actually rare. The ancients used it rather than hoarding it. But yes, we found about ten thousand lari worth of antique coin."

Rance dropped his spoon. It landed in his bowl and splashed broth on the tablecloth. "*How* much?"

"Ten thousand. And yes, that's a lot by any standards. But there was also jewelry, and gems, and...oh, all sorts of interesting things, all worth far more than the coin. And five spells, one of which no one's ever seen before."

Alcander whistled, which earned him a reproachful look from his mother. "That's practically priceless. Did you take it to the university?"

"Not yet. I scribed it into my spellbook and I'll study it—maybe I'll be the one to figure it out."

"But not all your finds are so impressive," Papa said. He had his eyes on Giles, who looked at Sienne as if she might be God's seventh avatar come to earth. "There's lean times, too."

"Yes. Sometimes we don't find anything, and not all our clients are willing to pay for our time when we don't return with a prize."

"That seems unfair," Felice said. Her voice was the same quiet alto Sienne remembered. She didn't look at Sienne, just at her soup, and Sienne shifted uncomfortably, as if her sister had slapped her instead.

"It's just the way it works. You learn quickly which clients are reliable, and they learn the same about you. We have a good reputation, and that translates into a steady income. Not all scrappers can say that."

"I thought you were a wizard. Why didn't you teach somewhere?" Liliana piped up.

That was a little too close to subjects Sienne would prefer not to address. "I—"

"That's enough pestering Sienne," Mother said. "Why don't the rest of you tell her what you've been doing? She hasn't seen you in over a year, after all."

Sienne had never been more grateful to her mother for anything. "Yes, please do," she said. "Alcander, are you still studying law?"

"For my sins, yes," her brother said. "It's still interesting. Next year I have to choose a field to focus on. I've been thinking, inheritance law." He flicked a quick glance at Felice. Sienne realized she hadn't asked if the rest of the family knew about the other reason they'd come to Fioretti. Alcander did, at least, and she could imagine her parents discussing it with the whole family. Whatever their faults, Pontus and Clarie Verannus had always believed in family unity, no matter the crisis.

"I think it sounds boring. If it were me, I'd want to study criminal law," Erianthe said. Her chestnut hair, exactly the same shade as Sienne's, was falling down over her forehead as it always did.

"Are you going to be a law-speaker too?" Sienne asked. Her sister was, what, sixteen now? Erianthe had never shown interest in anything but horses, but times changed. She wondered how Erianthe would react if she knew Sienne had ridden a unicorn. Not that she'd been in a position to appreciate it.

Erianthe nodded. "I'm off to school in two months."

"That's great! I hope you like it."

"I keep telling her it's a lot of boring reading, but it hasn't dissuaded her," Alcander said with a grin, "so I have to conclude she's serious."

Sienne leaned back as a servant removed her empty soup bowl. Another servant placed a delicious-smelling beef roast in front of her father, who took up knife and fork and began to carve. "And Quentinus is making a name for himself as a gardener," he said.

Sienne turned in surprise to Quentinus, whose dark olive skin was unusually flushed. "Oh," she said, unable to think of anything else to say. She'd always thought of Quent as the dumb twin, prone to sticking his foot in his mouth and then laughing awkwardly about his mistakes in a way that made everyone around him uncomfortable. "Um...does that make you Papa's favorite child?"

Everyone laughed. Quent said, "I'm not allowed to touch the roses. But I have my own garden at the estate, and I'm working toward establishing my credentials so I can maybe take on commissions someday soon."

"That's..." *unexpected* "impressive. I never would have guessed any of us would follow in Papa's footsteps. I don't have a black thumb so much as a black fist."

"It's hard work, but I like it."

It was fortunate her parents didn't have any foolish prejudices against their children working, like some nobles Sienne had grown up with. They were too poor for such scruples. *Of course*, she thought, looking at Felice's elegant gown that probably cost three times as much as her own dress, *poor is a relative term, when it's the nobility*.

"And Phebe and Liliana are still being tutored at home," Mother said.

"But I want to go away to school like you did, Sienne," Phebe said.

Mother tensed. Papa said, "We're still discussing it. School is costly."

"Yes, but you did it for Sienne and Erianthe, and I can't see why you won't do it for me," Phebe pouted.

"Wizards need special training to make the most of their abilities," Papa said, "and law-speakers must be accredited at one of only a few institutions. You don't have anything you're burning to study. Your needs might be as well met at home as anywhere else."

"I'm as old now as Sienne was when she left," Phebe said. "If we don't decide now, it might be too late."

"I had many classmates who didn't start at Stravanus until they were fifteen or sixteen," Sienne interjected. "You still have plenty of time."

"Just because you like Sienne better than the rest of us," Phebe said in a low voice.

"Phebe, don't talk nonsense. You know your father and I don't have favorites. We love you all equally," Mother said. Phebe ducked her head, but Sienne could see her scowl. It was a lie, though. Her parents might love all of them, but Sienne was under no illusions about her relationship with her mother. She took another bite of roast and tried to enjoy it.

"Felice, you've been quiet. Did you..." Alcander's voice trailed off.

Felice fixed him with her hazel eyes, chewing placidly. She swallowed, patted her lips with her napkin, and pushed back from the table. "I feel rather unwell," she said. "I think I should retire."

"Do you want me to come with you?" Rance said. He sounded unexpectedly eager.

"No, I'll be fine. You shouldn't interrupt your meal for me." Felice rose. Her gaze went from Alcander to Sienne, and Sienne once again felt awkward. She made herself sit up straight and return her sister's regard placidly. This was not her fault. She had nothing to feel guilty about.

"But your sister's just returned! Don't you want to...that is, I'm sure the two of you have much to talk about," Mother said.

Felice shook her head, the minutest movement. "Some other time," she said, and left the room. Rance looked like he might follow her despite her instructions, but in the end, he remained seated.

An uncomfortable silence descended over the table, heavy and oppressive like wet wool. Finally, Sienne couldn't bear it any longer. "You said Liliana has a dress for tomorrow night," she said. "What's tomorrow night?"

"Liliana's birthday party," Papa said. "You should come. There will be so many people who'll want to see you."

"I didn't want a party here," Liliana said. "I wanted a party at home with my friends. This one will be stupid."

"Don't be rude," Mother said. "And you know we had to be in Fioretti for the celebrations. You were the one who chose not to delay your party until after we returned home."

"I don't see why we couldn't have two parties," Liliana pouted. "Marinna had two parties."

"Marinna is a spoiled brat," Erianthe said. "And so are you."

"Mama!" Liliana said, bursting into tears.

"Liliana! Control yourself! And Erianthe, apologize to your sister immediately."

"Sorry," Erianthe muttered.

Sienne felt laughter, unexpected and light, bubble up inside her. She covered her mouth, but it emerged as a giggle that set everyone to staring at her again. "I'm sorry," she said, "it's just that everything's so *normal* still, even with everything that's happened. I didn't know I missed it until just now."

Papa chuckled. "What, missed the bickering and pouting and tears?"

"And the laughter and the jokes." Sienne laughed again. "I shouldn't have left like that. I missed you all."

"Not enough to do the right thing," Rance said, undeterred by a quelling look from his mother-in-law.

Sienne's laughter vanished. "I had my reasons," she said, aware that they'd been bad reasons.

"Rance, it doesn't matter," Papa said. "What matters is that Sienne is back, and everything can return to the way it was before."

A sick feeling started in Sienne's stomach. "But I'm not coming back," she said. "It won't be the way it was before. I have a new life."

"But you're the heir," Alcander said, his brow furrowing. "You'll need to return to Beneddo to start learning what you need to know to rule the dukedom someday."

"I'm not the heir yet. There's still...anything might happen."

No one spoke. Rance pushed back from his seat. "I'm going to check on Felice," he said, and disappeared out the door.

"I thought Sienne had to be the heir," Phebe said. "Is it a wizard thing, or a scrapper thing?"

"Both. Neither," Sienne said, feeling a little desperate. "I don't want—"

"This isn't a conversation for the dining table," Papa said. "Right now we're going to talk about other things. Sienne, I think you should bring your...companions, is it? Bring your companions to the party tomorrow night. We'd love to meet them, and it's a perfect opportunity."

"All right," Sienne said, grasping this conversational change like a drowning man clutches a rope. "Is it formal dress?"

"It's a fancy dress party," Liliana said, suddenly enthusiastic. "I'm going as Kitane the Warrior!"

"Like half the city," Erianthe murmured. Liliana glared at her.

"That sounds fun," Sienne said. "We'll come. I'd like you to meet them." And she could introduce Alaric to her parents. She couldn't decide if she was eager about it, or terrified.

Giles looked ecstatic at the prospect of meeting real scrappers. Alcander said, "It's at the park north of here, at seven o'clock. Liliana will demand a present. She always does."

"I do not!" Liliana bit her lip, and added, "But I do like presents."

"Understood," Sienne told Alcander.

"Then it's settled," Mother said. "I look forward to meeting your friends, particularly your...Alaric." She didn't look pleased. She looked like she'd bitten into an orange and discovered too late it was a lemon. Sienne smiled pleasantly at her. So Mother wanted a chance to judge Alaric, did she? Well, Sienne didn't need her good opinion. Fortunate, since history told her she was unlikely to get it.

7

The strange potential clients had taken rooms in a lodging house on the south side of Fioretti, in a neighborhood rapidly sliding into poverty. "I don't know how they can afford to hire us, if this is the lodging their purse allows," Sienne murmured to Alaric. The streets smelled strongly of burned meat and animal waste ripened by the true summer sun, but the men and women thronging the streets didn't seem to be breathing through their mouths as Sienne was. Anniversary fervor had struck this neighborhood as well; every other door had a forsythia wreath, or one studded with red berries. If the forsythia was a little wilted, or the berries wizened, it didn't dampen anyone's patriotic spirit.

Alaric led them down a side alley that opened on a courtyard paved with cracked stones. A weathered fountain at the center tinkled merrily as if unaware of its surroundings. High above, lines of laundry blocked the sunlight, making the courtyard cool and pleasantly dim. Children ran past them, screaming in some game. Their screams faded when they saw Alaric, their eyes growing wide and their small mouths falling open in astonishment. Alaric kept walking without acknowledging them, then suddenly turned on his heel, crouched, and said, "Boo."

The children shrieked with delight and fled, glancing over their shoulders at the big man. Alaric watched them go. "Funny how they're the same wherever you go," he said. "This place isn't as grindingly poor as it looks, or they wouldn't have the energy to run."

"Have you seen true poverty, then?" Perrin asked. He, too, had his attention on the fleeing children, and Sienne thought he looked wistful. They probably reminded him of his own children, forbidden to him by his father and an unjust law.

"In Concord, the free city," Alaric said, turning to walk on. "It's a hard place to live and doubly hard on children. I can't think of anything worse than a child so abused and starved he's afraid to do anything but hide."

"That sounds terrible," Sienne said. "I feel guilty now at resenting my younger sisters. I had to help care for them when they were infants, and I thought it was the worst punishment my mother could have devised. But I still loved them. Even Liliana the brat."

"It's her birthday party we're going to tonight, right?" Dianthe said. "It sounds strange, adults attending a child's party. Is that normal for the nobility, Sienne?"

"Yes. All our birthdays used to be excuses for our friends' parents to come together and drink my father's wine and bitch about taxes, or gossip about who was sleeping with whom. And half the people our own age who came were only there because their fathers were landholders under the duke. Sometimes the parties were fun, but mostly I spent mine trying to avoid Laella Tavenus, who only wanted to be my friend because I was noble."

"It's awfully short notice for fancy dress. What are you going as?"

Sienne hooked her arm through Alaric's. "We're going as the Old Man of the Mountain and Sylvie Dell. Simple, but recognizable, and I only have to cast *camouflage* to make us look good."

"Creative," Perrin said. "And with the advantage that it declares you openly a couple. At least, I presume you see it as an advantage."

"You presume correctly," Sienne said. "I don't want my parents thinking I'm ashamed of who I am, and Alaric is part of that. Also, he flatly refused to go as a wisp."

"I'm not built like a wisp," Alaric said in his deepest voice.

"But I could have made our clothes glow...oh, now I see how stupid that idea was."

Dianthe laughed. "I'd love to see Alaric glow."

"You're going to wait a long time for that," Alaric said. "This is the house. Second floor, third door on the right."

The lodging house smelled of boiled cabbage, an almost pleasant scent after the stink of the streets. The door opened on a long, narrow hallway lined with doors that hung crookedly in their frames. Somewhere nearby, a dog barked, startling Sienne, who wouldn't have thought animals were allowed indoors. Someone coughed, a hard, rattling sound that made her chest ache in sympathy. A door opened as they passed, and a small child, naked except for a breechclout, stared up at them with dull eyes. Sienne remembered what Alaric had said about poverty and quickly looked away, then made herself look back, wishing she had some way to help even as she felt grateful as never before for her own upbringing.

Narrow, splintered stairs at the far end of the hall went up into darkness. There were magic lights in the stairwell in unbreakable glass bulbs, but they were dark, and from the dust Sienne judged they hadn't been tended in months. The stairs creaked even under her slight weight and groaned terrifyingly under Alaric's feet, making Sienne want to step lightly. Though her friends had been here the day before, and the stairs hadn't broken then...which might mean they were just waiting for their moment.

Sienne fingered her spellbook and thought about casting *drift* on Alaric, making him light as a feather, but then they'd have to tow him up the stairs to keep him from floating away. She left her book in its harness and tried not to think about how much falling would hurt.

The second floor looked the same as the first, except for a grimy window at the far end of the hall. Alaric went to the third door on the right and knocked. Presently, it opened. "Ah. Please, come in," the tall man said. He stood beside the door as they filed inside and stared openly at Sienne. She pretended not to notice.

The lodging was a single room with two narrow beds with iron frames flanking the one window. The whitewashed walls were peeling, and flakes of the stuff scattered across the worn rag rug between the beds. Through the open window, Sienne saw the walls of the building next door. It was almost close enough to touch. A rickety table with a single drawer stood next to the door, atop which was an enameled basin and pitcher.

The room made Sienne feel uncomfortable. She'd taken rooms worse than this in the weeks before coming to Master Tersus's house, but those had only been temporary. The knowledge that some people lived like this all the time reminded her that even at her lowest point, she'd had a better home to return to. The people in this neighborhood had no such escape.

Another man rose from the bed where he'd been sitting. "My lady, thank you for coming," he said. He had skin darker than usual for a Rafellish and hair only a few shades lighter than his skin, and his accent was unfamiliar. He gestured toward the man who'd opened the door, who resembled him closely, though his eyes were hazel instead of dark brown. They both looked to be in their late twenties. "My name is Jaceus Adorno, and this is my cousin Lucan. I'm sorry we can't offer you a seat."

"We won't stay long," Alaric said. "We're all here. Make your proposal."

Jaceus stepped forward, his eyes on Sienne. "Lucan and I come from eastern Rafellin," he said. "Our family and a handful of others settled near the Bramantus Mountains, near the border—or past it, we're not entirely sure. It might be in the Empty Lands. At any rate, the settlement is thriving. But there's a problem. There's a ruin some ten miles north of the settlement, not a big one, but it's mostly intact. And there's something living in it."

"How do you know?" Dianthe asked.

"People have gone there and not returned. You know how young men and women are, convinced they're immortal. It's become popular among the younger set to dare each other to go to the tower, even after the disappearances. Some of those who return report strange lights and noises, and others have watched their friends enter the ruin and not come out again. Our leaders have forbidden it, but there's always someone...anyway."

"And you want us to clean out the ruin," Alaric said.

Jaceus looked up at him, clearly startled that Alaric had spoken. "That's right," he said. "The settlement keeps expanding, and the best and most fertile land is in the direction of the ruin. So far, whatever's there hasn't attacked us, but who knows what will happen if we encroach on it?"

"We're prepared to pay for your time," Lucan said, "and of course anything you find in the ruin is yours. We did our research—that's the standard contract."

"My lady," Jaceus said, returning his attention to Sienne, "Lucan is right, we did our research. Your team has a reputation not only for being honorable, but for taking on unusual jobs. We think there's magic in that ruin, and we know that's something you care about. Please, help us."

Sienne shifted uncomfortably and glanced at Alaric. "We weren't planning on taking any new jobs during the festivities," she said. "And, not to be rude, but your job isn't all that unusual. Clearing ruins for new settlers is common."

"But...there's magic there. We know that's something you seek out."

"Certain kinds of magic," Alaric said. "Ritual. That's no secret."

"All right, ritual. There might be something of that kind in the ruin." Again Jaceus ignored Alaric. Sienne's discomfort turned to irritation. They couldn't have done much research if they thought Sienne made the decisions for the team. And she didn't like how desperate they sounded, like they'd manufactured the claim of magic specifically to appeal to them. How stupid did the Adornos think she was?

She turned to face the others. "What do you think?"

Kalanath shrugged. Perrin said, "We do not need the money."

"Then do it for compassion," Lucan said. "I mean, of course we'll pay you, but think of how you'd be helping a community in need."

"I don't think so," Alaric said. "Your cause may be just, but Perrin's right, we don't need the money. And as Sienne said, we weren't planning to take any jobs until the celebrations are over."

"We can wait."

Alaric shook his head. "Sorry. We're not interested."

Jaceus's lips tightened. "You let him speak for you?" he said to Sienne, sounding surprised and a little disdainful.

"Ah...yes? He's our leader. Why do you keep talking to me?" Sienne asked.

Jaceus took half a step back, his eyes wide. "But he...you're the daughter of a duke! Why would you let him lead?"

Sienne laughed. She couldn't help it; his consternation was too funny. "Alaric has far more experience with scrapping than I do. If your research didn't tell you that, I have to say I don't think highly of it. And my birth means nothing when we're on a job. If Alaric says no, then no it is." That wasn't strictly true. Whenever any one of them had a strong opinion on a job, Alaric generally didn't override it. But Sienne didn't feel she owed the two men an explanation.

Lucan turned toward the window and gripped the sill, bowing his head as if in the grip of some strong emotion. Jaceus looked so crestfallen Sienne felt an unexpected sympathy for him. "Look," she said, "why don't we make some recommendations? There are a lot of good scrappers in Fioretti, and I'm sure one of them will be willing to take your job."

Jaceus nodded. "I suppose...thank you. But if you change your mind—"

"We won't," Alaric said. "But we wish you luck. We know how hard it is to make a living near the Empty Lands."

Jaceus nodded and opened the door. Sienne, leaving last, avoided meeting his eyes.

Back on the street, Dianthe said, "That wasn't as funny as I thought it would be. Maybe we should have taken the job."

"I didn't like how practiced that speech was," Alaric said. "It was tailored to appeal to us."

"I don't know," Sienne said. "Is it so bad that they wanted us enough to figure out what would intrigue us? Not that I want to take that job. I'm ready for a few days' rest. But I don't think there was anything sinister about them."

"I didn't say sinister, I said practiced."

"Well, it's sort of the same thing." Sienne sighed and looked up. The Adornos' window wasn't visible from the front, but she imagined she could feel them watching her anyway.

"I did not think we would be popular," Kalanath said. "It is interesting."

"Indeed," Perrin said. "I half expect to be hailed in the street as a conquering hero."

"If news gets around about the find we made, that might not be so farfetched," Alaric said. "Let's go home. Some of us have to go shopping for a gift for Sienne's sister."

"I almost forgot about that," Sienne said. "Now I'm trying not to be resentful that she's essentially blackmailing the family for presents."

"Not blackmail, surely," Dianthe said. "Undue pressure, maybe."

"I'm sure she's threatened to make everyone's lives miserable if she isn't satisfied."

"Sienne, you have not seen your sister for a year. You cannot know she is so unscrupulous," Perrin said.

Sienne sighed again. "All right, I don't know. Maybe she's changed. I'm just afraid she'll be a brat until she's twenty, and I don't feel like waiting around for her to grow up." It occurred to her that if her parents had their way, she'd be in a position to watch it happen. The thought irritated her.

"At any rate, I know what I'll get her," she went on. "Alaric, you'll come with me?"

"Always," he said, taking her hand. "Where are we going?"

Sienne smiled. "You'll have to tell me."

———

SHE USED MORE THAN A FEW CONFUSIONS TO MAKE HER AND ALARIC'S costumes perfect. The story of Sylvie Dell releasing the Old Man of the Mountain from the transform an evil wizard had cast on him was one of her favorites, and Alaric was built to play the part of the powerful creature he'd been turned into. Funny how no one ever wanted to dress as the prince he became once he was free. Or maybe not so funny, considering how Sienne preferred the giant Alaric to any more conventionally-sized man.

They walked arm in arm through the streets, following Dianthe dressed as Lady Time, whose gauzy robes fluttered in the evening breeze. Behind them, Perrin and Kalanath carried on a low-voiced conversation whose subject Sienne couldn't make out.

"You're not nervous, are you?" she asked Alaric.

"Nervous? About meeting your parents? No. They're just people, after all. I'm afraid I'm not awestruck by nobility."

"I noticed that when we met the king. Why do you suppose that is?"

Alaric frowned. "I've never thought about it. I suppose it might be because I know what true power looks like. The wizard who created and enslaved my people wields tremendous power over them. He's capable of making them do whatever he desires. Your king, your parents...they can exert pressure, they can take away your options, but in the end, you still have the ability to choose, even if the choice is death. I realize that sounds overly dramatic."

"Yes, but it's true. Alaric, what am I going to do if I can't get out of being the heir?"

"You could run away again. We'd help you disappear thoroughly."

"I don't think I can. It's not like before, when I was responsible only to myself. Now I have a responsibility to the dukedom, and to my family. Do I really have a right to throw them into turmoil again?"

"You'll have to speak to the king, then."

"I know. Tomorrow I'll ask for an audience. It may take a few days, what with the celebrations, but we have time." She sighed. "What ill fortune rules my life that I walked through the market just as Rance did?"

"He'll be here tonight, won't he?"

"Probably. Please don't start a fight."

"I have self-control, Sienne. I wouldn't ruin your sister's party. Unless he threatens you, in which case I'll break both his arms."

"He won't threaten me."

"Let's hope not."

They passed the Plaza of Sighs with the briefest stop to watch the confusions being cast outside the chapel of Gavant as part of their nightly worship. While confusions weren't anything a priest's blessings could manage, there were plenty of wizards who worshipped Gavant who were willing to contribute their wizardry to the cause. The control the wizards demonstrated impressed Sienne, whose early training in confusions had given her an appreciation for elaborate ones. This was a light display, curtains of gauzy red and blue and gold dancing in the air above the chapel, smaller sparkling lights winking within the curtains like jewels. Despite her reservations about Gavant's worshippers, Sienne had to admit they knew how to put on a show.

The park lay a few streets on from the plaza. It was as brilliantly lit as the chapel, but with white and silver lights that made the park as bright as day. Larger lights, waist-high spheres, dotted the lawn, pushed this way and that by laughing children. The older ones had organized races; younger children ran their spheres into each other, making them flash blue briefly when they collided. Sienne wished she were young enough to participate.

Men dressed in the fashion of fifty years earlier, with blousy knee breeches and full-sleeved white shirts under tightly-fitting black doublets, moved throughout the crowds of adults with trays of glasses. The adults had embraced the idea of a fancy-dress party with varying degrees of enthusiasm. Some wore costumes from various eras of Fioretti's history, making Sienne wonder if any of those men were mistaken for servants in their knee breeches and doublets. Others, more daring, had come as characters from popular plays. A few had gone for a more classic style and were representations of the avatars, or the virtues, or, like Dianthe, personifications of Time or Fate.

Sienne's parents were near the park entrance, greeting guests.

They were dressed, quite appropriately, Sienne thought, as the King and Queen of Staves from a hazard deck. Sienne swallowed her nervousness and led her friends in their direction.

Mother saw her first. She glanced once at Alaric and did a double take that would have been funny if Sienne's stomach hadn't been in knots. Then she nudged Papa, who was chatting with someone dressed as the Spirit of Winter.

"Sienne!" Papa exclaimed. "Thank you for coming. And these—" He caught sight of Alaric and his eyes widened. "These must be your companions."

"Yes. Mother, Papa, let me introduce Dianthe, Perrin, Kalanath, and Alaric. Everyone, these are my parents, the duke and duchess of Beneddo."

"What a pleasure to meet you," Perrin said, sweeping them a graceful bow.

"It's our pleasure," Papa said, unable to take his eyes off Alaric. Sienne hoped he wasn't about to start shouting things about the Ansorjan scrapper defiling his daughter. "We're grateful that Sienne made such good friends. We were terribly worried about her safety."

"We look out for each other, your grace," Dianthe said.

"She's a valued member of our team," Alaric added.

"I hope you don't mind my saying, but it was a complete surprise to learn what Sienne has been doing for the past year," Mother said. Her eyes were fixed on Alaric as well.

"I can imagine," Alaric said. "But she's taken to the life well. Saved all our lives more than once."

"It's what we do for each other," Sienne said.

Mother's gaze flicked past Alaric and back again. "I wish we could speak longer, but we shouldn't neglect our other guests," she said, and to Sienne's surprise she sounded sincere. "Please, enjoy yourselves. Sienne, Felice is here somewhere—you really should talk to her."

Sienne's desire not to talk to her sister warred with her feeling that her mother was right. "I'll...see if I can find her," she said.

Her father hugged her and kissed her cheek. "You look lovely," he said. "It's an interesting choice of costumes. Suits you—both of you."

It was the closest he was going to come to an acknowledgement of Alaric's presence in her life, at least in public. She smiled and hugged him back.

"Should we try to find your sister?" Kalanath said. "The one whose day it is, I mean."

Sienne squeezed the squishy paper-wrapped package under Alaric's arm. "We can at least find where to leave this."

They made their way across the lawn to a fountain topped by a bronze fish spraying water from its mouth. Other partygoers glanced at them, glanced a second time at Alaric, then continued their private conversations. Did Alaric ever get tired of being stared at? Sienne thought she'd probably lose patience with it after about five minutes. But Alaric never showed sign that he even noticed.

Packages wrapped in bright cloth and covered baskets made an untidy pile on a white sheet near the fountain. Liliana, dressed in armor made from quilted silver satin over a frilly party dress and expensive-looking boots, sat on the fountain's rim with her head propped on her hands. Kitane's sword and shield lay on the ground nearby. She looked so disgruntled Sienne had to suppress an annoyed reaction. It was her birthday, after all, and Sienne remembered her own birthday parties and decided disgruntlement wasn't an inappropriate reaction. "Not having fun?" she asked.

"Marius Kentarre is here," Liliana said.

"I don't know who that is."

"He's just the most annoying boy in Fioretti. His papa is an old friend of Papa's, so they had to invite him." Liliana scowled harder. "But he took over the game I was playing and made it all boring rules and the like. It's *my* party and we should do what *I* want! I don't think it's spoiled to want that."

"I agree," Alaric said. "You should start a new game and leave him to play by himself."

Liliana looked up at him. "Who are you?"

"This is Alaric," Sienne said. "He's my...friend." Alaric smirked. "And these are Dianthe, Perrin, and Kalanath. We're all scrappers."

Liliana eyed Alaric again. "Are you Sienne's lover? I heard Erianthe and Phebe talking about it where they thought I couldn't hear. Are you going to get married?"

Alaric's smirk became a real smile. "Maybe someday. But yes, Erianthe and Phebe were right."

"Oh." She turned her gaze on Kalanath. "You're Omeiran, aren't you? I heard Omeirans don't believe in avatars. Aren't you afraid they'll strike you down?"

Kalanath looked startled at the direct question. "Omeirans worship God differently," he said, "and the avatars do not seem to mind."

"I think you're handsome. Why isn't he your lover, Sienne?"

"I...Liliana, that's not—" Sienne took refuge in rudeness. "That's none of your business!"

Liliana's interest had already moved on. "Is that for me?"

Alaric presented her with the package. "It's half your present."

"Only half?"

"It's a dress like mine, with a skirt that sparkles," Sienne said, trying to regain her composure. "The other half is for me to use magic to fit it to you perfectly. You'll have to try it on the next time I visit."

"Oh!" Liliana's eyes were wide. "Thank you, Sienne!" She dropped the package and flung her arms around her sister's waist. Sienne, startled, tentatively hugged her back. It was hard to remember that Liliana was almost a young woman, given that she acted much younger than her age. At that moment, Sienne almost liked her.

"Now," Alaric said, "I think we should do something about a new game. These spheres are almost the right size for catch-and-carry. Maybe we could figure out how to make it work."

"But you're adults. Why would you want to play games?"

"Because it's more interesting than standing around and talking."

Liliana glanced around at the nearest adult guests, none of whom were paying them any attention. "They don't think so."

"Then they, too, are boring," Perrin said, "and we can at least cheer you on."

Liliana smiled. "I'll tell Sofie and Amabel. They don't like Marius either. Oh, and there's my friend Delphine."

Sienne turned to see a pretty, dark-haired girl dressed much as Liliana was, complete with sword and shield. Beside her, Perrin swore viciously under his breath and half-turned away. "What is it?" Sienne asked.

The dark-haired girl dropped her sword and shield and raced toward them, screaming, *"Papa!"*

8

"Papa, Papa!" the girl shrieked, and flung her arms around Perrin's waist, burying her face in his antique waistcoat. Slowly, Perrin put his arms around her, bowing his head so his long hair concealed his face. "Papa, where have you been? We missed you!"

"I have missed you too, sweetling," Perrin murmured. "I—dear Averran, Noel too?"

A young boy perhaps six or seven years old, dressed in a cut-down version of Gavant's famous many-colored robe, had emerged from the crowd and was running as fast as his stocky legs would take him toward the pair. Perrin crouched to take the boy in his arms and hold both children close. "Oh, how I have missed you. Is your mother here?"

"Mama is ill with a headache. Brinton brought us. Do you know Liliana, Papa?"

Perrin stood and detached himself from his children, though he kept hold of each of their hands. "I am a friend of Liliana's sister."

Sienne thought he looked relieved at hearing the children's mother wasn't present. She herself felt like a strong breeze might knock her over. What a horrible or beautiful coincidence that Perrin's children had been invited!

"I thought your father was dead," Liliana said. "Isn't that what Master Lanzano said? I heard him tell Rance that we had to be nice to you because your father was dead."

"He is *not* dead!" Delphine shouted, gripping her father's hand more tightly. "He had to go away and now he's back! Aren't you, Papa?"

Perrin's face looked cut from stone. "I fear not, Delphine," he said. "My...the thing that keeps me away is still in force. Forgive me."

"But Mama has us pray for you every night. She tells us to ask Averran to send you home," Delphine said.

"She...what?" Perrin's impassive expression gave way to confusion. "Surely that can't be right."

"You can't leave, Papa," the little boy said. "There are sweets, and punch. Come and have some with us."

Perrin was looking into the distance. "I wish I could, but I think my time with you is over," he said.

Sienne followed his gaze to a middle-aged man, not dressed in costume, striding toward their little group like an oncoming storm. He came right up to Perrin and grabbed the front of his shirt with both hands. "You were warned," he said. "I don't know how you got in here—"

Alaric wrenched the man's hands off Perrin and hauled him away by the collar. "He was invited," he said, dropping his voice to its most menacing rumble. "Based on your clothing, I'm guessing you weren't."

"I am the Delucco children's attendant, Althus Brinton," the man said, trying to slip Alaric's grasp and failing miserably. "This man has no legal right to have contact with them. He is forbidden to speak to them. I'll have the law on all of you for collusion."

The noise was drawing the attention of nearby guests, all of whom looked like this was great entertainment. "It was a coincidence," Sienne said. "But I'm glad it happened. Perrin is—"

"Sienne, please do not make a scene," Perrin said. He let go of Delphine and Noel's hands and stepped back.

"It's too late for that, Perrin." Sienne took a step closer to Brinton.

"It's cruel to keep them separated. I don't know what laws are responsible for it, but they're unjust. I don't see what's so wrong about them having a few moments together."

Brinton glared at her. "Oh? And who, pray tell, are you?"

Sienne drew herself up to her full height. "Lady Sienne Verannus. My parents host this party. And they personally invited Perrin Delucco. So don't you dare throw around threats, or I'll have you evicted."

"The law is on my side, Lady Sienne, not yours." Brinton clapped his hands. "Miss Delucco, Master Delucco, we are leaving."

"No!" Delphine and Noel screamed as one. They turned and threw themselves at their father again, clinging to his legs and waist like a couple of tearful monkeys.

Perrin looked like someone who'd been knifed through the heart. "Children," he said quietly, peeling them away from him, "Brinton is right. You must go. I will...see you again."

"You openly declare your intent to violate the law?" Brinton exclaimed.

"No. My hope for the future," Perrin said. "But if you ever summon my children as peremptorily as that again, I will break every one of your fingers."

"And I'll hold you down while he does," Alaric said. "Leave now."

Brinton had been about to clap again, but instead extended his hands to the children. Noel took his hand hesitantly, looking over his shoulder at Perrin for approval. Perrin nodded slightly. Delphine, tears streaming down her face, slapped Brinton's hand away and ran, disappearing in the direction of the park's entrance.

Perrin watched until long after all three were gone. In the bright lights, his face looked as pale as Alaric's, his jaw rigid. Then he turned and strode toward one of the servers, snatched a tall glass of wine from his tray, and drained it in one gulp.

"Perrin!" Dianthe exclaimed.

"I make no excuses," Perrin said, taking another glass. "I cannot bear this. Averran will have to understand." He drank only half of the second glass, then held it up to the light so its pale contents glowed.

"Please make my excuses to your parents, Sienne. I need to be alone." He set the glass on a different passing tray and walked away, deeper into the park until he disappeared beyond the lights. The guests who'd been watching the family drama play out drew into little knots of three or four, murmuring and casting glances toward the remaining companions.

"Sisyletus have mercy," Alaric said. "I don't blame him for anything."

"Should we go after him?" Sienne asked. "What if something happens to him?"

"Whatever he chooses to do, it is a thing he needs to be alone for," Kalanath said. "But I worry that he will drink until he forgets, and that will be much to drink."

"I'll go," Dianthe said. "I can keep an eye on him without intruding or him knowing I'm there."

"Do that," Alaric said. "He really shouldn't be alone, whatever he thinks."

Dianthe nodded and ran off after Perrin. Kalanath said, "Is it too much coincidence that his children come to this party?"

"He said once that he knew the Lanzano family," Alaric said. "If he meant he was related to the Lanzanos...it's not surprising that Rance's relations were invited, particularly relations whose children are the right age."

"Delphine's mother is Rance's cousin," Liliana said.

They all startled. "Were you eavesdropping?" Sienne exclaimed.

"I was here the whole time. It's not my fault you didn't notice. Does that man drink a lot?"

"No," Sienne said, "and it's private. You understand private, right? You hate it when people tell your secrets, so you should respect other people's secrets too."

"I'm not stupid, Sienne. Why can't he see his children? I really did hear Master Lanzano telling Rance that Delphine's papa was dead. Did he do something wrong?"

"Who's Master Lanzano? You mean Rance's father?"

"Yes. I don't like him. He always wants me to sit on his lap even though I'm almost as tall as him."

Sienne filed that away as information her father should have. "Perrin did something his father didn't like, and his father disinherited him. Legally, in some ways, Perrin is dead. But that doesn't mean he doesn't want to be with his children."

"That's awful. I like Delphine." Liliana turned her attention on Alaric. "Do you still want to play catch-and-carry?"

"I do," Alaric said, "and so does Kalanath."

Liliana smiled at Kalanath, almost coquettishly. "I *definitely* want him to play."

Sienne concealed her smile at Kalanath's discomfort behind her hand. "I'm not good at—" She stopped. From across the lawn, Felice was approaching, seeming to drift between groups of chattering people, all of whom ignored her. She was dressed as the Seer from a hazard deck, though she hadn't bothered with the token veil, so Sienne could see clearly that her sister's eyes were fixed on her. She took two steps toward Felice, then hesitated. She had no idea what to say to the woman from whose dashed hopes she benefited, if benefit it was and not curse.

She felt a warm, large presence at her elbow. "Is that Felice?" Alaric murmured in her ear. She nodded, feeling unable to speak. "I thought so. You look alike."

"We do not. She's prettier than I am."

"You're the most beautiful woman I know, but I won't argue the point. Talk to her. We'll keep Liliana occupied."

Sienne turned her head to look up at him. "You don't have to sacrifice your evening."

"It's no sacrifice," Alaric said with a smile. "She's the youngest child of a large family and I'm sure she doesn't get enough of the right kind of attention. And it *is* her birthday. Though I feel sorry for Kalanath, since she looks like he might be her true love."

Sienne laughed and kissed him. "Thank you."

She walked across the lawn to meet Felice, who slowed her steps as Sienne approached. She was looking past Sienne at the little group near the fountain. "Is that him? The tall one?" she murmured.

"His name is Alaric."

"He couldn't be more different from Rance. That's not why you chose him, is it?"

Irritated, Sienne said, "You make it sound like I went trolling for a lover out of spite. Falling in love with Alaric was a complete surprise."

"Sorry. I didn't mean it that way. I know Rance hurt you, and I thought you might have gone off short, dark Rafellish men." She smiled. "It was a poor joke. Come, let's get away from the crowds. I'm sure someone will try to listen in." She hooked her arm through Sienne's and drew her away from the lights and the people, moving in the direction Perrin had taken.

Outside the circle of lights, the park was dimly lit along its many gravel paths. Moths fluttered around the lamps, bumping against them and falling dizzily to the ground. Soon they were far enough from the party that the crunch of gravel underfoot was the only sound in the still night. Ahead, a trellis covered with brilliantly white moonflowers sheltered a marble bench. Felice steered them that way. The sweet fragrance of the flowers came to Sienne's nose, reminding her of other nights when she'd left the bedroom window open so the scent of moonflowers climbing the walls of Master Tersus's house filled her room. It was hard to stay irritated when the moonflowers bloomed.

Felice sat on the bench and folded her hands in her lap. "Well. I imagine you have good reason to hate me."

"I don't hate you," Sienne said, surprised to find it was true. Whatever anger she'd felt toward her sister for stealing her lover felt dim and distant in the peaceful night. "I'm surprised you don't hate me for stealing your birthright."

"That's hardly your fault. I don't imagine you want it." Felice closed her eyes and breathed in the scented air. "It's strange. I spent twenty-six years, more or less, knowing what I would do with my life, and now...nothing. It's terrifying and beautiful at the same time."

"Papa said it was your idea, being disinherited. You really don't have to. I don't mind..." Sienne remembered that she didn't intend to remain the heir. She felt awkward about saying so, as if her rejecting the thing Felice was forced to give up cheapened both the inheritance and her sacrifice.

Felice was shaking her head. "It would be too difficult to be the heir, and then the duchess, knowing you were waiting for me to die so you could get on with your life. This is better for everyone."

"I wouldn't—"

"You would. Maybe not right away, but eventually."

Sienne couldn't think of a response to that.

"I feel I should apologize to *you* for ruining your life," Felice went on. "By what Papa and Mother have said, you're happier as a nobody scrapper than you were as a lady."

"I am happy. I don't want to be a duchess."

"And you don't want to marry Rance. That's a change."

"Rance never loved me. I was fortunate Mother and Papa refused to change the marriage contract." Sienne hesitated, then added, "I'm sorry Rance wants to annul your marriage."

"Rance?" Felice chuckled. "It was my idea, though I might have manipulated him into thinking it was his. Frankly, it's a relief."

Sienne blinked. "I thought...you don't love him?"

"Why would I love him? This was a political marriage. Rance is handsome enough, but he's shallow and far too easily influenced by his father, who I don't mind telling you is a piece of work. Both his parents care more for their social standing than for petty concerns like love and loyalty."

"I didn't realize." Sienne chuckled. "I suppose I was so obsessed with him I couldn't imagine you not falling in love with him. I was jealous of you for so long."

"It would have been hard for me to fall in love with him when I was already in love with someone else," Felice said.

Sienne's mouth fell open. "Felice...how awful! Why did you agree to the marriage? You could have turned down the alliance!"

Felice shook her head. "I couldn't marry the one I loved, so I didn't think it mattered who I did marry. Rance isn't so bad, for all he's shallow. And we needed the money from the marriage settlement. I figured it was the least I could do for the dukedom I would eventually inherit."

"That's so unfair! Who is he, that he's so unacceptable?"

Felice regarded her steadily. "*Her* name is Violette Pierobo."

Sienne blinked. "Violette? Oh. *Oh.*"

"You see why it was impossible."

"I do. Felice, I'm so sorry."

"Don't be. Once my marriage is dissolved, I intend to move to Fioretti to live with her. She's a dancer here with a well-known troupe." Felice sighed. "I feel guilty at being so...relieved, really. I never resented my obligations to Beneddo as heir, because I was raised to put my own needs aside for the good of the dukedom. It wasn't until it was clear my infertility couldn't be cured that I began to consider what *I* wanted, and realized how much of myself I'd sacrificed on that altar. I only regret the turmoil it's caused. And that you've been pulled into it."

"I'm going to petition the king to have me disinherited."

"He won't do it. Not without a good reason. And there are no good reasons. You're healthy, intelligent, presumably fertile—you know they'll want to check that immediately—"

"I already did."

"So there's no grounds for appeal. I'm sorry." Felice took Sienne's hand. "But there's no reason you can't marry your Ansorjan scrapper. Papa and Mother will make a fuss, but there's no law against it, and ultimately the decision is yours."

"I can't. Alaric...can't have children."

Felice's hand closed convulsively on Sienne's. "Are you sure?"

"Positive. We can't have children together."

Felice's mouth twisted in a mirthless smile. "What a tangle. Then our parents will put enormous pressure on you to marry Rance."

"They know I don't love him. I already told them I wouldn't."

"I don't think you realize the financial situation we're in. Once I divorce Rance, he'll go back to his parents, and we'll have to repay most of the marriage settlement he brought with him. It won't bankrupt us, but it will leave us in straitened circumstances. There likely won't be money to send Erianthe to school, let alone Phebe. Keeping Rance in the family..." She bit her lip. "I suppose you and Rance could come to an agreement, take lovers on the side..."

Sienne shook her head. "No. Not a chance. I'm not going to keep Alaric like some kind of...of concubine. I'll just have to find a way to convince the king to free me of this obligation. Alcander would make a wonderful duke."

"He would. I don't think he realizes that. He certainly doesn't want it, which in my opinion ought to be the first consideration for an heir's suitability. Of course, that makes you incredibly eligible, since you want it less than he does. What's it like, being a scrapper?" Felice sounded almost wistful.

"Exciting, mostly. Sometimes it's boring. Occasionally it's terrifying." She thought of the acid jelly cube and suppressed a shudder. "But what I love is being part of a team. My friends...you don't know how close you can be to another person until you've risked your lives together. I love them. Giving that up just to rule a dukedom—"

Felice's laughter interrupted her. "It's possible you're the only woman in Rafellin who's ever said that."

"Only because most people think a noble title is glamorous."

"People like the Lanzanos." Felice's mouth twisted in a genteel scowl. "I will be glad to be free of them."

"Master Lanzano has apparently been making inappropriate advances toward Liliana. Does Papa know?"

"I don't think so. Parts of Master Lanzano would have shown up all over town if he did. I'll tell him. And speaking of inappropriate behavior, what was that little contretemps I saw with the Delucco retainer? He ran past me dragging the Delucco boy like he was going into battle."

Sienne's heart ached for Perrin once again. "One of my companions is Perrin Delucco, the children's father. The retainer took exception to him being here."

"That's a nasty business. Lysander Delucco is a vindictive man. He might try to bring the law against your friend."

"But it wasn't Perrin's fault! We had no idea his children would be here, and no reason to believe it. Besides, it's an unjust law that deserves to be broken."

"Nevertheless. Maybe we can put Alcander on it. He's driven to extirpate injustice wherever he sees it. You should have heard him when it turned out I couldn't inherit. He went on and on about those inheritance laws being the relics of an earlier, more desperate time when civilization was still clawing its way out of the wreckage of the wars and reproduction was urgent. Maybe he'll even succeed in changing them someday."

"Not if he becomes duke."

"Please, Sienne, don't put your hopes on that. The likelihood that King Derekian will grant your request is small."

"There's still a chance. I'm not giving up before I've even tried."

Felice nodded slowly. "No, you wouldn't." She squeezed Sienne's hand once more before releasing her, and stood. "I'm sorry I couldn't talk to you before. I felt guilty for so long at marrying the man you loved. I don't have an excuse to offer you, except that I thought I was doing what was best for our family. And Rance..." She bit her lip.

"What about Rance?"

"It's not important now. Just...you were fortunate not to have married him. I'm not sure he loves anyone but himself."

"That's probably true. And you're right, I feel fortunate. Now that I know what love is really like, I can't believe I ever imagined myself in love with Rance."

"So you're happy with Alaric?"

"Deeply happy."

Felice once again linked her arm with Sienne's and they strolled back toward the party. "He seems worth it. Look at him." She pointed. "I can't imagine Rance ever playing a rough and tumble game with children, let alone ones he's not related to."

Alaric had appropriated two of the large glowing spheres and was in the middle of a huddle of children. Kalanath stood several yards away with his own huddle, which included Liliana, Sienne was amused to see. They were too far away for Sienne to hear what they were saying, but suddenly the two teams broke apart and ran screaming at each other, each bouncing and kicking a sphere to make it roll in front of them. Alaric ran behind, waving his arms and herding the children in the right direction, while Kalanath did the same, if less enthusiastically. It wasn't catch-and-carry, but a game Sienne didn't recognize that seemed to require the teams to defend their own ball while trying to capture the opponent's. It also, apparently, required lots of screaming. Sienne couldn't help laughing at the melee.

"It's too bad he can't have children," Felice said. "He's good with them."

Startled, Sienne looked at her. "I...he is," she said. "I didn't know." Alaric had booted his team's sphere back into the scrum, and stood alongside, laughing. Sienne's heart ached with love for him. What had the divine Octavian said? Sometimes we don't know what we want until we've lost it? But Alaric hadn't been upset when he'd told her they couldn't have children. Yes, he was having fun tonight, but that was because he felt sorry for Liliana...wasn't it?

Alaric caught sight of her and bounded over to her side. "They took to *mylluste* like they were born Ansorjan," he said. "Of course, a real game of *mylluste* would have three sides, but there weren't enough players. I'm afraid young Marius is still playing whatever boring rules-heavy game he came up with, him and a handful of similarly stodgy children who will probably grow up to be tax collectors."

Felice chuckled. "Thank you for enlivening my sister's party."

"It was my pleasure, Lady Felice."

"Just Felice. You're part of the family, after all."

Alaric put his arm around Sienne. "I'm not sure your parents would agree."

"They can't dictate who we love. I'm glad you're with my sister." Felice hugged Sienne who, startled, hugged her back. "Come to dinner sometime. We all want to know you better." She nodded at Alaric and walked away.

"That was unexpected," Alaric said. "I take it you've both made amends?"

"I...think so. She has reasons for not being upset about losing her birthright and her awful husband."

"Speaking of the awful husband, is Rance here?" Alaric looked around.

"Probably. I hope he won't approach me. He might be under orders to convince me to marry him."

"Does he know about me?"

"I have no idea. If my parents gave him those orders, they might not have told him. Rance may not have scruples, but he has to believe courting me when you're in my life won't be successful."

Alaric's brow furrowed. "You don't really think your parents would encourage him?"

"Not really. It's more likely his father would push him that way. Either way—"

"If he makes a pest of himself, I'll remind him why that's a bad idea. And no, I won't start a fight, but I'll finish it if I have to." He flexed his arms, though by the way he was once again looking about him, he'd done it unconsciously.

"Thank you. Um..."

"Yes?"

Sienne found she couldn't meet his eyes. "You're enjoying yourself?"

"Of course. Liliana's friends are interesting, for children. Though I'm worried about Perrin."

She grasped this conversational thread gratefully. "Dianthe will keep an eye on him, and make sure he gets home all right."

Alaric frowned. "I was thinking more of what will happen if he gets seriously drunk. Averran might not be willing to look the other way more than once."

"There's nothing we can do about it, though. Except maybe pray."

"Praying never hurt." He kissed her. "I have to go. My team needs rallying so we can crush Kalanath and his minions!"

Sienne laughed as he ran toward the melee, which had gone

quieter in his absence. Everything was fine. Perrin would return, he would eventually recover from his heartache, so far as that was possible, and Sienne would find a way to get out of this inheritance. And Rance would find some other titled heiress to marry and she'd never have to see him again.

She drank wine, and watched the game, which slowly drew the attention of the adult guests. Their idle interest soon turned avid as they realized their children were engaged in something parents could decently choose sides in and, more importantly, shout threats at other parents. At one point, Liliana raced past, her quilted armor torn at the shoulder and her wooden sword raised high. She met Sienne's eyes and smiled, her eyes alight with happiness, and Sienne smiled back, feeling friendly toward her sister for the first time in her life. Maybe she'd stop being a brat sooner than Sienne thought.

It was probably close to eleven o'clock before the game wound down and people took their leave. Dianthe hadn't returned. Neither had Perrin. Sienne, Kalanath, and Alaric said goodbye to the duke and duchess and walked home in silence. Kalanath and Alaric were too exhausted to speak, and Sienne felt emotionally drained and lightheaded from too much wine. The celebrations in the city were still going strong, but no one tried to get them to join in. Sienne hoped it wasn't because they looked weary. Looking weary was a good way to get jumped by someone with much darker intent than a desire for a dance.

The house was dark except for the lights behind the kitchen window. Alaric pushed the door open for Sienne to enter. "Is Leofus still up?" she asked. "Leofus?"

"It's us," Dianthe called out.

Sienne entered the kitchen. Dianthe sat at the table next to Perrin. Her gauzy robes were torn into fluttering ribbons. He had his face buried in his hands and his hair hanging loose around it. "It's all right," Dianthe said. "We walked for a while."

"A very long while," Perrin said, his voice muffled. "I could not succumb to the desire to drink myself into a stupor while I was on my feet. Then I was assaulted, and Dianthe made herself known.

Together, we fought off my assailants. It was enough to bring me to my senses. We returned here not ten minutes ago. Dianthe has been kind enough to remind me that I have a duty not only to myself, but to you."

"I can't imagine how terrible it was for you to see your children," Sienne said. "How can we help?"

Perrin raised his head and chuckled. "You would not be yourself if that were not your first instinct, to help in an impossible situation. I will recover. I am trying to remember the joy in seeing them for even a few minutes and not the horror of having them torn from me."

"Your daughter said they have been praying for you," Alaric said. "To Averran."

"Yes, and that has puzzled me. For Cressida to encourage them in such an action...I thought her solidly in my father's court. I cannot understand it."

"It is not a thing she should do?" Kalanath said.

"She worships Gavant as I once did. Believes my father was right to cast me off. She was antagonistic toward Evander, my mentor, and dismissive of Averran's worship. It is not so much a thing she should not do as a thing I cannot imagine her doing."

Alaric pulled out his chair from his usual place at the head of the table and sat. "Something must have happened."

A knock, soft and diffident, sounded at the back door. They all looked at each other. "It is nigh onto midnight," Perrin said. "Who could be calling at this hour?"

Kalanath disappeared down the hall, and Sienne heard the door open, then the quiet murmur of voices. Then Kalanath returned, trailed by a lovely woman wearing a cloak much too warm for the weather, even the coolness of a true summer night. She put the hood down as she entered the kitchen. Perrin shot to his feet, his face pale. "Cressida," he said.

"This is..." Sienne began, but she already knew who it was.

Perrin answered her anyway. "Cressida Delucco," he said. "She used to be my wife."

9

"Not by my will," Cressida said. Her voice was deep for a woman's and as husky as if she'd spent a lifetime coughing. "Perrin, you are in danger."

"I, in danger? Cressida, do you not know how dangerous it is for a woman alone to cross the city at this hour?" Perrin took a few steps toward her, his hand outstretched, then let it fall. "How did you know where to find me?"

"I hired a woman to follow you, after you...after Father Delucco expelled you. I asked her to keep me informed as to your lodgings, in case...I do not know what contingency I wanted this information against." Cressida looked as pale as Perrin. "I could hardly ask Brinton to accompany me."

"Then you should not have come."

"I had to. Father Delucco intends to punish you for daring to break the terms of your disinheritance. You need to leave the city."

"You mean, because he spoke to his children?" Sienne exclaimed. "That wasn't his doing, it was an accident. There are witnesses, starting with me and my friends. If Lysander Delucco wants to make it a matter of the law, he'll find those witnesses are not insignificant."

"He knows that," Cressida said. "I heard him talking about it with

Brinton. Even if he could bring suit against you, it would make him look the fool to do so. I am certain you know how much your father dislikes looking a fool."

"I am aware, yes," Perrin said. "But you need not fear for me. We are well capable of defending ourselves."

"Against dozens of ruffians, none of whom can be traced back to him?" Cressida's fists were clenched tight as if she wished she could use them against someone. "He does not know where you are because he, as he put it, refused to sully himself with the knowledge of the location of a reprobate. But in the morning he will set out to discover your location, and if I could find you, he certainly will. Can you protect *all* your friends? The owner of this house? No, Perrin. You need to leave until his anger has cooled. A week, possibly two, and he will have forgotten its immediacy. *Please.*"

"I am not certain," Perrin said, "why you should care. You yourself told me I had to choose between you and the avatar I serve. I betrayed you, as far as you were concerned."

Cressida seemed not to remember there was anyone in the room but her and Perrin. Sienne thought about clearing her throat as a reminder, but decided against it. It was bad, she knew, but this was not a conversation she wanted to miss. "You think I wish you harm, just because you...because we were not one? That I wanted you cast out, disgraced and disinherited?"

Perrin's jaw tightened. "But you agreed with my father."

"I believed there should be no straying from the worship of Gavant. I didn't know how we could manage a household split between two faiths. I did not think...Perrin, how can you believe I wanted any of this? You left me with no choice but to follow your father's will."

"And yet, Delphine said...they pray to Averran nightly."

Cressida lifted her chin. "I hoped he would have mercy on the children of one who gave up everything to serve him. And I hoped I would someday understand the kind of faith that puts God above more earthly loves."

Perrin closed the distance between them, but still didn't touch her. "I chose Averran over you," he said. "It didn't mean—" He glanced around, seeming for the first time to remember his friends. "Excuse us," he said. "We will use the sitting room."

When they were gone, the others sat in silence for a while. Sienne wished she could hear the rest of the conversation, even though the wish was self-indulgent. This was far, far worse a difficulty to get past than Sienne's problems with Felice. It had never occurred to Sienne to see Perrin's choice in that light, but of course it was true: he'd chosen Averran over his own wife and children. Cressida might have wounded him by demanding that he choose, but he must have broken her heart when he chose wrongly, at least from her perspective. Sienne wasn't sure those were the sort of betrayals that could be easily forgiven.

Finally, Alaric said, "Mistress Delucco is right. We should consider leaving town for a while."

"Run away?" Sienne exclaimed. "And give Master Delucco the satisfaction?"

"I'm with Sienne," Dianthe said. "Running makes us look weak."

"It is not weak to find a better place to fight from," Kalanath said. "We do not know what Perrin's father can do, what resources he has. We are on the defensive, and that is not a good place to be when we lack knowledge."

"And we don't care how it makes us look to Lysander Delucco," Alaric said. "The alternative is that we never go anywhere alone and have to be constantly on guard against ruffians whose faces we don't know. And if Perrin remains in Fioretti, Delucco will be reminded that Perrin thwarted him, and he'll never stop trying to hurt or possibly kill him."

"He wouldn't try murder, would he?" Sienne said. "He has his social status to think of. He can't risk the accusation."

"That will be no comfort if Perrin is dead," Kalanath said. "We should go."

"All right," Dianthe said. "And I know just the job."

"We can—what job?" Alaric said. A look of distaste crossed his face. "Not the Adornos. I told you, I don't like how desperate they were."

"But it's a job we don't have to go hunting for," Dianthe said, leaning forward to emphasize her words. "The Bramantus Mountains are a week's journey away. A week out, a week back, and however many days it takes to clear out the ruin, and Master Delucco forgets all about us."

"I don't think it's quite that easy," Sienne said.

"Sure it is. We're still provisioned, mostly, from the Nocenti job, so it won't take much time in the morning to get ready. And who knows what kind of treasure might remain in a ruin that might have been occupied by a wizard once?"

Alaric scowled. "We could just go to Tagliaveno for a holiday. We've earned it."

"You know you never last more than a day with nothing to do."

"She's right about that," Sienne said. "And I did feel sorry for the Adornos."

"So did I," Kalanath said.

"Fine," Alaric said. "But when this goes horribly wrong, I reserve the right to say I told you so."

"Fair enough," Dianthe said. "You and Sienne can go to the Adornos in the morning, since they're so awed by Sienne—"

"Why do I have to—" Sienne began.

Footsteps in the hall silenced her. Perrin paused in the doorway. "I must walk Cressida back to her home," he said. "I will return shortly. Pray, do not wait up for me."

"Don't be late," Alaric said. "We're leaving Fioretti in the morning."

Perrin took a few steps into the kitchen. Cressida hovered behind him, her face betraying nothing of what had passed between them. "We are not leaving on my account, are we? I refuse to flee from my father."

"We're taking the Adornos' job," Alaric said, "which coincidentally gets us out of town. This is no time to be proud, Perrin. Lysander

Delucco is a dangerous enemy who believes you've flouted his authority. We're not going to stay where our presence rubs that in."

"If he has not attacked me in all the time I have lived here, I do not see why we should be afraid now."

"You did not encounter his grandchildren until now," Cressida said. "He sees them as his property, close to whatever passes for his heart. He fears your influence on them."

"And yet you have dared secretly to expose them to a different faith. Cressida, you—" Perrin stopped and pinched the bridge of his nose, closing his eyes against some horrible vision. "We will return you to your home. Alaric, if you are determined to protect me, I do not see how I can dissuade you. I will be quick."

"Should we go with you?" Sienne asked.

"I doubt my father will be able to marshal his forces quickly, and he is unlikely to set thugs to roaming the streets on the off chance they will encounter me. But if I do not return in an hour—"

"Understood," Alaric said. "Good evening, Mistress Delucco."

Cressida nodded once, and then she and Perrin were out the door. When it closed behind them, Sienne said, "I feel so awful for them. Do you think they can ever reconcile?"

"Some things are broken beyond repair," Dianthe said. "I hope their relationship isn't one of them."

"They did not look like two people who love again," Kalanath said.

Sienne had to agree with him. She wished she knew how to help them. She'd settle for knowing if they wanted to be helped.

———

A LIGHT RAIN FELL THE NEXT MORNING, AND SIENNE HUNCHED HER shoulders against it. She enjoyed how it swept away the stink of animal waste in the courtyard outside the Adornos' lodging house. "What if they've already left?"

"Why would they have left? They still have a job to hire out,"

Alaric said. He strode as if the weather were clear and fine, though rain beaded his short blond hair.

"All right, what if they've already hired someone else?"

"Then we go to Tagliaveno instead. I'm starting to regret agreeing to this. Tagliaveno is cooler than Fioretti in true summer. Or Sileas. Damn, I could have suggested we visit Dianthe's family."

"Why are you so opposed to this job? It can't all be because they were desperate."

Alaric held the door of the lodging house for her. "There's just something off about it. They were more interested in convincing us to go, regardless of the details, than they were about finding a solution to their problem. Like we were the job, and it didn't matter what they sent us after so long as we went."

"That's convoluted, Alaric. I'm not sure you can know all that."

He shrugged. "I could be wrong. Tell me I have an overinflated opinion of our worth."

"I never dismiss your instincts. You've been right too many times." Sienne stopped outside the Adornos' door. "It's not too late to go home."

Alaric stared at the door. "No," he finally said, "no, whatever's really going on, I think I want to know about it. Anyone that desperate will find a way to get what he wants, and I'd rather have the Adornos in front of me than behind me." He rapped sharply on the door. "Too bad it's too late to pretend you're the team leader. It might have been useful to hold me in reserve against any treachery they plan."

The door opened. Lucan Adorno stood there, his clothing in disarray like he'd only just risen. His pleasant, curious expression gave way to one of confusion. "Yes?"

"Do you still need scrappers?" Sienne asked.

"We, ah...yes." Hope dawned. "Do you mean you changed your mind?"

"I was convinced of the rightness of your cause," Alaric said dryly. "May we come in?"

"Yes, yes, of course." Lucan stood aside for them to enter. Jaceus, more tidily dressed than his cousin, turned away from the window. He looked from Lucan to Alaric and then at Sienne. "Jaceus, they've agreed to take our job!"

"They—but that's wonderful!" Jaceus came forward and clasped Sienne's hand, then offered his hand to Alaric. Alaric hesitated only a moment before accepting it. "Thank you. I promise you won't regret it."

"Our only condition is that we have to leave immediately," Alaric said. "It won't be a problem for you, will it?"

"No, of course not. We travel light." Jaceus still looked stunned. "Where—what do we do next?"

"You'll meet us at the Lizzorno stables in two hours. You have horses?"

"We don't. We walked here. Is that a problem?"

"That depends. Can you show me where your settlement is?"

"We didn't bring a map, but it's about fifteen miles north of Yvona's Breach. Does that help?"

Alaric's gaze grew distant, and Sienne could almost see him following the map in his head. "It's a day and a half by horseback to where we'll have to set out across country," he said. "Two days if you're on foot. You can rent horses—"

"We don't know how to ride," Lucan said, in the voice of someone proclaiming an unshakeable truth. "We'd just slow you down and the benefits of riding would be wasted."

Alaric grimaced. Sienne said, "We could rent a wagon. It would be easier on Button if he didn't have to haul our gear the whole way."

He said nothing, but Sienne knew him well enough to recognize when he was reining in his temper. "All right," he finally said. "But it's coming out of the client's pocket."

Jaceus turned to the bed, where a backpack hung from the end. "I can pay you now."

"That's not necessary. Later is fine."

"No, I want us to begin as we mean to go on." His strange accent was thicker when he was excited. He withdrew a small purse from the pack and shook a few coins into his palm. "Half now, half on completion, isn't that right? And something extra to hire the wagon."

Alaric tucked the coins away without looking at them. "We'll discuss the details on the road."

"But we've already told you everything."

"There are things we'll find useful that probably never occurred to you to think were important. But we'll have plenty of time to work that out. Also, while we're on the road, you'll follow my orders."

"Orders?" Lucan said. "But—"

"Alaric is responsible for keeping our team together," Sienne said. "Following his orders keeps us safe. While we're traveling together, you're part of the team, sort of. And I trust him completely, if that helps."

Jaceus and Lucan exchanged glances. "If you say so, my lady," Jaceus said. "Whatever you require."

"Then we'll see you in two hours," Alaric said.

Back on the street, Sienne said, "See? They didn't act strange at all."

"I'm trying not to come up with reasons that that's strange behavior in itself," Alaric muttered.

"That would just be paranoia speaking."

"I know. Which is why I'm trying not to." He sighed and took her hand, and they headed off down the street. "And yet they did still defer to you. I wonder what gave them such respect for the nobility."

"Some people are like that. I try not to take advantage of it. Or did, back when I was still Lady Sienne."

"I imagine it's quite the temptation, if people put themselves in your power."

"Mostly it happens by accident. Someone's generous to you, or asks your opinion frequently, and it's hard to tell right away if it's sycophancy or just niceness. And people in general respond well to flattery, noble or common."

"I dislike flattery. It's so insincere. I'd rather someone was rude to my face."

"Oh, but you're so good at being straightforward, it encourages people to be honest with you."

"Am I? I suppose—" He stopped in the middle of the street. "That was flattery, wasn't it?"

"Just making my point, love."

Alaric rolled his eyes. "All right, flattery is effective. That's not a weapon you wield often, is it?"

"No. And never on you. I have other ways of getting you to do what I want." She looked up at him through her lashes in a coquettish way, smiling a little half-smile. He laughed and squeezed her hand.

"It's too bad we're in a hurry," he said, "or I'd let you demonstrate. As it is, we'd better get back and pack up quickly. Every moment we're here is one in which Lysander Delucco could find us."

"You don't think he'd try to kill Perrin, do you?"

"I don't. I think he'd try to leave him permanently maimed, as a reminder." Alaric sighed. "I hope getting out of sight for a while works."

Sienne nodded. She'd never spoken with Perrin's father, but she knew his reputation as a hard man and felt certain Alaric's assessment was correct. Leaving town was the right thing to do. She tried to ignore the niggling feeling that told her they needed a more long-term solution.

Long-term solution. Sienne stopped in the middle of the road and cursed, causing a passing woman, her untidy gray hair straggling into her face, to stare at her disapprovingly. Sienne didn't care what her vocabulary made the rising generation look like. "I forgot," she said.

"Forgot what?" Alaric had stopped with her and looked concerned.

"Forgot that I should tell my parents where I'm going. I can't just pick up and leave anymore. Damn it, Alaric, when am I going to have time to see the king?"

"It will have to wait until you get back. You don't think they'll try to stop you, do you?"

"I don't know. They might." She swore again. "I've been trying not to think about it, but...you don't want to be a concubine, right?"

"I have to say that's not one of my life goals, no." Alaric took her other hand and made her face him. "This is something we'll figure out. Right now, we have to worry about keeping Perrin safe. Rituals, and your inheritance, will have to wait a few weeks."

"I'd forgotten entirely about your quest. I'm sorry."

"You've had a lot to think about. That's natural." He drew her into his arms and held her, right there in the middle of the street, ignoring the catcalls and whistles. "I'll go with you to speak to your parents. They're not unreasonable and you have obligations. They may not agree with those obligations, but based on what you've said, that's something they understand."

"I hope so." She hugged him tightly. What had she done before he'd entered her life? Pined miserably after a selfish bastard, right. "Let's hope they're understanding enough."

10

After the punishing heat of the lowland plains, the coolness of the forest felt like an avatar's blessing. Narrow, straight pines like soldiers in green and brown massed in front of the mountains, guarding the majestic peaks and filling the air with their rich scent. Even the ground, carpeted with fallen needles, felt softer than the short, stiff grass of the plains. Already Sienne felt revived from the five days it had taken to walk this far and ready to walk another five days. Even so, she was grateful that only another two or three would get them to their destination.

Sunlight slanted through the trees, golden and almost tangible with the dust motes in the air defining the rays. She hoped Alaric would call a halt soon; she was hungry for something more filling than the bread and cheese they'd had at their midday rest, and Kalanath had caught rabbits then and was carrying them slung over one shoulder. Rabbit was one of her favorite foods...no, that wasn't right, it was only when they were in the wilderness that she relished it, symbolic of her joy in her companions.

Ahead of her, Alaric shrugged his pack off and let it fall to the ground. "We'll camp here," he said. "Here" was a place where the trees were slightly wider spaced than elsewhere, which meant they'd have to squeeze the tents in wherever they could. Sienne set her pack down at the base of a pine whose bark was deeply scored by the claws of some animal and scuffed away needles in a large circle near the center of the widest spot, using her small magic called invisible fingers to whisk away more of them. Around her, the others began pitching tents and unloading supplies.

Alaric dumped a load of dry branches beside her improvised fireplace. "There's a fallen tree over there," he said, "so we'll have plenty of fuel. Do you need anything else?"

"That should be enough." She glanced over his shoulder at Jaceus and Lucan, engaged in setting up their small tent. It had no poles, just heavy canvas thrown over a taut rope between two trees that, when folded, a single person could carry easily. "They've done well."

"No reason to think they wouldn't. They are settlers, after all, and used to hard living."

"I meant they've been friendly and helpful, and they do whatever you tell them without complaint."

Alaric chuckled. "Only after looking to you first."

"I know." Sienne squatted back on her haunches and sighed. "It's embarrassing. Especially when they call me 'my lady.'"

"I promise never to call you Lady Sienne." He stroked her hair briefly. "I'll get the cook pot."

She watched him walk away and regretted briefly their mutually agreed-on policy of not sharing a tent while they were in the wilderness. It would increase Button the donkey's burden, for one, adding a third tent to his load. More importantly, noises that in the privacy of their room were discreet were much louder outdoors, as they'd found one memorable night. Alaric had said something about professionalism Sienne wasn't sure she agreed with, but she *had* agreed they were both capable of containing their baser passions for a few days or even weeks. It certainly made sex more exciting when they returned home.

She arranged the wood in a solid base that she filled with dry pine needles. This fire would smell incredible even before the soup pot went on. Dusting her hands off, she set the needles afire with her spark and teased the small flame with a magical breeze. Building a fire filled her with satisfying warmth that had nothing to do with the flames. She, Sienne Verannus, scholar and pampered daughter of a duke, was capable of accomplishing this basic survival need. She didn't think that feeling would ever grow old.

"My lady," Lucan said, "Alaric asked me to bring you this." He held the cookpot in one hand.

"Thanks," she said. "Will you find a couple of sticks to hold it up?" She prodded the burning tinder and rejoiced to see the heavier branches catch fire.

Lucan began working a forked branch into the earth beside the fire "pit." "Is this what it's like, being a scrapper?" he asked.

"Is what?"

He gestured with one hand. "Living off the land, camping at night...it seems so ordinary."

"Most ruins are far from civilization, or at least the ruins worth investigating are. Some teams use magic to get from place to place. I don't know any of the spells that will do that, not to mention you have to know a place before you can get there." She'd been so eager for *ferry*, thinking it would be the end of their transportation problems, until she discovered her magical reserves were too limited to allow her to cast any other spells after she'd *ferried* them all. And *transport* was even harder to find.

"So you travel the long way," Lucan said. He crouched to sift through the pile of wood Alaric had brought and grunted when he came up with a second suitable stick. "We appreciate your willingness to help."

"Well, you *are* paying us," she said with a smile.

Jaceus came to join them. He had a smudge of dirt on one dark cheek that he wiped away. "Yes, but the benefit we get from that payment is tremendous," he said. "It means the survival of our settlement. We can't have this danger threatening our borders."

Sienne shifted uncomfortably. Gratitude was one thing, but the Adornos sometimes sounded almost groveling in their praises. "That's up to you, once we're gone. And there will be other threats."

"True," Jaceus said. "Just none so overt."

Sienne turned her attention to the pot so she wouldn't have to meet his avid eyes. She summoned a glob of water to fall neatly into the pot with not even a splash, then lifted it to hang from a thick branch she wedged into the forks of the two uprights Lucan had placed. "Where's your settlement from here?"

"Oh, we were thinking we should take you directly to the ruin," Lucan said. "That saves half a day's travel."

Sienne's eyes narrowed. It was reasonable, but the quickness of the response sounded almost pat. "All right," she said. "Then where's the ruin?"

"Northeast another forty-five miles," Jaceus said. "We'll probably reach it around evening two days from now, given the terrain and the time we've made so far."

"That sounds right," Alaric said, approaching from the far side of the fire. He had Kalanath's rabbits in one hand and a clump of slightly withered carrots in the other. "You two can help Sienne by cutting these up."

Jaceus accepted the skinned rabbits without a trace of squeamishness. Sienne didn't know why she kept expecting them to cavil at the basic requirements of roughing it. They weren't city boys by a long shot, they were used to taking care of themselves—they'd made this journey alone, going to Fioretti—so why did she have the constant feeling that cutting carrots and building fires were new experiences for them? Maybe Alaric's paranoia was rubbing off on her.

She left the Adornos to prepare the food and collected her pack to stow it in her tent. Dianthe had already arranged her bedroll for her and was sitting on her own, rubbing her feet. "It's day five," she said.

"I know. The day when you question your life choices because there's no foot bath in sight and no Denys to rub your sore feet." Sienne plopped down on her bedroll and stretched. "Tomorrow will be better."

"It always is." Dianthe sighed, a long, put-upon sound, and worked her feet back into her boots. "It's nice having someone else to help prepare dinner. I'm really not fond of cooking."

"Is Denys a cook? Or will the two of you eat out all the time when you're married?"

"Denys *loves* cooking. He's always trying new things. He cooks, I do the dishes. I'd wash up forever if it meant never having to cook again."

"I like cooking over a campfire, but that's the only kind of cooking I've ever done. I'm afraid to ask Leofus to teach me. He'll either refuse on the grounds that I can't possibly treat his kitchen with proper respect, or be painfully enthusiastic." Sienne rummaged in her pack for a washcloth. "I want to wash up a bit before dinner. Day five is when *I* regret the lack of a bathtub."

Her hand fell on a red-lacquered box a little larger than her palm and fingers. She pulled it out and set it aside. Dianthe reached for it and slid open the lid, tipping the deck of hazard cards into her hand and fanning them out. "This would be valuable even if it weren't magical. A complete deck, at least four hundred years old...my mother would say it was especially potent."

"Why is that? Is there some superstition about hazard cards, I don't know, ripening with age?" The washcloth had slipped all the way to the bottom of the pack. She dug it out, then set about rearranging her other things.

"Don't ever say that in front of a serious hazard reader. The superstition part, I mean. Hazard cards are supposed to pick up the aura of the owner and become responsive to their questions. It's insulting to call it a superstition." Dianthe turned over the top card, the Ruby. The brightly colored gem glowed against the dull background of Dianthe's bedroll.

"Interesting. I wonder if it's true? Then you could learn something about the owner by examining her deck." Sienne held her hand out for the cards. "I just wish I knew what it does. I'm afraid to ask anyone about it in case someone knows Master Samretto had it and thinks we stole it."

"We did steal it. Sort of."

"He was an evil necromancer. It was lawful salvage. Sort of." Sienne shuffled the deck, something she had trouble with because the cards were slightly too large for her hands, and laid out three cards: the Two of Swords, the Duke of Coins, and Fate. The image on the last card of a hand tossing rune-engraved stones in the air made her uncomfortable, particularly since the stones seemed to be the source of the light in the painting. "What does this mean?"

"I'm not sure. Past, present, future...the Two of Swords means partnership in the face of danger, the Duke of Coins indicates a changing situation, or a man who isn't what he seems, and Fate..." Dianthe went silent.

"It means something inevitable in the future," Sienne said. "I don't believe in fate. I changed my future once, when nobody thought I could be anything but a duke's daughter. I can change it again."

"Your parents weren't happy about you leaving on this job," Dianthe said.

"No, but even if I am their heir, that doesn't mean I'm bound to them. They just want it to mean that." Sienne scooped up the cards and restored them to their box. The angular, unfamiliar letters engraved on its lid mocked her, hiding their secrets as well as if they'd been invisible. She spoke three languages and could read most of a fourth, not counting the spell languages; she ought at least to recognize this one's alphabet. But no, it was as opaque to her as if it were a code, which she suspected it was.

She closed the tent flap and took her shirt off, soaking the washcloth in warm water summoned from the air. "Anyway," she went on, sponging herself off, "I'm going to make a case to the king that Alcander will be a better heir than I. He's got all that legal training, understands the laws pertaining to ruling, and he always was good at being nice to the landholders. I'm easily annoyed and the only laws I understand relate to salvage and property rights."

"Let's hope that's enough," Dianthe said. She lay back on her bedroll with her arms behind her head. "I don't know what we'll do if..."

Sienne, too, felt afraid to put that contingency into words, as if that might make it come true. She put on a new shirt and sighed at how clean she felt. "I'm going to wash this. Do you have anything that needs cleaning?"

Dianthe shook her head. Her eyes were closed, and her face had begun relaxing into sleep. It was one of those things Sienne envied about her, her ability to fall asleep anywhere in the space of two breaths. She let out her first snore as Sienne left the tent.

The Adornos were still working at the soup pot, which smelled of hot water and nothing else. Kalanath had disappeared, probably to hunt more game. Alaric was tending to Button, talking to the animal in a low voice. Perrin sat in front of the men's tent, his eyes closed and his hands loosely open on his knees, meditating. He had prayed for blessings earlier that day, so this must be purely for the sake of communion. Sienne wondered, as she often did, what the avatar's voice sounded like. Maybe it was an actual voice only Perrin could hear. Or it could be thoughts that sounded like his own internal monologue, but different enough to be recognizable as such.

She took her shirt a short distance away, rinsed it, scrubbed it, rinsed it again, and held it up with her invisible fingers while she heated the remaining water soaking it to evaporate away. It was peaceful, mindless work that would be monotonous if she did it for a living.

She listened to the noises of the forest: the inevitable birds she never could identify, twittering at each other in challenge or courtship; the whoosh of the wind in the tops of the trees, high above, that sent occasional needles down onto her head; and the nearer sounds of people moving around camp. No speech; after five days they'd refined their system to a wordless harmony. Her fears for the future dwindled into the distance and hardened into a resolve not to let moments like this go.

That night, they ate rabbit soup in the same companionable silence, then sat around the fire in a bubble of light and warmth and listened to Lucan tell stories. He was good, professional quality, and he knew stories Sienne had never heard before: "The Owl and the Nighthawk," or "Swallowing Stones," or the haunting "Grizel and the

Howlers." Sienne wasn't sure she believed howlers were real, but Lucan swore the tale was true.

"Howlers are born from the places of magical contamination in the Empty Lands," he said now, continuing the friendly argument they'd started the day before. "It's said that a man or a woman witnesses horror, the death of a loved one maybe, within one of those places, and the horror takes hold of them and turns them into something evil. And then they can't not be drawn to where tragedy will occur, like sniffing out blood."

"Knowing the future is the province of the avatars," Perrin said. "I think it unlikely they are willing to grant such powers to inhuman creatures."

"Animals have senses humans don't," Lucan said. "How do birds know how to fly north in summer? I don't think howlers sense the future so much as they pick up on people's fear and anger. And far too often fear and anger turn into violence."

"They don't sound dangerous, anyway," Dianthe said. "Sad, maybe. Standing outside windows and howling like a werewolf."

"They do far more than that," Jaceus said. "A howler's wail makes your blood congeal with terror so you can't do anything but cower or flee. The ones they don't just tear apart, they make mad with lust for the flesh of their own kind. And once their victims have killed, they become howlers themselves."

"See, that just sounds like a story to frighten children," Dianthe said. "It's almost too terrifying. A howl that makes you frightened, maybe, but when you add cannibalism, it's too much."

"You didn't believe in carvers, either, until we encountered them," Sienne pointed out.

"That's true, but they also turned out to be different from the legends," Dianthe said. "If there are howlers, they're probably not as bad as the stories make them sound."

"Our people—I mean, the people in our settlement, they stay well away from anything that howls in the night, just in case," Lucan said. "Maybe the stories aren't entirely true, but the least of them are enough to make us wary."

"Yes, because things that howl in the night might be dangerous even if they're not howlers," Sienne said. "*There's* something dangerous. Were-creatures, I mean. Maybe howlers are imaginary, but there's plenty of evidence that werewolves and the like are just vicious."

"They defend their territory just like humans do," Jaceus said. "Protect the pack. Nothing vicious about that."

"You must never have seen were-creatures," Alaric said. "They're quick to aggress given the slightest provocation, and sometimes with nothing we'd call provocation at all. And since they're barely more intelligent than an animal, their attacks are particularly cunning."

Jaceus and Lucan exchanged glances. "We've seen were-creatures," Jaceus said. "They're more intelligent than people give them credit for. They're capable of learning human words, for one—not many, but enough to communicate on the level of, say, a four-year-old child. And humans have attacked them so often over the centuries, is it any wonder they're quick to retaliate?"

Kalanath scooted closer to the fire and extended one arm. "That is the bite of a werebear," he said, turning his arm to display a pale ring of scars around one biceps. "A team I was with three years ago went into the wilderness seeking salvage. We do not—did not attack the weres, but we entered their territory unknowing. They killed some of us before we fight them off. That is not intelligent. Or, to say, intelligent creatures know danger and act, for good or bad, by how much danger it is. We were not dangerous."

"It's not always easy to tell when something's dangerous," Lucan said. "Haven't you ever fought anything simply because it might be a threat, and the dangers in being cautious and dead outweighed the possibility that you could be wrong?"

"Sometimes," Alaric said, "but with most creatures, human experience tells us how to react. Carricks, for example, are deadly no matter how cautious you are in approaching them. And were-creatures are the same. There are stories of people finding them as cubs and taming them, but mostly those are just stories."

"You think they're evil, then," Jaceus said.

"Not evil. They lack the human capacity for choosing good or evil. But dangerous, certainly."

"I agree with that," Lucan said. "But we've settled the Empty Lands, and that's where were-creatures call home. We have to learn to live with them."

"Or clear them out," Sienne said. "I'd be afraid to live near weres, especially if there were children in my village."

"I'd hope it didn't come to that," Jaceus said.

Dianthe yawned. "I'm off to bed," she said.

"Me too," Sienne said. "Probably to dream of howlers, thanks."

Lucan, who'd looked very grave, smiled at this. "Dream of how Grizel found a way to defeat them, and ended their torment."

"That's more cheerful."

But sleep eluded her. She lay wakeful in her bedroll listening to Dianthe snore, which was normally a soporific sound, but tonight put her on edge like a saw cutting through metal. Finally she rose, put on her boots, and crawled out of her tent. As an afterthought, she removed the ash wand from her pack and tucked it into her belt. She'd carried it the whole time since finding it and occasionally made an effort to work out what it did. Now was as good a time as any for another trial.

Perrin, pacing the far side of the fire, said, "Is something wrong?"

"Can't sleep. I'm going for a walk."

"Do not go far."

"Don't worry, I'll stay within sight of the fire."

She summoned her magical sense of true north and walked southwest, away from the camp, until the fire was a dim glow at her back that did nothing to illuminate her surroundings. The sound of her footsteps was louder in the darkness than the daytime, her feet crunching across the needles and sending up whiffs of crisp pine scent wherever she trod. Insects chirred a constant high-pitched whine in the background, so pervasive she was only occasionally reminded of it when the wind brought it more loudly to her ears. She turned south and began walking around the camp, mindful of her promise to Perrin.

She took out the wand and examined it. In the dimness, all the crystals were dark, though eight of them were darker than the others. She touched each one with her index finger. Simply waving the thing had no effect, which was probably for the best, but it left her none the wiser as to how it was activated. Averran had refused to tell Perrin what it was, and Perrin had only said the avatar thought it would do them good to figure it out themselves. So Sienne kept trying. Sometimes wands had a command word, but that could be anything. Or it might require a combination of gestures. Or maybe the command word had to be thought.

"Go," she said, brandishing the wand. "Begin. Start. Commence." Nothing. She couldn't remember how many of those she'd tried before. "Open. Yield. Comm—no, I did that one." Open. Maybe...

She held the wand flat on her palm and closed her eyes. There was a small magic, not a spell, that let her open her spellbook directly to any spell she wanted. It wasn't faster than turning the pages by hand, at least not for someone who knew her spellbook as well as Sienne did, but if her spellbook were across the room, she might use invisible fingers to bring it to her and use the opening magic to make it be open to the spell she wanted when it arrived. With a thought, she turned the opening magic on the wand.

It twitched in her hand. She opened her eyes. The crystals were glowing with a soft blue-green light, all but the eight dark ones. Carefully, she reversed her grip so she was holding the wand to point away from her. The radiance didn't falter, but its rich intensity made it look as if the wand were hollow and the crystals were holes drilled into it to let the light at its core out. She waved the wand tentatively. The crystals left trails of light in their path. She tried again, waving the wand harder.

A jolt like a hard puff of air struck her. One of the crystals went dark. And every noise stopped.

Sienne froze in place. The sounds had cut off sharply, not dwindled away. She looked up and saw the trees move in a silent wind. So the wind hadn't just died, and probably all the insects hadn't fallen over dead. Fear that she'd been struck deaf hit her, intensifying when she couldn't hear the sound of her labored, terrified breathing. She made herself calm down and thought. It couldn't be *deafen*, because how stupid to create a wand that turned on its holder, which meant… of course. *Silence*. A perfectly ordinary confusion. The wand had cast *silence* on the area, and if she walked far enough, she'd come out of the effect.

The lights had faded back to nothing, and the wand looked just as it had, except that there were now nine dull, black stones instead of eight. Sienne started walking back to camp and tried not to feel unnerved at the total silence. Just to be sure, she tried singing a few notes of a wordless melody. She felt her vocal cords working, but again, no sound emerged. She walked faster. Damn, she should have kept track of how many steps she'd taken. She could experiment later. Now she just wanted to be back in the world of chirruping insects and hissing breezes.

The firelight glowed more brightly as she approached, turning the tree trunks into black exclamation points against its ruddy glow. She realized two of the trunks were actually shadowy, dark-skinned people just as her foot came down with a crunch on pine needles. The insect chorus came alive once more, sounding like a shriek after the unnatural quiet. "—won't listen," Lucan was saying to Jaceus. "We'll have to try—"

Jaceus held up a hand. "Sienne," he said. "We didn't hear you."

They both looked so furtive Sienne was instantly suspicious. "It's a spell called *silence*," she said. "You're not out here plotting something nefarious, are you?"

"Why, were you snooping on us?" Jaceus said.

That made Sienne feel defensive as well as suspicious. "Of course not."

"We were just talking about what to do when we reach the ruin," Lucan said. "We shouldn't go in with you, but you'll need us to show you where the settlement is when the job is done. For the rest of your pay."

It was so smooth he had to be lying. Sienne hesitated, debating whether to call him on it. Finally, she said, "Once we see the ruin, we'll know where to have you wait to be safe."

"Of course." Lucan and Jaceus regarded her with dark eyes. She stared back at them, willing them to break. Neither moved. It was Sienne whose nerve finally cracked.

"I think I can sleep now," she said. "Good night." She moved wide around them and hurried toward the fire, and Alaric's tent. With only a brief wave for Perrin, she ducked inside. Kalanath was a dark lump on the far side, sleeping as soundly as he usually did, but Alaric came awake the instant she put a hand on his knee.

"Sienne?" he said. "What's wrong?"

"I don't know," Sienne whispered. "I just caught our clients outside camp, acting very suspicious. They claimed they were having an innocent discussion, but why wouldn't they have it in their tent?"

"Did you hear any of what they said?"

"Just a few words. Something about how someone wouldn't listen, and they'd have to try...something else, I think."

"That could mean anything."

"I know. I don't like it."

"Neither do I." Alaric took her hand and ran his thumb across the back of it absently. In the dimness, she could barely see his face, but he had the still pose that meant he was thinking hard about something. "We'll have to be alert for signs of treachery. It's possible their story about a ruin is to lead us into a trap. They were pretty adamant about wanting to hire us specifically."

"I'm so angry. I liked them."

"It could still be nothing. We just have to be careful." He cupped the back of her head with his free hand and drew her close for a kiss, his lips soft and gentle on hers. She returned his kiss, letting go his hand to caress his cheek. He made a little noise in the back of his throat that never failed to drive her wild with desire, and she pressed herself against him and felt him chuckle against her mouth just before pulling away. "It's been too long, sweetlove," he said.

"It's only been six days."

"An eternity, then. Go to bed before we do something that will make Kalanath profoundly uncomfortable."

"I am already uncomfortable," a voice said from the far side of the tent. Sienne giggled and scooted out backwards.

She was taking off her boots before she realized she'd forgotten to tell Alaric her other news—that she knew how to activate the wand. It was good news and bad: good because *silence* was not in her spell-book, bad because it seemed one had to be a wizard to turn the thing on. So much for someone else having magic to hand. She also didn't know how useful it would be. She hadn't measured it exactly, but she knew the wand's *silence* affected a larger area than the spell, so there was that.

Dianthe might appreciate it, since if you cast *silence* on a person, it moved with them; that would be useful to someone who relied on being able to move stealthily. And *silence* could stop a wizard casting spells, since it effectively stopped one from speaking. She fell asleep trying to work out how to avoid having it cast on her.

11

A storm rolled in late the next afternoon, prompting Alaric to call an early halt so they could make camp before it rained. Sienne kept a close eye on the Adornos, but they behaved exactly as they had the whole week previous—friendly, helpful, and open. She didn't quite start thinking she'd imagined things the night before, but she did feel that perhaps whatever secrets they were hiding weren't dangerous to her friends. Alaric didn't behave as if he suspected anything, either, but she knew him well enough to recognize that he kept a careful eye on the cousins all through their rather damp meal. Tomorrow they'd discover whether their caution had been justified.

They traveled all the next day through the rain-soaked trees, which smelled more strongly of pine when they were wet and made the air feel cool and comfortable. Sienne walked beside Button, who stepped out smartly, as if the air invigorated him, too. She patted his neck. "This has been a nice journey, hasn't it?" she told him. "No monsters, just a pleasant stroll across the hills and through the forest. If you—"

Button lurched, stumbled, and went to his front knees, crying out in fear and pain. Sienne gasped and stepped back, her mind filled with the image of Button coming down on top of her. Button's hind legs collapsed, and he made another horrible shrill cry of distress.

Then Alaric was there, kneeling beside the animal. "What happened?"

"I don't know. He just fell." Sienne joined him and watched as he felt along Button's front legs. Her eyes swept the ground, seeking something that might have tripped the donkey.

"I think his leg is broken," Alaric said.

"There is a hole here," Kalanath said, prodding it with his staff. "It is not large. Bad luck."

"That's terrible," Lucan said. He and Jaceus were standing well away from the companions, who'd clustered around the fallen Button. "Does that mean you'll have to kill him?"

Sienne sat back on her haunches and regarded the two. She thought they might be afraid of Button, however ridiculous that seemed, because they never touched him and always walked wide of him when they camped. Maybe it was just the tension of seeing Button in pain, but that comment struck her as odd—like they didn't know what usually had to be done for a donkey with a broken leg.

"That will not be necessary," Perrin said, nudging Sienne to the side. "The rest of you, ease his burden by removing our things."

Sienne helped unload Button and tried not to think irritated thoughts about the Adornos, who continued to stand well to one side. True, it wasn't their burden, but it wasn't as if unloading a donkey was that much work. Alaric squatted near Button's head and spoke soothingly to him, keeping him calm as they worked. Aside from a few spastic movements of his undamaged legs, Button didn't seem distressed. How much of that was due to Alaric's presence, Sienne didn't know, but she was grateful for it.

When all the equipment was unloaded, Perrin took a green-smudged blessing from inside his vest and pressed it to the leg Alaric indicated. "O mighty Lord, have patience in your crankiness, and grant me this blessing."

Button went very still as green light flooded up his injured leg. His large brown eyes regarded Sienne placidly, as if this were perfectly normal instead of the first time they'd had to use a healing blessing on him. The light faded, and Alaric and Kalanath helped the donkey rise in an awkward scramble.

"Miraculous," Lucan said. "Your avatar is willing to heal an animal?"

"The avatars grant us healing blessings and expect us to use our wisdom in invoking them as we see fit," Perrin said. "They do not enjoy seeing creatures in pain, even those lacking in human intelligence."

Sienne started handing things to Alaric and Dianthe to load back onto Button. "Did you think God only reserves Her gifts for humans?" she asked.

"Actually, I hadn't thought about it, but yes," Lucan said. "I've never seen blessings invoked on anyone but humans."

"God loves all Her creations, or so I was taught," Perrin said, "and we are expected to reflect that love in our treatment of them."

"That's the last of it," Alaric said, tightening a rope. "Let's head out." He tugged on Button's lead, and the animal stepped out as if nothing had happened.

"I don't understand," Jaceus said. "How do you justify killing things if they're God's creations?"

Alaric looked over his shoulder at them. "Most monstrous creatures are man's creation, not God's. And I doubt God expects people to lie down and be eaten rather than defend themselves."

"But what about the creatures that came about...all right, not naturally, but through contact with the contaminated spaces in the Empty Lands? It's hardly their fault they were created."

"Jaceus," Lucan said.

"No, I want to understand this. If God is so understanding, why would She allow the creation of creatures that fall outside Her protection?" Jaceus sounded angry for the first time since Sienne had met him.

"I am still relatively new to my faith," Perrin said, unfazed by Jaceus's tone, "but I worshipped Gavant for more than thirty years before my conversion, and a priest of Gavant would say it is not our place to decide which creatures partake of God's grace. Gavant's priests and divines spend many hours in study of God's love, as Gavant was known for his charity and kindness to all and his ability to see beauty in the ugliest of creatures. Gavant taught that we should endeavor to see others the way God, who delights in our imperfections, sees us, and not to fear creatures who seem monstrous simply because they are other than ourselves."

"Which doesn't explain why you kill monsters."

"We aren't monster hunters," Alaric said, a little impatiently. "We don't kill except in defense of human life. I don't think any avatar would object to that."

"That makes sense," Lucan said, swiftly cutting off Jaceus's reply. "Killing in defense of one's own...that's something everyone can understand, right, Jaceus?"

Jaceus frowned. "I suppose so."

"We don't kill unless we're aggressed on," Sienne said.

"But *you* would never kill, would you, my lady?" Jaceus asked. It was almost a plea.

Sienne suppressed memories of a green ray, turning men to ash. "I've killed," she said shortly. "It's not something I like to dwell on. They would have killed me, so I don't regret...no, what I regret is that there wasn't another option."

Jaceus fell silent. She thought he looked disappointed, and felt momentarily guilty at having ruined his worshipful image of her. Then she felt stupid. She wasn't any better than anyone else just because she'd been born noble, and if this knocked her off the pedestal the Adornos had erected for her, so much the better.

As if the accident had dampened their spirits as thoroughly as the rain had soaked the trees, nobody spoke for the rest of the afternoon. Sienne caught herself looking past Alaric's broad back eagerly, as if their destination would be visibly different from the rest of the forest. If they would only have a few hours of daylight when they reached the ruin, Alaric would probably want them to get an early start exploring the next morning instead. She tried not to walk faster than the rest of them in her impatience.

After a few hours, Jaceus and Lucan took the lead. Alaric dropped back to walk next to Sienne. "Try not to look conspicuous," he said, "but I think you should have your spellbook ready."

Sienne tucked it into the curve of her left arm. "Do you really think they intend treachery?"

"I don't know. This is a long way to go for a simple ambush. But I want us to be on our guard." He dropped back farther to speak to Kalanath in a low voice Sienne couldn't make out. Beside her, Perrin caught her eye and nodded. Whatever happened, she and her companions would be ready for it.

The slender pines made the sun invisible, but it was easy to tell when the light began to fade. Jaceus and Lucan didn't show signs of slowing at all. "How much farther?" Alaric asked.

"Not much," Lucan said. "We can reach the ruin by sunset. There won't be time for you to explore it, but you'll be close."

"Maybe we should camp sooner than that," Sienne said. "It's not like we need to be right next to it at night, and making camp is always harder in the dark."

"But—you don't want to see it? We've come all this way," Lucan said.

"We'll see it in the morning," Alaric said. "Half an hour more, and we'll make camp whether or not we've reached the ruin."

"All right," Jaceus said. Sienne caught the glance he threw Lucan, a warning look she didn't understand. Whatever was going on, Sienne was sure there was something strange about the ruin the Adornos hadn't told them.

Half an hour passed with no ruin in sight. The light dimmed until Sienne had to squint to see her companions, dark blotches against the trees except for the fair-haired Alaric. "We'll stop here," he said, lowering his pack to the ground. Sienne gratefully followed suit and cast about for a place to put a fire. Her awareness that an ancient wizard's ruin lay nearby made her feel even more than usual the need for a fire's comfort and security.

They ate in silence seated around Sienne's fire, then sat in silence, with even the talkative Lucan quiet. Sienne leaned against Alaric and breathed in the smell of wood smoke. It was one of her favorite smells, reminding her of good times with her friends and the peace of an evening following a long day's hike. And if her parents had their way, she wouldn't have this anymore.

"What's wrong?" Alaric murmured. "You just went tense. Did you see something?"

"Just thinking about my parents, and the dukedom."

"There's nothing you can do about it now."

"I know. But if the king won't listen to my petition, I don't know what else to do."

"You intend to speak to the king?" Lucan said.

"I hope to, yes."

"It's because you are a duke's daughter, right? The king won't speak to just anyone."

"Anyone can petition for a moment of the king's time. My being a duke's daughter makes it more likely that he'll see me."

"That seems unfair," Jaceus said.

"Maybe." Sienne stretched and felt Alaric's arm go around her more securely. "The king is busy, and he'd be overwhelmed by petitioners if he heard the pleas of every person who approached him. It's not so much that he respects his nobles more than commoners as that he has a better idea of the seriousness of our requests because he knows us better. That makes it easier for him to decide who to see. He might turn down my petition regardless."

"We thought...you wouldn't have to worry about that. That the king would listen to you," Lucan said, exchanging another of those strange glances with Jaceus.

"I don't think he'll turn me down. What I have to ask is important to the future of my parents' dukedom."

"He did not strike me as irrational, when we met him," Perrin said. "I am certain he will hear you."

"You...the rest of you have met him, too?" Jaceus exclaimed.

"It was memorable," Alaric said dryly. "He's a brave man, for all I dislike him."

"Dislike your king?"

"He's not my king. And he hit Sienne. I haven't forgiven him for that."

Jaceus and Lucan wore identical shocked expressions that made them look more related than ever. "He...hit you, my lady?" Lucan whispered.

"He was pretending to be angry with us to get information," Sienne said. "It was...complicated."

"Even so—"

"We saved his life," Dianthe said, "but we had trouble proving it."

"He was generous even though he did not need to be," Kalanath said. "He is not my king either, but I think he is a good one."

Jaceus sat back, propping himself on the heels of his hands. "So he's generous and rational, but complicated?"

"Yes," Sienne said. "I think he's doing a good job, as king."

"Then..." Lucan said, but didn't complete his thought.

Dianthe yawned. "I'm ready for bed, and an early start. I'm eager to see this ruin."

"You won't be disappointed," Jaceus said.

Sienne kissed Alaric and followed Dianthe to their tent, removing her boots and leather vest but otherwise staying fully dressed. "Did Alaric warn you about possible treachery?" she asked.

"He did. But it's hard to picture either of the Adornos betraying us, however strange they are. Didn't you think it's odd how upset they got at the idea of killing monsters?"

"Yes. Especially for two people whose settlement is most of the way into the Empty Lands. Compassion for monsters that eat babies isn't a survival trait." Sienne lay back with her spellbook cradled in one arm. "I don't know what to make of it."

"We just have to be alert, like always," Dianthe said, settling into her own bedroll. Moments later she let out a gentle snore. Sienne lay awake for a while, listening to the night sounds of insects and people shuffling around, until she, too, fell asleep.

She woke to someone shaking her foot. "Alaric?"

"It is me," Kalanath said. He was little more than a dark shape in the light of the banked fire. He shook Dianthe's foot. "The Adornos are gone."

That woke Sienne fully. She clutched her spellbook and sat up. "How long?"

"I do not know. I had a...feeling, and I looked inside their tent. They are not there. Alaric said to wake all."

Sienne didn't press him for details on his "feeling." Kalanath was prone to moments of insight whose source he refused to talk about, and now wasn't the time to address it. She pulled on her boots and crawled out of the tent, followed by Dianthe. Alaric and Perrin stood beside the fire. Alaric's head was lifted as if he were a blond pointer hound, scenting the wind. "We don't know how long they've been gone," he said. "With the way their tent is constructed, they could have crept out the back without anyone noticing."

"*I* would have noticed," Dianthe said. "I put some dry branches back there, just in case they tried something like that. They must have taken advantage of the change of watch when I went to wake Kalanath."

"Then they've been gone about half an hour. Perrin?"

"I have one scrying blessing left that will give us the presence of sapient minds," Perrin said, taking out his riffle of blessings. "But the range is not far. Half an hour might put them outside it."

"Do it anyway," Alaric said. "If they went to get compatriots, they'll be returning soon, and I want fair warning."

Perrin nodded. He crouched to draw a circle near the fire with a thin stick, then tossed the stick aside and invoked the blessing. The circle filled with sapphire blue light that pulsed several times, then faded. Alaric swore. Sienne looked, and felt a chill shiver up her spine. Five blue dots of light grouped at the center of the circle. That was her and her companions.

Surrounding them, thronging the outer edge of the circle, were dozens of blue lights. They packed so closely together in places they were a single mass of light, indistinguishable as individuals.

"We have to move," Alaric said. "We can't let them surround us."

"They're already surrounding us," Dianthe said. "Kitane's eyes, there must be a hundred of them."

Alaric took the stick Perrin had used and pointed. "There are fewer of them on the northwest. We'll have to run for it. Leave everything but Button. Let's go."

Stumbling in the darkness, they ran northwest, not pausing even for Sienne to cast *cat's eye*, which would have given them the ability to see in the dark. Beside her, Perrin urged the donkey on. Button ran in silence, as if he could feel the urgency and didn't want to waste his breath. She tripped, caught herself, and ran on, her chest aching with exertion. She hoped whoever, or whatever, was converging on them had as much trouble with the darkness as they did.

Alaric stopped in front of her, and Sienne ran into him before she could stop. He grabbed her arm and hauled her in front of him. "*Fury*," he said.

Sienne's spellbook fell open to the powerful evocation. Ahead, she saw movement, several lumbering forms that came toward them with ponderous inevitability. She made a light and began reading out *fury* almost before it illuminated the page. The enemy faltered as if the light had startled them, then continued moving. She didn't dare look up from the book to see what they were, but as she read, Perrin said, "Those are no mere animals."

"Werebears," Kalanath said, his voice hollow. "What did those men lead us to?"

The evocation built in her chest, pressing on her heart and lungs and making her voice go thready from lack of air. She spat out the last acid-edged syllable and the spell leapt away from her, fracturing into half a dozen bolts that flew to strike their targets. Six massive forms staggered and fell. The other werebears roared, and charged.

Alaric put himself in front of Sienne and drew his sword. "Break through the line," he shouted. "Sienne, get behind them!"

Sienne flipped to *jaunt* and started reading the sharp, jagged syllables that filled her mouth with blood. She prayed silently that she would reach her destination; *jaunting* when you couldn't see clearly could simply fail, and it was crucial she not fail. Beside her, Perrin held a blessing ready. Dianthe and Alaric drew their swords, and Kalanath stood poised, ready to attack. Button shifted nervously, surrounded by clawed and fanged enemies. His fear echoed her own.

"*Stop!*" someone screamed from behind them. "Don't do it!"

Sienne broke off the summoning midstream and turned to face this new threat. Jaceus Adorno raced toward them, stumbling over hidden branches and catching himself through sheer willpower. "It's not what you think!" he shouted. "They won't hurt you!"

Alaric hadn't turned around. The werebears had halted some twenty feet from the companions, some of them standing on their hind paws, all of them looking black in Sienne's magic light. "And why should we believe you?" he said.

Sienne screamed, "Jaceus, look out!"

Behind Jaceus, one of the werebears ran ponderously toward him, rearing up on its hind legs to attack. Sienne turned to *force* and began reading, her heart in her throat. She would be too late, and Jaceus would die.

Then she stopped, astonished. The bear's body stretched impossibly wide and tall, like wax softened in the summer sun, then shrank down to a slightly shorter, slimmer human form. Dark brown fur receded and became darkly tan skin. The werebear's muzzle shrank and shifted to become a human face, and its small black eyes turned brown and wide with fear. Sienne found herself looking at the naked form of Lucan Adorno.

Sienne's nerveless fingers let the spellbook fall to hang loose in its harness by her side. "What..." she began, her voice almost inaudible.

"We need to talk," Jaceus said.

12

Swifter than thought, Alaric crossed the distance between them and put the edge of his blade to Jaceus's throat. "You led us into an ambush," he growled. "That says more than any amount of talk could."

Jaceus swallowed, making his throat rise and fall against the sword, but otherwise looked far too calm for a man in his position. "It's not an ambush," he said. "We weren't going to hurt you."

"Dozens of you against five of us," Dianthe said. "Why so many if you didn't intend to kill us?"

Jaceus said nothing.

Sienne exclaimed, "You're were-creatures! Weres aren't intelligent! How can you possibly exist?"

"Most weres aren't intelligent," Lucan said. "We're the exception."

"I don't care," Alaric said. "Tell your friends to back off. You're coming with us until I'm satisfied we're well away."

"We weren't going to hurt you," Jaceus repeated. "We brought you here so we could talk. We've put ourselves in your power so you'd trust us. Please, just five minutes, and if you still don't believe us, you can go."

Alaric laughed. "Are you that naïve, or do you think we're stupid?

You can't let us go. We know your secret. We might tell the king, and he'd send an army to wipe you out." He pressed the blade closer, and Jaceus went up on his toes trying to get away from it.

"Alaric," Perrin said. "We should listen to them."

"What?"

Perrin moved toward the big man. "The Adornos, or whatever their true names are, did not need to reveal their identities. They might have remained in bear shape and fought us with the rest. Instead, they, as he said, have put themselves in our power. And I admit to some curiosity as to how they can exist at all."

Alaric didn't move. "He's right," Sienne said. "They went to a lot of trouble to get us here. Doesn't it make more sense that it was because they want something than that they wanted us dead?"

Alaric's grip on the sword relaxed. He lowered the blade, but kept it pointed at Jaceus's heart. Jaceus raised a hand to rub his throat where the sword had pressed against it. He said, "Thank you. I'm sorry about all this. You weren't meant to know the others were there until we'd explained the situation."

"Don't underestimate us," Alaric said. "Five minutes. Talk."

Lucan came to stand beside his cousin. He didn't seem to care that he was naked. "Shift, everyone," he called out.

A rustling noise like a hundred birds flapping their wings went up from the surrounding creatures. Each werebear stretched out and shrank in on itself, their bear forms melting into human bodies. They were all tall, Sienne observed, though not as tall as Alaric, and all were powerfully built. Some were as blond as an Ansorjan, others were as dark as Kalanath, some with reddish skin and others with a gray cast to their faces. Sienne saw one...could she call him a man, when he was a were-creature? He had iron gray hair, though he didn't appear older than Jaceus. He stared back at her as if in challenge, though he made no movement. All of them seemed to be in their prime. They were also all extremely naked, and Sienne had trouble knowing where to look. She settled for keeping her eyes focused on Jaceus as the werebears surrounding them lowered themselves to sit on the ground.

Jaceus still didn't look nervous, though his death was only inches away. "Were-creatures too far outside the human norm aren't intelligent. Werewolves, for example...they're small in their two-legged form, and they're about as bright as a four-year-old. Their heads just aren't big enough for a human-sized brain. But the bigger ones, like wereboars, they're no smarter even though their brains are much bigger than humans. And there are types of werebears that are bigger even than that, and they're even stupider."

"This is not the time for a comparative anatomy lesson," Alaric said.

"I'm just trying to explain why we're different," Jaceus said. "We aren't like other weres. Could you carry on a conversation like this with a werewolf? We can learn to read, we can reason, we even create art. We have families. Maybe we're not human, but when we're in this form, can you really tell the difference?"

Of course, after more than a week traveling in the Adornos' company, the answer to that was "no." Sienne watched Alaric, who was still poised to attack, and wondered if he saw himself in Jaceus's argument. After all, Alaric wasn't human, though in every essential he might as well be.

"What's your point?" Alaric said. "That you're not monsters just because you're capable of human speech and intellect?"

"That is exactly my point," Jaceus said. "We don't know how we came to be, whether some wizard of the before times thought it would be fun to breed half-human creatures, or whether we arose spontaneously from the Empty Lands. It doesn't matter. We're just like you, with one difference. And we want the same thing you do—to survive."

"And you dragged us out into the wilderness as part of that need?"

Jaceus shook his head. "We chose you deliberately," he said, and now he was addressing Sienne, ignoring the sword pointed at his heart. "Only scrappers will go willingly into the Empty Lands, so we needed to find a scrapper team, one with a reputation for fairness and honor. And when we heard about a team with a duke's daughter at its head, we knew we'd found the right one."

"But I'm not the leader," Sienne protested.

"We didn't realize that before. It doesn't matter. Your team has a connection to the king. That's all we care about."

"Why? What do you want with the king?" A horrible thought shot through her mind. "You're not going to try to kill him, are you?"

"No." Jaceus shook his head. "We want you to plead our case with him."

Alaric said, "What case?"

Jaceus returned his attention to Alaric. "Our land is being encroached on by human settlers," he said. "We've had to relocate three times in the last ten years. We're tired of it. We want King Derekian to recognize us as Rafellish citizens and give us the same protections he gives his human subjects."

Alaric burst out laughing. "You have to be joking," he said. "You're were-creatures. You can't live in harmony with humans—they'd always be wondering if this is the day you take someone's head off."

"That's just prejudice talking," Lucan said. "We aren't any more violent than the average human. Less so, because any time we attack a human, we reinforce that belief that weres are evil and vicious. We don't want to move into human settlements—we just want the right to claim and defend our territory."

"I agree," Sienne said.

Alaric lowered his sword and turned to stare at her. "You can't possibly."

"Why not? Were-creatures are dangerous because they lack human intelligence and can't be reasoned with. They're no more than animals. But these people...if he's telling the truth, they're capable of passing for human, and maybe that's deserving of being treated like humans."

"But I do not understand," Perrin said, "why you do not simply live among humans. Would that not solve your problem?"

"We're still weres," Jaceus said. "Three days a month, we're forced to take bear shape, no matter where we are. That's not something that allows us to live in a city. But more than that—this is what we are, and we're not ashamed of it. We don't think we should have to pretend to be something we're not."

"Where are your women?" Kalanath said.

The abruptness of his query startled Jaceus, who looked as though he'd forgotten Kalanath was there. "They—oh. Our women don't fight. It's hard for us to have children, and the women are too precious to risk in combat. Swift and I—" He waved a hand at Lucan. "We were granted the authority to treat with you on behalf of our matriarch, Clever. It was a great honor."

"I'm not sure we're deserving of the honor, given the mess we're in," Lucan muttered.

"Then we should talk to your matriarch," Kalanath said.

"Hold on," Alaric said. "We haven't decided we're going to treat with them at all. They haven't been honest with us."

"We're sorry we had to lie about our identities, but we wanted you to get used to us as people before revealing we're werebears," Jaceus said.

"Not about that." Alaric gestured with his sword hand at the silently watching men surrounding them. "You brought a damn army with you. Don't think I don't realize our deaths are in the offing if we don't agree to your terms. You can't afford to let us go."

Jaceus and Lucan looked at each other. "Told you so," Lucan muttered.

"I swear that's not what we intended," Jaceus said. "Everyone just wanted a look at you. Talk to our matriarch. If you aren't convinced, you can leave. We'll just ask you to swear you won't tell anyone about us."

"You'd accept that?"

"I told you, we did our research. Your word is as good as a blood oath. If you swear it, you'll do it."

"Not that we won't uproot our people and move where no human will ever find us, if you leave," Lucan said. "Some of us aren't as trusting as others."

Alaric lowered his sword. "Stay there," he said. "Sienne will turn you into a greasy pyre if you so much as start to shift."

Sienne swiftly turned to the evocation *burn*, hoping she looked alert and fierce despite feeling completely lost. Werebears. *Intelligent* werebears. And they wanted political recognition. If the trees had suddenly come to life and demanded equal representation in Rafellin's government, she wouldn't be surprised.

Alaric retreated a few paces to stand at Sienne's side, and the others moved to join him. "I think he's lying," Alaric said, "at least about them just wanting a look at us. They have us surrounded— that's a tactical move that says they want to cut off any line of retreat."

"I agree," Dianthe said. "But I think he's sincere in what he's asking. It makes sense, in an insane way. I can imagine how hard it would be to stay hidden from humans, given how rapidly we're spreading east. How much easier if they didn't have to?"

"But we don't have that kind of power," Sienne said in a low voice, not turning away from Jaceus. "I can ask the king for an audience, but he's not bound to listen. I don't think we can give them what they want."

Dianthe nodded. "But we can't tell them that. Most of them don't look friendly, and I think *Jaceus* may be sincere, but I wonder how well he can control the others."

"Then we'll have to go along with them until we can find a way to escape," Alaric said.

"I think we should take them at their word," Perrin said.

"What, that they won't kill us?" Alaric retorted.

"No, that they are interested in treating with us. It harms us not at all to listen, and it is possible, however unlikely, that we might succeed in bringing their request before the king." Perrin glanced over Alaric's shoulder at Jaceus, who looked like he might be trying to listen in. Sienne wondered how good a werebear's hearing was.

"I can't believe we're even having this discussion. They're *were-creatures*, for Sisyletus's sake!" Alaric's voice rose, drawing the attention of the nearest werebears. He lowered his voice and added, "The king will never listen to a request to give them citizenship."

"I think that is for the king to decide," Perrin said. "But that is in the future. Let us first speak with their matriarch, and then make a decision."

Sienne heard Alaric sigh. "Do you remember how I said I reserved the right to say I told you so when this went horribly wrong?"

"It's not gone horribly wrong yet," Dianthe said. "That would be if we were torn to pieces by a pack of angry werebears."

"It's just past midnight. There's still plenty of time." Alaric walked past Sienne to where Jaceus still stood. "What's your name? Your *real* name?"

"Wit. And my cousin is Swift."

"Is he really your cousin?"

"Our mothers are sisters. But it's also true we call each other cousin no matter how we're related. Is that really what you want to know?"

"I'm just curious as to the depth of the lie. Now would be a good time to be forthcoming with anything else you haven't told us. Is there actually a ruin, or was that part of the ruse?"

"There's a ruin, but it's empty. I'm sorry."

"It doesn't matter. Since it's clear that's not why we came."

Jaceus—Wit—took a step forward. "Does that mean you're willing to talk?"

Alaric sheathed his sword. Sienne, watching the crowd in case she needed to defend against a rogue were, saw the men closest to him relax slightly. "We'll talk," he said. "Don't think that means we're on your side."

"You messed up," Lucan—Swift—said in a low voice. Wit elbowed him hard in the stomach.

"I'm sorry you felt threatened," he said. "Thank you for listening. Our home is about half a mile from here. Do you mind if the others shift back? Walking through the forest with no protection is uncomfortable."

Alaric hesitated. "Go ahead," he said. Sienne could guess what he was thinking: it took them only seconds to go between one form and the other, and keeping them relatively harmless in human form would only work for those few seconds.

Most of the men shifted back into bear form. A few dozen, including Swift, stayed human to carry their *fury*-blasted cousins. Sienne felt a small twinge of guilt that she instantly suppressed. They had only Wit's assurance that the werebears wouldn't have attacked them, and suppose Sienne's spell had been a greater deterrent? She kept her spellbook open to *fury*, just in case.

Walking through the midnight forest felt like a dream, not the pleasant kind and not a nightmare but one in which Sienne had to accomplish some task that kept multiplying. A distant howl threaded through the night, leaving Sienne feeling chilled, as if winter had reached out a cold finger and stroked her spine. Weariness, and inexplicable fear, struck her, and she wished she dared take Alaric's hand for reassurance. But that would have made her look weak, and showing weakness to these creatures could be deadly.

The werebears blended with the darkness, even the gray ones, leaving Sienne with the unsettling feeling of being watched by something just beyond the limits of her vision. They didn't move silently, though; the noise of their passing was loud enough to drown out the sounds of the insects. Or maybe the insects went silent as the horde went by. Sienne guessed the weres were being loud on purpose, possibly to put their unwilling guests at their ease. She couldn't imagine them avoiding humans if this was how they walked all the time.

After a few minutes of walking, Sienne saw a warm orange light in the distance, then another, until firelight illuminated the last feet of their journey. She walked faster, not because she was eager to reach their destination, but because she wanted free of the dreamlike state that left her feeling disconnected and edgy. Beside her, Dianthe put out a warning hand. "Let Alaric go first," she murmured. Sienne slowed and kept her eyes on Alaric, who strode as if he weren't surrounded by potential enemies.

Then they were through the trees and into a clearing—no, it was too big to be called a clearing. Raw earth around its edges showed where trees had recently been uprooted to enlarge the place, which was filled with ramshackle tents made of every conceivable material, from traditional canvas to heavy twilled cotton and even patched leather. The tents were pitched in groups surrounding campfires still burning brightly despite the late hour. Their "escort" began shifting, two and three at a time, back to human shape, peeling off from the group to duck inside tents. Other tents rustled, and women wearing shapeless belted tunics emerged, blinking in the firelight. They stood beside their tents as if guarding them, watching the companions with a wary calm Sienne didn't understand.

Farther back in the clearing, someone exclaimed, and darting movement flashed between the tents. A woman cried out. Alaric drew his sword and took a defensive stance, tension bleeding off him like noon heat haze. A naked child, no more than two, scampered out from between the tents and was snatched up by one of the men, who backed away from Alaric with his eyes locked on the big man. The child struggled to get down, then, with a convulsive full-body stretch, turned into a bear cub. His protector, startled, nearly dropped him, instead handing him off to a woman who appeared at his side, out of breath. Alaric lowered his sword. The woman backed away, stumbled over the corner of a tent, and caught herself before she could drop the cub. Then she turned and fled.

"Why didn't you wait until morning?" Alaric said to Wit. "You've woken the whole camp."

Wit shrugged. It was hard to tell in the firelight, but Sienne thought he looked embarrassed. "We were going to wait. You found out we were gone too soon."

"I told him you wouldn't be fooled for long," Swift said. He and Wit exchanged scowls, then Swift added, "I'm going to find some clothes. Don't do anything exciting while I'm gone."

"I'm going to take them to see Clever," Wit said. "Does that count as exciting?"

Swift snorted. "She's awake and we've been invaded. What do you think?" He loped off through the tents, dodging motionless women and men emerging dressed in the same kind of tunics as the women.

Looking at them, Sienne couldn't help wondering what they did in the winter. They might have to stay bears the whole time, hibernate —was that even possible?

"That's rich, calling us an invasion," Alaric said.

Wit gestured at the silent audience. "You're the first outsiders who've seen our home in...it must be over fifty years. And they all know why you're here. They're more afraid of you than you are of them."

"I'm not afraid," Alaric said.

"Then it's doubly true." Wit gestured. "This way."

He led them around the outskirts of the camp, past dozens of silent men and women and even children, most of whom looked like they would rather have been sleeping. They looked so human Sienne had to remind herself it was an illusion. And yet...they were were-creatures, yes, but they spoke and thought just like humans, so if there was a difference, it was subtler than she could manage to tell at this time of night.

They came to a place where the clearing narrowed, or maybe it was just that there were more tents filling the space. At the center lay a much larger tent, a proper tent like the ones her father's troops used on practice maneuvers, golden in the light of the bonfire blazing before it. Two women tended the fire, adding wood to make it burn hotter and brighter. It felt like a welcome, and Sienne wasn't sure why.

"This is the speaking tent," Wit said. "It's where Clever meets with her advisers and with people who've broken laws. Like a judgment seat. She'll let us know when she's ready."

"Keeping us off balance by making us wait," Perrin said.

"No, she just doesn't wake readily. She needs a few moments to come fully alert." Wit stretched unselfconsciously as a cat. In his Rafellish garb, surrounded by his more simply-dressed "cousins," he looked like an exotic bird in a field of sparrows even though his shirt and tunic were of an ordinary, dull make.

Sienne looked around. The werebears hadn't been so obvious as to follow them through the camp, but they'd shifted perceptibly in their direction and weren't pretending not to watch the companions. The woman with the child/cub had vanished. Wit had said the were-bears didn't have children easily, which made her wonder how many more cubs were in the camp. The little one had been adorable, the way most infant animals were—but it wasn't an animal any more than it was human. The thought made Sienne uncomfortable, as if she were trying to justify treating the child as a monster. She thrust it away and tried to think of something else.

At that moment, the tent flap opened, and a woman dressed in the ubiquitous tunic emerged. In addition to the tunic, she wore a sash that in the firelight was greenish, but Sienne thought it might actually be blue, a deep royal blue probably. The woman examined each of them in turn, then said, "Clever will speak with you now. Wit, you will remain outside."

Clever. No honorific, no title, just the odd name. Alaric approached the tent flap, but stopped when the woman held up a hand. "The women first," she said. "It is our custom."

Sienne couldn't see Alaric's face, but his back was tense the way it got when he was deeply unhappy about something he was powerless to change. He looked back at Sienne, and she could read his expression clearly: *if this is an ambush, I can't protect you.* He stepped back and gestured for Sienne to precede him.

A second woman had come forward and held the tent flap open for them to enter. Sienne ducked automatically, though the opening was taller than she was, then kept moving to get out of Dianthe's way. The tent was brightly lit with lanterns whose glass was tinted faintly yellow, enough to warm the tiny flames beyond their own heat. Three more women and a single man stood grouped to one side as if they'd been having a conversation that cut off mid-word when Sienne entered. The women looked much alike, with dark skin and brown hair nearly the same shade, and they, too, wore blue sashes. The man was much older than the ones she'd seen so far, his black hair streaked with gray and his ebony skin wrinkled. He was also gaunt, his blue sash hanging loose around his narrow hips.

Sitting on a camp stool opposite the door was an attractive

woman with red hair and dusty cinnamon skin. Had she been human, Sienne would have said she was in her mid-forties, but she had no idea how werebears aged. The woman wore a blue sash as well, but tied crosswise across her chest, and although her tunic was no fancier than the others, on her it looked majestic. Sienne had met King Derekian once and been impressed at his air of quiet authority. This woman had something of the same mystique.

The woman rose from the stool and stood with her hands clasped behind her back. "Are you the duke's daughter?" she asked. Her voice was a husky alto.

"I am, but—" Sienne began.

"I speak for our team," Alaric said from behind her. "Are you Clever?"

The woman smiled, one corner of her mouth quirking up in a self-deprecating expression. "I am called Clever," she said, "and I hope that name describes me well, because my people have need of it now. Please, sit. We have much to discuss."

13

The two women who'd greeted them outside the tent had entered and begun setting up folding stools in a circle. Alaric eyed them skeptically. "That's not going to work for me," he said. Sienne silently agreed. The stools were sturdy enough, but small, and there was no way they'd support Alaric's weight.

"I apologize for not being able to give you proper respect," Clever said.

"I don't mind standing."

Sienne was sure this was true. Standing, Alaric commanded the room and was more than a match for Clever's quiet authority. Sienne took a seat opposite Clever's and watched the other werebears settle in to either side of the matriarch. The man moved as if his joints pained him, making Sienne wonder again how werebears aged. She would have put his age at over sixty if he were human. The female weres, on closer inspection, didn't look at all the same once you got past their identical coloration. One looked younger than Sienne, though that might be because of her large gray eyes that gave her an innocent appearance. The other two might have been near Clever's age. One had a narrow, alert face with the straightest nose Sienne had ever seen. The other was beautiful by human standards, with full lips and rounded cheekbones. She watched Sienne closely, a smile touching those lips, and Sienne looked away in discomfort. It had been a look that assessed Sienne's appearance and probable abilities and found both lacking.

The women finished setting up the stools and stepped back. One of them said, "Ready and Knowing have returned from investigating the howl."

"Ask them to wait," Clever said. She turned back to face Alaric. "These are my counselors. Bloom, my sister's daughter. Deft, who supervises the children. Bright, who is...from what Wit has told us, you would call her a law-speaker. And Test, who communes with God." She indicated each in turn. Bloom was the young one. Deft had the narrow face. Bright was the beauty. And the man was Test. Sienne examined him closely. The idea that were-creatures might have a relationship with God would have until that night seemed ludicrous. If Test had a relationship with God, it didn't show on the outside, not the way it did with, for example, the divine Octavian. And why God and not an avatar? She felt full to bursting with questions.

"My name is Alaric," Alaric said. "My companions are Sienne, Dianthe, Perrin, and Kalanath. Or did you already know this?"

"Wit had very little time to explain the situation before we sent him back to you," Clever said. "You are the duke's daughter, are you not?" She addressed Sienne. "The wizard?"

"I am, but I'm not the leader," Sienne said.

"I understand that. It is strange to us because we do not let the men lead our people." Clever eyed Alaric. "But they do lead in battle, and perhaps your scrapping activities are closer to battle than we supposed."

"Among humans, men and women are equally capable of leading."

"And we are not human."

"According to Jac—to Wit, that's why we're here," Alaric said.

"It is," Clever said. "You are angry about the manner of your coming here."

"Wouldn't you be? Though I suppose we should be honored that you thought we were so dangerous you sent an army after us."

Clever's lips quirked in a small smile. "I wondered if you'd draw that conclusion. Yes. We were prepared for the possibility you would reject our proposal and decide to tell the world about us."

"Wit didn't think that was the case," Dianthe said.

"Wit is an idealist," Bright said. Her voice was as sweet and beautiful as the rest of her. "He never sees the bad in anyone. It makes him a poor warrior."

"But an excellent diplomat," Clever said. "He persuaded you, didn't he?"

"He did," Alaric said. "But we're not on your side. You should start doing some persuading of your own."

Clever nodded. "You should perhaps know that our community has existed for over three hundred years," she said. "Before that, we lived in kin-groups, traveling the Empty Lands, as you call them, making our living as best we could. There are no records of how we came to be, so we do not know if we were created deliberately, or arose from the magic places in the Empty Lands."

"Though we suspect it was deliberate," Test said. His voice was as creaky and aged as his appearance. "The magic places are capable of altering creatures, but only to a limited extent. Carvers, for example—"

"We've met carvers," Alaric said. "Are you saying they used to be human?"

Test shrugged. "As far as anyone can tell, yes. But changes in bone and blood...those are a simple matter. Not like merging man and beast into a were-creature."

"Let us not be sidetracked," Clever said. "The point is that we have had civilization for as long as humans have, if one counts rising from the ashes of an earlier civilization as a beginning. We may be different in many respects, but we have the same needs and drives as any human. And one of those needs is for a permanent home. We had one until humans from Rafellin started encroaching on it. Since that time, we've had to move frequently to avoid contact with them. We believe the time has come for us to stop hiding."

Bright shifted as if she wanted to say something, but remained silent. Deft said, "Our children should not grow up feral. We want them to be free from fear that they'll be discovered. To have a home that isn't a tent or a cave."

"You want to be Rafellish citizens," Alaric said. "You want protection by King Derekian."

"Precisely," Clever said. "We want him to acknowledge our right to the land we've claimed. It's not a large piece of land, and we won't hunt over land claimed by other citizens. We won't encroach on them at all, in fact. But we need them to stop moving in on our territory so we can have peace."

"How much peace will there be when the humans know we exist?" Bright said. "They fear were-creatures too much to ever live alongside them in harmony."

"I was about to say the same thing," Alaric said. "I think you underestimate the human capacity for fearing what they don't understand. Were-creatures have haunted human settlements for too many years for them to welcome you."

"We have never attacked humans," Clever said. "We have fought them in self-defense, but we have never been the aggressors."

"They won't know that, and if they do know it, many won't believe it." Alaric shook his head. "You'd be better off moving somewhere far away from human settlements, so this isn't an issue anymore."

"Some of us believe the same," Clever said with a swift glance at Bright. "But there are problems with that solution. The first is that the Empty Lands are as deadly to us as they are to you. Moving deeper into them would endanger us, particularly the very old and the very young. The second is that humans are spreading rapidly. Every year they reclaim more of the Empty Lands. However far we go, eventually humans will catch up to us, and then we will be in the same position we are now. Continuing to flee is not a long-term solution."

"But you'd be endangering yourselves if you come out into the open," Sienne burst out. "Right now nobody knows about you, but when they find out, some brave idiot will think it's his duty to rid the world of the evil werebears who think they're people."

"Then we will fight," Clever said.

"And you'll die," Alaric said. "Taking some of them with you, sure, but how will that help your cause?"

Clever stood and took a few steps until she was nearly face to face with Alaric. Sitting, she hadn't looked tall, but now Sienne could see she was almost of a height with Alaric. "We are dying now," she said, her low alto even lower as if imparting a great secret. "We already are forced to spend the winter in bear form because we cannot build permanent shelters for our human selves. Our children cannot maintain that form for long and some die of exposure. We work so hard to survive we have no time for anything else. We might as well be living in the era just after your civilization collapsed, scrabbling to stay alive, with only one hope for a better life. We would rather face the world honestly, even if that means war, than endure this slow, agonizing death."

Alaric stared her down, his face expressionless. Clever said nothing more. Bright shifted again, drawing Sienne's attention. She looked angry for the briefest moment, then the anger slid away, leaving her as expressionless as Alaric. It was so complete a transformation Sienne almost doubted she'd seen it.

"I see," Alaric said finally. "This really is a matter of life or death for you."

"It is," Clever said.

Alaric turned and looked at Sienne. "Is this something you can convince the king of?"

Sienne blinked. "Me?"

"You're the one he'd be willing to hear from. Can you?"

"I...don't know. If I could get all of us in...Perrin is the one with the silver tongue—wait. Are you saying we're going to do it?"

"I'm saying," Alaric said, "that Clever is right. It's risky, but it's the only option."

"It is *not* the only option," Bright said, rising from her stool. "You overstate the dangers of the Empty Lands. If we go far enough north, we can build a settlement that will allow us to grow so when the humans find us again, we will be able to face them on our own terms. This will destroy us."

"Bright, enough," Clever said. "We have been over this already. Moving north simply defers the problem to a future generation. I choose not to have my name cursed by my descendants."

Bright scowled. It made her look much less attractive. "So you'd rather have your name cursed by your contemporaries."

"Everyone agrees with Clever," Bloom said. Her voice was soft and diffident, but she radiated a calm assurance that made Sienne rethink her estimate of her age. "We're tired of hiding."

"Not everyone agrees," Bright said. "This is a foolish endeavor. We don't even know if these people can do what they promise. Or whether their king will listen, let alone grant us what we ask for."

"I can promise the king will see us," Sienne said. "But you're right, we have no control over what he'll do about your request. Except...I don't know. King Derekian doesn't think like other people. He might see you werebears as the solution to some problem nobody knows about. I think it's worth asking."

"And, if I may," Perrin said, "we can make our request in secret, without revealing your location, so if the worst happens and the king attempts to eradicate you, you will have time to escape. Fleeing into the Empty Lands may be suboptimal, but it is better than death."

Bright cursed under her breath. "I do not support this plan," she said, and pushed past Dianthe and Kalanath to fling open the tent flap and storm away.

Deft stood and went to the door, but didn't leave. "She may be a problem," she said.

"She knows her duty and will do it," Clever said. "And she is not wrong that it is a terrible position for us to be in." She extended her hand to Alaric. "This is how humans seal an agreement, yes?"

Alaric clasped her hand. "It is. I hope our help makes a difference."

"If you can be convinced, perhaps others can, too."

"We are unusual, if you will permit me an immodesty," Perrin said. "Do not expect most humans to react as placidly."

"We do not intend to force our company on others," Test said. He rose slowly, as if his joints were unoiled hinges left unmoved for a century. "And God is on our side. She has guided us this far, and she will not desert us now."

"Do you worship God directly, like my people?" Kalanath said.

"I do not know who your people are."

"I am Omeiran. We live across the Ikh—the Bramantus Mountains."

"You are dark, for a human." Test looked Kalanath up and down. "We did not know of the avatars until recently. God's voice has always been distant, but clear—clearer to some than to others. She tells us we are not monsters, nor have we been abandoned by Her."

"I would be interested to speak further with you on this subject," Perrin said. "I am a priest of Averran, one of God's avatars, and your worship intrigues me."

"So would I," Kalanath said.

"We would show you hospitality tonight," Clever said. "Or would you prefer to return to your camp?"

"We don't want to put you out," Sienne began, but Alaric interrupted her with "That would be welcome, yes."

"Then allow me to give you a place where you can sleep, and in the morning we will discuss further," Clever said.

Sienne stood and waited for Clever and Alaric to pass, then followed Alaric out of the tent. Wit still waited there, standing as if he meant to go on doing so indefinitely. Two unfamiliar men, both as brown-skinned as Bloom and Deft were, waited nearby. "Did you—" Wit said.

"You presume much," Clever said, but she was smiling. "They will help us."

Wit's gaze went from Clever to Alaric. "That's—thank you! I was afraid you'd hold my eagerness against us."

"Next time, don't bring an army," Alaric said. He sounded stern, but Sienne could see the amusement in his eyes.

"I won't—well, there won't be a next time," Wit said.

"Take them to our tents and see that they're made comfortable," Clever told him. "And don't talk their ears off. It's after midnight and I'm going back to bed once I've spoken with Knowing and Ready." The two strangers came alert at the sound of their names.

"Sleep well, sister," Wit said. "Come with me, please."

The last was addressed to Sienne and her friends, so even though Sienne wanted to know if Clever really was his sister, she followed Wit through the encampment to a fire pit surrounded by a ring of tents. They looked no different from the others, but Wit behaved as if he were presenting them with a mansion. "There's a place for each of you. Or should be, if Swift did his job."

"You talk too much, cousin," Swift said, emerging from one of the tents. "Of course I did my job. Would you like us to go pack up your things and bring them here?"

"They'll be fine until morning," Alaric said. "Who did you evict so we could have tents to ourselves?"

"Just family," Swift said. "They've all gone to sleep with other kin groups." He lowered his voice. "Don't take this the wrong way, but most of us are afraid of humans. They'd rather not sleep near you."

"That's ironic, considering how much humans are afraid of weres," Dianthe said.

"Tell them we're grateful," Alaric said. "And we're not offended."

Kalanath yawned. "I think we do not need to watch tonight," he said.

"We'd take it as an insult," Wit said.

"Of course," said Alaric. "Sienne?"

Sienne almost asked him what he meant before noticing he was holding a tent flap open for her. She must be more tired than she thought. Well, if there were enough tents for them to sleep separately, she didn't need to bunk with Dianthe. Even if sex wasn't in the offing. She went inside and dropped to her knees on the bedroll. It was thicker than hers and smelled of a heavy musk Sienne guessed was the natural scent of a werebear. It wasn't much different from how Alaric smelled in unicorn form.

Alaric joined her and immediately began pulling his boots off. "That's not how I expected the night to go," he said. "Was I wrong to make the decision for all of us?"

"At the risk of sounding petty, you do that all the time." Sienne took a boot out of his hand and kissed him. "It was the right decision. These people are living in poverty. How would you like to have your permanent home be a tent? Or sleep on this bedroll forever? Granted, it's nicer than the bedrolls we have, but it's not a mattress. And I don't even want to think about what they'd have to do to get some privacy. Alaric, we have to help them."

"I might have known you'd say something like that. You're a one-woman crusade against injustice." Alaric put his arms around her and drew her down to lie beside him. "I wish we could do something more vigorous than hugging."

"Me too. But if I'm not willing to have sex in a tent surrounded by my friends, I'm even less willing to have sex in a tent surrounded by werebears." She snuggled in closer to him. "This is pleasure enough."

His breath stirred the hair over her forehead. "True," he said. "Sleep. Tomorrow will be a busy day."

She heard his last words distantly, as if they were wrapped in cotton wool, and then she was asleep.

———

Sienne woke to something heavy lying across her legs. When she moved them, the weight didn't shift at all. She opened her eyes and squinted at her feet. A ball of black fur lay curled up over her legs, its small sides rising and falling in rhythmic breathing. Sienne took in a quick, startled breath, waking Alaric. "What's wrong?" he said, pushing himself onto his elbow.

"No, don't, you'll wake it!" Sienne whispered, but it was too late. The ball of fur uncurled itself and rose to all fours. Its small black eyes blinked at them in the wan light coming through the canvas. It shook its head, rubbed one paw over its nose, and sneezed with its whole body. A shudder went through it, and then a black-skinned baby boy was there in its place. A human that size would have been about a year old. The boy pushed himself upright, wobbling a little on the uneven terrain of Sienne's legs, then fell hard on his naked bottom. His little face looked so surprised Sienne laughed. The boy's eyes squinched up, and he let out a howl enough to wake the whole camp.

Sienne tried to shush the baby, but Alaric gathered him up in his two large hands and held him close. "He's just startled," he said. Sure enough, the baby let out one slightly less offended wail, then regarded Alaric with large brown eyes. Alaric matched him gaze for gaze. "It looks like they don't have control over their shifting when they're this young," he said. "I understand now why Clever said the children were in danger from the cold winters."

Sienne regarded him, noted how carefully he held the boy, and a pang of unexpected guilt struck her. "How did you learn how to handle babies?"

"My mother had charge of the infants. Sassaven have to work, and the wizard wouldn't allow the women to stop working to take care of their babies, once they were past a certain age. So there are a few Sassaven who watch the crèches while the parents work, and my mother was one of them. She enlisted me to help until I was big enough to do a man's work." Alaric shifted the baby to his shoulder and rubbed its back. "I resented it for a while. Then I got used to it. Children are interesting, when they're not being unholy terrors."

"I had to care for my little sisters. I never got over resenting that."

"Well, this little one probably has someone looking for him." In that moment, the child sneezed again, and Alaric was suddenly holding a bear cub. It rubbed its black nose against his cheek, then buried its face in the crook of his neck. Sienne, her mouth open to speak, caught sight of Alaric's expression and her words died unspoken. Once more, she felt guilty, and didn't know why.

"Let's find your mama, shall we?" Alaric told the cub, and crept out, cradling the cub in one arm. Sienne didn't follow. She sat on the bedroll and stared at the place the cub had lain. Just because Alaric was good with children didn't mean he was required to have them. Or that he'd want them. Guilt was ridiculous, and besides, there wasn't anything to feel guilty about. But it took her several moments before she felt calm enough to leave the tent.

Alaric stood talking to a woman who now held the bear cub, or rather the baby it had turned back into. She wore the same drab tunic all the other werebears did, but her hair was red like Clever's and fell in thick curls down her back. Alaric turned and gestured to Sienne to join them. "This is Faith," he said, "and her baby is named Stalwart. Faith, this is Sienne."

"It's good to meet you," Faith said. She had the air of a startled rabbit, as if she meant to bolt if Sienne said the wrong thing.

"Your baby is sweet," Sienne said, though in truth she liked it better in its bear cub shape.

"I apologize for the intrusion. I didn't think Stalwart would stray so far—but the tent you slept in is normally ours, and he must have been drawn to it."

Now Sienne felt guilty again, this time at having evicted a woman with a child from her own tent. "We're sorry—you shouldn't have had to—"

"No, it's an honor to host you," Faith protested. "My sister asked us all to show hospitality, and it was my pleasure. Though we did not know any of you were paired."

Alaric put his arm around Sienne and drew her close. "Your sister?"

"Clever is my sister. And Wit is my brother. You might have met my daughter Bloom; she's one of Clever's counselors."

Sienne didn't think Faith looked old enough to have a daughter Bloom's age, but she couldn't think of a polite way to ask about it. "She seems...young for such a responsibility," she said instead.

"She is, but I think Clever intends her to take her place someday, so she's grooming her early." Faith looked over her shoulder. "Here's Wit, with breakfast. I hope you like porridge with honey."

Alaric tactfully kept his mouth shut. Sienne, who knew how he disliked porridge, said, "Thank you for feeding us. I'm sure it's delicious."

Wit carried a big iron pot that looked like it could brain someone if swung hard enough and set it on the ground near the fire. "Swift's bringing bowls and spoons," he said. "Will you start back to Fioretti today?"

"There are still things to be worked out," Alaric said. "We need to make arrangements for a werebear liaison to the king. I need the details of what Clever wants us to request. We'll probably take half a day in discussions and head out tomorrow."

"Clever may want to send emissaries," Faith said, "which probably means you, Wit."

Wit shrugged. "If she says so. She might want Bright to do it. She's got more authority."

"Bright isn't fully behind this proposal. She might sabotage it."

"Sabotage?" Alaric said.

Faith, who'd relaxed somewhat when Wit appeared, tensed again. "I spoke out of turn. Bright's loyal. She wouldn't jeopardize our people by disobeying."

"Hmm," Alaric said, but held his peace. Sienne thought he wasn't so sure about Bright's loyalty. *She* wasn't sure about Bright's loyalty. The werebear counselor had been vocal about her doubts about Clever's plan...but that didn't mean she was disloyal just because she disagreed. Even so, Sienne thought Bright bore watching.

"Then if you're staying for the day, do you want to look at the ruin?" Wit said to Sienne.

"I thought you said it was empty."

"It is, empty of creatures, I mean. But it really did used to be a wizard's home. There's a room with mystical writing all over the walls. It might interest you."

"Writing?" Sienne and Alaric exchanged glances. "You mean, ritual?"

"I don't know what ritual looks like. But magical, certainly. And it would make me feel less guilty about lying to you if it turns out there's something there you want," he added with a grin.

"Well...yes. I'd like to go, if you don't need me today?" she asked Alaric.

"I would just have sent you with the others to pack up the camp. Go. Maybe we'll get lucky."

Sienne nodded. She still felt hungry, but the prospect of investigating a magical ruin overrode that feeling. And if she found something...it wasn't as if the trip were a waste of time, but it would certainly make her feel better to bring back something that would benefit their quest.

14

After breakfast, Sienne and Wit headed north and west, into the forest. It took less than a minute for Sienne to feel swallowed up by it. This was true forest, untouched by man. No one had ever taken an axe to these trees; they grew close together, narrow and spindly, their branches interlocking to block out the sun. Nothing else grew beneath their spreading limbs but some scruffy ferns that drooped in despair of ever getting enough sunlight. Sienne rested her hand on one of the tree trunks briefly, and it came away flecked with fresh, green moss that smelled of first summer. She tried not to think about what a fire would do to this forest, with all these trees clinging to each other for support.

The image brought to mind another image, that of the werebears fleeing from a fire burning out of control. "Do you worry about fires?" she asked.

Wit glanced over his shoulder at her. "Of course. This place is just waiting for a lightning strike to go up in flames. It's another reason we don't want to live here—well, unless we could clear out some of this wood, make permanent buildings."

"*Is* this where you want to live?"

"It's as good as anywhere else. Mostly we want to be able to settle down. I think Clever would like us to relocate a little farther south, but that might be impractical, the way the humans are moving. But even the clearing our camp is in now could be a good starting place for a real settlement."

"It must be hard, not having a permanent home."

"The warriors don't mind. Our men have traditionally been fond of the nomadic life, only settling down because the women require it. But I think most of them would like home and hearth for the winter. That's still possible, if your king grants our petition soon."

Sienne squirmed inside. "I hope Clever understands it's not a given that the king will give you what you want. He makes decisions based on criteria nobody else understands."

"She knows. And we're not expecting you to work a miracle. We just want to be heard." Wit slowed his steps. "We're almost there."

"I thought you said it wasn't inhabited. Why are you whispering?"

"I don't know. This place makes me uncomfortable, is all." Wit shrugged. "It's been unoccupied for centuries, probably, and there aren't any creatures living in it, but it has this...you'll have to see for yourself."

Ahead, the trees thinned out and then ended. Sienne and Wit emerged into a clearing just barely being lit by the sun, finally rising high enough to peep over the tops of the trees. Ferns and tall grasses covered the ground, waving in a slight breeze that came from nowhere. Ahead, a pile of black stone stretched toward the sky, trying to reach it before the trees did and failing. Sienne suspected when the building, whatever it had been, was new, it had been taller. Now smaller piles of stone lay scattered around the foundations, covered with moss and a few shoots of hopeful plants. Sienne walked forward and laid her hand on one pile. It was cold, far colder than the lack of sunlight could account for, and she yanked her hand back as if expecting to leave skin behind.

"The entrance is over here," Wit said, beckoning. Sienne followed him around to the east side of the stone pile. From there, it was more obvious that this had once been a keep or a large tower; the walls were less ruined, and there were a couple of intact window holes, the glass long gone. Sienne judged it had been two very tall stories high.

Whatever doors had once guarded the keep's entrance were gone, though metal hinges contorted by enormous pressure still clung to the walls, twisted enough to suggest a forced entry. Sienne's steps slowed as she passed through the gap, but nothing leaped out to grab her. Instead, she found herself in a small courtyard, paved with regular cobbles whose edges were worn down to give the ground a lumpy, uneven feel. "There's no grass here," she said. "Usually grass springs up between the cracks when a place is abandoned long enough. Why no grass?"

"Take a look at the forest," Wit said.

Sienne turned and looked back at the forest. "What about it?"

"Notice the way the clearing begins?"

"I don't...wait." She took a few steps back toward the forest. "It's a perfect circle."

"Oval, actually. But yes. It's like the trees don't want to come any closer."

Sienne shivered. "Do you really think this place is so...malicious?"

"Not malicious. Just watchful. Like an old man who still has dignity even though his warrior days are behind him."

Sienne turned and looked up at the black stones. "That's not so bad. And I don't feel any sense of danger. I hope I'm not wrong."

"My people come here all the time, for, um, privacy." Wit ducked his head in embarrassment. "Nothing's ever happened to them."

"Let's see what else is here," Sienne said.

The courtyard bore the remnants of horse stalls and what Sienne thought might have been a guard post. A door on the right led to a smaller tower, round and narrow, that was now open to the sky and filled with rubble. Another, similar tower on the left didn't even have a door remaining. An arched double door made of some wood that rang like iron when Sienne knocked on it yielded to their pushing, slowly creaking inward. "Why is this intact when the outer door wasn't?" Sienne asked. "Since that was clearly battered down."

"No idea," Wit said. "But we always close it behind us when we leave. It feels right to do that."

The space beyond was lit only by the light coming in through the open door. "I forgot to bring a lantern," Wit said.

"No need," Sienne said.

She made half a dozen lights and sent them flying toward the ceiling. Wit's mouth fell open. "I forgot you could do that," he said. "I'm not used to thinking in terms of wizardry."

"That's magic, not wizardry," Sienne said. "But your people *are* magic. That transformation... nothing wizardry can do conserves mass the way a were-creature does. It might be a lost spell, but I wonder if it was something wizards could only do by creating new magical creatures. Assuming that's what were-creatures are. I'm sorry, I don't mean to talk about you as if you're a thing."

"No, I understand," Wit said. "We don't have wizards among our people, and I've always wondered why not. We have those who commune with God, like your priests, but no wizards."

His words struck a chord within her, but it was fleeting, abandoning her before she could capture the thought and examine it more closely. "I can't think why you wouldn't," she said. She took a few steps through the doorway. "I want to see what's in here."

"This is just the antechamber," Wit said.

The barren room had a high enough ceiling that Sienne had to call her lights back so they would illuminate the immediate area. In their cold, white light the black stones looked darker, pools of ink that sucked in light and didn't give it back. The flagstones underfoot, by contrast, were a light gray that felt almost spongy underfoot, soft and yielding in a pleasant way. Doors to the left and right hung open on spaces as dark as the stones, and a plain, blocky staircase at the far side of the room led up into more blackness.

"Most of these are kitchens and storage rooms," Wit said, "but over this way is the room I told you about." He gestured to the right. The door was slightly larger than the others and banded with iron as they were not. Sienne pushed it farther open and sent a few lights ahead of her.

Beyond the door lay a short hallway that would have terrified her if she'd been the least bit claustrophobic. It smelled of old stone and damp, but not rot or animal waste. She hadn't seen signs of any animals, no birds or mice, not even insects. She suppressed memories of the acid jelly cube—it couldn't fit in here anyway—and kept walking. Behind her, Wit stumbled and cursed quietly.

They reached the end of the hallway, and Sienne stopped just before entering the vast chamber beyond. "Is it just me, or does this seem bigger than it was on the outside?" she whispered. Wonderful. Now she was doing it.

"We think it is," Wit said, "but nobody's ever measured it to be sure."

Sienne took another step forward and looked up, far up, to where the domed ceiling made a midnight sky over the chamber. It was definitely taller than two stories, and the ceiling was intact, something Sienne was sure hadn't been true of the keep she remembered. She made more lights and sent them out into the room, then had to make more lights because the room was much bigger than she'd first thought, at least a hundred feet on its longer side. The spongy flagstones put a little bounce in her step as she walked into the room, gazing up at the ceiling. A few lights darted around it like miniature moons, revealing that it was painted a very dark blue rather than black. It really did remind Sienne of a moonless, starless night sky. Round windows high in the walls let in a wan light that seemed filtered through gauze, or a screen of pine branches. It wasn't enough to allow her to dispense with the magic lights, but it did reassure Sienne that they hadn't stepped into some other world of permanent night.

"Over here," Wit said. He'd gone right, toward the wall, and now stood with his hands on his hips, staring up at it.

Sienne joined him and took a long look. "Huh," she said. White lettering covered the stone walls, broken and interrupted like chalk, except chalk wouldn't have lasted this long. "It doesn't come off, does it?" she asked anyway.

"No. That is, you could break the rock and get rid of it that way, but it doesn't wipe or smudge and it smells...take a sniff." Wit pressed his nose to the wall and inhaled. Sienne eyed him dubiously, but imitated his actions.

Instead of old, damp stone, she smelled fresh air and roses, and under that the musty smell of old paper. She breathed it in again and said, "This is definitely magic."

"So what does it do?" Wit asked.

Sienne stepped back so she could see more of the writing. "It's a ritual," she said. "That's like...a set of instructions for doing wizardry more powerful than a spell. The ancients used them—at least, that's what we've learned in our studies." No need to tell Wit they had a more recent witness to non-necromantic ritual in Alaric. "I think this is for summoning rain. That's supposed to be impossible!"

"Could you do this ritual?"

"I don't think so." Sienne ran her fingers across the lines of text. "It's in Ginatic, and I don't read that very well. No one does, really. But I can tell this calls for spells I don't have. And this—" she tapped one line—"calls for a spell I've never heard of. So summoning rain will have to stay a mystery."

"Well, there are lots of them," Wit said, gesturing at the room. "They're spaced far apart, but they're all in the same handwriting and they all have the same structure."

Sienne moved to the next one. "I can't tell what this is for. The next one is to summon...something. I think it's to call a creature to the place where you perform the ritual from wherever it is in the world. That's powerful wizardry. Wit, this place is *amazing*."

"Is it? So it's useful?"

How could she explain the weeks and months of searching for evidence that non-necromantic ritual existed, let alone that the particular ritual they wanted could be found? "It is," she said, her heart too full for more words.

She examined another set of words. "I think this must have been a school," she said absently, half her mind occupied with translating the Ginatic text. "Everything written on the walls, for easy reference... and these all do very basic—"

She stopped, numb with shock, in front of the next ritual. A single phrase had leapt out at her as if outlined in gold—*I am forever faithful.* The words engraved on a ritual cup that had started them on this quest. She reached out to touch the letters, written just at the level of her eyes, with a shaking hand.

From the center, to the heart, to open what is closed, I am forever faithful. That the center will accept the offering, let this cup by my hand open the path. That was it. The full litany.

She traced the lines back up the wall to the beginning, almost too high for her to reach. This was the scrap of ritual she'd found, this beginning: two people pricking each other's fingers, each drawing a symbol on the other's palm. The scraps she'd found hadn't showed the symbol, like it was so common it wasn't necessary, but here it was, a spiral with a diagonal bar through it. It wasn't the same ritual; the one she'd found, that she'd named the binding ritual, called for the two participants' wrists to be bound together symbolically, by a ribbon or scarf, and this didn't mention anything like that. But there were the words, that this ritual said were spoken by one and repeated by the other: *From the center, to the heart...*

"Dear Averran," she murmured. "This is it."

"Are you all right?" Wit asked. "You're crying."

Sienne shook her head and dashed a few tears away. "I'm fine. This is...I've been looking for this for so long." She reached for her pack and realized she'd left it in her tent, her actual tent, not the one she'd borrowed from Faith. "Damn it. I have nothing to write with."

"I don't either," Wit said. "Sorry. You need to remember this?"

"I can memorize it, but I'll feel more secure if I write it down, too." Sienne opened her spellbook and leafed through it as if a blank, untreated page might leap out at her. She drew in a deep breath and willed herself calm. "All right. I should look at the rest, just in case. But then I have to memorize this one."

She made her way around the room, which was a big oval she was increasingly sure was bigger on the inside. Moving slowly and examining each ritual drove her mad with impatience to get back to the one that mattered, but she made herself pay attention to them at least long enough to establish she didn't know what they were for. Another three down the line, she found the binding ritual—the full ritual, not the fragments she'd pieced together. That one, she also knew by heart, and it was nice to see she'd guessed properly.

Finally, she raced back to *her* ritual and read over the lines, committing them to memory. This had to be the ritual the wizard had corrupted, and thanks to Alaric, they knew a few of the alterations. But the entire second half of the ritual—the wizard's ritual, the one that bound the Sassaven to him even as it unlocked their full magical potential—was a mystery. Or had been. She still wasn't sure if the wizard had made alterations to that second half, but at least they now knew what the original was.

She closed her eyes, turned her back on the wall, and recited what she'd memorized. "Is that what it says?" Wit said. "It sounds...I don't know. Ordinary and extraordinary all at once."

"I'm coming back with paper and pencil," Sienne said, opening her eyes. "Though I won't try to *jaunt* into this place. I think the best I could hope for is that it would just fail, and the worst...this place isn't natural."

"You see what I mean," Wit said. "I take it you want to go back to camp."

"Can we? I mean, if there are other things to see..."

"The rooms upstairs are where some of us go for sex. Not something you'd be interested in." Wit grinned at her, and she laughed.

"No, not now. Once we get outside, I can *ferry* us back to your camp."

"You really are in a hurry."

The words of the ritual bounced around inside her head, fighting to spring free and vanish from memory. "You have no idea."

After the spongy flagstones, the hard, bumpy cobbles of the courtyard were almost a comfort. They strolled across to the gate, but before they got there, Sienne turned and looked back over the keep. "I wonder what magic does it," she mused. "Or if that corridor is some kind of *transport* that takes you elsewhere. If you climbed out through the windows, where would you end up?"

"Now it makes me nervous to go there again," Wit said.

"It's probably perfectly safe. Unless it does lead somewhere else, and you were inside when the little hallway collapsed. And it doesn't look in danger of that."

Sienne turned to find Wit had stopped. Facing them, outside the gate, was a werebear with iron-gray fur, standing on its hind paws. It reminded her of the man she'd noticed the night before, the one with gray hair who'd stared back at her. Wit was very still. "Is something wrong?" Sienne asked, pitching her voice so the bear couldn't hear her. She hoped.

"I don't know," Wit said in the same low voice. "Silver, shift forms and greet our *guest*," he called out, emphasizing "guest" in the way Sienne's mother had always used to warn her when she'd violated protocol in some way.

Silver stood watching them. He made no move to shift into human form. Five more bears, dark or reddish-brown or even pale gold, emerged from the forest behind him. Sienne's heart pounded faster. Six werebears against the two of them. It felt like an attack. Their silence unnerved her more than a screaming rage would have.

She took a step forward and brought her spellbook up, letting it fall open to *fury*. Silver dropped to all fours and charged.

15

The other werebears immediately followed Silver's lead. Sienne forced herself to read calmly, even though Silver had closed half the distance between them and she wasn't sure she'd finish the spell before his jaws closed on her throat. Beside her, Wit was taking off his boots and swearing viciously. He flung the second boot away and shifted, disregarding his remaining clothes. As his body transformed, the clothes tore along the seams, not quite falling off him, but definitely ruined. He roared, and ran at Silver.

Silver checked in his run and altered his course to attack Wit. Sienne wished she could curse and cast spells at the same time. Wit was going to be caught in the spell, and there was no way to warn him.

The spell burst away from her as she spat out the last acid-etched syllables. It fractured into half a dozen bolts of magical energy that sang through the air with a chime like steel striking steel. Each bolt slammed into a bear, making them sway before collapsing motionless on the ground. That left one bear standing. Unfortunately, that one wasn't Wit. It was the golden-furred bear, who'd been farthest back when they began their charge. He halted now, taking a few stumbling steps until he lost momentum and stopped.

Sienne flipped the pages to *scorch*. "You've seen what I can do," she said, hating that her voice shook with anger. The bear might mistake it for fear. "That's just the beginning. Come any closer, and it's going to smell like burnt hair around here for *years*."

The bear stood poised to advance. He put a single foot forward. Sienne began reading, casting swift glances at her enemy in between syllables. The bear put another foot forward. Then he turned and ran. Sienne lowered her book and breathed out in relief. She had no qualms about defending herself, but she'd never been in a fight without her friends to back her up, and she felt unexpectedly afraid.

She hurried to Wit's side and tried to check his pulse, but in bear form that turned out to be impossible. Nervously, she lowered her cheek to rest near his nose and relaxed when she felt air sighing in and out. As far as she knew, a *force* bolt couldn't kill by itself, but hit someone who had a heart condition with it, or a child, and that fact would be cold comfort.

Now she needed to get Wit back to camp—or was that best? If weres had attacked them, might they also have attacked her friends? Or was she the lucky one because she'd gone merrily into the wilderness without her team? She shook her head. That was crazy thinking. They should go to the camp, and everything else could follow from there.

Wit was far too big for her to carry, even in his less bulky but taller human form. For the briefest moment, she thought about leaving him to *jaunt* back to the camp and fetch help, but without knowing what the situation was there, she couldn't be sure she could return immediately. Leaving him surrounded by enemies, any one of whom might recover from *fury* sooner than he did, was a bad idea.

She walked around him, considering, then opened her spellbook to *float*. The honey-sweet taste of the transform filled her mouth, calming her somewhat after the terror of the short battle. If you could call it that. The last syllables drifted away on the morning breeze, and Wit's recumbent form floated three or four inches off the ground, shifting slightly in that same breeze.

Now, getting him back… Sienne nudged him with her toe, then gave a slightly harder shove when that failed to move him more than an inch. Normally when she had to move a load lightened by *float*, she tied a rope to it, but she had no rope and, again, no means of getting one short of abandoning him. She sighed. This was going to take *forever*.

She squatted and got her hands under his shoulders. With a heave, she shoved Wit higher so he now lay canted diagonally in the air, his feet brushing a spotty fern and his shoulders just above Sienne's waist height. She repeated the maneuver on his feet so all of him was at the same height. Then she pushed on his body until he rotated so his feet were pointed in the direction she wanted to go. Walking slowly, she took hold of Wit's furry shoulders and pushed him away from the keep's gate and toward the woods.

She hadn't been paying much attention to their path earlier, a fact she now cursed herself for. She was fairly certain she knew where they'd entered the unnaturally circular clearing, and she headed that way, around the southern end of the keep. Wit wasn't heavy in this state—*float* took care of that—but he still had mass, and he tended to keep moving in the direction she pushed him unless she stopped him. The first time he hit a tree, she winced. The fifth time, she wearily accepted it as collateral damage. The last time she'd done this, she'd been towing a corpse that hadn't cared if she slammed it into walls. Wit was probably going to be bruised after this, no matter how well padded he was with fur.

After about ten minutes of pushing, cursing, and bumping into trees, she was regretting her decision to take Wit along. How long before he regained consciousness? The response to *force* or *fury* varied by individual. She hadn't dared cast the weaker version of the spell that left someone conscious but immobile, so she was stuck with waiting for him to wake up. And now she was lost.

Quickly, she worked the small magic that told her where true north was. If she'd had that working when they came, it would have been far more helpful, but with Wit as her guide, what had been the point? She knew they'd headed north and west, so she aimed south and east and prayed the camp was big enough that she'd hit it even if she was a little off.

The sound of birds in the trees maddened her, all those cheerful little chirps singing out in complete disregard for her troubles. Too bad they couldn't be useful, guiding her toward camp or warning her of—

She stopped, and grabbed hold of the hair on Wit's shoulders to stop him as well. Ahead, two dark shapes slinked through the trees, lumbering toward her. They stopped as well, and one werebear rose up on his hind legs, front paws dangling before him in a limp-wristed way that would have been funny if she hadn't been painfully conscious of the terrible sharp claws tipping those paws. "Hello?" she called out. "Wit needs help. Are you…"

The bears didn't shift into human form. The one lowered himself to the ground and raised his head, sniffing the air. Sienne opened her spellbook and began reading *fury*. At the sound of her voice, the two ran at her, slowing to dodge the skinny trees but otherwise terrifyingly fast. Her heart pounding, Sienne spoke the final syllables, and *force* bolts blasted away from her. Two slammed into the werebears, dropping them both just feet from her. The others impacted on the trees, leaving fracture lines and splitting one completely in half. It crashed to the ground with a solid thump.

Sienne took in a deep, green-scented breath and waited for her heart to slow. That had been close. She hadn't appreciated before how much she depended on her companions to protect her. As they depended on her. She wished they were with her now. She wished even more she knew what had happened at the camp.

She let her spellbook fall to hang at her side and steered Wit around the fallen bears. If they were hunting her— She stopped again and cursed herself. If they were hunting her, she needed to be impossible to find.

She turned to *vanish* and began reading off the confusion, blinking away the doubled images the spell left behind. Laying her hand on Wit's shoulder, she let the spell encompass him, rippling around his body and turning it first translucent, then invisible.

Keeping a hand on him so she didn't lose him, she read it off again, this time turning it on herself.

Vanish did the strangest things to one's perceptions, making sounds echo slightly and giving objects a faint rainbow aura. She drew in a couple of calming breaths, then tucked her spellbook away inside her vest as she'd carried it back when she was starting out as a scrapper. Her invisibility only extended to things she was wearing, not to things she held in her hands, and even the stupidest werebear would notice a floating book.

She fumbled about a bit until she got a good grip on Wit, then began pushing. Almost immediately, his invisible body hit a tree, jarring her. She clenched her teeth and steered him for the biggest gaps between trees. This was going to take forever, and she might not have forever. *Averran*, she prayed, *protect my friends, wherever they are.*

Her whole world narrowed down to her invisible hands gripping Wit's invisible fur and trying to guess which way he'd drift. She soon fell into a fugue state, in which her feet scuffing the dry fallen needles echoed a hollow chorus of rustling that reminded her of birds flying north for the summer, their wings beating the air into submission. Her arms and legs ached with effort. She pushed Wit a little to the right, following her internal compass, and prayed again, though she didn't think Averran was required to listen. She remembered what Octavian had said, about asking Perrin about Averran's guidance for her personally, and wished she'd thought to do it when she had the chance.

The rustling grew louder, breaking through her stupor. She grabbed Wit's shoulders more firmly and brought him to a halt. More bears, three of them this time, headed her way. Sienne held onto Wit and tried to calm her breathing. Breathing. Smell. Didn't were-creatures have an excellent sense of smell? She cursed silently and fumbled her spellbook halfway out of her vest, then paused, torn by indecision. If these weren't the enemy, blasting them would only give her three more unconscious bodies to wrangle.

The bears were going to pass well to the left of her. They lumbered along, their heads swaying—oh, by all the avatars, they were casting about for scent! One raised its brown head, then halted. The other two stopped. She didn't know if they could communicate in bear form, though it was unlikely they were capable of human speech in that shape. And yet the way they stood, tense and with their heads tilted slightly, told Sienne clearly something was passing between them.

The first bear swiveled its head to look directly at her, or at least at the space she occupied. She held her breath. It turned back to its comrades, and again there was a voiceless communication. Then they moved on, slowly, still scanning the ground. Sienne waited for them to pass out of earshot, then went back to pushing. If that many bears were out looking for her, maybe the camp wasn't friendly territory, but it was all she had left. She was barely sure she could find the camp, and dead positive she would never find the place where she and her friends had camped the night before.

Minutes passed. She saw no more bears, heard nothing but the inane chatter of birds high above whose songs the echoes of *vanish* turned discordant. Bright. This had to be Bright's doing. Though why she would try to kill Sienne...no, it made sense. With Sienne and her companions dead, there was no one to speak on the werebears' behalf, and the bears would be forced to follow Bright's plan. But surely Clever wouldn't let Bright get away with it? Which would be small comfort if Sienne were dead.

She smelled wood smoke, and for a moment her addled brain pictured fire sweeping the forest, out of control. But it wasn't strong enough for a forest fire, she saw no raging flames, and realized it was someone's camp. The werebear camp.

In the next moment, she was out from between the trees and grabbing firmer hold of invisible Wit to keep him from floating away into the open space. Small tents surrounding campfires greeted her, with women moving around the fires, preparing food or chastising small children. Some of those children were bear cubs. It didn't look as if the camp were in an uproar. Sienne began to dismiss the *vanish* spell, then stopped. If no one yet knew that someone had tried to kill her, she might be able to use that.

She steered Wit's body wide around the edge of camp, trying to identify the tents they'd slept in last night. Everything looked so different in the bright morning light. She didn't recognize anyone, which wasn't a surprise given that she only knew a handful of weres to call by name, and there were several hundred people in the camp. She didn't see many men, and the ones she did see were all at least as old as Test. Either the younger men were out hunting, or they were out hunting her and her friends. She couldn't believe the whole camp was in on the plot. It wouldn't have been nearly so placid if they were.

Across the sea of canvas roofs, she saw Clever's much larger speaking tent. She changed course and headed for it. Either Clever was there, and Sienne could hand the whole problem to her, or Bright was there, and Sienne could find out if she really was behind the attempts on her life. In which case, she would show her why wizards should not be trifled with.

She thought about stashing Wit somewhere. The idea filled her with unexpected cheer. She'd started resenting his awkward burden and feeling irritated that he'd flung himself into combat without thinking. She had to remind herself he wasn't a scrapper, and had no experience fighting alongside a wizard, but it was hard not to imagine how much differently that fight would have gone if he'd had the sense to let her attack first. But she still didn't know when he'd wake up, and it probably wasn't safe to dispel *vanish* while he was still unconscious if they really were surrounded by enemies. Not to mention she had no idea where to leave him. Sighing, she set about crossing the camp to the speaking tent.

There weren't many people moving between the tent groups, but even those few made Sienne want to scream with frustration, getting in her way and stopping to talk for what felt like an eternity. She very nearly ran Wit into someone who stopped abruptly in her path, sniffing as if she could perceive them though she was still in human form. Sienne's heart, already beating faster from exertion, sped up. She was so on edge, if she'd had her spellbook open, she would have *force*-blasted the woman from pure nervous exhaustion. Finally, the woman moved on, and Sienne shoved Wit the last few feet into the open space surrounding Clever's tent.

With a final few pushes, she maneuvered Wit into the lee of the tent, well away from the two women who stood sentry before the door flap. People were talking within, not loudly enough for Sienne to make out anything but that there were three speakers involved in the conversation. One had a deep voice she recognized, and it made her leaden, exhausted heart light. Alaric was safe, at least. She spared one last prayer for her other friends, then walked around the corner and into the tent. The flap was ajar enough that she didn't disturb it much on entering. She caught sight, out of the corner of her eye, one of the sentries looking at the moving flap curiously, and then she was through.

Alaric, Clever, and Bright stood talking at the center of the tent. "Wit is a perfectly acceptable emissary," Clever was saying. "He's already familiar with human culture and his open demeanor gives him a trustworthy appearance."

"Yes, but a woman would have more authority," Bright said. "You can't go, but what about Bloom?"

"Bloom's too young."

"The king won't know anything about your culture to appreciate the difference between you sending a woman or a man," Alaric said. "My advice is you send someone who won't be overwhelmed by being among humans. I don't know your people, but Bloom struck me as a little too diffident for the task."

The flap opened. "Bright, could I speak to you for a moment?" said a man Sienne didn't recognize.

Bright's eyebrows went up. "Excuse me," she said, and left the tent.

"She came around fast," Alaric said.

"I beg your pardon?" Clever said.

"She was adamant about not supporting your plan last night. Now she's all for it."

Clever shrugged. "Bright is intelligent and forceful, used to getting her way. It sometimes takes her a while to accept a decision that runs counter to her own understanding. But I trust her, and rely on her."

"*What?*" Bright exclaimed, loudly enough to carry clearly into the tent. "When was this?"

Sienne couldn't hear the muffled reply. "I see," Bright said. The tent flap opened. "How long have your people plotted treachery?" she said, addressing Alaric.

"Treachery?" Alaric said. He was facing Clever, so Sienne couldn't see his expression, but his back tensed the way it did when he was ready for a fight. "That's a strong accusation, considering *your* people dragged us out here."

"Burr reports a slaughter out at the ruin," Bright said, her voice furious. "Many of our people killed—by magic."

"That's impossible," Alaric said. "Sienne wouldn't use magic on anyone who wasn't attacking her."

"We have no reason to attack any of you," Clever said. "Bright, do you have proof?"

"Burr saw the bodies himself," Bright said. "The wizard is gone. Where are the rest of these...scrappers? Killing more of us?"

Sienne knew a good straight line when she heard one. "The wizard is right here," she said, "and if any of your people are dead, they deserve it for trying to kill me."

All three of them startled and spun around, searching for Sienne. "Where are you?" Alaric said, with a note in his voice that said he was close to snapping.

Sienne concentrated and dismissed *vanish*. "Here."

Alaric took a step toward her, reaching for her, then stopped, glancing at the werebears. "Why were you invisible?"

Sienne came forward, pulling her spellbook out of her vest. "Wit and I were attacked out at the ruin," she said. "I *force*-blasted most of them and scared off the last. Then we were attacked again in the forest. I didn't kill those two, either."

"Why would any of us attack you?" Clever exclaimed.

Sienne glared at Bright. "I think *she* knows why."

Bright's perfect lips compressed in a tight line. "I have no idea what you are talking about."

"So it's just coincidence that if we were gone, everyone would have to follow your plan instead of Clever's?" Sienne opened her book at random. She didn't intend to cast a spell on Bright, but it felt good to have the option available. "I bet if you ask those weres when they wake up, they'll tell you Bright put them up to it."

Clever looked Bright up and down. Bright said, "You can't possibly take this accusation seriously."

"I know you are deeply loyal to your people," Clever said. "I also know it is the kind of loyalty that might not think humans are deserving of the same consideration."

Alaric's hands were clenched into fists. "You ordered them to kill Sienne?" he growled.

Bright faced him square on. "I owe you no answers."

Alaric roared and swung at Bright, catching her below the jaw and knocking her backwards to stumble over one of the stools. Sienne screamed, grabbed his other arm, and was dragged along as he pulled back for another blow. "Don't!"

"I don't hit women who aren't trying to kill me," Alaric snarled, "but I'll make an exception for you." He grabbed Bright and hauled her up, her head lolling dazedly.

"*Stop!*" Clever roared, and the end of the word turned into an actual roar as she transformed into a red-furred bear that towered over Alaric and Bright, her tunic shredding around her. She slapped Alaric across the jaw, sending him reeling. Sienne staggered as he nearly fell, then threw her arms around him and pushed as hard as she could to keep him away from Bright. It was like trying to move a mountain.

"Clever!" someone shouted from the doorway. "Clever, it's coming!"

Clever shrank back into human form. "What is? Is it the humans?" She clearly didn't care that she was naked.

The woman shook her head. Her eyes were wide, and she breathed in short, panicked gasps. "Not the humans," she said. "It's the howler. It's on the move."

"Howler?" Sienne said. "I thought those were a story."

"I would to God they were," Clever said. She reached out a hand to help Bright to her feet. "Did you hear the howls last night? We have been tracking this one for a week, waiting for it to move on."

"Where is it?" Bright said, ignoring Alaric, who still looked poised to attack her.

"Five miles due east. It's headed southeast."

Bright and Clever shared a look filled with meaning. "But that's good, isn't it?" Sienne asked. "South and east takes it away from your camp."

Clever pursed her lips. "There is a human village some six miles from here. South...and east."

"So howlers are real," Alaric said. "How real? How much of the legend is true?"

"We don't know," Clever said. "Enough of our people have been killed by them that we stay well away. Those who encounter them... they are never in a condition to tell us details. We know a howler's scream strikes its hearers numb with fear, forcing them either to flee or to freeze where they stand. It can fill its victim with an intense hunger for the flesh of its own kind, making them turn on those they call friends or kin. And we have seen it rend those it does not corrupt. Whether it is capable of turning someone into a howler, we cannot say."

"The rest is quite enough," Bright said. "This one will not threaten our people."

"Yes, but what about the humans?" Sienne said. "Shouldn't someone warn them?"

"They will not listen to were-creatures," Clever said. "There is nothing we can do."

"Are the others back?" Alaric asked Sienne.

"I don't know. I came straight here. Mostly."

Alaric took her hand and pulled her close. "We're leaving," he said. "If we come back, we're going to renegotiate. Attacking my team makes me disinclined to help you."

"We did not attack you," Clever said, but she glanced at Bright. Bright's chin, which was turning a spectacular purple, lifted high in defiance. "And if we did," Clever went on, "I assure you it was not an authorized attack. I would not jeopardize my people's future that way."

"You're all going to die," Bright said. "No one faces the howlers and survives. Running is the only option."

"Then we'll make the settlers run," Alaric said.

"You should help," Sienne said.

"They are not our problem," Bright said. "They hate and fear us. Why should we help them?"

"Because you're people, not animals. And that's what people do for each other." Sienne released her spellbook. "How better to show them who you really are?"

Clever shook her head. "We are too small a force to make a difference. And my first duty is to my people's survival."

"You wanted us to plead with the king for your people's survival," Sienne persisted. "Give us something to show him you're committed to being citizens. It's not just about what you get from the country, it's what you give, too. Help save that settlement, and King Derekian won't need much persuading."

For a moment, Sienne thought she'd reached her. Then Clever shook her head again. "Persuasive," she said, "but it is impossible. I wish you luck."

"Yes. You'll need it," Bright sneered.

Alaric steered Sienne out of the tent in silence. They'd taken only a few steps when Sienne said, "Wit. I forgot."

"What about him? Was he hurt in the fight? Sienne, were *you* hurt?"

She shook her head. "Just a minute." She felt around until she found Wit's foot, concentrated, and dispelled *vanish*. Wit lay in midair, gently breathing as if he were only asleep. Sienne shoved on his midsection until he lay on the ground, then dispelled *float* as well. "That's all I can do for him."

"Why is Wit unconscious? Sienne—"

"He did what I'm always telling you not to do, which is run into the middle of *fury* without ducking. Alaric, what are we going to do?"

"Find the others. They were supposed to be back by now with our things. Then we're going to run for that settlement and hope we can find someone to listen to us."

"It's hopeless, isn't it."

"Probably. Would *you* listen to strangers spouting children's tales about monsters that freeze the blood and turn people into cannibals? But we have to try."

They walked swiftly through the camp until they reached familiar territory. Alaric didn't have any trouble remembering where they'd spent the night. To Sienne's relief, Perrin, Dianthe, and Kalanath were all there, seated around the fire and eating meat off skewers. Swift sat with them, laughing at some joke Dianthe had told. "Ho, the negotiator returns!" he said. "You—" His joking tone vanished. "You don't look happy."

"We have to leave," Alaric said.

"So soon?" Dianthe asked. "Don't we need to wait for the weres to supply an emissary?"

"We're not going back to Fioretti," Alaric said. "The short version is that howlers are real and one is going to attack a settlement several miles from here. We're going to warn them, and possibly get ourselves killed by a mythical creature. Is everyone in?"

"You can't be serious," Swift said. "Nobody attacks a howler."

"Attacking is not the plan," Alaric said, "but if that's what it takes to protect that settlement, then we'll do that too."

Dianthe stood and wiped her mouth. "Our things are all here, but I imagine we'll want to travel light. Is it all right if we leave the other stuff in your camp, Swift?"

Swift stood as well. "Sure. But I'm coming with you."

"It's not your fight," Alaric said.

"There's nothing that says that howler might not head our way eventually," Swift said. "And I find, after my time pretending to be human, I'm more interested in your people's fates than I used to be. Besides, there are only five of you, and you could use the help. Where's Wit?"

"Still unconscious. It's a long story," Sienne said when Swift gave her a puzzled look.

"I have been wondering why this morning's blessings had a decidedly martial tone," Perrin said. "What do we know of this creature? Is Swift's tale accurate?"

"Let's move, and we'll talk on the way," Alaric said.

———

SIENNE RESENTED THE TREES, GROWING SO CLOSELY TOGETHER SHE AND her companions couldn't go faster than a brisk trot. She hated not knowing things, and not knowing where the howler was or how much faster it was moving than they were filled her with a dread urgency that the stupid trees thwarted. Swift, in the lead, lived up to his name, darting between the boles like he was a deer rather than a bear. Were there such things as weredeer? Common knowledge said the only weres were predators, but common knowledge also said all weres were mindless monsters, so common knowledge could be wrong.

Her small compass magic told her they were heading more east than south. How fortunate that Swift had come along, because Perrin had no blessings that would lead them to a destination. She tripped over a tangle of ferns, caught herself before it could become a fall, and ran on. Her lungs were a sharp pain in her chest, her heart thudded against her ribs like a captured rabbit, but she made herself maintain the jogging pace that could go on for miles. A year ago this would have been impossible for her, untrained in wilderness travel and soft from years of doing nothing more strenuous than dancing.

Despite what Alaric had said, there hadn't been time or energy for talk before the running pace had made speech impossible. The others hadn't had many questions, though Kalanath had asked, "So we are not to fight this thing? How is that a good solution? It will only be free to return."

"Howlers are opportunists," Swift had said. "They're like...those pieces of metal that attract other metals. When they're close enough, they're drawn to groups of people to feed, but far enough away they pass right by. They tend to move in straight lines. This one, if we can keep the humans away from it, will end up in the mountains where it's harmless."

"There are mining camps," Dianthe had said. "Humans are all over the Bramantus Mountains. It's hardly harmless."

Swift's cheeks had reddened, but he hadn't responded to that except to say, "No one's ever taken on a howler and lived. There's only so much we can do."

Now Sienne considered this. Whatever Alaric said about just getting the settlers out of the howler's path, she was sure it would come to a fight. The likelihood of the settlers listening to them was small, and probably they wouldn't believe it until the howler was upon them. Which meant Sienne and her friends would have to keep it busy while the settlers fled. She felt resentment again, this time at the werebears who'd attacked her and Wit, forcing her to cast spells and use up her precious magical reserves. She didn't know what would work on a howler, whether *force* or *scorch* or *shout* would have an effect. *Change* was probably pointless, since it was less effective the more magical a thing she used it on, and howlers had to be filthy with magic to be as powerful as Swift suggested.

She was so preoccupied with planning her strategy that she didn't at first realize they'd come out of the forest. Alaric loomed before her, unmoving, and she stumbled to stop herself falling into him. "Where now?" he asked Swift.

Swift pointed. "It's another three miles. We—"

An unearthly howl shivered through the air, faint but unmistakably inhuman. It touched Sienne's heart with a terrible chill. Long-dormant memories surfaced, of huddling terrified in her sister's bed as thunder crashed outside their window, of fleeing from a snake she'd nearly stepped on, and she clenched her hands into tight fists until they felt numb. By the look of her companions, they, too, were lost in their own fears.

Alaric shook his head like a dog coming out of deep water. "That's nothing," he said. "We've faced worse fears than those."

"Don't be cocky," Swift said. "That's just the edge of the effect. When you're within sight of it...I've seen brave men lose control and run into danger just to get away."

"I was going for confident defiance rather than cocky, but I'll take it," Alaric said. "The point is that those fears are groundless. We need to remember that when it gets bad."

"I have a blessing that will help," Perrin said. "We used it against the carvers."

"I thought that prevented the carvers taking control of us," Dianthe said.

"That is one effect. Its general efficacy is against magic that works on the mind. Whether it will be truly effective depends on whether our fears are grounded in memory, or in our instincts. But it is worth trying."

"When we reach the settlement, let's do that," Alaric said.

"Then we should go quickly," Kalanath said.

They still couldn't run as fast as Sienne wanted without exhausting herself. She didn't even dare *ferry* herself and, by preference, Perrin of the silver tongue to the settlement to give their warning, because she needed all her magical strength to fight the howler, if it came to that. It didn't matter, because she didn't know the settlement at all, and she needed to have a clear picture of anywhere she used *ferry* to reach, but impatience had her in its claws and she wanted to move faster, *faster*.

Swift stumbled to a halt, and Sienne raced past him before she could stop herself. "What's wrong?" Alaric said.

"Someone's coming," Swift said. He untied his tunic and stripped it off over his head. "I can—it's hard to hear in this shape."

His body stretched, thickened, and shifted into his bear form, falling to all fours. The bear raised his head and sniffed the air, taking a few steps back toward the now-distant forest. Then he sat back on his haunches and let out a sound halfway between a bark and a howl.

Something replied, longer and louder. Sienne shielded her eyes against the bright afternoon light and saw a dark shape approaching, low to the ground and coming fast. After a few seconds, it was recognizable as a bear, loping along at a ground-eating speed. It carried something in its mouth.

Swift changed shape and picked up his tunic. "It's Wit."

Relief coursed through Sienne that Wit had recovered. It was irrational—everyone woke up from *fury* eventually—but she still had that image of him lying helpless and unconscious, surrounded by enemies. She watched with the others as Wit ran up to them, changing into human form at the last minute and dropping what he held. Wit bent to pick the small bundle up and shook it out, revealing it to be a tunic. He shrugged into it, saying, "You could have waited for me."

"We didn't know when you'd wake up," Swift said. "Didn't Clever forbid you to come?"

"She did," Wit said, "but I didn't listen. She knew I wouldn't, too."

"But she is your matriarch," Kalanath said.

"And not the keeper of my honor," Wit said. "I told her she was wrong to let the humans be destroyed when we have a chance to stop it. She and Bright were still arguing about it when I left." He stretched. "We should move. Howlers aren't fast, but once they get whiff of their prey, they're implacable in their pursuit."

Alaric shook his head. "You do realize we're all probably going to die, right?"

"Better to die a hero than live a coward," Wit said. "Besides, you all fought carvers and survived that. I have a feeling this howler is going to find us a greater obstacle than it expects."

They ran on, Sienne clutching her spellbook so it wouldn't bang against her thigh. Wit's arrival had cheered her more than the simple fact of his lone assistance could account for. Maybe it was his calm confidence, maybe it was just his faith in them, but in any case, the fears the howler had raised were gone.

Soon thin plumes of smoke scarred the cloudless sky. Alaric slowed, and said, "We'll need to find their leader. I don't suppose you know who that is?"

"We stay well away from humans," Wit said. "We only know this place is here because we watch it for signs that they're spreading out toward us."

Another howl, closer now, threaded toward them on the slight breeze. Alaric drew in a deep breath and let it out slowly, as if controlling himself. "It's close," he said.

Sienne shivered and closed her eyes against old nightmares. "That blessing would be nice right now."

"Gather around, then," Perrin said. He removed a paper from his riffle of blessings and held it high where he stood in the middle of them. The murmured invocation set the paper afire with rose-colored flames. Sienne didn't feel any different, but she'd expected that from the last time he'd used that blessing.

"It's reassuring," she said, and *It's reassuring* echoed in her mind like doubled vision, half a second after she spoke.

"I didn't feel—oh, that is strange," Swift said.

"It will not last long, perhaps an hour, so we should move quickly," Perrin said.

Another five minutes' jog brought them to the settlement. It was small, perhaps fifteen or twenty houses clustered together around a road that showed signs of being formed not deliberately, but by the passage of many feet taking the shortest route to their destination. To the south, fields of grain, mostly wheat and barley, spread out as far as Sienne could see. Dark blotches marked where people worked the fields. More people, mostly women, tended yards or fed chickens behind the houses. Small children ran and screamed in some game whose rules Sienne couldn't discern. Possibly there were no rules. It was all so domestic Sienne despaired. These people would never believe them.

Alaric strode up to the closest woman, stopping well away so she wouldn't feel threatened by the Ansorjan giant accosting her. "We need to speak with your leader," he said. "Your head man, or wise woman—whoever makes the decisions for your community."

The woman clutched her broom like a weapon. "Why?"

"We have a message. It's imperative that we deliver it quickly. Where should we go?"

The woman looked at each of them in turn. She reserved her longest looks for Swift and Wit, who did look odd in their shapeless tunics and bare feet. Finally, she said, "You scrappers?"

"Yes," Alaric said.

"We don't have anything scrappers would want. You should leave us be. There's a ruin west of here—try your luck there."

"We're not here on a job. We just have a message to deliver. Please, mistress."

She eyed him again. "Yannick's as close to a leader as we have. Fourth house on the right from here. He might be in the fields, this time of day, but you can check his house if you want."

"Thank you." Alaric saluted her and trotted in the indicated direction. Sienne hurried after him, counting houses.

The fourth one on the right didn't look any different from the others, which was probably a good sign; it meant Yannick didn't think he was superior just because he was the leader. Alaric rapped sharply on the door. "Perrin?"

"We want them moving west, correct?" Perrin said.

No one had come to the door. Alaric rapped on it again. "West is probably safest. I think this man must be in the fields. It's going to take us forever to find him if he is."

On his last words, the door swung open. A short, round man with an enormous moustache that split his face in half regarded them warily. "Yes?"

"Are you Yannick?" Alaric asked.

"I am. You're scrappers, aren't you? Is there something I can do for you?" His tone indicated he didn't think that was possible.

"We have a message for this settlement. May we come in?" Alaric hadn't bothered staying back to give the man room. Yannick swallowed hard as he looked up at his looming presence.

"A...message? From scrappers?"

"It's a complicated story I'd rather we told you indoors. And it's urgent."

Yannick looked past Alaric at the rest of them. He sagged slightly. "All right, come in."

Yannick's home was even simpler than its outsides indicated. It was a single room with a bed in one corner and an iron stove in another. A table with a lone chair was drawn up beneath the room's one window. And even this was far more luxury than the werebears possessed. Sienne felt a moment's anger that she quashed. Now was not the time to protest injustice, and the werebears' condition was only very peripherally this man's fault.

With all of them inside, the room felt very cramped. Yannick said, "I'm sorry I can't offer you seats. Now, what is this message?"

Perrin stepped forward, drawing Yannick's attention to himself. "Sir, what do you know of howlers?"

"Howlers? You mean, as in the children's story?"

"They are very much not a fable, and one of them is coming this way. Your settlement is in its path. It will destroy all of you if you do not leave."

Yannick's mouth fell open slightly. "What proof do you have of this?"

"Ah..." Perrin looked as if this was not the response he'd expected. Sienne felt the same. She'd expected Yannick to either command them to leave or laugh himself silly. "You must have heard the howls of an unearthly creature, yes?"

"We hear howls all the time. Wolves, bears...it's what you expect when you live on the frontier of the Empty Lands."

Wit pushed forward. "Sir, my people—our settlement, that is—we have seen howlers and fled from them. We tracked this one from a distance and confirmed where its path would take it."

"Your settlement? There isn't any settlement other than ours for miles. You came all this way to warn us?"

Wit glanced at Swift. "No, sir. We did not come from far away. We live in the forest a few miles from here."

"Then why haven't we heard of you?"

Sienne willed him to make something up. This man might be willing to listen to their tales of howlers, but who knew what he'd make of were-creatures living on his doorstep?

"We aren't human," Wit said. "We're weres."

Yannick's mouth fell open again, wide enough this time to catch flies. "You're *what*?"

"Were-creatures. Werebears."

"Impossible. Weres are brutes, lacking in human intelligence."

"That's a discussion for another time," Alaric said. He clearly felt as Sienne did, that Wit was, despite other evidence, an idiot. "If we can get your people far enough west, the howler will pass this place and you'll be able to return when it's gone. But we have to move quickly."

Yannick's gaze was still stuck on Wit. "You haven't attacked us," he said. "Why?"

"Because we're not monsters." Wit took a step forward. "We just want to be left alone, to live in peace."

Yannick didn't back away at Wit's approach. "Prove it."

Sienne wasn't sure what he wanted Wit to prove—how could Wit show, by himself, that weres wanted to live in peace? But Wit took it as instruction to remove his tunic and gesture the others to stand back. Yannick's wide-eyed stare took in Wit's nakedness, but he said nothing. Then Wit changed shape. The crowded room became positively claustrophobic. Wit sat back on his haunches and stared at Yannick. Yannick grabbed hold of the table he'd been forced against when Wit changed and looked like he needed it to keep from falling. Wit snuffled, a quiet, almost peaceful sound, so ordinary Sienne almost couldn't believe it had come from the bear.

Yannick reached out his hand to Wit. Wit nosed it and snuffled again. Yannick lowered his hand and said, "Kitane's left arm. There are more of you?"

"Many more," Swift said. "And none of us wish you any harm. Which is why my cousin and I are here."

Yannick closed his eyes briefly. "Kitane have mercy," he said. Then he let out a deep breath. "They're going to think I'm mad, but I believe you. How close is the howler?"

"Close enough. A couple of miles," Swift said.

"It might not be enough time. Most of us are scattered in the fields this time of day."

"We'll buy you time," Alaric said. "Wit, change back. We need to move."

Wit stood up on his hind legs, shuddered, and was his human self again. "We can help spread the word," he said, donning his tunic, "but I'm not sure your people will listen to strangers."

"I'll get the women working on telling people. You can help the children start their escape." Yannick stroked his moustache. It looked like a nervous habit. "Thank you. And—you didn't have to reveal yourself," he told Wit.

"We want to live openly," Wit said. "That has to start sometime. And if—" He shut his mouth before he could finish saying what Sienne was sure would have been *we're all going to die.*

"Go," Alaric said.

Yannick strode rapidly down the street. "Susa, Lannie, come here. Terian, go to the fields and have the men return. Tell them it's an emergency. I'll explain it all when they get here."

Sienne stood with Alaric and watched the children, still running and playing with no regard for the strange grownups in their midst. "It's not going to work, is it," she murmured.

"We'll get some of them away, and that's what matters," Alaric replied.

"But there aren't enough of us to defend them."

"We do our best. You know that." He shielded his eyes and looked to the west. Sienne, glancing up at him, saw a fierce smile spread across his face. "And I think we'll have plenty of help."

Sienne followed his gaze. There was movement across the western horizon, a wave of browns and reds and golds sweeping toward them, backlit by the setting sun. Her heart beat faster, this time with excitement, as an army of werebears loped across the unbroken fields, coming straight for them.

17

The bear in the lead had dusty red fur like cinnamon and was bigger than the others. She loped up to them, changing shape mid-stride into Clever. "This is a fool's errand," she said when she was close enough. "Hitching our fortunes to theirs."

"But it's the right thing to do," Sienne said.

The howl sounded again, so close Sienne looked around wildly for its source. The howler couldn't be far now. Just as she realized the fear hadn't struck her with such power as before, Clever said loudly, "Remember it is not a real fear. But if it strikes you, do not stand against it. Flee rather than be taken by the lust for flesh." She turned back to Alaric and said, "That applies to you and yours as well. The howler can cause such terror it inspires a desire to rend one's allies, to taste their blood. One becomes a danger to one's friends when that happens."

"We'll remember," Alaric said.

"The blessing works," Kalanath said. "We can defend against it."

"You—ah, I'm sorry, I don't know your name," Yannick said.

"Perrin," Perrin said. He quickly introduced the others and added, "We have gained allies."

Yannick looked out over the massed werebears and blanched. "They, um, there are certainly a lot of them," he managed.

"They will guard your retreat. Have you summoned the others?" Perrin asked.

"They're coming." He gestured to a pair of women who were corralling children. "Susa and Lannie will take the children now."

The fairer-haired of the two women looked up and saw the bears. She screamed and clutched two children to her. Alaric cursed. "No, it's all right, they're..." Yannick's words faded into silence.

"Ladies!" Perrin exclaimed, walking toward them. "You have nothing to fear. These creatures are here to help."

"Help with what?" the darker-haired woman said. "Yannick says something dangerous is coming—they look dangerous to me!"

Behind Clever, a brown bear shifted, became Bright. Both the settlement women screamed. Bright strode forward. "We do not mean you harm," she said, "but there is no time to convince you. You must trust that man who is your leader, and later will be the moment for discussion. But move quickly, because I did not want to come and I wish to be gone when the howler arrives."

A child of about five broke away from the women's protective huddle and ran toward the bears. The dark-haired woman screamed and tried to follow her, got tangled up in the rest of the children, and was too late to stop the girl from running to the nearest bear, shouting, *"Dog!"*

"Not a dog!" the woman cried. "Lilia, stop!"

Lilia threw her arms around the bear, who sat back on its haunches and regarded her with some bemusement. Then it nosed the child's ear, making the girl laugh and rub her face against the furry one. The woman stopped a few feet away, astonishment making her face a still, frozen mask. "Come back," she whispered.

The bear shivered, stretched wide, and turned into a black-skinned man crouched on the ground nose to nose with Lilia. Lilia jerked back, astonished. The man offered her his hand, which she took tentatively. He rose and led the child back to the woman. "My daughter is this young," he said. "She is also fearless."

The woman snatched the child into her arms, but didn't back away. "Were-creatures don't speak," she said, still whispering. "What are you?"

"Creatures who wish you no harm," the werebear said.

The woman's gaze flashed lower, then back to his face. Her cheeks reddened. "We are used to...more clothing than you are," she said.

The man smiled. "We apologize for our...immodesty. I will shift back if that will ease your mind."

The woman hesitated, then nodded once, sharply. The werebear stepped back and transformed, falling to all fours. They regarded each other closely. Then the woman, hesitating again, held out her hand palm-first to the bear, who pushed his black nose against it.

"I do not wish to interrupt," Perrin said, "but time is against us. The sun is setting fast, and we should not fight in darkness if we can help it."

The woman nodded. "We'll take the children west," she said, motioning to the other woman.

Clever turned to face the werebears. She said nothing, but a moment later ten of them left the formation to gather around the women and children. "Do you...speak mind to mind?" Sienne asked Wit in a low voice.

"Yes and no," Wit said. "It is a combination of mental speech and body language. Harder to speak in human form, but we're still capable of communicating that way."

"I do not understand," Kalanath said. "Why do they not fear?" He gestured toward the gathering settlers. "And why do they accept our story?"

"You see all sorts of strange things on the borders of the Empty Lands," Swift said. "They may have thought howlers were a story, but they've probably encountered enough monsters to believe in the impossible when someone they trust vouches for it."

Another howl split the air. It was so close and loud Sienne shivered despite the blessing. The massed ranks of werebears shuddered, and a few broke away to flee westward, not stopping even when Clever shouted after them. "It's here," Alaric said.

"It's too late," Dianthe said. "They'll never get away."

"That's why we're here," Alaric said. "Perrin, tell Yannick where we're going and that he needs to get the rest of his people moving westward. Don't bother with possessions, just flee. Everyone else..." He didn't have to finish the sentence.

Sienne opened her spellbook to *fury*. She wiped her sweaty palms one at a time on her trousers. Alaric caught her nervous gesture and smiled at her with such tender amusement it reassured her. They would win. They had to. Even if winning meant their deaths.

They left the settlement and walked north, surrounded by the werebear army. It was all open terrain for miles, with the forest a deep green mass on the horizon below the darkening sky, and there was no one in sight besides themselves. Sienne wiped her palms again. She didn't dare cast *sharpen,* to enhance her vision, or *jaunt,* to take her closer to the enemy, because even that small expenditure of magical energy could be fatal in the long run. Besides, there was no one to *jaunt* to.

Far in the distance, something pale moved against the darkness of the pines. It bounded, rose high into the air, and floated down again, a white blotch against the indigo sky. "It can fly," Dianthe said, despair touching her voice. "How are we supposed to stop something that can fly?"

"Sienne?" Alaric said.

"It's not flying, it's floating. Maybe enough *force* bolts will keep it on the ground," Sienne said. "I can cast—"

This time, the howl shook her to her core. She dropped her spell-book and covered her ears, cringing like a child in a thunderstorm. The werebears went wild, stampeding in all directions. Most of them ran toward the oncoming howler, others fled, and a few turned on their allies, snarling and tearing at their throats. A hand clamped around Sienne's arm. "Run," Alaric said, and dragged her stumbling along after him.

"That howl is going to destroy us before we can reach the monster," Dianthe shouted as they ran.

"If we could stop that, we might have a chance," Perrin said.

Sienne stopped, wrenching away from Alaric, and patted her legs frantically. "What's wrong?" Alaric exclaimed.

Sienne's hand landed on the thin, rigid shape of the *silence* wand. "I can shut it up, but I have to be close," she said. "And I don't dare use resources on *jaunt* in case I'm wrong."

Alaric looked around. "Is anyone watching?"

"They're all busy running or fighting each other," Dianthe said. "But you'll have to hurry."

Alaric took a couple of steps away. His body vibrated, making Sienne's eyes water. Then he was gone. In his place, a tall, powerfully muscled unicorn stood, the last light of the setting sun making his black horn gleam as if oiled. He bowed his head to Sienne. Sienne swallowed, let go of her spellbook, and with a boost from Kalanath pulled herself across the unicorn's broad back. "This is never not going to feel strange," she told Alaric, who tossed his head in agreement.

Then they were flying across the fields, Sienne clinging desperately with legs and hands to keep from being flung off by the speed of their passage. Carefully she let go with one hand and felt along her trouser leg where the *silence* wand lay. It was too bad she didn't share the kind of mental communication with Alaric that the weres did with each other, because she didn't know what to do after they reached the howler and she used the wand on it. Blast it with *fury*, yes, but she was terrifyingly aware of how unprotected her soft, human body was, and the howl was certainly not the creature's only weapon.

The howler was now distinguishable as a creature, and it was *enormous*, twice Alaric's height and so heavily muscled it looked deformed. Its huge hands were tipped with claws stained dark with old blood, and fresher blood outlined its mouth, full of jagged teeth that would tear its own flesh as well as its victim's. Cold poured off it like the heart of winter. In the growing darkness, it looked like something out of nightmares. Sienne drew the wand from its sheath along her trouser seam. If it howled when they were this close, even Perrin's blessing wouldn't protect them.

The howler's mouth opened. Alaric put on a final burst of speed. Sienne worked the opening magic on the wand and slashed it at the terrible creature. Blue-green light flared. The howler's mouth opened wider—and no sound emerged.

Alaric skidded to a halt and shrugged Sienne off. She landed on all fours and scuttled away as Alaric became human again, drawing his massive sword and aiming a swing at the howler's head. One of the howler's huge arms came up to block the blow, and the sword bounced off it like it was steel beneath the skin. "Sienne!" Alaric shouted. "Hit it *now!*"

Sienne's spellbook opened at a touch to *force*. Not as powerful as *fury*, but she couldn't risk hitting Alaric. She read through the spell as fast as she dared, for once relishing the acid-tinged taste of the sylla-bles, feeling the magic course through her until it shot away from her in a single burst. It took the howler square in the chest, shaking it so it didn't block Alaric's next swing. Once more the sword rebounded off the thing's hide. Alaric cursed and changed his grip, thrusting rather than slashing.

The howler let out another silent scream. Sienne cast *force* again, barely missing Alaric when he stepped between her and the howler. "Don't *do* that!" she shouted. Alaric ignored her, all his attention on the howler. Then Dianthe was beside her, and Kalanath, and half a dozen werebears, and she lowered her spellbook, breathing heavily. Too many people blocked her line of sight. She backed away, waiting for her moment.

The howler moved in a silence almost more terrifying than its howls had been. It snatched up a bear and flung it at the others, bowling three bears over. It grabbed another bear and buried its mouth in its throat, tearing it out in a gout of ruby blood that splat-tered Alaric and Dianthe. Throwing the corpse aside, it bounded forward, its cold black eyes fixed on Perrin, who held a blessing aloft. He invoked the shield just as the howler swung at him. Its clawed hand skittered off the surface of the pearly gray shield. Sienne, caught inside the shield with Perrin, felt her hands shaking from the nearness of their escape. "I think," Perrin said, his breathing labored, "it is drawn to me. Or, more accurately, to the power of Averran."

"I can make you invisible."

"That likely would not help. Whatever it senses is beyond things like sight and smell. We must kill it, and quickly."

"How can we kill it? Swords just bounce off," Sienne said.

"Magic, perhaps. The werebears' claws do damage—look there." Perrin pointed. One of the werebears had gotten behind the howler and reared up on his hind legs to slash the creature's back. It howled, or tried to, and spun with remarkable agility for something that bulky to swipe at the bear, who leaped back. Blood, darker red than a human's, trickled down its back from four parallel cuts.

Shreds of filmy gray drifted down from where the howler's claws had scored the shield. Sienne paced its confines. "Don't take this the wrong way," she said, "but this shield is far too effective."

Perrin smiled. "How unfortunate that there is not a personal version of it."

Sienne opened her book to *burn* and continued pacing. The howler tore at the shield again. Alaric thrust for its belly, and Sienne saw the skin yield—a little, just a little, but enough that the howler turned its attention from the shield and lunged for Alaric. Sienne screamed as it got one hand around Alaric's wrist and lifted him high in the air. She threw herself at the shield, drawing her belt knife and hacking at it. It felt tough, like gristle, and her knife barely penetrated. With its other hand, the howler grabbed Alaric's leg and pulled. Alaric screamed, a hoarse sound that hurt Sienne's heart. She slammed into the shield and finally felt it part, shoved her way through the slit, and brought up her spellbook to cast *burn*. *Scorch* was more powerful, but it would catch Alaric in the blast, so she settled for the fire that burned inside her, filling her until it lashed away from her to strike the thing in the face.

The howler's mouth contorted in agony. It had felt that. It dropped Alaric, who landed like a stone and didn't get up. Sienne wanted to go to him, but she was experienced enough to remember the best way to help a fallen companion was to kill the thing that had hurt him. Once more she cast *burn*, rejoicing at how the creature recoiled. They were winning, by Averran!

The howler crouched, then leaped high into the air, flying back toward the forest. "We can't let it get away!" she shouted, racing after it. It bounded off with great sailing leaps that took it farther away with every moment. She staggered to a halt. One last chance.

Swiftly turning pages, she began reading a new evocation, one that burned her tongue and lips with acid. The howler had nearly reached the forest. Orange light grew and coalesced in front of her, its heat scorching her face and hands. She spat out the last syllables, putting as much power into it as she could, and a ball of fire shot away from her, flying faster than the howler, expanding as it flew until it was fifteen feet across and blazed like a tiny sun.

It struck the howler in the back and engulfed it, clinging to its deformed body and sending flames licking along its limbs. This time, when the howler screamed, she heard its cry, not the terrible frightening howl but an agonized shriek. The creature plummeted to the ground and lay still.

Sienne collapsed to her knees, breathing heavily. It all seemed so unreal—the bears still fighting their maddened kin, the burning corpse lighting the evening like a cheery bonfire and not the remains of a terrible creature, and Alaric—

She pushed herself to her feet and staggered back to where she'd left her friends. Alaric lay unconscious, his arm in an unnatural position. "Dislocated," Perrin said. "We will have to restore the joint, and then I can heal him."

Kalanath had already arranged Alaric's body to give himself a good grip on the dislocated shoulder. With a quick lift and twist, it popped back into place. Alaric groaned and tried to sit up. "One moment," Perrin said, removing a healing blessing from the riffle of papers. Sienne knelt at Alaric's side and held his hand as the green light played across his body. Alaric winced, then opened his eyes. He sat up quickly and pushed himself to his feet. "Where is it?"

Sienne pointed. Alaric lowered his sword. "*Scorch,*" he said. "It's dead." The next moment, he shoved Sienne to one side, shouting, "Look out!"

Sienne fell to one knee, twisting to see what was behind her. The roar of a maddened bear split the night as something coal-black and slavering bore down upon her. She forgot about her spellbook and screamed, raising her hands to defend herself in a futile gesture. Then Alaric was between her and the bear, sword raised. "Don't hurt him!" she shouted. "It's not his fault!"

Alaric changed his grip on the sword and smashed the hilt, with its enormous round pommel, into the side of the bear's head. The werebear staggered backward, shook its head, and charged again, this time straight into a punch that knocked it to its knees. It stared up at Alaric, its small black eyes dim with confusion. "Wake up, you idiot," Alaric said. The bear sagged lower, and then it was a man, lying face-first on the ground and moaning.

"We have to stop the mad ones from hurting anyone," Dianthe said, and took off toward the settlement.

Alaric took a few rapid steps after her, then turned. "I think I should make sure the thing is dead," he said. "Sienne?"

They ran hand in hand toward the burning corpse, which smelled horribly of rot and burning tar. It was clearly dead, its face eaten away by flames, but Alaric prodded it a few times with his sword just to be sure. "How did you know the wand would do that? You took a terrible risk," he said.

"Because that's how *silence* works when you cast it on...oh." Sienne's cheeks felt warmer than the fire could account for. "I guess I never remembered to tell anyone I figured out what the wand does. Though it's true it might not have worked on something so powerfully magical."

"It's almost miraculous. The perfect weapon for this battle. Without it, we would likely all have died, either at the howler's hands or at each other's."

"Averran steered us toward Nocenti's treasure. Do you suppose this was why?"

"Who knows how avatars think? Aside from their priests." They turned and headed back toward the settlement. "I certainly believe Averran could have seen this conflict in our future."

The fighting was all but over when they returned. Too many people, werebears and humans, lay motionless near the settlement. Sienne was grateful none of the figures were tiny. They found Clever in human form talking to Yannick. Someone had found her an overlarge shirt that barely came to the tops of her thighs, but neither she nor Yannick seemed bothered by her state of undress. "We must carry our kin to where they can be honored," Clever was saying. "Then we will return and speak further."

"Do you bury your dead? It seems so human," Yannick said. Sienne winced. Clever ignored his gaffe.

"It is a private thing," she said. She saluted Alaric, one leader to another. "Your deeds are now the stuff of legend," she told him. "We thought killing a howler impossible."

"Thank Sienne," Alaric said. "And the artifact we believe Averran gave us."

"An avatar?" Clever looked Sienne over. "Then that is truly a marvel. As was the creature you summoned."

"Creature?" Sienne said.

"The horned beast that carried you into battle. I thought unicorns a myth. I suppose magic can do many things."

Sienne swallowed. "Yes, it can."

"Find the others, would you?" Alaric told her. "I'm going to make sure the children return safely. It's getting dark."

Sienne nodded and went in search of her friends. Near the closest building, she found Perrin tending to the wounded. "It is both good and bad news," he said when she approached. "Few people are seriously wounded enough to require divine healing. But that is because everyone seriously wounded was killed, either by the howler or by maddened allies."

"Did those people, the ones the howl made mad, did they recover?"

"They have been subdued and taken to where they cannot injure themselves or others. If they do not recover..." He shrugged. "It breaks my heart to think of them permanently in that state. Death may be the only option."

"Where's Dianthe and Kalanath? And Wit and Swift?"

"Kalanath is assisting with carrying the bodies for burial. The human bodies, that is. I believe Dianthe went in search of the children. I have seen neither Wit nor Swift."

"I'll go look for them. They were close to the howler—it might have injured them."

It was getting too dark to see, so she made a few lights and set them hovering around her shoulders. It probably made her look like Delanie, the Lady of Light, and she hoped no one would think her blasphemous. All around her, naked men and women carried the fallen bodies of their kin, most of them still in bear shape, back toward the werebear camp. She was struck by their silence, how no one was weeping or shouting the way humans might when confronted by premature, violent death. It felt surprisingly fitting that they should mourn that way.

She saw Wit, crouched beside a dead werebear with his back to her, his naked shoulders heaving as if he were crying. She approached him quietly, then thought maybe sneaking up on someone who was grieving was a bad idea, and tried to make more noise. "Wit? Is everything all right?" she asked.

Wit didn't respond. He was shaking, though the evening was warm and there were no breezes to cool the air. "Wit?" She laid her hand on his shoulder.

Wit jerked away and turned on her, snarling. His mouth and hands were covered in blood, and he clutched something rubbery that trailed tufts of brown fur matching that of the dead werebear in front of him. He raised it to his lips and tore off a hunk of flesh, chewing and slobbering over it.

Sienne took an involuntary step backward. Horror flooded through her as she realized he was eating his dead kinsman. Her mind gibbered in circles, paralyzing her. Just as she had the one coherent thought that she should stop him, he lifted his head and let out a soul-shattering howl.

18

She ran. The need to flee, to escape the horror before her, took control of her legs and propelled her away from the settlement, toward the distant mountains. Nowhere was safe. Another howl pierced the night, but she was already gone, her lights trailing behind her like comets chasing the moon.

She reached the forest and plunged into it, welcoming its shelter. It couldn't find her here. A nagging pain tugged at her midsection, an ache she didn't have time to fill. Hunger. It was hunger. Not an ordinary desire for comforting food, but a driving emptiness that only one thing could fill. She didn't know what that one thing was, but when she found it, she would sate herself on it and everything would be all right again.

She stumbled and fell, scraping her hands on the rough earth and pine needles underfoot, pushed herself to her feet and ran again. The terror that had propelled her into the night hadn't faded; something pursued her, something that crashed through the trees and breathed too heavily to be human. She couldn't scream, couldn't cry, because those were weaknesses that would open her to the Thing that followed her, would sap her strength and steal her breath and leave her helpless in its path. Her chest ached with a sharp, stinging pain, her feet hurt, but she kept running, praying that the Thing would lose interest if she ran far enough.

The lights had vanished, unable to keep pace with her. It was full dark under the trees, and she darted out of the way of one tree only to slam face-first into another. It knocked the breath out of her, and she clung to it, trying to suck in air and struggling to find her footing. Then she stopped moving and listened. The Thing was gone. Its heavy footsteps and labored breathing had vanished. Sobbing finally, she pressed her abraded cheek against the rough tree bark and tried to remember who she was. She had a name, she was sure of it, and she would remember it eventually.

When she felt confident she could stand without falling, she let go of the tree and stood rubbing her hands together. The ache in her stomach was growing. She peeled a strip of bark off the tree and bit it, wondering if this was the food she craved. It was bitter, and resinous, and she spat it out and went looking for something else. Dirt wasn't the answer, and neither was moss. She contemplated a couple of tiny stones she found beneath the moss before deciding they were inedible. She rubbed her stomach, wishing the small pressure could ease the hunger pains. Nothing worked.

She turned until she was facing west, then wondered how she knew which way west was. Something exerted a pull on her, telling her the way north, and it was easy to work out the other directions if you knew one of them, but where did the pull come from? *Magic*, she thought, and froze. Was she in the habit of thinking her thoughts in words? Yes, she was. Whoever she was, she could do magic and she carried on conversations with herself. She was strange.

She began walking westward, sniffing the air in case her craving manifested itself that way. Nothing smelled particularly appetizing. Nothing smelled nasty, either, which was probably for the best. She didn't like nasty smells, though she guessed most people didn't and that wasn't going to help her recall her identity. Magic, conversations, pleasant smells. It wasn't much to build a personality on.

Why was she going west? She vaguely remembered having fled eastward, and that there were people in the place she'd left behind.

Maybe one of them would know her. That felt right. Other people, friends—

Memory struck. Her name was Sienne, and she had friends, and a lover, and she'd run terrified into the woods away from all of them. Her stomach burned with hunger. She sped up, nearly ran into another tree, and stopped. Conjuring some magic lights, she took a look around. How far had she gone? She trotted on, fast enough to appease the part of her that was desperate to return to Alaric but not so fast that she collided with anything.

She came out of the forest and saw the settlement in the distance, with lights coming on at most of the windows. It was too dark to tell if all the bodies had been removed. She stumbled onward, feeling incredibly weary but unable to stop moving. She felt she might die of hunger. Maybe one of these people in the cottages would give her something to eat. She still had no idea what would assuage her burning need, but the hunger was great enough she didn't care.

She put on a final burst of speed and fetched up against a wooden door. Pounding on it with both fists, she called out, "Is anyone there? I'm so hungry!"

She heard wood scrape across wood, then footsteps crossing a creaky floor, and the latch slid open. A middle-aged man peered out. "Who are you?"

"Sienne. I helped kill the howler. Please, is there anything to eat?"

The man smiled. "You're one of our heroes! Come in, come in. Where are your friends?"

Sienne shook her head. "Somewhere. I need food, please, anything will do."

The man opened the door wider, and Sienne entered. Immediately she knew she'd found the right place. A delicious scent filled the one-room cottage, seeming to come from everywhere at once. It smelled like nothing she'd ever smelled before, but every other memory of good smells was dim and flat by comparison. It warred with the homelier scents of rabbit stew bubbling on the hearth and the piney aroma rising from the log walls. Sienne inhaled deeply, and the ache in her belly stabbed her once, making her double over.

"Miss? Are you well?" the man said, putting his arm around her shoulders for support. Sienne nearly choked on the delicious smell. It came from the man himself.

"Very well," she said, turning to bury her face in his side. The man jerked away, startled. Sienne followed him.

"Miss, I don't think...miss, you need to stop that, you're scaring me," the man said, once more edging away. Sienne wiped away a trace of saliva trickling from the corner of her mouth. She needed to eat, was desperate for it, and if this man could sate her craving, so much the better.

"Just one bite," she said, and lunged for him.

The man let out a cry somewhere between a shout and a squawk and ran for the door. Sienne beat him there. "I'm so *hungry*," she said. "Just let me feed."

Someone knocked on the door. "Sir? Is our companion within?" Perrin said.

Delight overrode the demands of her stomach long enough to let her turn and open the door. Of course they'd come looking for her. Perrin probably had a location blessing just for that. She flung herself on Alaric, who held her tightly. "Don't ever do that again," he whispered.

"She's sick. Something's wrong with her," the man said. "She said she wanted to...to eat me!"

Alaric's arms went rigid. Sienne burrowed into his embrace. He smelled even better than the man did. "I'm so hungry," she said, drew her knife, and stabbed Alaric's thigh.

The big man yelped and let go of her. Sienne raised the knife for a more direct hit. Someone grabbed her from behind, immobilizing her arms, someone who smelled delectable. Someone else broke her grip on the knife and took it away. That made Sienne panic, because how was she supposed to get food if she didn't have her knife? Her stomach hurt so badly it felt like it was caving in from hunger.

Tears slid down her cheeks. She stomped her heel on the foot of whoever was holding her arms and heard Kalanath shout. She twisted, and his hands slid just enough to let her get one arm free.

Then Alaric had her again, but this time his grip was rough and merciless. She kept fighting, though she knew there was no way she could break free of his grasp.

"Tie her," Alaric said. "She can't get free again."

Sienne screamed and thrashed as rope went around her wrists and ankles, trussing her securely. She managed to smack Kalanath in the face with the back of her head, but he just grunted and wrapped more rope around her wrists. Sagging, defeated, Sienne wept hot tears of fear and pain and tried once more. "I'm so hungry. Please. I just need to eat."

"We're sorry about this, sir," Alaric said to the settler. "She didn't hurt you, did she?"

"No. Just sniffed me and said some crazy things. She's not going to turn like the were-creature did, right?"

"Not if I can help it," Alaric said grimly. He hoisted Sienne over his shoulder and ducked out of the cottage's low door, carrying her away down the makeshift street.

The delicious smells were coming from every one of her friends. She just needed one of them, and then...wait, then what? If their flesh was what would satisfy this horrible hunger, didn't that mean she'd have to kill one of them? "No," she shrieked, "no, I won't do it! I won't! *I'm starving!*"

"Is it too late?" Dianthe asked.

"If she is still hungry, she has not fed, and there is still hope," Perrin said. "At least, that is my understanding of what Swift said."

"But what about..." Kalanath began, and fell silent.

"There's nothing we can do for Wit," Alaric said, his voice still flat and emotionless. "We have to save Sienne now."

Sienne, slung over Alaric's shoulder like a rolled carpet, couldn't see where they were going, so it was a surprise when they entered another house. This one was larger than the other man's, but not by much. Alaric deposited Sienne to lie on the room's one bed and stood back, hands on hips, examining her. "Sienne, how hungry are you?" he said.

The scent coming off him was overpowering. Sienne closed her eyes and tried to calm her breathing, which was coming in quick, sharp pants. "It hurts, Alaric, please, it hurts so much. I need to eat. I *need* it, don't you understand? To eat and eat and eat until I'm full."

"That's bad," Alaric said. "What can we do?"

"What we did for Wit," Perrin said. "Wait until morning, when I can pray for a blessing that might remove the curse. Keep her from feeding."

"But if she's that hungry, couldn't that starve her to death?" Dianthe's eyes were red, as if she'd been crying.

"Do you have a better solution?" Alaric asked. Dianthe turned away. In moving, she revealed something Sienne hadn't seen before: Wit, bound as she was as well as gagged, lying on the floor under the window. His eyes observed the room brightly, and Sienne shuddered, because there was no human intelligence behind them anymore.

Alaric crouched beside Sienne and stroked her hair. "Sweetlove, the howler turned Wit into one of its own," he said, "and Wit's howl touched you the same way. So long as you don't eat human flesh, you'll recover. It will be all right."

Tears spilled over Sienne's cheeks and dampened the blanket under her face. "But I'm so hungry," she whispered.

Alaric's own eyes were bright with unshed tears. "I know. You can't eat. Tomorrow everything will be better. We won't leave you alone tonight, I promise. You just have to be patient."

"Alaric, you are still bleeding," Perrin said. "Let me bind the wound. I fear I have no healing blessings left."

"Make it quick," Alaric said. "And then everyone should get comfortable. It's going to be a long night."

Sienne closed her eyes. A howler. She was this close to becoming a howler. She noticed Alaric hadn't said anything about *Wit* getting better. Was there any hope for him? She opened her eyes and found Wit staring at her. His inhuman eyes gleamed with malice, and she could almost hear him thinking at her: *You and I, we will hunt together. Feed, and we will be one. We will share the big one.* She shuddered and looked away, to where Perrin was bandaging the knife wound she'd given Alaric. "I'm sorry," she said, and felt almost relieved at the pang of guilt she felt. It was a real, clean emotion that had nothing to do with the hunger that claimed her.

Alaric smiled at her. "It's just a scratch. I'm glad I haven't taught you how to strike with a knife for real. Then we might have had a problem."

Sienne tried to smile, but her momentary feeling of relief had passed, and dread once more consumed her. Her stomach screamed at her to feed it. She struggled against her bonds once, and her friends all went still, watching her. It made her feel self-conscious and stupid and bitterly angry. Alaric was right, this was going to be a long night.

How long, she couldn't have guessed. The hunger kept her from sleeping, drove her to alternating bouts of shrieking at her friends to free her so she could feed on all of them and sobbing fits in which she cried hard enough to forget the pain briefly. Sometimes she varied the pattern by begging them to kill her. At one point, she tried untying her bonds with her invisible fingers and got as far as freeing her hands before they noticed and bound her more tightly.

Alaric never left her side. When she cried, he spoke quietly to her, reassuring her; when she shrieked, he ignored her curses and vicious threats and waited patiently for her to cycle around to crying again. To her babbled apologies he said only, "It's not you, sweetlove. This will pass." Her heart ached, her throat was raw with screaming, and still the hunger wouldn't let her sleep. Whenever her eye fell on Wit, the hunger redoubled, as if he had some way of intensifying it, but she couldn't stop watching him. Nobody else paid attention to him, a thing she thought, in her more coherent moments, was a mistake. She wasn't sure, but she thought he looked bigger than before, more muscular. Whatever had happened to him, she feared it wasn't something Averran could fix.

She was looking at Wit during one of her bouts of sobbing when her eye was drawn to the window above him. The night sky was fading, turning pale rose and gold. Morning.

Alaric noticed the direction of her gaze and looked to Perrin. "I don't know how much longer she can endure this," he said. "I know it's early, but..."

"I will try," Perrin said. "Were I a priest of Sisyletus rather than Averran, I am certain my request would be answered immediately, as Sienne has demonstrated tremendous endurance these past hours. But Averran..." He shook his head. "I will do this outside. I fear I would be distracted here."

That made Sienne feel even more guilty. Despite Perrin's words, she didn't think she'd shown much endurance, what with the screaming and the crying and the begging. She closed her eyes, tried to ignore the hunger, and prayed, *O Averran, I can't take much more of this. Please wake early, just this once.*

Peace touched her heart briefly, startling her so much she forgot to think about her hunger. She drew in a surprised breath, and Alaric said, "What? What's wrong?"

"Nothing's wrong. For a moment, I felt...better."

Alaric brushed hair away from her face. "Everything will be all right. I swear it."

"Should you swear a thing you cannot control?" Kalanath said. He sounded as weary as Alaric.

"I will turn this world upside down to find a cure for her," Alaric said.

"We still don't know what to do with Wit," Dianthe said. She jabbed a thumb in his direction. "If he can't be cured..."

"Then we'll let Clever deal with him," Alaric said flatly. "She has the right."

"It's her brother," Dianthe said. "Isn't that cruel, to make her... dispose of him?"

"Crueler to pass the duty to someone else," Alaric said.

The door opened. All eyes turned to Perrin, who was sweating, his long hair falling loose around his face. He was also smiling. In one hand, he held what looked like a flat orange cake. He crossed to kneel beside Sienne. "Help her sit," he said.

When she was upright, he brought the cake to her lips. "You must eat it all," he said. Sienne shied away from it. It smelled greasy, like rancid oil. "No, do not flinch," Perrin commanded. "Eat, and you will be free of this curse."

Sienne looked at Alaric, who nodded encouragement. She opened her mouth, and Perrin held the cake so she could bite into it. It tasted worse than it smelled, not only of rancid oil but of dust and raw meat and mold. She gagged on the first bite and made herself swallow, then, breathing heavily, took another bite. If this was Averran's sense of humor at being roused just after dawn, she didn't want to be around when he was truly angry at someone.

Nothing changed. Her stomach still burned with the need for human flesh, and the gagging didn't help. She controlled her tears and took another bite. Crying wouldn't help and it would just make her friends feel worse. She caught sight of Wit, who for once didn't have that malicious gleam of humor in his eye. In fact, he looked afraid. The sight gave her strength to take another bite, and another, chewing more rapidly as the end neared. Finally, she let Perrin put the last of the cake in her mouth, and swallowed it almost without chewing.

Orange light filled her vision. She cried out, but it didn't hurt, just blinded her briefly. A feeling of peace swept over her, clearing away the pain and terror and filling her with happiness. She realized the aching hunger was gone, leaving her not only free from the nagging lust but from the aches of having her arms and legs bound. She closed her eyes and breathed out a long sigh of relief. "It's gone," she said. "The hunger...it's gone. I feel wonderful."

Dianthe produced a knife from somewhere and swiftly cut Sienne's bonds. The instant she was free, Alaric took her in his arms and held her so tightly she squeaked. "I won't apologize for that," he said.

"Don't let go."

"I won't." He kissed her forehead, then looked up at Perrin, who stood watching them both. "You look grim."

"Averran was quick to grant my request for curing Sienne," Perrin said. "But no amount of pleading produced a similar solution for Wit. I am afraid it is too late for him."

Wit once more had the cunning, hard look about his eyes. There was nothing left of the man they'd come to know. Sienne buried her face in Alaric's shirt so she wouldn't have to look at Wit. "That means he has to die, doesn't it," she murmured.

"He's a howler," Alaric said. "Wit is already dead."

19

The following morning, just as dawn turned the eastern skies rosy, Sienne and her friends stood at the edge of a new clearing and watched the werebears bid farewell to their fallen kin. The pyres lay close together, enough that walking between them when they were burning high would be impossible. The weres had died in bear form, and hadn't reverted to human when they died. Sienne wasn't sure why she'd expected that. It wasn't as if one form were more natural to them than the other.

The nearest pyre bore the lone human form among the dead. Wit's face was peaceful, not vicious and mindless as it had been the last time Sienne saw him. The small gash where Clever's knife had taken him in the chest had been cleaned of blood. It looked so innocuous a thing to have caused a man's death. She stared at him, willing herself to remember him as he'd been and not as the monster he'd become. Alaric was right; Wit had been dead the moment he'd taken his first bite of werebear flesh. And she'd come so close to joining him. She wiped tears away, not sure who she was crying for, Wit or herself.

Alaric put his arm around her. "Try not to think about it," he said. He understood her mind better than she did. "You're safe, and Wit's body won't be used to commit any more horrors. He would have welcomed death if he'd known the alternative."

"It's hard when there's no one to blame," she whispered. "It's so senseless."

"Death usually is."

The watching weres, all in human form, moved to allow Test passage between them to the first of the pyres. He was followed by a younger were with golden skin who carried a burning torch. Test turned to face the others, regarding them silently. That they were communicating in the way Swift had described became clear when the crowd shifted to bear form as one, squatted back on their haunches, and let out a short cry something between a bark and a howl. It echoed through the clearing and floated away into the sky. Sienne hoped the avatars were watching, and that the cry would touch their hearts. It was impossible now to think of werebears as being any less deserving of God's mercy than a human.

Test took the torch from his assistant and touched it to the nearest pyre. Sienne didn't know what they'd treated the wood with, but it went up as readily as if it had been drenched with oil. The smell of wood smoke curled up from the pyre, rousing her hunger—they hadn't yet eaten. It embarrassed her, made her feel weak and disrespectful of the dead. And she hadn't yet come to terms with her body's demands for food, remembering all too clearly the terrible lust for human flesh that had consumed her. That specific craving no longer troubled her, but she irrationally feared its return.

Test moved on to the next pyre, and the next, and the crowd returned to human form and fractured into small groups, each attending a different pyre. Sienne no longer felt discomfort at seeing so many naked people all together. She wished she'd known the weres who'd died, to honor them properly, but she had to settle for looking long at each group and wishing peace to his or her kin.

A woman detached herself from the rest and approached them. "Thank you," Clever said. "More of us would have died if not for you."

"None of you would have died if you hadn't joined the fight," Alaric said. "We owe *you* thanks."

"You spoke truth. We are people, not animals, and if we wish to be accorded those rights, we ought to behave as such." Clever turned to Sienne and bowed. "I have a thing to ask of you. Test is...concerned about the state of Wit's soul. He believes an ordinary pyre might not be enough to cleanse his flesh of the howler's taint."

"You want a magical fire?" Sienne nodded. "Of course. I'd be happy to."

"No human has ever participated in our funeral rites before. It marks another change." Clever smiled. "Bright would not be happy."

"I'm sorry for your loss," Sienne said, only partly meaning it. "I'm sure her death is a tremendous blow."

"Her death in battle restores her honor," Clever said. "She knew she would have far to go to regain my trust. That she acted against you, Sienne, believing she did what was best for our people does not change the fact that she tried to kill a guest. That is a serious breach of our laws—something a law-speaker would have known. I apologize again on her behalf."

"Thank you," Sienne said. "What about the ones I had to attack? What happens to them?"

"They believed they were authorized to attack you, and were horrified to learn Bright was acting alone. I believe their penitence and choose to forgive them. I hope you will accept my apology for them as well."

"It makes me glad I didn't use something more deadly."

"I as well." Clever inclined her head to Alaric. "Are we still in agreement? You will speak with the king for us?"

"We will. Who will you send with us? Swift?"

"Yes. It will give him something to distract him from his grieving. And he understands humans better than the rest of us." Clever turned in response to a signal Sienne couldn't hear, lifting her head as if listening. "Test is ready. The other pyres are all lit."

Test was crossing the clearing toward them, his path weaving to avoid the stumps of the trees sacrificed for the pyres. "She will do it," Clever said when he was near enough.

"Thank you," Test said in his creaky voice. "It is fitting."

Sienne walked toward Wit's pyre. It was waist-high to her, its logs forming a solid foundation like a campfire she herself might have built. Like the fires she'd built for Wit to cook on while they traveled. She swallowed tears and cleared her throat. "I'm sorry it ended like this," she said. "I hope Perrin is right, and God's mercy encompasses you."

She read out the spell *burn* with calm deliberation, savoring each syllable despite the bitter acid tinging them, the last gift she could give her friend. The power built within her, burning her chest until it shot away from her in a streak of blue fire. It struck the pyre and spread as rapidly as the ordinary fire had, burning hot and fierce enough she had to take a few steps back as it scorched her face. Wit's body looked gray in the blue light and crackled as it was devoured.

She felt her friends' presence as they came to join her. No one spoke. It seemed fitting to let Wit burn with only the voice of the fire as a final tribute. They watched in silence until the pyre collapsed, burying what was left of Wit in its remains. Test said, "It is enough. Will the fire burn itself out, or is it magical?"

"It will die when it's out of fuel," Sienne said.

"Then you need not stay longer," Test said.

Alaric put his arm around Sienne and steered her away from the pyre. She was grateful for his guidance, because she felt she might otherwise stare at the blue flames until they were gone. "Food," he said, "and then we start for home."

"No," Sienne said. "We have something else to take care of first."

———

THERE WAS NO QUESTION, THIS TIME, THAT THE ROOM FILLED WITH ritual was not anywhere near the ruin. The small round windows showed not midday light, but a starless night that blended with the domed roof. Sienne stood in front of her ritual and scribbled the details in her notebook. Its contents were now more precious than all the treasure in Nocenti's chest.

"We should copy all of these," Alaric said. "Who knows what value they might have?"

"You don't suppose we went back in time as well as moving elsewhere, do you?" Dianthe said. "Given how well-preserved this place is."

"Pray, do not give me more to worry about," Perrin said. He was walking around the center of the room, examining the floor. Sienne had seen only that it was a mosaic of some sort before the writing on the walls had claimed her attention. "I do not care for this image. It is unsettling."

"What is it?" Kalanath asked, going to join him.

Perrin scuffed away dust with the toe of his boot. "People praying, or at least that is how I interpret their kneeling, penitent stance. And this, in the middle—it is a symbol, but not one of any avatar I know."

Kalanath crouched and swiped his hand across it. "*Good God,*" he said in Omeiran. Sienne's head jerked up. She'd never heard Kalanath blaspheme before.

"What did you say?" Perrin asked.

Kalanath stood and walked away. Sienne finished writing the ritual in her notebook and turned to watch him. He strode to the doorway and stood with his right hand clenched on the frame. His left hand held his staff so hard his knuckles were pale against his dark skin. Then he thrust himself away from the door and paced before it, turning rapidly in his agitation.

"Kalanath?" Sienne asked. "Is something wrong?"

"I do not know if I should say," Kalanath said.

"If it's something important, we should know about it," Dianthe said.

"It is not—no, it may be important. But it is not for me to speak. It is sacred."

Alaric approached him. "You mean, something you're sworn not to reveal."

Kalanath nodded. "I do not follow my religion as I once did," he said. "In some ways, I am no longer Omeiran. To be Omeiran is to be one with God—do you understand?"

Sienne shook her head, but Perrin said, "Do you mean that being Omeiran is in part a religious observance, and not just a matter of birth or homeland?"

"Yes. That is it. We are Omeiran and we are one with God. I am not—" He resumed pacing. "I rejected God when I left. It is not a thing I can share now. Please understand."

"But there are plenty of Omeirans in Fioretti," Sienne said, "and they have places of worship and follow your dietary code."

"Yes. No. It was not leaving that did it. It was that who I am—that I was the one who left. And the way I left."

"You don't have to tell us now," Alaric said. "You have a right to privacy. But we're your friends, and I hope you know that if you can tell anyone, you can tell us."

Kalanath nodded again. "I...think I will. But not in this place. Not with that—" He jabbed his staff in the direction of the mosaic —"watching."

"All right, Kalanath, you *have* to tell us something," Sienne said. "Because now I'm scared."

Kalanath let out a deep breath. Slowly, he walked back to the mosaic, his staff held ready to strike. "You know that we believe God is one," he said. "That She speaks to us without the need to appear in human form. But we also believe God is many." He shook his head. "Not many people. Many...intents. Many powers. God as creator. God as healer. God as defender. That is how She is many. And since we do not show God as human, we have symbols to show Her in Her many powers. That is one of them."

"An Omeiran religious symbol in a Rafellish ruin?" Perrin said. "Then perhaps we are elsewhere, after all."

"What symbol?" Alaric said. He was watching Kalanath closely, regarding him like an owl stalking a mouse.

Kalanath drew in a deep breath. "God as destroyer," he said.

All of them took an involuntary step back. Perrin took two more steps so he was no longer standing on the mosaic. "People worshipping God as destroyer?" he said. "Or does it have a different significance in your culture?"

"It does," Kalanath said. "We believe God does not destroy as a whim. She destroys to make room for something new. This means change, this picture. But it is not pleasant change. God sees far enough that She knows what will make us happy for a long time, not what will make us happy now. And the kind of change that makes for long happiness hurts. To worship God as destroyer..." He appeared to be searching for words. "It is when you reach beyond your grasp. To take pride in being given challenges because you think you are too good to fail."

"Hubris," Perrin said. "You mean it is prideful to worship God in this...power?"

"Yes. We are not to fear God as destroyer, because She loves us to give us this change, but we are not to seek Her out. This—" He tapped the symbol. "This makes me wonder what the reason for this room was. Knowledge, because of the rituals, but knowledge for what?"

"I wonder," Alaric said, but whatever his thought was, he didn't complete it.

"But it doesn't mean the rituals are evil, right? I mean, that's not an evil thing, if it's about God," Sienne said.

"I think the rituals are just rituals," Kalanath said. "And they used the rituals for gaining knowledge that would make a change."

"And yet everything's written in Ginatic," Alaric mused. "Why Omeiran symbols in a pre-Rafellish building?"

"We don't know how much contact there was between Omeira and the ancients," Sienne said. "They might have worked together on scholastic things. Or even magic."

"Omeirans do not have wizards," Kalanath reminded her.

"They don't *now*. Who knows what things were like four hundred years ago? Besides, don't you think it's strange that no Omeirans are born wizards? It's not like you're not human, and even people from the southern continent and from Chysegar can be wizards."

"I do not know," Kalanath said. "This suggests they knew something of magic, if this place is as old as you think."

"Sienne, copy as many of the rituals as you can make out," Alaric said. "Perrin, can you sketch the mosaic? Kalanath, is it blasphemous to copy that symbol?"

"Not blasphemous, but not safe," Kalanath said. "To carry it with us is like asking for God's presence in that power. We do not want to call down destruction on ourselves. Besides, I know it and will not forget it."

"All right. Don't copy the symbol, Perrin. Let's wring as much knowledge from this place as we can, and then I want to be on the road no matter how late it is."

Knowing what time it was inside the midnight chamber was impossible, but Sienne was still surprised to find it was just after noon when they emerged. She stopped to look back at the ruin just before they left the clearing to return to the werebears' camp. "Do you suppose we should warn the werebears?" she asked. "If that ruin takes you to some other place, or some other time—"

"They've been using it for years and nothing has ever happened," Alaric said. "We can tell Clever what we suspect and let her decide what to tell her people."

Sienne wasn't sure that was good enough, but she had to admit she hadn't felt any evil coming from the place. Even the symbol had felt innocuous, Kalanath's story notwithstanding. She turned to follow Alaric into the forest. With the notebook and its precious contents stowed safely in her pack, she felt confident in a way she hadn't felt in the weeks since she'd begun actively searching for rituals. Knife, goblet, sedative potion, and full ritual. Now they just needed to know if the wizard had altered the second half of the ritual, and they'd be in a position to figure out how to undo the binding the Sassaven were under. It filled her with heady delight.

Back in the camp, they tracked Swift down at the speaking tent. "Clever and Yannick are talking," he said in a low voice. "She asked you to enter when you arrived."

Alaric raised his eyebrows, but pushed open the tent door for Sienne to go first. Clever and Yannick sat opposite each other on the tiny stools, their conversation breaking off when Sienne entered.

Yannick rose, but Clever remained seated. "Thank you for speaking with me before you leave," Clever said.

"Not to be rude, but is there anything left to say?" Alaric said. "We have an understanding between us that we'll take to the king, along with Swift as the first emissary of your people."

"Yannick and I have discussed further," Clever said, "about the relationship between weres and humans, or at least between this camp and the human settlement."

"I'd like you to tell the king that we support the weres becoming citizens," Yannick said. "If he knows at least some humans are willing to accept them as people, he might be more willing to grant their request."

"That's...generous of you," Alaric said. "Are all the settlers in agreement?"

"Most of them. Enough that we intend to help them build a permanent home."

"What if the king rejects their plea?" Sienne blurted out. "They won't be citizens and they'll still live nearby."

Yannick shrugged. "This is the frontier. Not a lot happens out here for the king to get upset about. We tend to live our lives free from government interference. By the time the king finds out we're living cheek by jowl with intelligent weres, it will be a settled thing. And maybe that will change his mind."

"I'm sorry," Dianthe said. "I find it hard to believe your people are that well-adjusted."

"That howler went a long way toward reminding us what the real monsters are in this world," Yannick said. "The weres have saved our lives, protected our children, and we've never seen a single bear attack since the settlement began. Some of us are more wary than others, but they'll come around. Particularly once a few more of us have seen this place. No offense," he said to Clever, who inclined her head in acknowledgement.

"We will work together to build permanent homes," Clever said. "With the humans' help, we should be protected come the winter. It is a start."

"Thank you," Alaric said, clasping Yannick's hand. "Let's hope the king is as understanding as you all are." He saluted Clever. "And that he's willing to hear us out."

"We owe you much," Clever said. "Return someday, and we will honor you with a feast that lasts three days."

"I think even I could eat my fill in that time," Alaric said with a smile.

Swift rose from where he squatted on the ground when they emerged. "Time to go?" he said. "I'm past ready."

"Time to go," Alaric said. "I hope you have some stories to pass the time."

"Plenty of stories," Swift said. "But I'll never tell 'Grizel and the Howlers' again."

20

A rare true summer storm brought them within sight of Fioretti seven days later. They took shelter at the nearest waystation and sat in the common room, listening to the rain pound the roof and crash against the windows. It had blown in from the east, and Sienne thought about the werebear camp and wondered if they had stayed dry when it struck. How far had they gotten in building homes? Those snug little one-room buildings would be such a comfort when it rained, or snowed.

"I wish the damn rain would give up and go drown someone else," Alaric griped. "This is ridiculous. It's like the sky is begging for attention."

"You're just impatient because we're so close to home," Dianthe said.

Alaric glanced at Sienne. "Nothing wrong with that."

Sienne blushed. It had been far too long since they'd made love, and she'd felt the need for the reassurance of sex ever since that long, hungry night. Alaric's intent gaze told her he was thinking the same thing.

"How long before we can see the king?" Swift said. He was once again dressed in ordinary Rafellish clothing instead of a shapeless tunic, courtesy of the men at the settlement, and looked perfectly human, if a trifle dark-skinned for a Rafellish and too pale for an Omeiran.

"I'll make my request as soon as we reach Fioretti," Sienne said. "After that, I don't know. Either the festivities mean he's too busy to see anyone, or he'll have plenty of time because no one dares approach him during the festivities."

"I can't believe they're still going on," Alaric muttered. "You'd think two weeks was enough of a celebration for anyone, but no, they have to go on nearly a full month."

"You're in a mood," Dianthe said. "You've been nothing but irritated ever since we headed west."

"Have I?" His brow furrowed. "I don't know. I suppose I'm just ready for this to be over."

"I'm glad the celebration is still going on," Sienne declared. "We still haven't gone dancing."

Alaric's frown deepened. "I was hoping you'd forgotten about that."

It stung. "Oh," she said. "We don't have to, you know."

"We—" Alaric closed his eyes and let out a deep breath. "I'm sorry. I don't know what's wrong with me. You know I don't mind dancing with you."

Sienne managed a smile, but the hurt didn't fade. It was always a joke between them, Alaric putting up resistance to going dancing, but still a joke. That hadn't felt like joking. She wished she had him alone to figure out what was really troubling him.

Perrin stood and walked to the window. "The rain is letting up. I believe we might continue, if we do not mind becoming slightly damp."

Alaric stood, shoving back his chair with unnecessary force. "We'll dry. Let's go."

Fioretti after a hard rain looked bright and new, the smells of thousands of people and animals in one relatively small space swept away, replaced by fresh, damp air mingled with the briny ocean breezes. Sienne patted Spark's mane. "Ready for home?" she said. "I know they took good care of you at the outpost, but it's not the same as your own stall." Spark nodded agreement, making Sienne laugh.

The rain had cleared away much of the traffic, but men and women were once again taking to the streets, and Sienne found herself caught up into an impromptu parade by a string of revelers in costumes topped by elaborate animal heads. Worshippers of Lisiel, probably, the avatar who loved guile and trickery in the cause of justice. She let them sweep her along toward the stables, then fought her way free, laughing at the broad-shouldered men who turned cart-wheels and handsprings around her, begging her to stay. How they kept their ungainly deer or cat heads on while they were upside down, she had no idea. Maybe it was a blessing that did it.

She passed the men and women who loitered at the stable yard gate, chatting and watching the passersby, and dismounted beside Dianthe. "That was fun," she said. "It must be exciting, worshipping Lisiel. All those parties."

"All that deception, you mean," Dianthe said. "I don't think I could stand it, keeping track of the stories I'd told people."

"I didn't know Lisiel encouraged lying."

"Not lying. Not to your friends and family. But Lisiel likes a good story well told, and if you do it in the service of justice, she likes it even more. Though I've heard her priests and divines never turn away a dedication, even if they suspect it was stolen." Dianthe shook her head. "I've never really understood how Lisiel's worshippers think."

Sienne privately thought Dianthe, with her less-than-legal skill set, ought to be a prime candidate for a worshipper of Lisiel. "I think it's interesting, how the avatars are all different faces of God," she said as she led Spark to her stall and handed her reins to a stable hand. "And how they can seem to be at odds with each other."

"To enhance our understanding of God, no doubt," Perrin said, coming up behind them. "Though I will leave such contemplation to the priests of Delanie, who say the search for knowledge is of para-mount importance. I have enough to do divining the will of one avatar, let alone several."

Alaric and Kalanath approached from the far side of the stables. "Sienne," Alaric said, "what next?"

"Why are you asking me?"

"Because the next step is down to you. Do you want to go immediately to the palace to request an interview? Or home, to clean up? And I suppose you should at least send word to your parents that you've returned." Alaric's tone of voice told her clearly which of those options he preferred.

"I think we should all get cleaned up, and talk to Master Tersus about renting Swift—I mean, *Lucan*—a room," she said. "Because there's the very slim possibility the king will be able to see us at once, and I'd rather not show up looking disheveled."

"I do not think he will mind," Kalanath said. "He is not usual."

"No, but *I'd* mind," Sienne said. "It probably won't matter. It's more likely we'll have to wait a few days. But cleaning up...oh, how I want a bath!"

The cluster of people around the gate was heavier than usual. The Lizzorno stables were a Fiorettan landmark, being large and easily noticed from a distance, and people frequently gathered there to meet friends or listen to the latest gossip. Sienne followed Alaric, who as usual broke the crowds with no effort, and gasped as someone laid a hand on her arm. Rance, again? She jerked away reflexively and turned on her would-be assailant. But the stranger, dressed in her parents' livery of green and gold, quickly withdrew his hand and bowed. "Lady Sienne?" he said. "Your parents wish you to wait upon them immediately."

"How long have you been waiting here?" Sienne asked. Surely her parents wouldn't have set someone to watching the stable for weeks, waiting for her return.

The servant bowed again. "Master Macchari had an augury indicating that you would return on this day, at this hour."

"Sienne, what's wrong?" Alaric said. Sienne turned away from the servant to find her friends gathered around her. They were all blocking the entrance, which Sienne was sure the stable master wouldn't like.

"My parents want to see me," she said, moving away from the gate and drawing the rest of them, including the servant, with her. "I have to get cleaned up," she told the servant. "I'll be there in a couple of hours."

"My lady, I'm afraid my instructions are to bring you immediately," the servant said.

Alaric laughed. "How were you planning to do that? Carry her away?"

The servant, who was short and slight, bowed to Alaric. "I would not lay hands on Lady Sienne. I was instructed to remind her of the duty she owes her parents, and inform her that they are unconcerned about her state of attire. You have been gone nearly three weeks, my lady, and the duke and duchess are naturally concerned."

Sienne closed her eyes and mentally bid farewell to her hot bath and comfortable bed with Alaric. "Did they say why they wanted me to come?"

"I was not privy to that information, my lady."

"Of course not." She sighed. "All right. I'll come."

"Should we come with you?" Dianthe asked.

"No, it's all right. This won't take long." She kissed Alaric, whose brow looked like thunder. "Save some hot water for me?"

To her surprise, the servant had a carriage waiting down the street. Sienne hadn't ridden in a carriage in...she counted back the months. Well over a year. She tried not to come into too much contact with the satin upholstery, in her trousers that hadn't been washed in three weeks and her boots still mucky from the damp stable yard.

Fioretti looked different from this height, and not just because she had a better vantage than when she was walking. It was that everyone stared at her, or maybe it was just the carriage, painted in vivid dark green and gold with the Beneddo coat of arms on the door. The roof wasn't raised, and the cushions weren't so much as damp, so they'd trundled it out after the storm was over, which meant someone really had known exactly when she would return. The knowledge made her uncomfortable. She couldn't imagine what was so urgent that her parents needed to see her immediately.

The carriage drove up to the door of number 4, Plaza of Sighs, and the servant hopped down to help her out. She accepted his hand even though she hardly needed it, not wearing a gown. The servant then trotted ahead of her to knock on the door. Pagani opened it so quickly Sienne was sure he'd been standing there for an hour, waiting. "My lady," he said, bowing, "welcome. May I show you to the drawing room?"

Sienne, now thoroughly unnerved, let him lead the way even though she knew which door it was. To her relief, the room was empty. If her parents had been seated inside, that would have been too much for her to handle. She sat on an uncomfortable chair after Pagani closed the door and twiddled her thumbs in her lap to stop her hands shaking. She was being stupid. Her parents were probably just concerned that she'd been gone so long, even though she'd told them how long the journey was likely to take. And her mother consulted Lorne Macchari on everything, so asking him for an augury about Sienne's return wasn't unusual.

The door opened. "Sienne, you're safe," her father said, coming to embrace her. "We were worried."

"You shouldn't have," Sienne said, suppressing memories of a gnawing hunger. "I was fine. The job is almost over and—"

"*Almost* over?" her mother said. "Why 'almost'?"

"We just have one or two things to do here in the city. It's really nothing."

"Well, you're not leaving again," Papa said.

His tone of voice, so certain, irritated her. "Not any time soon, certainly."

"Sit," Papa said, and took a seat opposite her. Sienne sat, still irritated. "We've discussed the matter with our law-speakers, and they're in agreement. As the patriarch of this family, I have the right to forbid activities I deem detrimental to our family's well-being."

"'Forbid'? 'Detrimental'? Did they teach you that line?"

Papa didn't rise to the bait. "You're our heir, Sienne. The decree disinheriting Felice came through last week. It's official. And as our heir, you have obligations, one of which is to abstain from activities that might jeopardize your life. Which, according to law, includes scrapping."

Sienne shot to her feet. "You can't do that. I'm not a child anymore!"

"This has nothing to do with your age," Mother said. "You owe it to us not to risk your life in the wilderness. Lorne scryed you out—"

"You *spied* on me? How dare you!"

"We were worried, Sienne. And we wanted to reassure ourselves that you were well." Papa shook his head. "You were in the middle of a fight—attacked by werebears, and by that *thing* that nearly tore your Alaric apart—Sienne, you lied to us!"

"I did not. I told you scrapping was dangerous." Fortunately, they hadn't spied on her when she was in the throes of the howler's madness, or they would be far more distraught.

"But not that that danger included combat! We thought it was just the danger of the wilds, or the Empty Lands."

"I'm sorry you didn't understand what 'dangerous' meant." She sat down and tried to rein in her anger before she said something truly offensive. They meant well, even if they were going about it all wrong. "But I've survived every danger scrapping has thrown at me because I'm sensible and have reliable friends and I'm *powerful*. Did you see that part? I destroyed that monster with my magic. Me, Sienne Verannus. Yes, scrapping is dangerous, but it's not impossibly so. And it's certainly not something you need to worry about."

"I'll decide that, Sienne." Papa's voice was cold and not at all reassuring. "You've had your fun, and it's time for you to take up your responsibilities. I want you to move in here for the last week before we return to Beneddo. It's better you give up this life at once rather than drag it out."

For a moment, Sienne forgot how to breathe. Give up this life? "What?" she managed finally. "You can't be serious."

"What did you think was going to happen, Sienne?" Mother said. "That you could go on as you have been? You're not a scrapper. You're a lady, heir to a dukedom. It's time for you to settle down." She pursed her lips. "And get married. *Not* to your Ansorjan lover."

"There's nothing wrong with Alaric!"

"Except for the small matter of his being sterile." Mother met Sienne's eyes directly. "Lorne scryed out your future children. Your liaison with Alaric doesn't lead there. We know he can't have children."

Her vision was fogging over again because she'd once more forgotten to breathe. She had no idea what Lorne had seen, except that if he'd seen Alaric's true race, Mother and Papa would have gone at this differently. He'd seen children in her future? Impossible.

"You have to produce your own heir, Sienne," Papa said. He looked profoundly uncomfortable, probably because the idea of his daughter having sex was something he'd rather not entertain. "I'm truly sorry. We know you're attached to him. But—"

Sienne found herself on her feet without knowing how she got there. "I'm leaving," she said. "And I won't come back until you've come to your senses. You can't order me to give up Alaric and you can't order me to give up my life. I'm going to petition to see King Derekian and ask him to disinherit me. I don't care if that makes your lives difficult. I'd be a terrible duchess and I'll be an even worse mother to whatever brats I'd spawn from whoever you order me to marry, and I guarantee you would have to make it an order."

Her parents continued to regard her dispassionately. "We thought you'd say that," Papa said. "You won't be allowed to leave."

"Excuse me?"

"Lorne invoked a blessing on this house to prevent you leaving by magic. No transport spell will work within ten feet of it, in all directions. Including ten feet above the roof."

Sienne's jaw dropped. "You what?"

"We underestimated your abilities the last time you ran away. Not again." Papa's voice was calm, not at all as if he'd just aimed a knife at her throat.

"That won't stop me walking out of here."

"Our servants have orders to prevent you leaving," Mother said, "and we have guards posted at the doors to do the same. Not forever. Just until you come to your senses."

Sienne snapped her spellbook open. "How, exactly, did you expect to stop me *force*-blasting my way out? You should have taken my spellbook the second I stepped through the door. Not that I'd have made it easy on you."

Her parents looked at each other, then back at her. "You'd attack innocents just to get your way?" Papa said. "How far do you think you'll get after we set the law on you for illegal use of magic within city limits?"

Sienne opened her mouth to reply, then snapped it closed again. She could make a case for kidnapping, but they'd arrest her anyway while they sorted it out. And she had a sinking feeling that her father's words about his rights as patriarch might mean the law didn't consider it kidnapping at all. "Damn you," she said. "And don't you dare yap at me about my language."

"We've had a room readied for you," Mother said, "and someone will draw you a bath. You look as if you need it."

"I don't want a bath. I don't want any of this." A thought occurred to her. "They'll come looking for me. Alaric will break down that door and fight every one of your people if you don't let me go."

"He'll be arrested for assault," Papa said. "Is that what you want?"

"Then you should let me go to him. It's not fair to them for me to simply disappear. I have to explain."

"You can send a message."

"They deserve more than a stupid letter, Mother."

Mother pursed her lips. "Forgive me, but we don't trust you not to disappear again. You did it once with, I imagine, less provocation. A letter will have to do." She gestured in the direction of a writing desk. "There is paper and ink in the desk. I promise your message will be delivered immediately."

"And you'll read over my shoulder so I don't plan a daring escape."

"Sienne, this is for your own good," Papa said.

Sienne laughed bitterly. "It was for my own good when you wouldn't let me marry Rance, and that turned out all right, so this will too, is that it? At what point do *I* get to choose for my own good?"

"When you understand what that is," Papa said. "And when you stop thinking of your own selfish whims and start thinking of the good of the dukedom."

Sienne strode to the desk and slammed it open. "The dukedom," she said with finality, "would be better served by having a duke who wants to be there. Not a duchess whose heart is elsewhere."

Her parents said nothing. Sienne fumbled with the ink pot and pen and managed to irreparably blotch the first page. Swearing under her breath, she crumpled it, threw it aside, and started again. Her parents didn't join her, which relieved her mind, because the way she was feeling, if they tried to read her message, if they *dared* display such blatant mistrust, she'd take a swing at one or both of them. She'd never punched anyone in her life, but she was ready to learn now.

She scrawled out a few lines, hoping her handwriting was legible enough for them to read. Fury filled her, poured down her arm and through her pen into words she barely remembered writing: *forcing me to stay—don't come after me—will speak to the king.* That last made her realize it was possible her parents would prevent that, too, so she added another line: *You should probably request an audience with the king on my behalf, just in case.* She threw the pen to stick quivering, point-first, in the plaster of the wall, and blew on the page to dry the ink, then folded it in thirds and looked around for sealing wax.

"That won't be necessary," Papa said when she picked up the stick of green wax. "No one's going to read it."

"It's for their peace of mind, not mine," she said curtly, and used her spark to melt the wax. She dribbled it over the seam and swiftly pressed her thumb to the soft wax. It was better than a seal that had nothing to do with who she really was.

She handed the sealed paper to her father, who stood, followed by her mother. "Let me show you to your room," Mother said. "And you really will want to bathe before dinner."

That was too much. "You can lock me in," Sienne said. "You can prevent me seeing my friends. You can even force me to sleep here.

But I'll be damned if I eat dinner with you and pretend this is all normal. I'd rather starve."

Mother's eyes narrowed. "You dare speak to me—"

"Clarie," Papa said. "Enough. Sienne, if you want to eat in your room, we'll send something up."

"I said I'd rather starve."

"That's up to you."

"I suppose you're going to lock me into the bedroom for my own good, too?"

"The door has a lock. We'll give you the key."

It was like fighting a wall of wet sand, oozing back into place wherever she made headway against it. "I want to speak with the king," she said, hating how weak she sounded.

"We'll talk about that later," Papa said. "Excuse me. I'll have this sent."

Sienne's mother followed him out. "Your room is on the third floor," she told Sienne, gesturing toward the stairs at the back of the entry hall.

"So I won't climb out and run away, you mean?" Sienne responded.

Mother began climbing the stairs. "Because that's where the spare room is," she said.

The stairs ended at the second floor, where a brightly-lit hallway extended from the landing in both directions. Mother led the way to the left, but stopped, startled, as a door opened and Liliana came out. "Sienne!" she shouted, and flung herself on her sister. "You came! Are you here to fix my dress? You were gone a long time. Was it an exciting adventure?"

Sienne extricated herself from Liliana's embrace and clamped down hard on a cruel retort, barely aware that Liliana, brat or not, didn't deserve the anger that rightfully belonged to two other people. "Later," she said. "I'm...going to take a bath."

Liliana's nose wrinkled. "Good, because you need one. Are you..." She looked more closely at Sienne. "Are you *crying*?"

Sienne hadn't realized she was. She swiped furiously at the tears spilling from her eyes and said, "Something got in my eye. I'm fine. I'll talk to you later." She strode off down the hall, past her mother, and found another set of stairs leading up.

The third floor was darker than the second, but still well-lit enough that Sienne could make out several doors. Her parents must have struggled to find a house with enough bedrooms for their ravening horde. She realized she didn't know where to go just as her mother came up beside her and said, "Second on the right. I'll have someone find the key for you."

"I thought that was a lie."

"We wouldn't lie to you, Sienne."

"No. You'd just ruin my life. Again."

"Stop being so dramatic," Mother said, grabbing Sienne's shoulder and swinging her around to face her. "You think you're the only one who's given up things for the sake of the dukedom? Think of Felice—"

"Felice is *happy* not to be heir. Did she tell you her plans? That she's moving here to—" In time Sienne remembered that her mother might not be privy to Felice's romantic secrets. "To live? That she doesn't love Rance and is happy to be free of him? Don't you dare tell me about what she's given up."

"That's not what I meant. But it's none of your business." Sienne's mother threw the door open. "The bath is at the end of the hall. Someone will bring you a tray in a few hours, if you're really set on making a farce of your life."

"My life was fine before you intruded on it."

"I suppose your next words will be to tell me you're sorry you were born into this family."

"You said it. Not me."

Mother spun on her heel and stormed off toward the stairs. Sienne went into her cell and slammed the door shut. The latch didn't catch, and the door rebounded almost in her face. She caught it and slammed it again, less forcefully. This time it stayed closed. She leaned against it face-first and waited for the tears to fall. They didn't. Instead, she felt weariness seep into every muscle. Banned from her friends, banned from Alaric, trapped in this horrible life...would they even let her request an audience with the king? They might see it as one more way in which she would defy them, and forbid her to make the attempt. For her own good, probably.

Unfortunately, her audience with the king wasn't just for her anymore. Without her, how likely was it that the others could get in to see him? The werebears' plea would go unheard, and their people unprotected, just because her parents thought they knew better than anyone else how the world should run. It was vital she see the king, and she would have to find a way to convince her parents of it. Maybe she could make it a deal: she'd acquiesce to their wishes if they gave her one last appeal. They might respond to that.

She turned to survey her cell. It was nice, not at all an afterthought like most spare rooms, with a bed big enough for two—

Now the tears came.

21

The bathroom, tiled in blue and white, was chilly even in the heart of true summer. It would no doubt be glacial in winter. It didn't matter, because whatever happened, Sienne wouldn't be there to find out. She pumped the tub full and heated the water as hot as she could stand, scrubbed herself clean, then washed and dried her clothes. It wasn't as good a job as a laundry would have done, but she wasn't going to go begging to her parents for a change of clothing, and the thought of wearing her road-grimed shirt and trousers over her clean body made her cringe. She tried not to think of the rest of her wardrobe, safely tucked away in her dresser back at Master Tersus's house. It would be hers again, soon enough.

She went back to her cell and stood looking out the window for a while. The room looked out over the Plaza of Sighs and the chapel of Gavant, busy even at this hour, when most people were still at work. Of course, Gavant was most worshiped by the well-to-do, who could afford not to work, so maybe that made sense. She wondered if they put on that light show every night. Possibly they used different confusions, to keep the worshippers from becoming jaded. She scowled. That one, she *would* be around to see.

She tried to remember the wording of the message she'd sent her team. Would Alaric try to break her out regardless? She hoped not. If he were arrested for assaulting her parents' servants, it would be that much harder for them to see the king. She was sure she'd made that clear, but Alaric, otherwise sensible, often didn't display common sense when it came to her safety. She turned away from the window. There was nothing she could do about that now.

In addition to the large four-poster bed with heavy red velvet drapes, the room contained a small round table barely big enough for fancy work, a wingback chair, a clothespress, and a heavily embroidered footstool. The clothespress was full of clothes, mostly gowns in rich brocaded satin or fine silk, scented with the lavender sprigs tucked between their folds. Suspicious, Sienne pulled a gown out and held it up to herself. Her own size. One more part of her parents' evil plan. Was it a warning, or a bribe? Well, she'd wear her own clothes to rags before she donned any of it. *But they went to so much trouble,* a tiny part of her said, and she felt a flash of guilt at rejecting their offering. Her weakness infuriated her so much she slammed the lid of the clothespress, then opened it and slammed it again a few more times until she felt better.

The armchair was more comfortable than the one in the drawing room, which angered her all over again, so she sat on the bed, which she'd been avoiding ever since she'd stopped crying, and opened her spellbook. There had to be something she could do to get out of here. Really, her parents were either stupid or naïve to leave her with the ability to do wizardry. The window was large enough for her to climb out, so...*drift*, to let her leap weightlessly to the ground, *vanish,* so no one would see her do it, and she still had the wand, so *silence,* in case the guards were unusually alert. It made sense to wait until everyone had gone to bed, even so.

Having a plan cheered her. She got up and went back to the window, to test the fit. She'd have to squeeze to get through, but she was flexible and it wouldn't be too much of a challenge.

She unlatched the window and pushed on it. It didn't move.

Stunned, she shoved harder. Nothing. She stood on the footstool, balancing carefully on its overstuffed cushion, and examined where the window met the casing. Someone had nailed it shut. She ran her fingers over the nail heads, sunk so deeply they didn't protrude at all, and the anger that had faded with the slamming and the tears rushed through her with a white heat that found voice in a terrible scream a howler would envy. She slammed her fist against the window and screamed again, longer and louder until her throat hurt. Then she threw herself face down on the bed and beat her fists against the counterpane. They *dared* treat her like a prisoner? Never mind that she'd been planning an escape that justified their actions—she was their *daughter*, supposedly their heir, and they'd locked her up like some animal.

"Sienne?"

Sienne sat up. Liliana stood in the doorway, a bundle of midnight blue fabric in her arms. Her eyes were wide and her face pale. "Are you all right? You didn't hear me knock, so I came in anyway. I was hoping you'd fit my dress for me, but I can come back later..."

Sienne calmed her breathing. "No. It's fine. Come in and shut the door." She sat up as Liliana closed the door, and added, "Sorry you had to wait so long. I didn't have time before we went on that last job."

"It's all right. Was it exciting? I wish *I* could do exciting things. But I don't want to be a scrapper."

"Go ahead and put the dress on. Why don't you want to be a scrapper?"

Liliana took off the dress she was wearing and shrugged into the midnight blue confection. "I don't know. Probably because they go into the Empty Lands. I'm scared of the wilderness."

"It's not that scary. You don't really encounter many monsters, and when you do, you have your team to help you fight them." The dress was only a little too big. Sienne opened her spellbook to *fit* and prepared to read.

"You don't really wish you were born to a different family, do you?"

Surprised, Sienne lowered the spellbook and said, "Why would you say that?"

"I heard you and Mother arguing. How did she ruin your life?"

"Liliana, were you *eavesdropping*?"

"I never learn anything unless I do." Liliana scowled. "People think I'm too young to know anything, but I'm twelve now and that's old enough to know the truth. You don't want to be heir, do you?"

"No. I don't." Anger resurfaced, and she quashed it ruthlessly.

"Then why don't you run away again?"

She'd been planning just that, before the nailed-up window. "I... it's complicated."

"That's what people tell me when they don't want to explain. I'm not stupid, Sienne. I just don't understand why the heir has to be the oldest. Or the next oldest. Or why Papa can't just say which of us he wants to be heir. *I* think he'd choose Quent. He talks to him most."

"I don't really know why not. I think it's because, if he could choose, we'd all fight about it, trying to prove who was the best choice."

"Except you don't want to, and Felice doesn't want to, and I'm not sure I want to either. I don't know what I do want, but being duchess isn't it."

"You're so lucky it won't be you. Now, stand still." Sienne read the *fit* spell, shaping it with her thoughts, and the dress shrank to fit Liliana perfectly. It looked good on her, the dark blue fabric flattering her fair complexion. Liliana twirled to make the skirt flare and twinkle.

"Thank you. I love it most of all my presents." Liliana flopped down on the bed and propped herself on her elbows. "I knew Felice didn't love Rance. They never kissed or held hands the way lovers do. And Rance likes someone else. I saw them kissing in the shadows on the verandah back home."

So Rance had a lover on the side. It didn't surprise her. "Who was it?"

"I don't know. It was too dark."

"Too bad. Mother and Papa might be able to do something about the marriage settlement if they could prove Rance was unfaithful."

Sienne closed her spellbook and sat on the edge of the bed. "They probably want me to marry him."

"But you don't love him."

"I am fairly certain Mother and Papa don't give a damn about my feelings at this point."

"Why not? Sienne, why are you fighting with them?"

Sienne sighed. "They're making me abandon my friends, my whole life, because it's not befitting the heir to Beneddo."

"But you can't be a scrapper if you go back to Beneddo, and you have to go back to Beneddo to be the heir."

"I'm going to ask the king to disinherit me. Then I won't be the heir and I can go on living my life my way."

Liliana's eyes went wide again. "Would he do that?"

"I don't know. But I have to try. Do you—have you ever had something in your life that made you...complete? More yourself than anything else? That's what I have with my friends. If I have to give that up just to rule a dukedom, especially when I don't have any idea how to do that, I'll die inside." It was dramatic, but it was so true she felt tears rising inside her. She blinked them away and added, "Alcander will be a much better choice to rule."

"He won't like it either. He wants to be a law-speaker."

"There's no reason he can't do both. It's only scrapping that's incompatible with ruling."

"I guess that's true." Liliana rolled onto her back. "So what are you going to do?"

"I was going to escape. I'm afraid Papa won't let me speak to the king. But they nailed the damn window shut."

"Were you going to fly? Sienne, can you *fly?*"

"Sort of. I was going to make myself invisible and then float to the ground."

"Oh! You can use my window!"

Startled, Sienne said, "I can't do that!"

"Why not? It's not nailed shut. You can come to my room after everyone's asleep and escape that way!"

"But you'd get in trouble when they find out I'm missing. You know what Mother is like—she'll ferret it out somehow."

"I don't care. It's not fair what they're doing to you. And it's an exciting adventure!" Liliana bounced a couple of times.

Sienne hesitated. Then she stood. "Let's look at your window."

Like Sienne's, Liliana's second-floor room faced the plaza. The sky was darkening, and figures were gathered around the chapel steps, waiting for the nightly worship. Her father was probably one of them, and Alcander and Quent.

Sienne pushed on the window and breathed in the fresh, warm evening air. She hadn't realized how stuffy her room was until she felt breezes on her face. The window was bigger than hers, more than half her height, easily tall and wide enough for her to fit through. She leaned out to examine the front door, but it was sheltered by a narrow roof that blocked her view. It wasn't wide enough to obscure the two guards who stood at the bottom of the steps leading up to it. She closed the window and pursed her lips in thought.

"Will it work?" Liliana said.

"It will, but..." Her anger had subsided thanks to her excitement at once again finding her escape plan possible, and she could think more rationally. With her wizardry, escaping would be trivial. She could run home, collect her friends, and apply to the palace for sanctuary and an audience with the king. The problem was, her parents had the law on their side—the same unjust laws that allowed Lysander Delucco to annul Perrin's marriage and prohibit him from seeing his children. The king wouldn't grant her sanctuary if he knew the story, and with nearly three weeks to plan this, Sienne was sure the king knew the story, or at least her parents' side of it. She'd be lucky to get an audience with the king at all.

All right, so she'd run away instead. With her friends' help, she could disappear thoroughly, go to Tagliaveno or Marisse or all the way to Concord if she had to. Problem solved. And yet...she remembered how Dianthe had been on the run for nine years, how hard it had been for her, and she hadn't been the heir to a dukedom. Sienne would never see her siblings again. And she'd leave Beneddo in turmoil, because so long as they couldn't prove she was dead, she'd still be the heir, and when her father died...no. She couldn't run away.

She closed her eyes and breathed out a curse. "I can't," she said. "The only way out of this is to see the king. And if he denies me..."

"But you can't give up! Don't you love Alaric? You can't be with him if you marry someone else!" Liliana exclaimed.

"I know." Sienne opened her eyes, but everything was blurry, so she closed them again and blotted away tears. "I have to hope the king will listen to me. I'm not the only one whose fate is on the line." She'd temporarily forgotten the werebears' plight. Their problem was even more important than hers.

"I don't understand," Liliana said, pouting.

"Don't pout, Liliana. You're too old to get your way by pouting. It just makes you look stupid and weak."

"I'm not stupid and weak!"

"Then don't act like you are."

Liliana frowned. "I'm glad you're not leaving. You're the only one who talks to me like I'm a grownup."

"That's because I'm not good with children. Alaric's the one who knows what to say." The thought of him hurt her heart.

"I like him. Why don't you marry him?"

"Because I'm the heir." Explaining their inability to have children one more time was beyond her. She was tired, and miserable, and in that state she almost felt it would be good for her to leave Alaric, so he could someday marry a Sassaven woman and have the children she was sure he wanted. After they freed the Sassaven from the wizard who'd enslaved them. Which couldn't happen unless Sienne remained with them. The ache inside her redoubled.

"I'm going back to my room," she said. "I'll see you later. And... thank you for being willing to help me escape." She almost added *I guess you're not the brat I thought you were*, but realized in time how cruel that would be and refrained.

"Are you really going to eat in your room?"

"If I don't, I might kill someone with my dinner knife." Though if that someone were Rance, probably nobody would mourn too loud or long.

She trudged back up the stairs to her room, only realizing after she shut the door that the room was occupied by the one person she wanted to see less than her parents. "Rance!"

Rance turned away from the window. "They're not taking any chances with you, are they," he said, gesturing at the nails.

"I guess not. What do you want?"

His eyebrows went up. "Just to talk. You could be a little more polite. I haven't done anything to you."

A dozen possible responses sprang to mind, but she went with, "Not today, anyway."

"What's that supposed to mean?"

She shook her head. "It doesn't matter anymore. Rance, I'm tired and I'm not interested in conversation. If you have something to say, say it, and then please leave."

He took a couple of steps toward her. "I wanted to apologize."

It felt as if he'd knocked the wind out of her. "What?"

"I'm sorry for how I treated you. My parents convinced me I needed to marry Felice for my family's sake. I tried to tell them I loved you, but they didn't care. I should never have gone along with it."

Sienne blinked at him. Then she laughed.

Rance frowned. "Why are you laughing at me?"

"Because you're so good at pretending to be sincere. You're going to blame our mess on your parents? Let me guess. They want you to convince me to marry you so you can still be duke of Beneddo someday. If you'd tried this any other day, I might have believed you. Or did you think you should strike while I was at my low point?"

"Sienne, I'm telling you the truth. You were my first love, and I've never stopped—"

"Loving me?" Sienne stopped laughing and took a step closer, putting her within arm's reach of him. "Let me remind you of what you said the day you told me you were marrying Felice. 'Sienne, I know we've had fun together, but we always knew the day would come that we'd have to part. That's how these childish romances end. I hope, now that we'll be brother and sister rather than lovers, you'll feel the same affection for me I always have for you.' *Childish. Fun. Affection.* Those were your *exact* words, Rance. Did you think I'd forget? Because those words burned inside me every day for months."

Rance reddened. "I...was just trying to make the best of it. Pretending I didn't love you with my whole soul. I thought that would make it hurt less, but I was wrong. Being with Felice only made it worse, because you're so much alike and yet so different."

"If I were you, I wouldn't bring up the woman *you are still married to* when proposing to someone else. Aren't you a little early off the mark?"

"Our marriage was annulled three days ago. I would never do anything like that. I do have scruples, Sienne."

He sounded so offended Sienne backed off. "Sorry. Is Felice still here? Or did she move out?"

"She's still here. Did she say she was going to move out? I knew she had a lover on the side!"

"So did you, Rance. Don't get all high and mighty or I'll tell Papa."

Rance's red face went pale. "You wouldn't. Who told you? That bitch Lorana—I knew she couldn't keep her mouth shut."

"Lorana Doxus?" Sienne laughed. "You could do better than that. Maybe I will tell Papa, after all."

Rance grabbed her arm and squeezed hard. "You do, and I'll...I can make you suffer."

Sienne faced him without a hint of fear, barely feeling his rough grip. "No, you can't. And I won't tell Papa so long as you convince your parents not to ask for the marriage settlement back."

"I can't do that!"

"Of course you can. As if your family will even miss the money. Of course, you could have your affair become public knowledge. That will make it *very* hard for you to win a titled wife, since you know how noble houses feel about bastards, or scandals."

"Everyone has affairs. It's no secret."

"Yes, but *everyone* isn't someone like you, with more money than lineage. You're held to a higher standard than they are. I know, it's not fair, but nothing in life is, right?"

Rance released her. "They won't do it."

"That's up to you."

He tried once more. "Sienne, I thought we had something special. I was so happy to learn we could finally be together. Please, my darling, marry me."

"I don't love you, Rance. And I don't believe you love me."

He gave her a look of perfect wounded sorrow that made the laughter bubble up inside her again. "So you won't have me," he said.

"Rance, I wouldn't have you if you came gift-wrapped in a box full of puppies. Now—get out. And I hope you find happiness someday. It just won't be with me."

He brushed the back of his fingers against her cheek. "Are you sure?" he said, and leaned in to kiss her.

Even though she wasn't expecting it, even though she didn't want it, she had to admit Rance was a very good kisser. But although he'd probably intended his kiss to make her fall into his arms, all it did was remind her that the one she wanted to kiss was nowhere near, and if he was, he'd probably take Rance's head off for taking liberties. So she let him kiss her, patted his cheek, and said, "Goodbye, Rance."

Rance looked puzzled. She wondered how many women he'd tried that on, and how many had succumbed to his considerable charms. Then he said, "All right," and left the room. Sienne sank onto the bed and wiped her mouth clean of his kiss. She missed Alaric so much it hurt. Briefly she reconsidered running away. But no, this was still the option most likely to get her what she wanted. Even if it was agonizing in the short term.

She took off her boots, lay on the bed, and studied the mystery spell until someone knocked at the door an hour or so later. It was a servant with a covered tray. Her earlier defiance about eating with the family had faded as her hunger grew, and she was glad her parents hadn't taken her demand to starve seriously. She balanced the tray on the little round table and ate quickly, then set the tray outside in the hallway and returned to her bed. The room was growing dark, so she made a handful of lights and sent them flying around the room until that got boring, then opened the spellbook again.

The mystery spell was obviously a summoning; she could tell that by the language it used. So that limited the possibilities of what it might do. Summonings, unlike evocations, dealt with the physical world—calling creatures into being, yes, but also manipulating water or stone, not to mention the various transport spells. She was less familiar with summonings in general than she was with the other three spell languages, but she was certain this spell was meant to either bring something from somewhere else or possibly create something out of nothing. She didn't know how summoning creatures worked any more than she knew where the water she created with her small magic came from, whether it was actually created or was pulled from the air around her, as she'd always been taught.

She went back to tracing the sharp, staccato lines of the spell. No, it really did look as if it was intended to bring something from somewhere else, not create it. But what? The summonings she'd been shown at school all had elements that would constrain the thing they were summoning, but that was because they summoned things that might turn on the wizard if they weren't controlled—monsters, or swarms of vermin. The students had all whispered rumors of a spell that would summon one of the devils that carried away souls not deserving of God's grace, murderers and rapists and so forth. And this had no constraints written in.

Well. With no constraints, it probably wouldn't summon something dangerous. Or it would, and the ancients were so confident in their magic they felt equal to handling whatever they did summon.

Sienne rolled off the bed and stood with her back to the door. One thing she did know was how to alter a spell to last as long or as short as you wanted, and with a summoning, that meant limiting the time the summoned thing was present before it was whisked back to wherever it had come from. She'd once asked a teacher whether it was too disruptive to pull monsters out of their place in the world and then send them back, and the teacher had gotten angry and made her write an essay on the magical ecology of tree-cats. It hadn't been *that* irrational a question.

Now she cleared her throat and read off the sharp, jagged sylla-bles. They stung her lips and the insides of her cheeks, and she tasted blood. Swallowing, she pressed on, feeling the world stretch and pull around her. The air shimmered like heat haze, stronger than anything she'd felt before, and she blinked to moisten dry eyes before spitting out the last of the blood-flecked syllables.

The air contracted, thickened, and a small black shape shim-mered into being near her feet. It plopped down on its hindquarters and looked up at Sienne, breathing heavily. Its little tail wagged. "*Ohhhhh*," Sienne exclaimed, bending to pick up the puppy and cradle it close. It put its tiny paws on her shoulder and licked her face once, then let out an excited *yip*. "You are *adorable*. I can't believe the ancients had a summon puppy dog spell. It's just ridiculous, except you are so cute. Yes you are!"

She set the puppy on the bed and watched it walk around on unsteady feet, sniffing its surroundings. Surely this couldn't be what the spell was supposed to summon—but what else could it be? Spells did one thing, and you could alter their duration or shape or who they affected. And if you got them wrong, they did nothing but give you a bloody mouth or leave you tasting honey for a week.

She picked up the spellbook and retraced the lines. Now that she was looking at it again, she could see it was more ambiguous than any other summoning she'd learned. This syllable...well, what if you pronounced it differently? Or this one? It would still be a recogniz-able "word," if you could refer to a spell in such a mundane way.

With a pop, the black puppy vanished. Sienne felt a momentary pang before reminding herself that the puppy no doubt had a home somewhere, and it hadn't just been destroyed. She read the spell again, altering the central syllable, and watched the thickening air with excitement.

This time, what appeared in the shimmering air was much bigger. Sienne bit back an excited shriek. The wolf was full-grown, sleek and gleaming, with sharply pointed ears and a long nose that nudged her hand, looking for pettings. Sienne had seen wolves before, out in the wilderness, but they had been shy, feral creatures, rough-furred and dirty, not clean and alertly intelligent as this one seemed to be. She stroked its head and whispered, "This is incredible. A spell that summons more than one thing. I wonder if it's all dog-like creatures?"

It wasn't. After summoning a hawk, a raccoon, a giant blue frog, and, horribly, a dolphin that thrashed helplessly on her floor for a full minute before disappearing, Sienne had exhausted the pronunciation possibilities of the mystery spell and given herself the beginnings of a headache. She was too excited to care. A spell that varied depending on how you pronounced it...that wasn't just going to make their fortunes, it was going to make them famous. Assuming she was ever in a position to sell it.

She put her spellbook away and lay on the bed with her eyes closed, willing the headache away. There was so much more experimenting she wanted to do, if only she had the resources, and so many questions. How long could a summoned creature be made to stay? What could they be commanded to do? If the wolf was any example, the creatures were smarter than average and more inclined to obey their summoner. Though that might not be true of the dolphin. And, most importantly, did she summon the same animal every time? With the puppy, that would be easy enough to prove, if it aged as time went on...

She massaged her temples and tried to calm herself. If the king didn't summon her immediately, she would have time to work out the details, if only because she couldn't imagine her mother wanting her to accompany her on social calls, or her father asking her to sit in on ducal judgments. It would keep her from going insane with worry.

She dismissed her lights and lay in the darkness for a while, then rose to hunt through the clothespress for a nightgown. It felt like giving in, but she was tired enough and elated enough by her discovery that her angry resentment was dulled to a quiet ache instead of white-hot fury. She still wasn't going to wear the gowns. Tucked into bed, she let a few tears fall, but exhaustion caught up to her before she could do more than that, and she slept.

22

No tray appeared the following morning. Sienne sat cross-legged on the bed, getting hungrier and more annoyed by the minute. Finally, she got up and went to the door, slamming it behind her. She still feared her hunger enough that continuing to go without food felt worse than the humiliation of appearing to have given in to her parents.

Back in Beneddo, breakfast was a casual thing, with all the dishes laid out on the sideboard for the family to help themselves to and coffee and juice in carafes on the table. It turned out her parents had kept the tradition here in the capital. She was late enough to the table that only her brother Alcander, usually a late riser, was still there, along with a maid who was clearing plates. Alcander's eyebrows went up when he saw her. "Sienne! What are you doing here?"

She bit back a rude comment—she liked Alcander, and none of this was his fault—and said, "Apparently I'm staying here for the duration."

"Apparently? What does that mean?"

She filled a bowl with porridge and stirred in cream and sugar. She could take it to her room, avoid any more uncomfortable conversations like this one was sure to be, but that would make more work for the servants. "It means Mother and Papa have decreed I'm to give up my degenerate lifestyle and start behaving like the heir."

Alcander's eyes narrowed. "They forced you to return home?"

Sienne slammed the bowl on the table, making the porridge slop over the rim. "I have a home, Alcander. This is *not* it."

"We're your family, Sienne. This will always be your home, no matter where else you live."

He sounded so reasonable, so pained, she couldn't stay angry with him. She dragged a chair away from the table and sat, poured herself some orange juice, and took a bite of porridge. It was too sweet, but she choked it down anyway. That, at least, was her own fault and no one else's, not like everything else she'd endured since yesterday. "Why can't you be the heir?" she said.

"The same accident of birth that put you in that position," Alcander said. "It's sensible, really. Letting the dukes name their own heirs would cause a feeding frenzy as all their children fought each other for the honor. Think of how a titled father or mother could control their children's lives by dictating what behavior would please them most. This way is more sensible." He took a long drink of his coffee. "I suppose you could do something reprehensible, get Father to cast you off."

"I can't imagine anything I could do that would be that bad. I'd end up hating myself."

"Then you'll need a royal decree. Forgive me for hoping you don't get it. I don't want to be duke."

"You'd be a good one. You already know all the landholders by name and you understand the law."

"Yes, but I hate public speaking. I want a nice, quiet office somewhere I can advise people on drawing up their wills."

Sienne spooned up more porridge. "I guess it's Erianthe who wants to argue cases publicly. I hope she can go to school." She remembered her encounter with Rance and hoped he'd taken her threat seriously. She might hate her parents, but the last thing she wanted was for her sister to lose her chance at her dream just because they couldn't afford her education.

"I don't see why not. She's dogged in getting her own way." So Alcander didn't know about the financial situation. It reminded Sienne that she wanted to see Felice, find out what her plans were. Maybe if her parents were outraged by Felice's intent to live with her lover, they'd ease up on Sienne.

The door opened. "Sienne! Good morning," her father said. Sienne took another bite of porridge and ignored him. "I hope you slept well," he went on. He wasn't really going to try to pretend everything was normal between them, was he? Well, Sienne had mastered patience in the years she'd been a student at Stravanus. She could be silent for *days* if she had to.

Papa helped himself to a couple of slabs of ham and sat at the head of the table. "Your mother intends to pay some calls this morning," he said. "I'm sure she'd want you to go with her. They're all people you should know when you're duchess someday."

Sienne continued to ignore him, focusing all her attention on the last scrapings of porridge. Someone had painted a picture of cheerful daisies on the bottom of the bowl before turning it unbreakable. She traced the petals with the tip of her spoon and envied the bowl's maker, who probably loved her work and had never had anyone threaten to take it from her.

Alcander gulped down the last of his coffee, made a face as if it had burned his tongue, and pushed back from the table. "I'll just...I'll see you later, Sienne. Father."

Sienne nodded to him and scraped up a final bite of porridge.

"And she'll expect you to be properly dressed," her father said as if Sienne had answered him. "I'm sure you'll find something you like in the wardrobe we assembled for you."

Sienne drained her glass and set it precisely at the twelve o'clock position above her bowl, dropped her napkin to drape across the bowl, and shoved back from the table, all in silence. She was at the door before her father said, sharply, "*Sienne.*"

She was too accustomed to responding to that note of command, and stopped despite herself, but managed not to turn around.

Papa said, "Sienne, this is the way things have to be. We're trying to make it easy on you. If you keep fighting us, you'll just be miserable. We don't want that for you."

Her hand closed on the knob so tightly the blood wasn't flowing through her fingers. She couldn't think of a single response that wouldn't end with her trying to scratch his eyes out. She left the room in silence and didn't slam the door.

She went back to her cell and lay on the bed, staring at the canopy and trying not to think of how much the color looked like fresh blood. That much blood would have overpowered the room with its smell. As it was, the room smelled of lavender, pleasant but not overwhelming, from the clothespress. If she were home, she'd probably be out negotiating for the sale of the summoning spell. Would they let her name it? *Drajanek,* "companion," that would be good. Or *prajatela,* "friend." Or maybe it already had a name, and she'd match it to a lost spell, and wizards everywhere would celebrate.

Someone knocked at the door. Sienne waited, but the person didn't enter. That meant it wasn't her mother. "Come in," she said.

The door opened. "Mother told me you were here," Felice said. "I'm supposed to get you to see sense, but I'm sure you don't see anything sensible about this situation."

Sienne sat up. "Rance asked me to marry him."

"Of course he did. He's gone back to his parents' house. Left last night in a huff. Really, I don't know what you ever saw in him. No offense."

"None taken. I don't understand it either. How shallow was I?"

"Not shallow. Young and inexperienced." Felice sat on the bed beside her. "What will you do now?"

"Ask the king for an audience. Let him make the decision."

"Sienne—"

"It's not just about me. My last job left us with something only the king can rule on. I have to speak to him about that. And if that puts me in a position to plead my own case, so much the better."

"I see." Felice frowned. "I'm not sure Mother and Papa will agree to it."

"When I can stand to speak to them, I'll make them a bargain. I'll be an obedient daughter and heir if they give me this one thing. And I'll abide by whatever the king decides."

"That might work." Felice hesitated, then said, staring at the door-knob, "You've really upset them. I don't think they realized how angry you'd be about the situation."

"How could they not? I stayed away from home for a year because I was happier where I was than I ever was in Beneddo!"

"Because it's hard for them to believe anyone would prefer to live in squalor—"

"I do *not* live in squalor!"

"As far as they're concerned, living anywhere but in a mansion might as well be squalor. And they can't believe you don't miss all the privileges and luxuries of a titled existence."

Sienne blew out her breath in an explosive *pah*. "That probably explains the wardrobe."

"What wardrobe?"

Sienne pointed at the clothespress. "Mother has never accepted the fact that I don't care about clothes the way she does. I bet she thought it would break down all my resistance." She shook her head. "I suppose I should have expected this. After all, they were completely clueless about my attachment to Rance. Why should they understand me any better after a year's absence?"

"All I'm saying is you might try to be a little understanding of their position. Or do you think they want you to hate them and fight them on everything?"

"I don't hate them. I know they're doing what they think is right. But they've given me no opportunity to make it *my* choice."

"Because you wouldn't choose them."

"Children are supposed to leave home and strike out on their own! It's not about choosing sides!"

To Sienne's surprise, Felice put her arm around her shoulders and hugged her. "I'm truly sorry about all this. You never were intended to inherit. Mother and Papa never made the slightest effort —no, that's unfair. I remember the day you manifested magic. They were so proud of you. They never wanted anything but a wizard's education for you—never bothered giving you the lessons I had in ruling a dukedom because it was clear what your destiny was. I think they're struggling with this as much as you are, trying to do the right thing by everyone. But you're the one who'll sacrifice your life for their dream."

Sienne remembered looking up at Kitane's statue and thinking the same thing. She wiped her eyes and said, "I discovered a lost spell. It's amazing. It ought to be grounds for celebration. And all I can think is that I'll never do anything like that—" She covered her face with her hands and let out a sob. Felice's other arm went around her as she cried.

When she finally ran out of tears, she hugged her sister. "I'm happy for you," she whispered. "You're free to do whatever you want. Free of Rance, free to be with the one you love."

"I wish it hadn't come at so high a cost," Felice said. "I'd like you to meet Violette, eventually, when Papa and Mother aren't quite so rabid about keeping you locked up so you don't run away."

"I'd love that."

Felice hugged her once more, then released her. "Are you coming with us to pay calls?"

"No. And if Mother were thinking clearly, she wouldn't ask me to. Even if I didn't *jaunt* away, I'd just be sullen and rude to whoever she wanted me to impress."

"That's what I told her. I wish...but it doesn't matter."

Someone knocked on the door. "Lady Sienne?"

Sienne rose and opened the door. A servant in Beneddo livery stood there, wringing her hands in agitation. "Lady Sienne, you have a visitor."

A *force* bolt of excitement struck her. Alaric. Of course he'd come. But—they wouldn't let him in, it was impossible. "Who?"

"A divine, my lady. An actual divine, here to see you." The woman's voice shook.

"A divine?" Felice said. "Why would a divine come here?"

The only divine Sienne knew was Octavian, and Felice was right

—why would he come to see her? For that matter, how would he know where to come? "Did you tell my parents?"

"Yes, my lady. He's in the drawing room." The woman's voice said clearly that she couldn't believe a divine could possibly be comfortable in anything as mundane as a drawing room.

"I have to go," Sienne said. "Please...make my apologies to Mother."

"It won't help, but I'll try," Felice said.

On her way down the stairs, Sienne wished briefly that she'd changed into something nicer than her rumpled scrapper's clothes. Then she reminded herself that divines were beyond such petty concerns. Unless...oh, by all the avatars, it wasn't a divine of *Gavant*, was it? Was her father capable of dragging a holy man into his house to lecture Sienne about her familial duty? He wouldn't be that desperate.

She slowed her steps as she approached the drawing room, anxiety gripping her heart. She didn't know what to hope for—that it was a stranger, come to bid her obey her parents, or Octavian, come to do the same thing. That would feel like betrayal.

She opened the door. Her mother sat on the sofa opposite Octavian, and withdrew her hands from his as Sienne entered. She looked awed, which made sense; she might have a tame priest of Kitane on call, but even she didn't have frequent contact with the divines of her own avatar. Octavian smiled and rose to greet Sienne. "It's good to see you," he said. "I take it your last expedition was successful?"

"It's not finished yet," Sienne said, "but yes, thank you."

Octavian gestured for her to sit beside her mother. Sienne did so, perching on the edge of the sofa and sitting as far away from Mother as she could manage without being overtly rude. "I received a visit from a very distraught young man this morning," Octavian said. "He was under the impression that you'd been kidnapped. And he said his friend, a priest of Averran, had been given direction that he should seek me out. I've never been the answer to another avatar's prayers before. It was...oddly satisfying, actually."

"Averran told Perrin to contact *you*?" Sienne's anxiety turned to confusion. "I'm surprised he was awake enough to tell Perrin anything."

Octavian laughed. "I know little of Averran, but that does seem like him. *I'm* surprised Alaric listened. He was not in a patient mood when he arrived. I believe he intended to come here next."

"I told him not to," Sienne said, just as Mother said, "We wouldn't have let him in." They glared at each other.

"I read the letter you sent him and convinced him to obey your wishes," Octavian said. "And sent him home in a rather more peaceful state of mind."

"Thank you. I was afraid he'd be upset no matter what I wrote."

"He loves you very much. Love does tend to disorder the senses."

Sienne blushed and glanced at her mother, whose face was stony. "And I love him," she said defiantly.

"I know. But I understand from what your mother has said that you have a duty that trumps your other attachments."

"Not if I can get the king to disinherit me."

"She said that too." Octavian looked at Mother. "Clarie, was there something you wanted to say to Sienne?"

Her mother's jaw was rigid. "There's nothing more I can say that I haven't already said," she ground out. "We want what's best for Sienne. She doesn't understand that."

"You want what's best for *you*," Sienne exclaimed. "If you wanted what was best for me—"

"And when have we ever not acted in your best interests?" her mother exploded. "We nearly bankrupted ourselves sending you to school so you could be a wizard. We protected your reputation when you disappeared for a year, a *year*, Sienne, in which we didn't know if you were alive or dead. We put up with your selfish desires and let you go out on that horrible journey where you were nearly killed. And now, when we finally expect you to do the right thing, you treat us like we're monsters!"

"I didn't ask for any of that!" Sienne shouted. "Why do you care what I do, anyway? Just because suddenly your lesser daughter is the important one? That must have killed you, knowing you had to hand over power to someone completely incompetent!"

"Why would you think that? We would never call you lesser!"

"*You did!*" Sienne balled her fists in her lap, itching to attack. "Did you think that was something I would forget? You said it yourself that you couldn't offer the Lanzanos the lesser sister when I begged you to let me marry Rance. When I wasn't crying over Rance's betrayal of me, those are the words that stabbed my heart, every night for weeks."

Sienne's mother gaped at her. Then she closed her eyes and let out a deep sigh. "Sienne," she said, her voice quiet, "I used the words the Lanzanos would have about you. They're social-climbing snobs so fixated on gaining a title for their son they would have mocked and belittled you for daring to do anything so gauche as fall in love. They're the ones who would consider you lesser. If you believed I could possibly consider you less important than Felice just because you were my second born, then I've failed you more than I ever imagined."

"But you..." Sienne couldn't think of how to end that sentence.

"We should never have made the alliance with the Lanzanos," Mother went on. "I still haven't forgiven myself for sacrificing my daughter like that, but we thought...it doesn't matter. Felice's infertility was like a second chance. We're free of the Lanzanos now, and you—Sienne, can't you see what a difference you can make for Beneddo? Someone well-educated, talented, with a thirst for seeing justice done? You are going to be a wonderful duchess someday. I know we're asking you to give up so much, but that's what it means to be of the nobility. You don't always get what you want."

"This isn't so much, Mother, it's everything I am."

"I know you think that now. You're in love and you think that's more important than anything. But there's so much more to life. I promise."

"How would you know? What did you have to give up?"

"My true love," Mother said.

Sienne blinked. "But Papa—you married your true love."

"I loved a man named Ged," Mother said. "He was a servant at our country house, but so much more than that... I intended to run away with him when my parents told me they'd arranged the match with the Verannus family. Then they told me the truth—that they were ruined financially, would be ruined socially, unless I married Pontus. I felt betrayed. Trapped. They'd put me in the position of being solely responsible for our family's survival. So I married your father."

"You didn't love him."

"I resented him at first. Then I grew to love him. And I realized I had so many more opportunities to help people than I would have as a servant's wife. I made a difference in the lives of the people of Beneddo, and it was a sacrifice worth making. But don't ever think it didn't break my heart to say goodbye to Ged."

"But—then why did you do it to Felice? You knew how she must have felt."

"I thought it was justified. I didn't realize the kind of man Rance is until it was too late. We made a mistake, but I still believe the principle is sound—we sacrifice for our families, for our people, and we're rewarded in the end."

Her mother's candor had left Sienne with nothing to say. It was impossible to imagine her as a young woman in love with someone who wasn't Papa, more impossible to think of Sienne's grandparents, who'd died a few years back, confronting her mother with the same ultimatum they'd given Felice. Even if her parents had dressed it up in nicer words.

"Sienne," Octavian said, and she jumped. He was so good at stillness, she'd forgotten he was there. "Do you understand better now?"

"I do. Maybe. But I don't agree."

"Sienne," Mother said, exasperation creeping into her voice.

"I don't! I understand making a sacrifice for the greater good. But you have eight children! Why do I have to be the sacrifice when there are six others just as good?"

"And that is the sticking point," Octavian said, forestalling Mother with a raised hand. "Clarie, why must Sienne be your heir? Is it simply an accident of birth? Or is she really the most qualified of your children?"

Mother sighed. "We've been through so much turmoil in the last few months. Losing Felice as heir...if Sienne isn't the heir either, what will prevent Alcander from making the same petition? Or any of our children? The law exists for a reason. It's sensible."

"I agree. But I also think having a recalcitrant heir is a mistake. Clarie, I believe you and Pontus meant well, but you must see you've hurt Sienne in the way you went about it."

Mother's lips pinched tight for a moment. "Yes. I know."

"Then, if you don't mind my making a suggestion, I think you should allow her to petition the king."

"Impossible."

"It's not impossible," Sienne said.

"We'd be giving in to this fantasy of yours that you'll be able to keep your new life."

Sienne shook her head. "Just let me talk to him. I swear I'll abide by his decision, whatever it is, and I'll be cheerful about it. At least, I'll try to be."

Mother, hesitating, turned toward Octavian. Octavian said, "I think it's reasonable."

"But we'll have allowed her to raise her hopes only to have them dashed."

"I think it's better we not anticipate what King Derekian will decide." Octavian took Mother's hand again. "I shouldn't have to remind you that Kitane understood sacrifice better than anyone. And no one ever tried to force her into it. Should we be any less understanding, just because we're human?"

"I suppose not," Mother said. She withdrew her hand and clasped them both in her lap. "Very well. You can ask Derekian for an audience. But you will stop being recalcitrant and you won't try to run away. And when he turns you down, you'll return with us to Beneddo without argument."

"I promise," Sienne said. He wouldn't turn her down. The king had to see the sense of her position.

"I'm glad everyone can be reasonable," Octavian said. "But I don't think you're finished."

"With what?" Sienne asked.

Octavian looked from one to the other. "With your apologies."

"I've said I'm sorry," Mother said.

"You have not," Octavian said. "And Sienne, you've let your distress lead you into behaving very badly to your parents."

"They nailed the window shut," Sienne said bitterly. "I think they deserved it."

"You wouldn't have found out about the window if you hadn't tried to escape through it," Mother shot back.

"*Enough,*" Octavian said, shutting them both up. "Does this continued argument make either of you happy? By my judgment, you've spent years misunderstanding each other and letting that build into festering resentment. She is your mother. You are her daughter. Those things will be true throughout your life, Sienne. If you want to go on fighting with her, no one will stop you, but a corner of your heart will always be bruised. And, Clarie—" He fixed Mother with his sharp blue eyes. "You must stop resenting Sienne for wanting to keep what you chose to sacrifice."

Mother's eyes widened. "I—I didn't—" She swallowed. "Do you think I'm that vindictive?"

"I think there's a part of you that never stopped loving Ged. You look at Sienne, with her inappropriate lover, and it hurts you to remember being in her position. Stop taking your pain out on her."

Mother looked at Sienne. "Oh, my dear child," she said. "I am so sorry."

Sienne blinked away unexpected tears. "I thought you hated me," she said in a tiny voice. "You said—"

"Please stop throwing my careless words back in my face," Mother said. "I truly didn't mean it."

"I'm sorry," Sienne exclaimed, and threw her arms around her mother. "You tried so hard, and I was so awful—"

"I never knew what to do with you," Mother said. "You left home, and you were such a stranger when you returned, it was like we'd already lost you. And then you ran away."

"Thank you for not letting me marry Rance."

"Thank you for coming home even though you didn't want to. Don't think I didn't realize what you could do with that spellbook."

Sienne wiped her eyes and drew back enough to look her mother in the face. "I think we might be a little too much alike for comfort."

"That's probably true. Your father told me you gave him the silent treatment this morning." She laughed. "I used to do that to him all the time, when he made me angry."

"I was so angry. I was afraid I might do something rash if I spoke."

"I understand." Mother wiped her eyes and let go of Sienne. "I don't know what else to say."

"There will be time for more words," Octavian said, rising. "Sienne, I promised Alaric I would tell you they haven't given up on you. Do you have any messages you'd like me to deliver?"

Sienne glanced at her mother, who didn't look upset at the idea. She contemplated the reality of a divine of Kitane playing messenger for her and said, "Tell them I'll send word when I learn the time of my audience with the king. And that I'll ask him to see all of us." She thought about asking him to deliver her love to Alaric, but she felt shy about that, so she only said, "Thank you. For everything."

"Averran in his wisdom acts in roundabout ways," Octavian said. "I'm happy to have been of service."

"I'll show you out," Mother said, opening the door. Sienne stood and tried to regain her calm. She wasn't sure this new understanding with her mother would last—they were, after all, very much alike—but she already felt happier and freer than she had for days.

Mother returned after a minute and let out a deep breath. "I'm exhausted," she said.

"Do you still want me to pay calls with you?" Sienne sighed. "I'll... change my clothes."

"Do you know, I don't think I feel like calling on anyone today?" Mother said. "Let's get everyone and go into the city. There must be a celebration somewhere we can join."

"Really?" Sienne smiled. "You aren't worried about insulting those women?"

"I'm the duchess of Beneddo. They should worry about insulting *me*." Mother held out a hand to Sienne, who clasped it. "It's past time we were a family again. You restored to us, Rance gone...I feel like celebrating."

Sienne laughed. Deep in her heart, she still ached for her friends, and her worry over the werebears' plight nagged at her, but for now, everything was all right. It was now down to the king to make the decision. Sienne could only hope he'd make the right one—and that they'd be in agreement as to what "right" meant.

23

It was three days before the message from the palace arrived: *Sienne Verannus, to receive audience with King Derekian Fiorus, at ten o'clock in the morning, Endweek.* She'd almost given up hope, had believed the king was so dismissive of her request he'd simply ignored it, but there it was, a palm-sized piece of thin card inscribed in gold lettering. Not *Lady Sienne Verannus*, and she didn't know what to make of that. Was it an acknowledgement that he'd already made his decision? Or simply an oversight on the part of the clerk? She tried not to read too much into it.

Endweek morning, she changed her clothes five times before settling on the simplest of the gowns her mother had provided, a seafoam-green silk with flowing sleeves and a narrow skirt. She'd wanted to wear her scrapper clothes, but even washing them a second time hadn't been enough to disguise the fact that they needed a true launderer's care, and that the trousers were worn in the knee to be three shades paler than the rest of the fabric. And it had felt too much like a challenge, like making the king's decision for him, and she didn't want to do anything that might set his back up. She had to admit the gown suited her. Sienne might not love clothes as much as her mother did, but she could admire her mother's excellent taste.

Her parents were in the hall when she went downstairs, dressed in court finery. "Oh, Sienne," her mother said, then bit her lip and went silent. Sienne didn't know if she'd been about to compliment her appearance or criticize her for not dressing more elegantly.

"Are you...you're not coming, are you? I promised I wouldn't run away." Sienne's heart, already aching with nerves, contracted at the thought of needing a chaperon.

"What the king decides affects us, too," Papa said. "We didn't want to wait here to learn the news. And...we thought you might need support." *If the king rejects you*, his eyes said.

"We know how hard this has been for you," Mother said. "If you want us to stay behind, we will. We want you to be..." Again her words trailed into silence, and Sienne wondered how she would have ended that sentence. Happy? Safe? Respectable?

"I want you to come," Sienne said, and both her parents looked relieved, which made her feel guilty all over again. Yes, she'd been fighting for her life, but how much hurt had she done them in exchange for the hurt they'd caused her? She suddenly felt tired and wished it were all over, even if it meant giving in and giving up. But no, this wasn't all about her. There was a whole magical race depending on her to take their case to the king. Giving up wasn't an option.

They rode in the green and gold carriage in silence, watching men and women take down banners and bunting and remove wreaths from doors. They looked as weary as Sienne felt, like four weeks of nonstop frivolity had permanently drained them of cheer. She never had gone dancing. She might not go dancing with Alaric ever again.

She suppressed the melancholy thought and went over possibilities for this meeting. If the king let her friends come with her, Perrin would do the talking, explaining about the werebears and the decision of the settlement to aid them. She and the others would add details as needed. And Swift could make a personal plea. But if the king insisted on seeing Sienne alone...she was terrible at trying to persuade anyone to do anything, because she let herself be caught up in the injustice of whatever it was she was trying to change, and it tangled her words so badly she often ended up only convincing the person that she was mad. This was too important for her to fail.

She closed her eyes and sent up a silent prayer: *O Averran, you've brought us this far. Don't let me let them down.*

When she opened her eyes, her mother was looking at her strangely. "Are you well?"

"Nervous."

"Derekian is intelligent and understanding. Even if he...tells you no, he won't make you feel a fool for having asked."

"I still say he could have told us you were safe," Papa grumbled. "How long did he know where you were?"

"Since the beginning of first summer."

Papa scowled and turned his attention to the passing scenery. Mother said, "It doesn't matter now."

Sienne nodded.

"How did he find out?" Mother asked.

"We foiled an assassination plot against him."

Papa sat up, astonished. "You did *what*? You mean, you and your companions?"

"Yes. I'm not allowed to share the details."

Mother said, "Is that...usual? I thought you fought monsters."

"We do. This was by accident." She had a flash of a memory, of an emerald falcon artifact digging its claws deep into her arm, and involuntarily tried to rub the memory away. "He was grudgingly grateful."

"I would think he would show you more respect than that," Papa exclaimed. "Grudging...that's typical of Derekian. He hates owing anyone anything."

"Pontus, be nice. A king owing favors can be dangerous." Mother turned to Sienne. "Is that why you believe he'll listen to you?"

"No. He said he didn't want to see us again. But I hoped it would be enough to gain the audience."

Her parents exchanged unreadable glances. Sienne settled back and watched a couple of women carrying a papier-mâché statue of Delanie around the back of a dressmaker's shop until the carriage took her out of sight. It seemed a rather permanent sort of decoration with limited utility. Maybe it would come out again on Delanie's name day.

"It seems there's more to scrapping than we thought," Papa said, drawing her attention back to him. "Or are you unusual?"

"I think we're unusual. Most scrappers just search ruins for salvage. We...we've fallen into bigger adventures. Mostly it's been by accident." Stopping an assassination, destroying not one but two evil undead creatures, killing a howler, acting as emissaries for a magical race...definitely not usual. And that didn't include their quest to free the Sassaven. Sienne's aching heart contracted again. Surely the king would have to see that what she had accomplished as a scrapper, what she would continue to accomplish, was far more important than making her rule a dukedom.

The carriage rattled over Half-Moon Bridge and trundled toward the palace, snug on its little isle that parted the Vochus River. Sienne preferred it at night, when magical lights in white and red turned it into a confectioner's dream, something so solidly real it was hard to believe in lesser buildings. By day, it was still impressive, with arched passages and domed roofs and two towers that dominated the skyline. Sienne had been inside exactly once, when the king had kidnapped all of them and interrogated them because he believed they were complicit in the assassination plot. She thought that had been in one of the side wings, and she didn't even know which one because the king's wizards had used *ferry* to take them directly back home from the rather stuffy drawing room they'd been held in.

Now, the driver took them to the grand front entrance, with the broad, shallow stairs flanked by rows of fluted pillars and the arched doorway flanked by liveried guards. The guards held ceremonial pikes that looked much deadlier and less ceremonial the closer Sienne came. She waited for the Beneddo footman to help her down from the carriage, fearing she would trip over the narrow skirt without a steadying hand, then walked ahead of her parents up the stairs and through the doorway.

The shady interior felt ten degrees cooler than the sun-drenched outer court. Frescoes in blue and green added to the effect, the murals depicting fanciful scenes of sea creatures cavorting on the waves. Sienne recognized kelpies racing from crest to crest and wondered if the artist had known they were real. She'd never seen one, but Dianthe had. "Majestic from afar, sure, but get up close and those hooves are razor sharp," she'd said. Sienne had dreamed of one day seeing them herself. That seemed unlikely now.

A woman dressed in scarlet and yellow approached them. They were Rafellin colors, but she looked unspeakably gaudy, like a tropical bird inexplicably interested in making friends. "Lady Sienne Verannus?" she said. "Come with me, please."

"My parents," Sienne said.

"You may all accompany me," the woman said. She made it sound like a privilege. Sienne followed the tropical bird, too nervous to pay attention to her surroundings. She was aware that the halls had ceilings high enough that the lights affixed to the walls didn't illuminate them fully, and that those lights were magical, but the paintings and sculptures lining the halls passed in a blur. Her mind ran a constant sequence of possibilities: facing the king with her friends, facing the king alone, sitting in an antechamber while her parents argued the king around to their point of view. That last was unlikely, since it wasn't their audience, but they were on a first-name basis with the king, they were a ruling duke and duchess, and maybe it wasn't so unlikely that he'd listen to them over her...

"You may wait here," the tropical bird said, and Sienne came to herself and realized she'd walked a few paces past the woman. *Here* was a room big enough to be an audience chamber by itself, but empty of everyone but themselves. A few chairs upholstered in scarlet velvet, their frames carved and gilded past the point of comfort, stood under several tall, narrow windows with palm-sized square glass panes. Some of the panes contained red or yellow glass rather than clear, making a random, blotchy pattern on the wall opposite.

One of the yellow blotches fell on a door that was so ordinary as to look out of place, as if it led to someone's linen closet rather than to, presumably, the king's audience chamber. Sienne swallowed. The door made it all horribly real.

"You'll be summoned when it's time," Sienne heard the tropical bird say, and was struck with fear that the others wouldn't get there on time. Would the king think they'd disrespected him, and deny their request before they'd even made it? She walked toward the door, stopped, and paced back toward the windows. The tropical bird was gone, and Sienne's parents looked at her in concern.

"Sienne," Papa said, "he's still just a man. We raised you to be respectful, not servile."

"I know." So much was riding on this. She made herself stop pacing and looked up at the windows, trying to find a pattern in what was meaningless. Who had thought the random panes were a good idea?

More footsteps sounded, and she turned in time to see another tropical bird, this one male, enter the antechamber, followed by Dianthe and Perrin, Kalanath, Swift, and Alaric, bringing up the rear. Her heart stopped for one agonizing moment, then lurched into movement, pounding so hard it made her shake.

She took half a step toward them. Alaric's eyes came to rest on her, fierce and burning, but he said nothing, just stood motionless near the door, tense as if he were a spring wound tight. She glanced at her parents, hating herself for not just going to him, but she'd promised, and suppose staying away was part of that?

Her mother looked her way. A sad smile touched her lips, and she nodded, so slightly. Sienne walked toward her friends, feeling that any moment someone would call her to heel. Then she was running, and Alaric came toward her to snatch her up and hold her so closely it soothed her aching heart. He was dressed more nicely than she'd ever seen him, even on the nights they went dancing. She sensed Dianthe's hand in his wardrobe. "Don't cry," he whispered in her ear. "You'll ruin this tunic."

She laughed damply and sniffled back tears. "I'm sorry. I'm so sorry."

"What are you sorry for?"

"I don't know. For not coming home."

"It's not your fault. Don't worry, Sienne. Everything will be fine." He brushed the hair back from her face and kissed her with such tenderness it nearly made her cry again. If she had to leave him... maybe her mother could find meaning in sacrificing love, but Sienne could only feel the sheer terrible waste of it.

She stepped away and hugged her friends, one at a time, even Swift, who looked like he wished to be well away from Sienne and her family drama. "Will the king see all of us?" he asked in a low voice.

"I don't know. The card I received was addressed only to me. Were you summoned?"

"We were not," Perrin said, "but when we presented ourselves at the front door, we were admitted with no demurral. I choose to take it as a good sign."

"They knew our names," Kalanath said. He looked almost naked without his staff. Sienne realized none of them were armed. "I think the king remembers us."

"Hard to forget," Dianthe said.

Alaric was glaring at Sienne's parents. "Alaric, don't," she said, putting a hand on his arm.

"They kidnapped you and made you miserable. That doesn't make me love them." He looked about two heartbeats away from erupting.

"They meant well. And the law is on their side. *Please*, don't start a fight."

"I'm starting to hate the laws of this supposedly civilized city," he rumbled, but turned his back on the duke and duchess. To their credit, Sienne's parents didn't look as if Alaric frightened them, though they watched him the way travelers watch a waterhole, looking for hidden carricks. She was sure they wanted her to return to their side, but it would have felt too much like deserting her friends, and expecting the two groups to mingle was about as likely as getting a lamb to snuggle up to a lion.

The small, incongruous door opened. A man dressed all in black with a tunic that screamed "secretary" stepped through. He surveyed the room. "There are certainly a lot of you," he said. "Which of you is Sienne Verannus?"

"*Lady* Sienne Verannus," Papa said.

"As you wish," the man said. "Lady Sienne?"

Sienne stepped forward, suddenly very grateful she'd worn the gown. "I am," she said, proud that her voice didn't quaver.

"The king will see you now," the man said, indicating the doorway.

"I—asked for him to see all of us," Sienne said.

"I am aware of this. His Majesty chooses to see only you, my lady." The man said "my lady" with the slightest ironic emphasis. Sienne heard her father harrumph with irritation.

Alaric squeezed her hand gently and released her. She walked away without looking back, certain if she did she would burst into tears. She'd never felt smaller in her life.

The black-clad man followed her into the next room and shut the door behind them. It wasn't a throne room. It wasn't even an audience chamber. It was a study, an ordinary if windowless study with a couple of bookcases, a claw-footed desk big enough to sleep on, and a globe on a stand. Two armchairs were drawn up to a fireplace in which a fire was laid but not lit. The only illumination came from a pair of lamps, lit by flames and not magic, that flanked the fireplace, shedding light on the deep chairs and turning their black velvet upholstery dark blue.

King Derekian Fiorus sat in the armchair facing the door. He wore simple but elegant clothes that again made Sienne grateful she'd chosen the gown, a belted rust-red tunic over a white linen shirt, plain wool trousers, and boots so finely made Sienne was sure she knew who his bootmaker was. His neatly-trimmed black beard concealed his expression, as did the hand he had raised to his mouth. She'd expected to see, if not the state crown, a coronet like the one her father wore on court days, but the king was bareheaded and his hair needed a trim. That relaxed her somewhat. *He's just a man, after all*, she reminded herself.

"Have a seat," King Derekian said, gesturing at the armchair opposite him. Sienne's nerves twanged again. She seated herself and smoothed the wrinkles out of her skirt. The king regarded her for some time, during which Sienne clutched her fingers together and waited for him to speak. Whether he was trying to disquiet her, or simply didn't know what to say first, she didn't know, but she had a feeling it was safer, with this man, not to give up any advantages. Speaking first might be a weakness.

"So," he said finally. "You have a request."

"I have two, your Majesty."

The king raised one eyebrow. It made him look like a satyr. "Daring."

"I told you we needed to speak to you about our last job. That's the important thing."

"Is it? Go ahead."

"I'm not the best one to explain it. Perrin Delucco—"

"Is not the one I've granted an audience to. Your time is short, Sienne. Make your case."

Sienne glanced at the black-clad man, who was seated behind the desk, pen in hand. "It's sensitive information, your Majesty."

King Derekian followed her gaze. "Benedict," he said, "are you comfortable hearing sensitive information?"

Benedict inclined his head once, but didn't look up from his paper. "Your Majesty may choose to dismiss me, if my confidence is in question."

The king turned back to Sienne. "Benedict Gambrus knows where all the bodies are buried," he said. "Take that as literally as you like. He is my confidential secretary, and having him present for this conversation saves me the effort of having to repeat it to him later. I assure you he's good at keeping secrets."

Sienne nodded. "All right. Your Majesty, we took a job—"

"Is this background necessary?"

"Yes, your Majesty. I'm sorry, but you have to understand how it all began for it to make sense." Sienne hoped he wouldn't lose interest. She was no storyteller, like Swift, whose people's fate was in her hands. "We were hired to clear out a ruin east, near the Bramantus Mountains..."

She told him everything she could remember, though she glossed over the fight with the howler and said nothing about nearly becoming a howler herself. Derekian's expression never faltered, though he did cross his leg over one knee halfway through her recitation, and stroked his beard a few times. When she started repeating herself, he held out a hand palm-first and said, "That's enough."

Sienne fell silent. Derekian said, "I thought you intended to ask me to disinherit you."

"I did. I mean, I do. But this is more important. It was why we all wanted to see you, not just me."

"I understand. You brought one of these were-creatures with you?"

"His name is Swift. He's in the antechamber—you can speak to him—"

"Not right now. I have a few more questions for you. What exactly do these werebears expect of my government? Recognition? Or support?"

"I'm...not sure what you mean. They want the same rights as any citizen. I suppose that means protection from assault, and recognition, yes, of their property rights, but they don't want any special favors."

"And yet that is exactly what they would have to have, in order to remain safe from humans who would see them as a threat."

"But they're not a threat! That settlement is willing to live peacefully with them, side by side. If they can do it, why not others?"

"Few humans are so understanding. We tend to fear what we don't understand, and kill what we fear. I would have to send troops for their protection, and Gavant help those troops if they fall victim to fear, too."

"It wouldn't have to be forever. People would get used to them."

"Not soon enough."

"So you're not willing to commit troops to the protection of these people just because they are a little different from you and me?

They're not deserving of living free and having a better life for their children?"

"Don't put words in my mouth, Sienne. This is a complex problem and you're not the one who will have to solve it."

"It seems pretty simple to me. They're people. They want to be treated like people. And they've turned to you because you have the power to make that happen." Sienne leaned forward. "I told them you're fair and honorable. I hope that wasn't a lie."

The corner of the king's mouth quirked up in a smile. "You're far more eloquent than I believed from our last meeting. Are you calling my character into question?"

"I think that's up to you, your Majesty."

Derekian laughed. "Benedict, are you getting all of this?"

"Every word, sir."

"Sienne Verannus, your words are being immortalized as we speak. How do you feel about that?"

Sienne swallowed. "Very small, your Majesty."

"And you don't want to be duchess of Beneddo."

"No, sir. But the werebears' plight is more important."

"I see. And you say they're living in tents now? What do they do in the winter?"

"I don't know, your Majesty. Clever said they hibernate, but that the very young children can't do that, and some of them die."

"This settlement agreed to help them build permanent homes."

"Yes, your Majesty."

"Making my agreement moot."

"I'm sure they didn't intend that, your Majesty." She didn't want to tell him how defiant Yannick had sounded when they'd warned him about that.

"I wonder." Derekian leaned back and steepled his fingers together. "And what will these creatures do for Rafellin?"

"I'm sorry?"

"What benefit do they bring to our country? How will they improve our economy, for example? Or will they simply take our resources and give nothing back?"

His question irritated Sienne. "Does it matter?" she said. "I mean, a baby is a drain on resources, and it doesn't give anything back. It's not until it's grown that you know what it can do. Who knows what these people might end up doing for Rafellin?"

"So we're to support them on the off chance they might end up benefiting us?"

"No. We support them because it's the right thing to do. We don't cast people aside just because they're not useful, whatever that means. They're people, like us, and they're struggling. We—Rafellin—we have a chance to embrace the only nonhuman intelligent race anyone's ever discovered that isn't trying to eat us. That has to count for something."

The king went silent, tapping one long finger against his mouth. "All right," he said. "Sienne Verannus, in recognition of the services you have rendered this kingdom, I grant you a boon. Ask, and I will give it to you."

Sienne's heart lightened. She smiled, and opened her mouth to speak. "Do not be hasty," the king said. "*One* boon, Sienne. Be careful what you ask for."

Sienne's mouth snapped closed on her quick reply. "I don't understand. You mean—if I ask you to recognize the weres as citizens, you won't...you won't grant me any other request."

"Ah, it appears you do understand."

"But that's not fair! Why can't you do both?"

Derekian rose. He wasn't a tall man, but he towered over her in her chair. "I am disinclined to set an example that inheritance law is a thing lightly set aside," he said. "And according recognition to the werebears will cause strife in my kingdom for years to come. You may have done me a service in the past, Sienne, and you may have performed acts that benefited our people, but you are not entitled to disrupt this kingdom twice. One boon."

Sienne's throat closed up. She swallowed hard, twice, trying to get it to open. The sheer monumental unfairness of it all made her wish she dared scream at this man. Faintly, she heard herself say, "You leave me with no choice."

"You always have a choice, Sienne."

Even if the choice is death, Alaric had said. It had sounded overly dramatic then. Now it felt like inevitability. "Then I choose for you to recognize the werebears as citizens," she said, and bid farewell to Sienne the scrapper.

24

The king's eyes narrowed. "That is not the choice I expected of you."

"It's the only one I could make, and keep my self-respect." Sienne's eyes ached with tears she would shed later, when she was well away from this awful room in the awful palace.

"I hope you aren't expecting me to change my mind just because you made the unselfish choice."

"No, your Majesty. I only expect you to do as you've promised."

"My word is law, Sienne." The king extended a hand to help her up. She thought about rejecting it, decided that was juvenile behavior, and let him assist her to her feet. Her knees trembled so much she was afraid she might collapse, and she leaned on him more heavily than she wanted. The king regarded her closely. "Are you well?"

"I'll be fine." She let go of his arm and clasped her shaking hands together.

Derekian still had his eyes on her face, studying it. She wondered what he saw there. "Sienne Verannus," he said, "shortly I will leave this room to speak to the were-creature you've told me about. I will give him the news that he and his people are now citizens of Rafellin.

You have until I open that door to change your mind, if you wish, and I will give him different news."

Sienne swallowed to moisten her throat, which had started to close up again. "Thank you, your Majesty," she said, "but that won't be necessary."

The king pursed his lips in thought. Then he inclined his head once to her, the bow of equal to equal, and gestured for her to precede him through the door.

She knew the look on her face delivered the news before she had time to speak a word. She didn't dare look at her parents for fear their obvious pleasure at having won would destroy her hard-won calm completely. Out of the corner of her eye, she saw Dianthe cover her mouth to hold in a gasp. Perrin lowered his head so his long hair obscured his face. Kalanath's mouth went grim, and he turned away, closing his hand as if reaching for a staff that wasn't there. Sienne saw all this in a blur, because her attention was all on Alaric. His eyes, filled with hope, went stony, and his jaw tightened. She couldn't think of anything to say. Nothing could make this better for any of them. Why she wasn't crying, she didn't know. One always wept over a death, yes?

"I assume this stranger is Swift," Derekian said.

"Yes, your Majesty," Sienne said. It came out as a whisper, and she cleared her throat and said, "Swift is the werebear matriarch's cousin, and her official emissary."

"Excellent. Swift, are you prepared to make binding oath on behalf of your people?"

"I am, sir. Your Majesty," Swift said. He alone among her friends was calm. Well, this wasn't a tragedy for him, if you didn't count how Wit should have been there to make oath as well.

"Then kneel, and raise your hands, palms together."

Swift knelt and raised his hands as directed. Derekian placed his hands on either side of Swift's, encompassing them. "Benedict?" the king said.

Sienne hadn't noticed the black-clad man following them. "Swift, repeat after me," Benedict said. "I, Swift, on behalf of my people, swear fealty to Rafellin and its monarch, to obey its laws, and to serve its needs, according to the requirements of its government."

Swift recited the words back without hesitation or mistake. For someone who kept the words to hundreds of stories in his head, one line was no difficulty.

"I, Derekian of the Fiorus family, by the grace of God King of Rafellin, accept the fealty of the werebear people, and swear to defend their lives as citizens of this country, according to them all privileges and rights appertaining thereunto." The king removed his hands and added, "You may rise."

Swift stood. "Thank you, your Majesty. My people thank you."

"Thank Lady Sienne," Derekian said. "It was her boon I granted."

Alaric stirred. "You made her choose, didn't you," he said, distantly, his eyes fixed on the multicolored wall.

"I did. Do we have a problem?" Derekian's voice was cool, but Sienne saw his fist clench, and it satisfied her to know he was a little afraid of what Alaric might do.

"I would never cheapen Sienne's sacrifice by fighting you over it," Alaric said.

Sienne realized her parents were standing close beside her. Neither of them touched her, for which she was grateful. Her face felt numb and her eyes hurt from unshed tears.

"I would like," Derekian said, "to see our newest citizen in his true form."

"This is my true form," Swift said, "or, more accurately, we're not more one than the other."

"However you put it. Will you shift here?"

Sienne said, "Um, your Majesty, my parents—"

"You convinced me that humans will learn to live with Swift's people," Derekian said. "Do you lack confidence in that assertion?"

"No, your Majesty."

"Sienne, what is he talking about?" Papa said.

"And—dear Kitane, why is that man undressing?" Mother added.

Sienne just shook her head as Swift finished disrobing and took a few steps away from everyone. It occurred to her that if this had all been an elaborate assassination plot centered on the king, she and her unarmed friends were in no position to defend him, and their lives would be forfeit. The thought was dull, distant, and Sienne discovered she didn't much care if it were true.

Swift's body distorted, and he fell to all fours, shifting into his bear form as he fell. Sienne's mother shrieked and grabbed Sienne, pulling her away from Swift. Papa stepped in front of them both, shielding them. "What in Gavant's name is going on?" he shouted.

"It's all right, Papa," Sienne said, removing her mother's hand from her shoulder. "Swift is a werebear. They're intelligent and not at all vicious."

Derekian hadn't moved. His eyes gleamed with calculating interest. "What an army you would make," he said. "Benedict, think how we could push back the borders of the Empty Lands with their help."

"I can think of more than one way in which they might benefit us, depending on how many of them there are," Benedict said. "He is not large, is he?"

"He is a true were-creature, so his mass is conserved when he shifts," Perrin said. "And he understands our speech in this form, so we should likely not refer to him as if he were not present."

"My apologies," Benedict said.

Swift extended both front paws and executed a perfect bow that made Sienne smile. It hurt the corners of her mouth. She couldn't imagine having much to smile about in the coming weeks.

"Was this the rest of your job?" Papa said. "You brought this...this werebear here to meet the king?"

Sienne nodded. Even that was painful. "The werebears came to us for help in gaining recognition as citizens, and as people. We agreed to help them."

"But...why you?" Mother asked. She still hovered behind Sienne as if afraid Swift, who'd now transformed back into human, might lunge for her at any moment.

"Because we have—had a reputation for honor, and because they thought if anyone could get them in to see the king, we could."

Sienne closed her eyes. "Is it all right if I say goodbye before we leave? I don't think I can bear much more of this."

"Sienne," Papa said, "why did Derekian turn you down?"

"He didn't. He let me choose. The werebears, or myself. Please. I'm so tired."

Papa and Mother looked at each other. "Derekian," Papa said, "thank you for your time."

"Pontus. Clarie. I hope this signals the end of your inheritance troubles," Derekian said, walking over to join their group.

"It doesn't," Papa said. "We still don't have a suitable heir."

Sienne, struggling to keep her tears in check, was shocked into staring at him. "What?"

"On the contrary. I think Sienne will make a fine duchess one day," Derekian said.

"I disagree," Papa said. "She doesn't know the first thing about ruling a dukedom, and she's too easily angered. She'll make rash decisions. She doesn't understand the law. She's a poor choice."

Derekian's eyebrows went up. "She's bright, and she'll have you to instruct her. I see no problem that cannot be resolved."

"But it doesn't change the fact that she's far better suited to the life she has," Mother interjected. "You would never have known about the werebears if not for her. She and her friends saved your life. I'm sure there are dozens of other events we don't know about. We have six other children, all of whom are just as capable of learning to rule a dukedom as Sienne, but none of them are going to continue to serve the kingdom as directly as she has."

"Don't try to manipulate me, Clarie," Derekian said. "I don't play games with the nobility."

"That is not true, and you know it," Papa said. "You've manipulated and schemed your way to a secure position, disposing of weak or corrupt nobles and putting your own people in power. There's no reason you can't designate whoever you want as our heir."

"Pontus," the king said, "you come dangerously close to treason."

"Derekian," Papa said, "you have never had a stronger supporter than Beneddo, even in the early days when everyone thought you would be just another weak Fiorus monarch. If that counts for anything, let it matter now."

Sienne heard it all in a daze, words tumbling past in a wind only she could feel. Her vision had tunneled down to nothing, just her parents and the king talking about things her addled brain only barely understood. "I," she said, her voice barely audible. It nevertheless drew their attention to her, searing her skin. "I don't understand."

Derekian sighed. "I sometimes think I might as well not be king, for all the respect my vassals fail to give me." He turned back to Papa. "And which of the many Verannus offspring do I want to choose as heir?"

"Giles," Mama and Papa said as one, then looked at each other with amusement. "He's smart, he's loyal, and he's at loose ends for what he wants to do with his life," Papa went on. "I think the focus of knowing he'll be duke will be good for him."

"I certainly hope so, because I'm not intervening in your dynastic squabble a third time." Derekian. "Sienne, you look as if you need to sit. I'm afraid these chairs are designed more to keep petitioners off-balance than to be comfortable."

"I'll be fine," Sienne murmured. Everything still seemed to be coming from so far away. She felt her father's hand on her shoulder, bearing her up, and finally the tears came. She threw herself into her parents' arms, sobbing uncontrollably, all the pain and worry of the past four days coming out in hot tears. "You didn't have to," she choked out between sobs. "I promised—"

"We only ever wanted the best for you," Papa said. "We were just bad at guessing what that was."

"It's remarkable what you've done with your life," Mother said.

"But—what you said about sacrificing—"

"The whole point of making that sacrifice is to gain something better," Mother whispered. "It's not to give up the something better for something less."

"We're still your family, no matter where you go," Papa said, tweaking her ear and startling a laugh out of her. "Lady Sienne."

Sienne nodded and, smiling, stepped away from them. "You leave in a few days," she said. "I'll stay with you until then."

Papa and Mother exchanged significant looks. "I think there's someone who needs you more than we do," Papa said. "But...bring him for a visit. Bring them all."

Sienne turned. Alaric looked as if he'd run into the middle of *fury* without ducking. "I will," Sienne said, and took three steps and threw herself into his arms.

———

THEY LAY AT LAST IN THEIR OWN BIG BED, TWINED TOGETHER IN A tangle of limbs and breathing heavily from exertion. "I can't remember how long it's been," Sienne gasped. "I was afraid I might have forgotten how."

"Never," Alaric said, brushing strands of sweaty hair back from her face. "I dreamed of you every night you were gone. Dreamed you'd been kidnapped, dreamed you'd accepted your inheritance, dreamed you'd simply up and left me. They were the worst nights of my life."

"I won't leave you again." Sienne twisted so she could lie curled up in the curve of his body.

"I never thought I'd be grateful to your parents after that trick they pulled, keeping you locked up. It turns out they really did want the best for you." He blew lightly across her temple, cooling her skin.

"They really did. I'm glad they figured out what that was." She felt so relaxed, like resin melting over a hot stove. "And to do them credit, they would have let me marry you if we could have had children."

"Mmm. Is that something you want? Marriage?"

"I don't think it would change anything, do you? Since there's no noble title or estate at stake?"

"Marriage isn't something Sassaven do. The wizard..." Alaric's arm tightened over Sienne. "He sometimes forces us to mate with someone who will produce acceptable offspring. We're not privy to what he thinks is acceptable. But it means we make our alliances in secret, in case he decides to punish us by taking us away from the ones we love. I'd never even heard of marriage before leaving the valley."

"That's horrible. It makes me even more eager to free them." She paused, then decided to go for broke. "But children...that *is* something you want."

"No. Not really."

"Liar. I saw you with the werebear children. And with Liliana and her friends. And even those snotty-nosed urchins at Wit and Swift's lodging. You want children."

She rolled over to face him and saw he'd gone very still, his eyes closed. "I'm sorry," he said. "I do."

A cold fist closed over her heart. "And we can't have them." He had his arms around her, so fleeing in tears wasn't an option. "Do you want..." She cleared her throat, which was suddenly tight and dry. "I understand."

"Understand what?" His eyes opened, but he wasn't looking at her, he was looking far beyond the walls of the room at some distant vista.

"That you need to be with your own kind."

His gaze came swiftly to rest on her. "What are you talking about?"

"To have children. You need a Sassaven woman—"

"I need—Sienne, that's not what I meant!"

"Alaric, it's obvious this means so much to you, being a father. I don't want to stand in the way of that."

Alaric released her and rolled onto his back. "It's not as simple as that. I haven't thought about having children, all these years, because —not just because I was away from the Sassaven, but because someone in my line of work, someone trying to defeat a powerful wizard who could possibly kill him, has no business bringing children into the world. Then you came along, and now..." He blew out his breath in a long stream. "Having you means giving that up. I thought I was at peace with it, but I think I grieved that loss all the way back to Fioretti."

"It doesn't have to be a loss." Breathing around the icy fist in her chest hurt more than she'd imagined possible.

"Of course it does. Lose my future children, or lose you. But it's not even a choice. I want you, Sienne. I have from the beginning." He buried his face in the curve where her neck met her shoulder. "I just thought, with such an obvious choice, it wouldn't hurt so much."

She put her arms around him and held him in silence for a long, long time. "I'm sorry," she whispered. "It's so unfair. If there was anything I could do—but it's not something magic can fix."

"Given that magic caused the problem in the first place, you'd think there would be something," he murmured. He raised his head and kissed her, the barest brush of his lips against hers. "I don't resent you. Don't ever think that."

"I was worried, a little."

"Well, don't. It's not like you won't have a horde of nieces and nephews, given the size of your family. And there are other compensations, and you are chief among them." He kissed the side of her face. "Besides, you'd be a terrible mother."

"I would not!"

"You'd get caught up in something, and forget we even had a baby. Don't deny it."

"I took very good care of my little sisters and never once forgot about them. All right, maybe once. There are eight of us! It's natural to leave one behind in the garden. For an hour. Stop laughing! I swear, Alaric, I'm going to—"

25

S ienne closed Master Tersus's back door behind her and leaned against it, finally giving in to the shakes that had threatened to overwhelm her ever since speaking to Mistress Givvani at the University of Fioretti's wizardry school. Fifty thousand lari. For a piece of ancient parchment.

She'd pushed herself to the limit of her resources demonstrating the potential of the mystery spell, then sat and listened to the wizards argue over whether it was truly a lost spell, or one they had records of. An hour later, they'd decided none of their records matched it, and allowed her to name it: *klica drajanek, summon companion*. With her name listed as discoverer. No wonder she was shaky.

Nobody was in the kitchen, so she went down the hall to the sitting room they rented from Master Tersus. Alaric had Sienne's notebook in hand and was frowning at it, probably studying the translations she'd made of the ritual. Perrin sat in the corner on the floor, cross-legged, meditating with his hands resting loosely on his knees. Dianthe had her feet propped on the low, awkward table and appeared to be asleep. Sienne knew it was a sham, because Dianthe wasn't snoring. "Where's Kalanath?"

"Out," Dianthe said without opening her eyes. "He said he needed to speak to someone, and he'd be back soon."

"Did they buy the spell?" Alaric asked.

"Yes. Guess how much. Never mind, you won't guess. *Fifty thousand.*"

Perrin's eyes flew open. Alaric let out a long, low whistle. Dianthe shot upright and said, "Is that even possible?"

"It's not the most anyone's ever paid for a lost spell, but this one— the price is as much for the new wizardry theory as for the spell itself. And they agreed to examine the hazard deck at no charge."

"Is that safe?" Perrin asked. "If Master Samretto stole it, and it is recognizable as belonging to someone—"

"It's worth taking the risk. I explained that we found it as legitimate salvage, which is true, and if it was stolen, they won't think it was us, because who would dare present stolen goods to the University of Fioretti? So at worst, the real owner claims it, and at best, we have an artifact we can actually use for something other than hazard readings. They said to come back in a few days and they'll have an answer."

"Good choice," Alaric said. Sienne took a seat next to him and snuggled under his arm. She still felt tender of him, the long days of enforced separation having left a mark. By the way he occasionally touched her hair, or her shoulder, for no reason at all, she thought he might feel the same way. She reached into her pack and pulled out the banker's draft, extending it to him. He took it and held it up to the light. "This is a lot of lari."

"It's almost too much to know what to do with," Sienne said.

"Oh, I assure you I can think of ways to spend it," Dianthe said, holding out her hand to look at it. Alaric passed it across. "Precious, precious lari."

Kalanath appeared in the doorway. "I hear Dianthe talking about money," he said. "Do we have some?"

"Fifty thousand," Dianthe said. Kalanath's eyes widened.

"I do not know what I can do with my share," he said.

"Dianthe will give you advice," Alaric said dryly. Dianthe mock-snarled at him and handed the banker's draft back. "Though as to that, if Perrin's ready, what we learn from this blessing may change how we spend that money."

Sienne stood with him and helped move the sofa back as Dianthe dragged the table out of the way. Kalanath lifted Dianthe's chair and set it against the wall. "You think it will need money?" he said.

"I think it's possible we may need to do more research, and that costs," Alaric said. "Perrin?"

"Everyone sit in a circle," Perrin instructed. "Sienne, put your notebook in the center, open to the page with the ritual we need, please." He settled down cross-legged again as Sienne laid out the notebook, cracking the spine so the pages wouldn't turn. Alaric handed her the writing desk that normally stood on a table under the window. She settled it on her lap, spread sheets of paper on it, and gripped a pencil, ready to write.

"Do not fear, Sienne. This will not hurt you," Perrin said.

"I hadn't thought it would until you said something, thanks." The shakes had returned. She held the pencil more tightly, willing them to vanish. Perrin was right, this wouldn't hurt her, though if she thought about it too long, she started to imagine the possible repercussions of allowing an avatar to work through her. She'd seen Perrin commune with Averran once, seeing the world as the avatar saw it, and it had nearly killed him. This wasn't the same, but the memory persisted nevertheless.

Perrin breathed in and out rhythmically, half a dozen times, and Sienne found her own breathing falling in time with his. "O Lord of Crotchets," he said, "hear my plea. You know the quest we have pursued these many months. We thank you for your guidance and ask your forbearance once more."

A tingling began at the base of Sienne's spine. The air thickened, became difficult to breathe. She made herself continue the slow, rhythmic breathing and relaxed her grip on her pencil. At least her palms weren't sweating. Yet.

"Before us is the ritual we discovered in the ruin," Perrin went on. "We believe your guidance led us to it, and we give thanks, o most cantankerous Lord. Now we ask that your wisdom extend to cover our ignorance. An evil man has warped this ritual to his own ends. We seek to undo what he has done. To this purpose, we ask you, o Lord, to reveal the ways in which the ritual has been warped. Please work through your servant Sienne, whose discovery this is, to show us wisdom."

The tingle spread up Sienne's spine and down her shoulders, through the long bones of her arms and into her fingers. Her right arm twitched. Then, without any direction from her, it rose into the air. She stifled a shriek. It felt as if she'd cast *drift* on only part of her body, to make it rise weightlessly and hang mid-air like a puppet's arm dangling from invisible wires.

Letters in Ginatic formed in front of her eyes, became words and then sentences in Ginatic she was only just capable of interpreting. A bubble of air pressed against her lips from inside her mouth, pushing them open. She released the bubble, which popped. The faint sound of the first syllable of the first word dancing before her drifted away. *One.* "One," she repeated, but in Fellic rather than Ginatic. "Drink deep of the well of slumber, and awaken the second self."

She felt her right hand, holding the pencil, write something on the paper. She risked a quick glance down and saw she'd written what she'd just said. The letters moved with her, dizzying her when she raised her head. Her hand had its own agenda, clearly, and another bubble of air was pressing against her mouth, so she decided to ignore her hand and give in to the urging of the letters. "Two," she said as the faint *two* puffed from between her lips. "Let the knife of binding draw us together, two hands as one."

She went on, reading the words that scrolled up before her eyes, barely comprehending what she read. The tingling in her hand grew to a burning ache, but it wrote on with no direction from her. The room's four walls receded from her until she felt she was in a vast white room, featureless, in which sounds and smells were absorbed into its bright walls. She'd never felt so alone, and yet it didn't frighten her, because she wasn't alone, there was a presence that lifted and guided her hand. She thought, *Averran*, and the room shook, nearly thrusting her out of it. She calmed herself and let the next word press against her lips until she set it free and resumed reading.

It was either hours or seconds before the last of the words slipped out; she knew it had to have taken time, because reading always did, but her body insisted it had been no time at all. She blinked, and realized she couldn't remember the last time she'd done so. Whatever force had moved her arm vanished, leaving it too heavy for her to lift. The pencil fell from her nerveless fingers and rolled a short distance away, where Dianthe picked it up. Sienne massaged her limp arm and let out a long breath. "I think Averran guided my hand. Literally."

"Something certainly did," Alaric said, taking her right hand and raising it to be level with her eyes. She gasped. The skin was pale, almost as pale as Alaric's, and there were four short, rounded red marks like burns across its back, with a fifth, longer mark running down the base of her thumb. Alaric placed his hand around hers, fitting his fingers to the marks. His hand was too large, but it was clear they were the marks of somebody's thumb and fingers.

"Astonishing," Perrin said.

"What did we learn?" Kalanath asked, leaning forward to look at the paper, which to him was upside down.

Sienne shook out her still-numb right hand and picked up the top sheet with her left. "I wrote what I said. Didn't you understand it?"

"Some words were in a foreign language. Probably Ginatic." Alaric held out his hand for the paper. "And some of it was very familiar. Was it the ritual?"

"I think so. Not this ritual." Sienne indicated the notebook, which someone had shut—or had it closed itself? She was ready to believe almost anything now. "The one the wizard uses. The altered ritual."

"But if Averran could tell us that all along, why hasn't he?" Dianthe took a turn looking at the paper.

"Presumably because we have never asked before," Perrin said. "And I think it likely that the altered ritual is meaningless without the original to compare it to. We are, after all, seeking a way to invert the wizard's ritual while retaining the parts of it that give a Sassaven his full power. We are now in a position to compare the two."

"What's this word, Sienne?" Dianthe asked, pointing at the bottom of the page.

Sienne looked, and felt numb again. "It's *prafladuo*," she said. "It means 'dominate.' It's a charm spell, or used to be—I don't think anyone still knows it. I hope no one still knows it."

"That carver wizard I killed knew it," Alaric said, his voice grim with unwanted memory.

"Well, no human still knows it, or at least will admit to knowing it. There are stories...it's the stuff of legends, or nightmares, casting *dominate* to make someone your willing slave. If that's what the wizard uses, it's no wonder the Sassaven are in thrall to him. But in the stories, there's always a way to break free of *dominate*. It doesn't sound like that's the case for the Sassaven."

"No," Alaric said. He had the page again and was following the last lines with his finger. "This says to cast *dominate* after another spell, one that alters the body, and then it's altered again. Like sealing in the spell to bone and blood."

Sienne shivered. "You made it sound dire, just then. I mean, of course it is, but that felt...like there was no hope. Like only death can undo it."

"I refuse to believe that's the case," Alaric said. He handed the paper back to Sienne and stood, towering over them. "We just have to figure out the reverse of this binding."

"Which could take another year, or five, or forever," Dianthe said. "I'm with Sienne. This seems hopeless."

"I think it is not," Kalanath said. "But it will be hard."

Alaric regarded him with narrowed eyes. "You know something."

Kalanath nodded. "I went to ask today," he said, "a...holy woman of my people. It is when you ask forgiveness so you will no longer have guilt."

"Absolution," Perrin said. "Why did you need absolution?"

"It is...absolution...before the thing." Kalanath put the chair back in place and leaned against it. "But she cannot give it to me because I am holier than she. So it must be my guilt if I am wrong to tell you."

"Tell us what?" Sienne asked.

Kalanath drew in a deep breath and let it out as if releasing a great weight. "Sit, and I will tell."

They straightened the furniture and settled in. It felt to Sienne like a campfire gathering, at night after a long day's travel, except that Kalanath rarely spoke then. Now, with the sunlight slanting across his face and making his high cheekbones seem sharper than ever, he looked unspeakably foreign, someone whose words would carry weight no matter their meaning.

"We have a practice you will not understand," he said. "It is...your words are not the same. You say, prostitute, or whore, and it is a shameful thing. In our temples, there are women who are God's vessels, open to men who want to worship—it is that they need guidance, or strength, and they commune with God through these women. Through sex." Kalanath drew another deep breath. "They have a thing that stops them having children, and the men as well. If a *madhi*, one of these women, has a child, it is only because God has a wish for this child. My mother was one of those women. And I was that child.

"I was born in the temple and it was my home for my whole life. They teach—taught me what a holy child, a *devesh*, must know. History, literature, mathematics. Religion. The use of the staff—it is meditation as well as fighting." He smiled. "The divines at the temple would say it is unholy to fight with the staff—no, that is wrong, they would say it is unholy that *I*, a *devesh*, fight with the staff. But they do not get to say, not anymore."

Sienne almost asked *Why not?*, but Alaric put a quelling hand on her knee. It warmed her inside that he knew her so well. And that she didn't have to leave. That wasn't going to get old any time soon.

"But that is ahead of the tale," Kalanath said. "I learned, was taught, many things, but for a *devesh* there is much forbidden. Things not to eat, things not to learn. I did not ever leave the temple so I would not be made unclean. But my mother...she did not believe being *devesh* made me less of a child. She told stories she should not, explained about the stars and their movements in the sky, many things I should not have learned. It was secret from the divines. We believed it would not matter.

"Then there was a day..." Kalanath's voice trailed off, and his bowed his head, gripping the back of the chair as if he could break it in two with his hands alone. "The divines came for me. I had a purpose, they said, and their training had prepared me for it. A *devesh* is a vessel for God, one who may speak with Her directly and hear Her voice. It is not like the cloudy visions of a priest or divine. Only a *devesh* is raised in purity to withstand God's presence." He glanced up, caught Perrin's eye. "I do not know if it is the same for you."

"I think not," Perrin said. "Please, continue."

"They gave me wine. I had not tasted wine before, so I do not know if it was drugged. Then they shut me in a little room with no windows, just one vent for air, and told me to meditate. I fell unconscious, I think. Unconscious, or asleep. And I had dreams I have never forgotten, so I know they were not usual dreams. They did not make sense, like someone speaking in a foreign language who believes you will understand. But I remember them still.

"When I woke, I was not in the little room anymore. I was in the temple and the divines were arguing. I think they did not expect me to wake so soon, because they argued about me, saying things about my impurity and that I was broken. When they realized I was awake, they stopped arguing and took me to my room. They locked me in and did not return for a day. I was frightened. I knew I was impure because of my mother's teachings, and I was afraid they would hurt her if they knew what she had done.

"But it was not about her. When they came back, they told me what I had overheard, that I was a broken vessel. But they believed my impurity was because I had not been faithful enough in my prayers and fasting. They almost...they were kind about it, and that frightened me more. Then they told me I could redeem myself through my children. They would choose women to bear them and they would raise them to be pure as I was not, that one of them might be the voice of God."

Sienne couldn't bear it any longer. "But they can't make you have children! Let alone with strangers!"

Kalanath smiled. It was an ancient, pitying expression that made him seem far older than he was. "There is a thing," he said, "a drug the men use sometimes when they cannot be ready for sex. They would give it to me, they said, and then I would not care who the women were so long as they were available."

"That's—"

"How old were you?" Alaric asked, cutting off Sienne's outburst.

"I was fourteen. Old enough to know I did not want to be used for breeding. Or for my children to be raised to the temple's purposes."

"I should hope not," Perrin murmured. "And yet I daresay they did not simply allow you to decline and walk away."

"That is true. I told my mother what they intended and she helped me escape. She used the same opening she used to bring me inappropriate things, and we fled. But she—" He closed his eyes. "We were trapped, and she let herself be taken so I might be free. I do not know if she is dead. She was alive when I saw her last, screaming at me to run, but they are not gentle with those who break the sanctity of the temple."

He fell silent. Sienne said, "But do you...you said you had true dreams. Does that...still happen?"

Kalanath nodded. "I do not always understand them. Sometimes it is years before I do. Sometimes it is immediate. But I never forget the ones that are true, not like other dreams that fade or are ridiculous in the light of day."

"And you've had another true dream," Alaric said. "Or a true dream from your past now makes sense."

Startled, Kalanath said, "How do you know?"

"It makes sense. This ritual, and the place where we found it, and that symbol on the mosaic, means something to you. Something you only just put together. What is it?"

"I saw the symbol, God as destroyer, years ago in a dream,"

Kalanath said. "I told you it means change, disruption. In the dream, I saw two people circling a room, doing things that made no sense, with the symbol hanging in the air above them. At first the people and the symbol were all I saw. Then I seemed to step back and saw the room. It was the temple, and yet not the temple—" Kalanath swore softly in Meiric. "I mean it is that Omeiran temples all look much the same in their building, but each is different, enough that you know which temple you are in by looking. It is what I was taught —I have never seen a temple but the one I lived in. This was not that temple, and when I stepped back again, I saw it was surrounded by desert wastes as no Omeiran temple could be. We do not live in the desert, except for the *pakhshani*. The dream showed me the people moving, and the symbol, and the temple, and until now it meant nothing. But that—" He gestured at the notebook—"and what Sienne said...it is the movements the people did in my dream."

Once again the room was silent. Sienne picked up the notebook and opened it to the ritual. "Omeira," she said. "Is the answer there?"

"It must be," Alaric said. "There's the mystery of why an Omeiran symbol was in a Rafellish ruin, after all. And if Kalanath saw our ritual in his dream...somebody in Omeira might be able to explain that."

"But we can't go to Omeira and wander from temple to temple, asking about foreign ritual," Dianthe said. "Never mind that they probably won't let us in, it would take forever."

"We don't have to wander. I know where the temple of his dream is," Alaric said. "It's the lost city of Ma'tzehar."

"That city is a myth," Perrin said, "and if it is not, it is at the very least impossible to find. I have not been a scrapper long, but even I know no scrapper has found it in over sixty years of searching. And most of the expeditions who sought it did not return."

"Except that Kalanath's dream says it's a real place," Alaric said.

"Why would anyone build a city in the middle of the desert?" Sienne asked. "It doesn't make sense."

"The stories say Ma'tzehar was settled before the desert shifted and encompassed it," Alaric said. "It was abandoned because it became uninhabitable. I don't believe it's a treasure city, filled with heaps of valuable artifacts, because the people had enough warning to get out with their possessions before the desert took over. But if it had a temple, and why wouldn't it, there's no reason that's not still there."

"And somewhere in that temple is the key to this ritual," Sienne said. Excitement bubbled up inside her. "Maybe the key to inverting it. That could mean change, wouldn't it? Destructive change, even?"

"That's what I was thinking," Alaric said. "I feel that symbol is important to us, terrifying or not."

"It is true," Kalanath said. "But I do not think I can go."

"Because you are a fugitive?" Perrin said.

"That, and because I have never dreamed myself returning to Omeira," Kalanath said. "I think it means I should not return." He sounded so young, and so forlorn, Sienne's heart went out to him.

"Do you want to go home?" she asked.

Kalanath looked thoughtful. "It does not feel like home anymore," he said. "Not like this place does. But I am still a stranger in Fioretti by my looks and my speech. Maybe it is that I do not belong anywhere."

"You belong with us," Dianthe said.

"That is true. That is why this is home." Kalanath sighed. "I feel fear when I think of returning to Omeira, and I dislike acting out of fear, but I cannot see another path."

"You're not old enough to have run out of true dreams," Alaric said. "Just because you haven't dreamed of returning there doesn't mean you won't someday. And I wonder if your dreams about the ritual and the temple don't mean Omeira isn't finished with you yet."

"And maybe—" Sienne almost said *you can find out what happened to your mother*, but realized in time what a tactless thing that would be to say and turned it into, "maybe it means there's more for you to learn there."

"That is also possible." A small smile touched his lips. "Then I will go, because I think you will be helpless without my staff."

"Almost certainly true," Alaric said. "So it's settled? We're off to Omeira?"

"I want to do some research first," Sienne said. "There must be something more than legend written about Ma'tzehar."

"It will take a few days to assemble everything we need for a journey of this length," Dianthe said. "We'll need passage on a ship, and the right kind of coin to provision ourselves when we reach Omeira—it's not like heading into the wilderness for a week."

"And I will attempt to scry the location of our lost city," Perrin said. "It is possible I will learn nothing, if the desert is as featureless as all accounts suggest, but any guidance Averran is willing to provide is welcome."

"Then we have a plan," Alaric said, rising from the sofa. "Sienne, let's see about redeeming this banker's draft, and then I'll join you in research. Unless you're going to the university library."

"No, I was thinking of starting at Madalynna's. She won't charge us anything to look."

"We're hardly impoverished anymore, Sienne," Dianthe said with a grin.

"I know, but frugality is a virtue, or should be."

She and Alaric strolled hand in hand through the streets, stopping for skewers of roasted meat and vegetables and washing the meal down with ale from Alaric's favorite tavern. Sienne controlled a burp and said, "I missed this."

"Such low tastes you have," Alaric teased. "It's fortunate you aren't going to be a duchess, because think of the horrible example you'd set your people."

"That's actually very low on my list of reasons it's fortunate I won't be a duchess."

"Am I at the top?"

"Of course. You and all our friends. You might be a little higher than the others."

Alaric took her hand again. "I'm glad Octavian convinced me to see sense. I was ready to break down your parents' door, throw you over my shoulder, and escape into the night. The problem was, it was daytime and I'd certainly have been arrested."

"That would have made things so much worse." Sienne breathed in the warm air of Fioretti, scented with roasted meat and ale and animal waste all stirred together by the salty sea breezes. A couple of small children ran past, laughing, and she looked at Alaric. He was watching an elaborate high-sprung carriage drive by and hadn't even noticed the urchins. Despite his reassurances, it would be a while before she stopped feeling anxious about the subject. For today, though, everything was fine.

"I've been thinking, though," he said, a little too casually. "About marriage."

"Oh? What about it?"

"It's a powerful promise, beyond the legal ramifications. An oath to be true to your love, now and for the rest of your life, said before witnesses. Not something you take lightly."

"No, it isn't."

"And I was thinking...it's not something Sassaven do because it's forbidden them. No—they don't even have the concept of marriage. For me, it would be an act of defiance as well as a binding promise." He stopped and turned Sienne to face him. "I still don't know how I feel about it, and I don't want to make you into a symbol of my defiance. But...when we return from Omeira, if I asked you to marry me, what would you say?"

For a moment, he looked as he had the first day she'd met him, pale blue eyes intent on her, mouth set in a firm line, shoulders filling the sky. She remembered that day, and all the days after that, flickering past so quickly they made a moving line tracing the path that ended with her loving him with all her heart. "If you asked me then," she said, "I'd say 'yes.'"

SIENNE'S SPELLBOOK

Summonings:

Summonings affect the physical world and elements. They include all transportation spells.

Castle—trade places with someone else

Convey—teleport an object

Ferry—teleport with one other person

Fog—obscuring mist

Jaunt—personal teleportation

Slick—conjure grease

Evocations:

Evocations deal with intangible elements like fire, air, and lightning.

Barrier—wall of fire or air

Burn—ray of fire

Force—bolt of magical energy, hits with perfect accuracy

Fury—six *force*-bolts, hits whatever is in range

Scorch—fireball

Scream—sonic attack, causes injury

Shout—sonic attack, causes short-term paralysis

Confusions:

Confusions affect what the senses perceive.

Camouflage—disguise an object's shape, color, or texture
Cast—ventriloquism
Echo—auditory hallucinations
Imitate—change someone's entire appearance
Mirage—visual hallucinations
Mirror—creates three identical duplicates of the caster
Shift—small alterations in appearance, such as eye or hair color
Vanish—invisibility

Transforms:

Transforms change an object or creature's state, in small or large ways.

Break—shatters fragile things
Cat's eye—true darkvision
Change—polymorph a living thing
Drift—feather fall
Fit (object)—shrink or enlarge an object; permanent
Fit (person)—shrink or enlarge a person; temporary
Float—levitation
Gills—water breathing
Mud—transform stone to mud
Purge—transmute liquid
Sculpt—shape stone
Sharpen—improve sight or hearing
Voice—sound like someone else

The Small Magics

These can be done by any wizard without a spellbook, with virtually no limits.

Light
Spark
Mend
Create water
Breeze
Chill/warm liquid
Telekinesis (up to 6-7 pound weights)

Ghost sound
Ghostly form
Find true north
Open (used to manipulate a spellbook)
Invulnerability

SNEAK PEEK: SANDS OF MEMORY (COMPANY OF STRANGERS, BOOK 5)

Sienne leaned over and tickled the copper-red puppy's nose with her knotted handkerchief. The little animal growled, a high-pitched sound closer to a purr than the deep-throated grumble of a dog, and fastened his tiny teeth in the knot. Sienne tugged against his grip and smiled as the pup's hind legs skittered on the shiny floorboards of Mistress Elodie Givvani's office.

Anywhere else, she would have worried about the dog wrecking carefully constructed piles of books or shelves full of artifacts, but Mistress Givvani displayed the kind of cleanliness Sienne normally associated with a professional laundry, though without the smell of boiling water. Nothing disrupted the well-scrubbed surface of her desk, the one bookcase was practically empty, and the only chair in the room was the one Mistress Givvani was currently sitting in. It was the only room Sienne had ever been in where the fragrance of soap was strong enough to be called a stink.

"You're sure the spell doesn't summon real animals?" she asked, teasing the pup by brushing the handkerchief across his nose.

"Positive," Mistress Givvani said. Her short gray hair flew in wisps around her face from the many times she'd run her fingers through it since Sienne had entered the office. It was the only disorderly thing about her and reassured Sienne that she was a real woman and not a marble statue. "They're realistic, granted, but they're creatures of magic, given form by the spell and released at the end of its duration."

"So why can't the duration be permanent?"

"That would usurp the power of God. Our best theorists believe She grants us this limited exercise of the power of creation to give us greater empathy and an understanding of Her nature. Bringing life into being...it's humbling, even if the being is something monstrous." Mistress Givvani ran her fingers through her hair again. "You'll notice none of those creatures has human intelligence. Nothing we can summon does."

"But these creatures all seem to understand what I ask of them. Even the frog will take simple commands."

"That's another reason we know they're not real creatures summoned from somewhere else in the world. The magic creates a link between summoner and summoned that makes the summoned creature inclined to obey. It goes both ways, too—you've no doubt noticed you understand their nonverbal communication."

"I do, a little." Sienne let go of the handkerchief and giggled as the puppy rolled backward tail over ears from the sudden absence of pressure. "It's a relief to know there isn't some child in tears somewhere hunting for his puppy."

"That would be cruel, yes." Mistress Givvani bent to scratch the puppy's head. It looked up at her, yipped once, and vanished with a faint *pop*. "You'll also find the more often you cast the spell, the longer the maximum duration will become as your reserves stretch to meet it. As is true of most spells with a limited duration."

"That's good to know. Thank you for your time."

"It's no trouble. You did recover the spell, after all, and provided us with a new line of investigation. Who knows what other spells have a versatility we haven't discovered yet?" Mistress Givvani laughed. "Probably not many, given the propensity of students to mispronounce the spell languages when they're learning. But it's a pleasant possibility."

"I never thought I'd be back in academia, when I became a scrapper a year ago," Sienne said. The office looked nothing like those of her teachers at her old school in Stravanus. Those had been packed with books and artifacts, not cleaned to within an inch of their lives. But it had the same feel to it, the sense that here was a place where knowledge happened.

"Life does take us unexpected places," Mistress Givvani agreed. "Like Omeira, apparently."

"Like Omeira." An odd thought struck her. "I don't suppose you know why there are no Omeiran wizards?"

Mistress Givvani's brow furrowed. "Aren't there?" Her eyes grew distant, and she tapped her fingers on her desk. "You know, I had never thought about it, but it's true we've never had a single Omeiran student in the wizardry school. Plenty of them in the other colleges, of course, but...well, that doesn't mean there are *no* Omeiran wizards."

"My companion Kalanath says there aren't. But he doesn't know why, either. I can't believe Omeira doesn't have any children born wizards. Even the southern continent has wizards."

"And no more nor fewer than we have up north," Mistress Givvani said. "I suppose it's something you could ask about while you're there. If it matters. I don't know that it's more than a curiosity, though some of my colleagues—the ones obsessed with theory, though you didn't hear me use the word 'obsessed'—would disagree." She stood and stretched like a cat, unselfconscious and relaxed. "Shall we see about the other matter?"

Mistress Givvani's office opened off her private lecture hall, which at the moment was empty of students. It was as tidy as her office, if more thoroughly furnished. Chairs and desks aligned at precise right angles to the walls and each other filled the high-ceilinged space, which was over-warm due to the sunlight pouring through the tall windows. The glass was thick and bubbly, not the thin modern glass sheets of the mathematics building across the courtyard, and it showed the world in colorful smears, some of which moved as students crossed the courtyard from one building to another. It took

Sienne back in time again, to years past when she was a student sitting at a desk like these, though the room she remembered had no windows and was always cold even in the heart of true summer. Perhaps all schools were alike on some level.

The halls of the wizardry school of the University of Fioretti were thronged with students, all of them wearing the lightweight blue gown that marked their school. They walked in groups of three or four, chattering away in conversations Sienne couldn't make out. Words came to her ear, fragments of sentences that together made no sense: *activated the hummingbirds in I asked for dinner*. She caught a few curious glances directed her way, assessing her trousers and shirt that said she was a scrapper, but no outright stares. She didn't look *that* out of place.

They passed through the rotunda, a tall, domed room from which corridors radiated like the spokes of a wheel, and down a new hall. This one was somewhat less packed with students and had no windows, instead being lit by giant versions of the lights Sienne could summon with a thought. The lights hung from the ceiling like moons in an alien sky, cold-white and casting sharp-edged shadows on the floor and walls.

Mistress Givvani opened a door about a third of the way down the corridor. "I'm as ignorant as you are about the thing," she said. "Let's see what they've discovered."

This room looked like a wizard's chamber, with its high ceilings and narrow windows whose glass was yellowed with age. Bookcases crammed with ancient tomes made a maze of the room, and more books piled on mismatched chairs made the path through the maze narrower. Sienne swept a hand across the surface of the nearest pile and sneezed at the cloud of dust that went up from it. The room smelled of dust and dry paper and, astonishingly, fresh apples. Sienne dusted her hands off on her trousers, leaving a pale smudge, and followed Mistress Givvani, who walked with a confidence Sienne didn't think the maze warranted. She felt she might be lost in this room forever.

"Vincentius? Joanna?" Mistress Givvani called out. "Don't tell me the books have finally engulfed you."

A thump, then a patter of louder thumps, sounded somewhere in the distance. Someone cursed loudly, making Mistress Givvani blush and say, "Sorry about that. Master Vitali isn't always careful about his language."

"I don't mind," Sienne said.

They came out of the maze into an empty space about ten feet in diameter, hedged in on all sides by stacks of ancient books and a desk big enough to seat ten to dinner. One of the piles had fallen over, and a thin, gangly man with a prominent chin knelt beside it, swearing softly now and stacking the books untidily. "There has to be a better way," he muttered.

"There is. It's called 'organization,'" Mistress Givvani said with some amusement.

"I can't be having with your organization, Elodie. It stifles the mind." The man looked up. "Who's this?"

"This is Sienne Verannus. The owner of the artifact I asked you to investigate?"

"Oh. You," the man said, as if Sienne were an expected, unwanted guest. "You're not planning to donate the artifact to the university, are you?"

"Um...no?"

The man grunted. "No one ever does, more's the pity. At least not until they're dead. Could I convince you to make the bequest in your will?"

"I...I don't have a will."

"No? And you a scrapper? At least I assume from your dress you're a scrapper. You of all people ought to have a will."

"Sienne's not here to discuss inheritance law, Vincentius. She wants to know what you learned about the artifact," Mistress Givvani said.

Vincentius rose to his full ungainly height. He looked like a stick insect unfolding, one slow joint at a time. "It's here somewhere," he said. "I'm sure it's here somewhere."

Sienne cast an eye on the piles of books, on the clutter covering the desk, and tried not to feel anxious over the fate of the hazard deck she'd given over to this man's care. It was in a bright red box, for Averran's sake, it ought to be visible!

Behind them, in what Sienne thought was the direction of the door, another sliding thump and a curse echoed through the room. "Joanna!" Vincentius called out. "Where's that artifact?"

"You'll have to be more specific," a woman replied. "Why do you have all these books, anyway? They should be in the library."

"Don't tell me my business, woman!" Vincentius roared.

"Don't call me 'woman' again or so help me I'll let you have one right round the ear!" the unseen woman shouted back.

"Treacherous whore!"

"Ignorant ass!"

"Maybe we should come back later," Sienne murmured, shifting uncomfortably in the direction of the maze.

"Don't worry, they talk to each other like this all the time," Mistress Givvani said. "Personally, I think they should just sleep together and get it out of their systems, but they seem to prefer the unresolved tension."

"Sex is a distraction from the essentials," Vincentius said, startling Sienne, who hadn't thought he could hear them over the shouted invective he was trading with his...colleague? "Joanna, come meet our guests."

A woman as round as Vincentius was thin emerged from the maze clutching an oversized book to her chest. "Guests? What guests? Nobody ever comes here. It's why I like your office better than mine."

"The owner of that artifact. You didn't take it, did you?"

The woman, Joanna, examined Sienne as Vincentius had. Sienne was growing tired of being stared at like a museum exhibit. "Of course not," Joanna said. "It's probably exactly where you left it." The clutter on the desk shifted without being touched, pieces of artifacts and small books rising into the air and shuffling into piles so the center of the desk was clear.

"You're a wizard," Sienne said.

"I am. I specialize in studying the magic of the before times, which is why Elodie gave me your artifact."

Sienne glanced at Vincentius, who gave his stack of books a final nudge to keep them from falling. "And...Vincentius...is a wizard, too?"

"No, an historian," Mistress Givvani said. "Oftentimes we learn more about artifacts from the histories than from arcane investigation. It's safer than working out an artifact's function by trial and error."

Something red caught Sienne's eye. Vincentius picked it up. "Here it is. Right where I left it. I told you that's where it would be."

Joanna rolled her eyes and let the rest of the mess return to the desk. "This is a powerful artifact. I don't suppose you want to donate it?"

"I already asked," Vincentius said. "She doesn't even have a will."

"I promise I'll draw up a will immediately," Sienne said, cutting off Joanna, who looked about to start in on a lecture. "What does it do?"

Vincentius shoved a pile of artifacts to one side and sat on the desk. His long legs swung gently, the soles of his feet brushing the floor. "There are records of hazard decks like that one occurring as recently as five hundred and forty-five years ago. They were never common, even among the ancients. Mostly they were used as divination tools in the time before the avatars, when God's voice wasn't as clear as it is today. So that's one use, if you know how to read a hazard deck."

"But that would be like using a cannon to swat a fly," Joanna said.

"*I'm* explaining it, harpy."

Joanna scowled at him and raised one hand for a prodigious slap she didn't deliver. Vincentius ignored her. "The real use, the magical use, took some doing to figure out, because the histories only referred to what it could do, not how to make it do it." He removed the lid and displayed it, with its black angular characters burned into it. "I couldn't find out what the symbol means, but based on other evidence, I think it's a name, or a house name—something identifying the owner."

He tipped the cards into his hand. His long, bony fingers curled easily around the deck. "First, shuffle the deck three times." He did so, the cards riffling through his fingers with a faint snapping sound. "Then cut three times, like this." He set the deck on the desk and cut it into three piles, then picked up the center pile, stacked it on the left-hand pile, and put both atop the right-hand pile. "Then you draw a card. No, not you. The person who shuffles draws a card. Otherwise the magic doesn't work. You can do it once every twenty-four hours."

Sienne waited. Vincentius continued to hold the deck loosely in one hand. "So...why don't you draw a card?" she finally asked.

Vincentius snorted. "Every card has a different effect, and not all of them are positive. I'm no gambler."

"Can I try?" Sienne asked.

"It's your artifact. Go ahead," Vincentius said, handing her the deck.

Sienne awkwardly shuffled the cards, which were almost too big for her hands, then cut the deck as directed. With only a moment's hesitation, she drew the top card from the deck and turned it over. Three staves against a golden background looked back at her. "I don't —" she began, then blinked. Everything had taken on crisp, sharp edges, like shadows on the brightest day in true summer. "Thirty-eight books on that shelf," she said. "Forty-two on that one. There are seventeen artifacts on the desk—I only looked at it once and I remember everything."

"Staves is the suit associated with intelligence and memory," Joanna said. "This one seems to have enhanced yours."

"And you just know that?" Vincentius said.

"I dabble in hazard reading."

"So how long will it last?" Sienne asked. Everywhere she looked she was conscious of numbers: numbers of books, numbers of nail heads in the floorboards, numbers of hairs on Mistress Givvani's head. It didn't dizzy her or make her feel overwhelmed; in fact, she felt her mind clicking along like a hummingbird's wings, zipping from thought to thought. It felt incredible.

"No idea," Joanna said. "We only know it's not a permanent effect. And that it seems to draw not only from the five spell languages, but from divine power as well. That is, the few effects the ancients recorded either duplicate a wizard's spell or priest's blessing, or do something related to those."

"I know priests can invoke blessings to enhance memory," Sienne said, recalling that Perrin had done something like that for Alaric once.

"Exactly," Vincentius said. "There's an implication, too, that the shuffling—randomizing the deck, as it were—allows God the opportunity to choose something most helpful to the wielder of the deck at that time. I don't know if I believe it, but it's an interesting theory."

"Wait," Sienne said. "You said *five* spell languages."

"All five," Joanna said. "Including charm. Another reason to be careful with it. It doesn't contain actual spells, so it's not banned, but you should take care how you use it."

Sienne nodded, torn between nervousness at handling such a powerful artifact and excitement at the possibilities. Charm...it was devastating, as she knew from personal experience, and she had no desire to cast *dominate* on anyone, but suppose the deck let her put enemies to sleep? Or frighten them away? Surely even the most rules-bound wizard could see the benefit to that.

Vincentius opened a desk drawer and dug around in it for a bit, coming up with a palm-sized notebook. "I've written down the effects I was able to uncover in my research. You can add to the list as things come up. It might not matter, since you can't invoke an effect by searching the deck for the card you want, but you might be able to see a pattern and decide if the odds are in your favor."

Sienne opened the book. Vincentius had remarkably neat hand-writing for someone whose office looked like the aftermath of an earthquake.

Five of coins—creates small gem. Records say it doesn't disappear.

The Seer—record of talking sword, giving advice about the future

King of swords—companion appears to fight for invoker—impossible?

"None of these seem bad," she said.

"I couldn't find specific evidence of cards that had a negative effect, true," Vincentius said, "but there's plenty of records of people referring to these decks as cursed, or of destroying them out of fear of what they might do. You should be careful."

"I will." Sienne put the cards into their box and tucked it away in her pack. "Thanks for everything."

"Don't forget about your will," Joanna said. "You scrappers all think you're immortal, but death takes us all, in the end."

"Don't frighten the girl, shrew," Vincentius said.

"Don't call me a shrew, you worthless excuse for a man!"

"Vixen!"

"Louse!"

"We can go now," Mistress Givvani murmured. Sienne was grateful to make her escape.

They walked together as far as the rotunda, where Mistress Givvani said, "Good luck to you. And feel free to return any time you have an artifact you need identified."

"I will. Thanks again. I don't know that the hazard deck will be useful to us, but we never turn down magical assistance."

She bade Mistress Givvani farewell and strolled across the courtyard to the gate. Unlike the halls, the courtyard was virtually empty at this early hour, and the sound of Sienne's footsteps on the cobbles echoed back at her from the walls of the surrounding buildings. Their cold, forbidding façades made her grateful she wasn't a student at the university, constantly watched over by the marble bas-reliefs carved into every conceivable surface.

Now she looked around for a quiet place to *jaunt* home from. Maybe it was an indulgence because being able to *jaunt* amid distractions was more useful to her team, and she ought to look for opportunities to practice, but *jaunt* took long enough to cast she didn't like being stared at while she did so. The portico of the library was empty; that would do as well as anywhere.

She tucked herself away in a corner of the broad, imposing

portico and opened her spellbook. Transport spells were all long and cut her mouth to ribbons, which was why she rarely used them. Today, she was in a hurry. She began reading the spell and immediately tasted blood. Swallowing, she read on. A quivering tension began in her stomach, radiating gradually outward until she felt something was gently pulling on her in every direction. The tension grew more intense until, spitting out the final syllable, she released it all at once and found herself in her own bedroom, breathing heavily. She swallowed more blood and closed her eyes as she recovered—another indulgence, since if she had to do this under pressure, she wouldn't have time to recover. Then she dropped her pack on the bed and headed downstairs to the sitting room.

The normally peaceful sitting room, rented from their landlord at a better than reasonable price, overflowed with backpacks and canvas bags. Dianthe sat on the sofa and studied the contents of one of them. "We have to reduce," she said. "This will cost far too much to ship."

"I thought we had enough money not to worry about that anymore," Sienne said, taking a seat next to her.

"No reason we can't still be frugal, as I believe *you* pointed out. And we still have to carry this lot." Dianthe leaned back and blew out her breath. "*And* we'll buy supplies for the actual journey in Chirantan, so you can multiply what you see here by five."

Three sets of footsteps sounded in the hall. "You're back," Alaric said. "Did they know what the hazard deck was?"

"Yes. It's exciting. Random, but exciting. I don't know how useful it will be."

"I prefer stability, myself," Perrin said, pushing his long hair back from his face. "Uncertainty may be the spice of life, though I am not certain that is the saying, but how much better to know one's path."

"You don't like surprises?" Dianthe said.

"Not at all."

"I agree," Kalanath said. "Surprises can be not pleasant."

"Or they can be exciting!" Sienne exclaimed. "I had no idea you two were so stodgy."

"It is not stodgy when surprise means, hello, I am here to kill you," Kalanath said.

"That almost never happens."

Distantly, she heard a knock at the back door. "Are we expecting company?" Alaric asked.

"I don't think so," Dianthe said. "I hope it isn't someone looking to hire us. I hate having to turn people down."

Kalanath turned and disappeared down the hall. Perrin entered the room and sat on the chair across from Dianthe. Alaric went to Sienne's side and leaned down for a kiss. "So, can you be more specific about the deck?"

"Well, each card—"

Kalanath returned, his eyes wide. "Perrin," he said, "it is a surprise for you."

Perrin looked up, startled.

"Papa!" two small voices shrieked. Delphine and Noel Delucco dashed into the room and flung themselves at their father. Perrin's arms reflexively went around them, surprise deepening to stunned amazement.

"Children," he said, "what are you—"

Another figure entered, more sedately. One look at Cressida Delucco's face, though, told Sienne she was anything but serene. "I'm sorry, Perrin," she said in her husky alto, "but we had nowhere else to go."

Perrin rose awkwardly, hampered by two children clinging to him. "Why should you need to go anywhere?"

"Because your father intends to take our children away from me," Cressida said.

ABOUT THE AUTHOR

In addition to the Company of Strangers series, Melissa McShane is the author of more than twenty-five fantasy novels, including the novels of Tremontane, the first of which is *Servant of the Crown;* The Extraordinaries series, beginning with *Burning Bright;* and *The Book of Secrets,* first book in The Last Oracle series. She lives in the shelter of the mountains out West with her husband, four children and a niece, and four very needy cats. She wrote reviews and critical essays for many years before turning to fiction, which is much more fun than anyone ought to be allowed to have.

You can visit her at **www.melissamcshanewrites.com** for more information on other books.

For news on upcoming releases, bonus material, and other fun stuff, sign up for Melissa's newsletter at http://eepurl.com/brannP

www.ingramcontent.com/pod-product-compliance
Lightning Source LLC
Chambersburg PA
CBHW070544260626
47161CB00002B/499